"YES . . ."

He kissed her slender throat and let his mouth roam until it caught the rosy tip of her breast.

It seemed to Kelsey that a wire was stretching within her, tightening with exquisite pain and pleasure. Her hands, clenched in the thickness of his hair, felt his pulse throb at a tempo matching her own. Then slowly, reluctantly, he raised his head to meet her gaze.

"Sweet Kelsey, are you sure?"

Her instant response left no room for doubt.

"Love me," she murmured, "Love me . . ."

FREEDOM ANGEL

Robin LeAnne Wiete

AN ONYX BOOK

ONYX
Published by the Penguin Group
Penguin Books USA Inc., 375 Hudson Street,
New York, New York 10014, U.S.A.
Penguin Books Ltd, 27 Wrights Lane,
London W8 5TZ, England
Penguin Books Australia Ltd, Ringwood,
Victoria, Australia
Penguin Books Canada Ltd, 2801 John Street,
Markham, Ontario, Canada L3R 1B4
Penguin Books (N.Z.) Ltd, 182-190 Wairau Road,
Auckland 10, New Zealand

Penguin Books Ltd, Registered Offices:
Harmondsworth, Middlesex, England

First published by Onyx, an imprint of New American Library,
a division of Penguin Books USA Inc.

First Printing, October, 1990
10 9 8 7 6 5 4 3 2 1

Printed in the United States of America

To my parents, Robert and Shirley Graff,
with much love.

1

October 1850

Sheldon Tremayne clasped his hands behind his back and stared at the broad expanse of well-manicured lawn and sturdy outbuildings of Riverview. He knew it was cowardly, turning away from confrontation, but he much preferred to contemplate this proof of his accomplishments than to face the bitter accusation in his wife's eyes as she waited behind him.

Riverview was prospering, he noted with pride. From the parapet topping the three-storied mansion he could sight the masts of the river schooners that had brought him his wealth, or turn to look out over the land that gave him his greatest satisfaction. The rich, fertile soil produced some of the sweetest fruits of the earth. Apples, grapes, pears, even peaches, all flourished here, coddled by the warm, moist air from Lake Ontario. Above the lake to the north, a sky the color of cornflowers hovered protectively. It was the same rich hue of the Caribbean Sea he'd once traveled, a blue so vibrant it made your heart ache.

With an effort, Sheldon forced his thoughts back to earth. To the east a border of poplar trees, shimmering sentries guarding his precious domain, hid the road to Lewiston. He admired their amber majesty, knowing in a few weeks the November winds would make them shiver and bend, and that soon the ground below would be littered with their tiny gold medallions.

As he pondered both his good fortune and his troubles, Sheldon's gaze eventually drifted southwest as it always seemed to do, to the place where the green lawns and artful shrubbery halted abruptly on the rim of a precipice that might have marked the edge of the world. Perhaps he was drawn to them because the stark cliffs of the Niagara Gorge reminded him of his boyhood home in Cornwall. The rushing, swirling river below constantly beckoned to him. He'd built his home within the sound of its roar; he forever turned toward its awesome power.

And now, in a way, it was the river that was breaking his heart. He sighed heavily.

"I won't stay, Sheldon. I won't stay and watch you destroy everything."

"Destroy, Mabelle? That's a strong allegation." Resignedly, Sheldon turned to face his wife, knowing by the sound of her harshly drawn breath that she was prepared to continue the argument that had raged about them in the past few months like the relentless flow of the Niagara.

Dressed in somber brown, Mabelle was but a shadow of the beautiful girl he'd married. Her dark hair was streaked with gray, her flawless skin pinched with worry. And yet he loved her still. Loved her even though she hated much of what he stood for.

Mabelle, too, wondered how the years had changed them both so. She'd fallen in love with a kind and doting young man, but ambition had turned his head away from her, and now this foolish notion stood between them like . . . like his damned trees! Pulling her already ramrod-stiff posture even taller, she dredged up the last weapon in her exhausted arsenal. "If you can't think of us, then at least consider Kelsey. What kind of future will there be for her when word of your idiocy gets out? It will, you know," she sniffed. "These things always do."

Mention of his only child brought a rush of apprehension to Sheldon, but he managed to show no sign of his doubts. His voice firm with conviction, he explained once again. "I *am* thinking of Kelsey's future, and the future of us all. Someday she'll understand why I've chosen this course. What she may not understand is why you've insisted on taking her away."

"Because in Europe she'll remain untouched by this sordid business. Besides," Mabelle intoned, "every young lady of quality is entitled to a season . . . something that's not available in this god-forsaken corner of the world."

"She's only fourteen," Sheldon protested.

"Fifteen!" Gloating triumphantly at this proof of his neglect, Mabelle continued. "She's fifteen now, and deserves better than to be subjected to the same life I've borne for years. At least in Europe she'll meet the right kind of people, and eventually make a good marriage."

This was the same reasoning Sheldon had heard on countless other occasions, and it never failed to raise his ire. Mostly because he feared Kelsey was beginning to believe it.

His daughter was adept at the social amenities, much to her mother's satisfaction, and was quick to mimic Mabelle's dogmatic attitudes. Only on a few occasions had he found reason to hope Kelsey would grow above such pettiness. One summer, when Kelsey was twelve, Mabelle had returned to Alabama to be with her dying mother, leaving her daughter at home. Out of necessity Sheldon had taken Kelsey everywhere with him and by the end of a month she was as comfortable working with the fruit pickers as she was climbing the roped ladder up the side of one of his ships. The two had grown closer than ever during those weeks, and Sheldon poignantly recalled her childish wish to grow up just like him.

But Mabelle, upon her return, had been livid when she'd spotted Kelsey's unruly braids and freckled skin. Despite the child's protests, Mabelle had vowed to undo all the damage her absence had allowed. And it appeared she had succeeded.

"We leave in the morning," Mabelle said, her voice low and firm. "Kelsey's bidding farewell to the Delbert family now. I suggest you join us for dinner tonight if you wish to say good-bye to your daughter."

Turning back to the railing in order to hide his desolation, Sheldon cleared his throat before speaking. It didn't help. ''You can still change your mind,'' he offered hoarsely.

''So can you,'' Mabelle retorted.

Again, Sheldon's eyes flickered left to the broad emptiness across the gorge, an emptiness broken only by the indistinct mass of gray in the distance that was the Canadian shore.

''No,'' he murmured sadly. ''I can't.''

Garrett O'Neill patted his hand absently along the sleek, piebald neck, then deftly unfastened the bridle and slipped it over his horse's upright ears. ''What is it, boy?'' he asked, leaning back as the huge head tossed nervously.

The sound of crunching gravel just outside the door caught Garrett's attention and he sauntered to the wide opening after turning the piebald into a box stall. His eyes squinted automatically as he peered out into the October sunlight.

No one there, he thought. An instant later he glimpsed a splash of vermillion as it disappeared behind the yew hedge. Intrigued, he quickly returned the bridle that dangled from his sun-browned hand to its place on the tack wall, then strode toward the spot where he'd last seen her. His steps were strong and sure, as in his mind he was sure he knew what he'd find.

Anticipation rose high in Garrett's chest, but if he told himself it was only because she amused him, well then, that was often the way of it for young men of nineteen years, when life was one immense cauldron of anticipation.

''Kelsey,'' he called softly when he rounded the corner of the squared-off yew and found she wasn't there. A giggle drifted over from where another large bush shielded a bed of low-growing roses. He moved around them, halting when again he found nothing but fragrant air. Tinkling laughter circled his head, but this time instead of following the sound he planted his feet wide apart and crossed his bare arms over his chest. "Don't waste my time, Kelsey. I'm too busy for games."

"Then why were you chasing me?"

The clear, teasing voice came from behind the wide trunk of an elm tree, and now Garrett spotted the edges of her skirt spreading too wide to remain completely hidden.

"I wasn't chasing," he replied with a superior tone. "I just wanted to see what spooked Prince."

Now the red skirt twitched once, and Kelsey Tremayne flounced onto the open, her pointed chin lifted high. "I did not spook him, and besides, Prince is a silly name for a horse."

Garrett was used to having her change the subject abruptly, but he was definitely not used to seeing her dressed this way. Overnight, it seemed, Kelsey had gone from pinafores and ruffled frocks to young womanhood, and while Garrett's first thought was that her mother appeared bent on rushing her through childhood, he couldn't help but feel a bit dazzled at the sight she made.

She wore a morning gown the color of a fresh poppy, and though red was generally considered unsuitable for the very young, it was somehow appropriate on Kelsey. Her dark brown hair glistened with auburn highlights and her cheeks glowed brightly, rivaling the cheerful hue of her skirts. A scooped neckline hung tantalizingly close to the tops of her high, firm breasts, drawing his unwilling gaze.

"Do you like my dress?" Kelsey singsonged as she picked her way toward him, stepping daintily over the grass where just moments before she had sprinted in boyish fashion.

Garrett felt the muscles in his chest tighten, but he was careful to keep his gaze focused on her black, gypsy eyes as she edged closer. "It's pretty," he grunted, "but you look like a little girl dressed up in her mama's clothes."

Kelsey squashed the retort that nearly sprang to her lips. Ever since she could remember, Garrett had responded to her many pranks with playful teasing, and even when she grew mad at him he always managed to cajole her out of a mood. Lately, however, the game had taken on a new dimension, and Kelsey was determined not to let him distract her by treating her like a child. Instead she formed her mouth into the moist pout she'd been practicing in front of the mirror. "And I thought you'd like it," she simpered. "I wore it just for you."

"You wore it for Justin Delbert, I expect." Christina Delbert was Kelsey's best friend and it was common knowledge that her older brother, Justin, already had his heart set on Kelsey—or the Tremayne fortune. Garrett snubbed out the flame of jealousy deep within him, letting his gaze sweep insolently from her face down to her hem, then back again to her blazing eyes. "Little girls are more to his taste than mine."

This time Kelsey couldn't resist stamping her foot. "And since when did you turn into such a man? At least Justin's studying in his father's office, while you're still mucking out stables!" The instant she saw his face cloud over, Kelsey regretted her impetuous words. She shouldn't have said that, but he could be so touchy sometimes. Though she often forgot that, as her father's employee, he was not considered a proper companion for a young girl of her station, Garrett was constantly reminding her. Like now. His blue eyes narrowed slightly and his full, lower lip drew thin.

"What do you want, Kelsey? I have work to do."

His words were abrupt but there was not nearly so much impatience in them as she might have expected. That was the way it had always been. Her first memory might be of her father lifting her onto the rail of his parapet, but her second was of Garrett pulling her to her feet after she'd stumbled while trying to keep up with him. Ever since, it seemed she'd been trying to capture his attention in one way or another, from competing to see who could find the best fishing worms to waiting behind the poplars each day after work to walk with him before he turned down the lane toward his own home.

Now Kelsey was no longer satisfied with those methods, or the results they produced. It had occurred to her recently, gradually, that if she wanted Garrett to see her differently, then *she* had to behave differently toward him. Exactly in what way she wasn't sure, but she had a vague idea how to proceed and hoped Garrett's reactions would clue her in on the rest.

Besides, there was no turning back now, she realized. She was fast running out of time.

What Kelsey did not know was that it wouldn't take schemes and trickery to gain Garrett's attention, since she had always had it. Few days went by when he did not strive to see her, if only for a few minutes, and few minutes went by when he wasn't thinking of her. She was as much a part of his life as the tall ships he loved so well, as intrinsic to him as his own name. Garrett knew this, but he resented it just the same.

"What do you want?" he repeated, though his tone had gentled a little.

Kelsey shrugged with pretended nonchalance, conscious that the motion made her breasts heave prettily beneath the thin fabric of her bodice. Gazing up through dark lashes, she spoke in a low, husky voice, also practiced in her room. "I came to say good-bye. Mother and I are leaving tomorrow."

Garrett's anger melted somewhat at her attempt to flirt. Did she really think all she had to do was bat her eyes to catch a man? Maybe one like that sissy in britches, Justin Delbert, Garrett thought disdainfully, but not a man of nearly twenty. Especially one who'd already had a taste of passion and had found it much to his liking. Besides, he knew Kelsey too well to be swayed by such games. Flirting worked only with strangers, or in the case of Justin, with friends who refused to open their eyes to reality.

"Leaving? For the springs?" Garrett asked, referring to Mabelle's annual trek to Saratoga.

Kelsey shook her head, pleased that his expression had turned to one of extreme interest. "No, to Europe. Switzerland and Germany first, then London and maybe even Paris. I'm to have a season,'' she declared.

Garrett tried hard to hide his dismay, but he must have failed because her eyes widened with surprise as he dropped his arms to his sides. ''For how long?'' he demanded.

Again, Kelsey shrugged, but some of the elation seeped from her, as if she were seeing the reality of leaving for the first time through his azure eyes. ''I . . . I don't know. A year, I expect. I never asked.''

Garrett lifted one sun-bronzed arm, raking his hand through hair the color of ripened wheat. Kelsey felt a tiny thrill race around her heart. He *would* miss her! she thought.

But her spirits plummeted when he looked over her shoulder in the direction of the lake. ''Your pa going?''

She spun away, startled by the sudden tears that stung her eyes. ''Of course not,'' she answered sharply. ''So you don't have to worry about your precious job!''

She should have known, Kelsey cried silently. She should have remembered all he ever thought about was work, work, work! Something her mother had once said leapt to her mind, repeating itself over and over. *Irish father and German mother: him drinking away every penny she earned.* Maybe Garrett couldn't help himself, but that didn't make things any easier now. ''I expect you'll both like it better with Mother and me gone,'' she said over her shoulder.

Garrett cringed at the partial truth in her words. He certainly wouldn't miss Mabelle's constant derision, and he had often wondered why Sheldon did not pay more attention to his daughter when Kelsey obviously adored him. But Garrett could not deny that, with Mabelle's resistance out of the way, it was likely he and Sheldon *would* spend more time together.

''And you'll probably like Europe so well you'll never come home,'' he said lightly, coaxing her back to her previous mood.

Kelsey peeked over her shoulder suspiciously. It was

hard to stay upset when Garrett was being nice to her. His charming grin made her stomach flutter, but it was the sight of him standing there, hands on narrow hips and broad shoulders thrown back so the muscles in his arms strained against his chambray shirt, that brought her around again.

An answering smile dimpled her cheeks. "Oh, Garrett! You're such a tease! I don't know why I talk to you?"

Because I'm in love with him, her heart responded quickly, confirming feelings that had begun as a childish infatuation but had recently blossomed to something new and wonderful.

Because I'm handy, he thought cynically, unable to give credence to the possibility for more. "Every little girl needs someone to talk to," he taunted. "Who will you confide in while you're in Europe? Your mother?"

Kelsey laughed then, a throaty, musical laugh that hinted more at the woman she would become than all the grown-up dresses in the world. "If you've noticed, I'm not a little girl now . . . but I guess I'll have to save my secrets till I get home."

After such a near admission of her true feelings, Kelsey couldn't resist testing further her newfound wiles. Stepping so close to him her breasts nearly touched his arms, which were folded across his chest again, she raised her face saucily. "Will you miss me, Garrett O'Neill?"

A knot the size of a fist lodged in his throat, making it more difficult to answer than it should have been. "Sure," he rasped. "It'll be quiet around here without you." He could see tiny freckles dancing across the golden skin of her cheeks, and the sweet fragrance of her breath fanned his chin, which he held firmly in place. A muscle twitched when she placed her hand on his arm, but otherwise he made no move, toward her or away.

"May I have a kiss good-bye?" she whispered, lowering her thick lashes just enough to look enticing—she hoped.

Disbelief surged through Garrett. Disbelief that this girl—this child!—was trying to seduce him, and disbelief that his own body was responding so eagerly. Anxious to end the encounter, he bent his head quickly, placing a dispassionate kiss on her brow.

"That's no kiss!" Kelsey exclaimed, forgetting for the moment her mature pose.

"What do *you* know of kissing?" Garrett scoffed. There was no way in hell he'd let this chit see how close he'd come to teaching her.

But Kelsey wasn't prepared to give up easily, not when she'd come this far. For years she'd tagged after him, ignoring her mother's frequent complaints that she had no business pestering one of her father's employees. And most of the time he'd seemed to enjoy her company, at least until recently when he'd remained distantly polite in her presence.

She was nearly a woman now; hadn't Mama and Justin both told her so? Then why did Garrett insist on avoiding her? Kelsey didn't relish being ignored. Pressing closer, she raised her hands to his shoulders. "I know it's much better if you kiss my lips instead of my forehead. You're not afraid, are you?"

Garrett let out a derisive huff, but part of it was aimed at himself. "I'm not afraid, but maybe you should be," he warned. "Didn't your mama ever tell you not to swim in water too deep?"

Kelsey tilted her head, her eyes twinkling saucily. "But *I*," she teased, "hardly ever listen to my mother."

Of their own volition, Garrett's hands dropped to his sides, then quickly bridged the distance to her waist. The flesh beneath the fabric of her dress was soft and warm, for despite her grown-up attire, she still wore no corset. He was also mildly surprised at the gentle curve of her hips; he'd expected hoops were mostly responsible for her feminine silhouette. Perhaps she truly *was* nearly a woman. Black eyes beckoned to him from beneath sooty lashes, shimmering with youthful vitality and something . . . something he couldn't put a name to. Unable to resist her upturned face, Garrett lowered his mouth slowly, intending only to brush the tempting, rose-hued lips long enough to satisfy her childish whim.

His gentle kiss sent a shock wave careening through Kelsey, for it was at once less and more than she had expected. Though his mouth barely traced a feathery trail over hers, she couldn't keep herself from trembling so violently that she was afraid he would think she was frightened.

And Kelsey didn't want him to think she was frightened. She didn't want him to think anything that would make him stop kissing her.

Instinctively , she leaned close to him, letting her hands slip higher over his chest until they spanned his wide shoulders. The rough fabric of his shirt couldn't block the heat that scorched her fingertips and she dimly wondered what his skin would feel like to touch. Would it be soft when the muscles beneath were so rigid?

Slanting his mouth over hers, Garrett deepened the kiss, sensing both her surprise and pleasure when he slipped the tip of his tongue between her slightly parted lips. The sweet taste of her spread through him like a flood of honey, the soft press of her breasts against his chest was nearly driving him mad, and he shuddered uncontrollably even while he kept telling himself he was teaching her a lesson . . . just teaching her a lesson.

When Garrett could finally drag himself far enough away from Kelsey to gaze into her wide, luminous eyes, he was startled by the expression of unabashed yearning directed toward him. At first he felt a surge of tenderness at the thought that, though she claimed sophistication, she was still innocent enough to wear her heart on her sleeve. But then reality stopped him from doing the same. He repeated the things he'd been telling himself for the past several months.

She was a child. He was a man.

She was the daughter of a wealthy family. He was her father's employee.

But most important, she was used to getting anything

she wanted, and he had long ago taught himself never to want anything he couldn't have.

Gently, insistently, Garrett eased her away.

It took only a moment for Kelsey to comprehend that the look of resolution on his face had nothing to do with kissing, or love, or any of the things she wanted him to be thinking about right now. Still shaken by the sheer force of his kiss, she gazed helplessly at him, unable to control her quivering chin. "What's wrong?" she whispered achingly.

Garrett felt a muscle in his jaw leap crazily and he forced himself to relax, releasing his hold on her waist and letting his clenched hands drop to his sides. "What could be wrong?" he answered with a lightness of tone he couldn't match with his eyes. "You wanted a kiss; now you've had one."

"And that's all?" Kelsey's voice quavered as she swallowed back the tears that filled her throat.

Garrett shrugged, turning his head slightly so he wouldn't have to see the wounded expression in her eyes. How could he hurt her like this, he chastised himself. She was so young.

Exactly, his mind warred. *Young enough that by tomorrow or next week or next month she'll have forgotten all about this whether you walk away now or make a fool of yourself again.*

"That's all," he quipped gently. "You shouldn't be disappointed. You did quite well for the first time."

Kelsey swung around, appeared to study the horizon for a few moments, then turned back to him with her chin angled high, the cool little smile on her lips belying the blazing fire in her eyes. "Then I thank you for the instruction," she replied levelly. "Since Mother intends that the purpose of this trip is to find me *suitable* beaus, I'm sure I'll have plenty of chances to practice my *lessons.* You can go back to the stable now."

Garrett resisted the urge to give her a shake, remembering instead how many times Mabelle had eyed him with the same look of withering displeasure. Anger raced through him, all the more cutting because it was edged with shame. It was his own fault his pride was taking such a blow. He had *known* better.

"You'd better watch out," he growled warningly, "that the next time you try to play at being grown-up someone doesn't mistake you for a *real* woman. You'll end up finding out the hard way that some men won't let it end with a kiss."

Kelsey turned her back to him again, speaking over her shoulder. "And some men, like you," she replied archly, "will never have the chance."

Only a few seconds passed before she heard him move, but to her disappointment he didn't snatch her back into his arms. Instead the rustling sound of his footsteps as they retraced the path to the stable jarred her as if he were stomping on her heart. Garrett was gone.

I won't cry! she insisted silently, wiping tears from her cheeks with the back of one hand. Using a trick she'd learned as a child to deal with her feelings, Kelsey let anger replace disillusionment. In a few weeks she'd be in England with handsome gentlemen and beautiful ladies to have as new and better friends. She would show him. She'd show him there were more important things for her. Why should she care whether she ever saw Garrett O'Neill again?

Would she see him again? she wondered dismally, her gaze sweeping over the lake in the distance as her thoughts returned to the place they always did. Would he still be here when she came back? It might be six months . . . maybe even a year.

A sudden ache for all she was leaving behind rushed through her, and she squeezed her eyes tight, trying to see if she could hold forever in her mind the sky as it was today. If she could only remember that, then maybe she wouldn't miss her home so much while she was gone. Kelsey could feel the October sun pouring over her, its subtle warmth burning her face. Her mother would give her a tongue lashing if she came in with reddened cheeks, but she remained standing that way until bright spots danced behind her eyelids.

And when she opened them, her heart was glad. It *would* work! A sense of calm settled over her as she knew with undeniable certainty that she'd always carry a piece of the northern sky with her. How *could* she forget the clear, rich blue that seemed to stretch all the way to heaven?

It was the exact color of Garrett's eyes.

March 1856

As he strode along the path between the stark, skeletal spires of the poplar trees, Garrett looked upward automatically, almost expecting to see the familiar figure of Sheldon Tremayne leaning over the railed parapet at the top of the house. So often when he'd returned from the fields, his friend had hailed him from high above, calling the latest news or just a simple greeting. Garrett knew Sheldon had used the tower to oversee his vast holdings, but he also knew that far above the rest of the world, the older man had been able to let his thoughts drift beyond the land to where his heart lay an ocean away.

Bitterness clung to Garrett's memory of his friend's last days, and his steps lengthened as anger drove him toward the house. What good had it done Sheldon to yearn for love that was never returned? he raged silently. How many months, maybe years, had been drawn from the noble man's life as he'd waited patiently for a message that never came?

The planked walkway that fronted the house shuddered beneath his bootsteps. He hurried forward, shoving the heavy door open so hard, it slammed against the wall with a resounding crash. Inside the spacious foyer two heads peeked cautiously through the kitchen doorway and two pairs of eyes widened with varying degrees of apprehension.

"Hannah! See that the north rooms are cleaned and aired," he ordered. "You'll have two hours. Send for another girl from town if you need help."

"But them rooms ain't been used since—"

"They will be now."

The withered, coffee-colored face nodded at him from the kitchen doorway. Hannah, Garrett knew, rarely stepped beyond the boundaries of her domain, and since Sheldon had made him promise to retain the older staff members, he was willing to concede to this one idiosyncrasy, so long as she carried out his wishes once he was gone. "There'll be guests for dinner. Two, I think, at the main table, and undoubtedly a carriage load of servants to be fed as well."

Trained by the original mistress of Riverview, Hannah was accustomed to obeying without comment, but she couldn't help wondering what all the commotion was about. She was often asked to cook up enough food for several extra mouths. But she'd never seen young Garrett in a stir on any of those occasions.

"Benjamin, come with me!"

Garrett's terse command was met with silence as he stormed into the study without waiting to see if he was being followed. Shrugging his bony shoulders at the old woman, Benjamin limped across the polished slate of the foyer and slipped through the study doorway, closing the door gently behind him. The gloom in the book-lined room was unrelieved by the wan afternoon light trickling through two tall windows, though it appeared to match perfectly the mood of its occupant.

Benjamin saw the tension beneath the gray wool covering Garrett's broad shoulders as the younger man stared out across the eastern lawn. "We gwine ta have another shipment?" he ventured, taking another halting step closer to his employer.

Garrett turned then, and the older man was shocked by the ill-concealed torment that changed his handsome face into a twisted mask. He hadn't ever looked that way, even when the master died, and everyone knew young Garrett had loved him like a father. For the first time, Benjamin noticed the crumpled piece of paper clutched in one strong hand.

"I wish it were so easy," Garrett said derisively, moving to the wide, mahogany desk that he'd so recently begun to use. Sweeping aside the plans he'd been drawing up for the new boat house, he seated himself behind the desk and laid the creased message in front of him.

The old negro waited patiently, deciding whatever news Garrett had received from the telegraph station must be bad, because he was staring at the small square of paper like it was a snake, and a poisonous one at that.

Garrett lifted his gaze to Benjamin's after a few ponderous seconds. The dark eyes peering back at him were so full of forbearance and aged wisdom that he was immediately ashamed of his own brusque behavior. He gestured toward another seat and watched as the man settled into the comfortable chair with an involuntary sigh of relief. Benjamin grimaced as he spent the next few minutes positioning his crooked leg, but before long his questioning gaze was riveted once again upon his employer.

"She's coming home," Garrett said without preamble. Long ago he thought he'd be saying those words with joy, and during the months of Sheldon's illness he'd hoped to utter them with reassurance. But now he could summon no other emotion but anger—at least none that he cared to permit—and the words hung in the air like a storm cloud, pregnant with stinging rain.

"Home?" Benjamin shook his head in confusion, then realization dawned on him and his eyes widened until they looked like two black pennies ringed with white. "Ah, the poor little miss," he whispered.

Garrett dismissed the sympathetic words impatiently, leaping up to stand at the window once again. "Save your pity," he said curtly. "She'd have come months ago if she truly gave a damn! Five years! She didn't even bother to send a wire of her own. That message . . ."—he pointed angrily at the paper on the desk—". . . is from Justin Delbert. He says he's meeting her train in Lockport and will bring her to Riverview himself."

Benjamin wondered briefly if part of Garrett's anger stemmed from the fact that the missy hadn't sent for him instead, but he curbed the disloyal thought. The young master had every right to be disturbed about this change in plans. No one knew that better than he. Shuffling to his feet, the old man paused to add a word in defense of the loving child he remembered. "Mebbe she couldn't ketch no boat. Leastways she's comin' now."

Garrett heard the imploring note in Benjamin's voice, but he steeled his heart against it, and against the yearning for something long dead that tightened his chest.

"She's coming now, all right," he acknowledged coldly. "But she's too late."

I'm too late.

The words stung Kelsey's brain like one aching, endless wound. *I'm too late.*

She'd had time for the painful knowledge to settle into her heart. From the moment she'd heard the news of her papa's death from Christina Delbert in New York City, she'd berated herself for not coming sooner, though that would have been impossible. Impossible, she mourned, because of her own foolishness.

Her sorrow, then, was tinged with guilt, but the two seemed inexorably bound together like ingredients that are harmless alone, but when combined form a lethal potion. Knuckling a stinging teardrop from her cheek, Kelsey drew herself up straighter in the smartly equipped buggy. It had been one thing to succumb to tears while alone in a hotel room, but now that she was home, she would not reveal her anguished shame among those who remembered her father with affection and respect.

"Lewiston." At her side, Justin Delbert guided the buggy round the corner onto the main road, announcing this superfluous piece of information as he did.

Mentally shaking herself from her despairing thoughts, Kelsey looked around at the town, amazed by how much was changed as well as by how much had stayed the same. Freshly painted new buildings vied for her attention with the familiar landmarks that seemed to her like old friends lined up along Center Street to welcome her home.

Home. It was strange she couldn't feel much beyond the stifling blanket of grief enveloping her heart, but then less than a year ago she hadn't expected to see her hometown ever again. Now she was here, fast approaching the moment when she'd reach her beloved Riverview, and she was finding it difficult to pretend enthusiasm.

Not that it mattered, she thought absently. Justin was eager enough for them both. "And wait until you see the bridge!" he said, unaware that Kelsey was barely paying attention. "They'd just begun when you left but now it's one of the finest suspension bridges in the world. You've been gone much longer than anyone expected. Christina and I thought you would be gone for only a few months."

"That's what I thought, too," Kelsey sighed. "But mother had other plans."

"Then why didn't you come home when she died? It's been almost a year now, hasn't it?"

She realized he was only trying to lend friendly support, even if his questions hit a bit too hard. She decided that telling him a small part of the truth might not be such a bad idea. "I was sadly short of the funds necessary to make the trip," she admitted. "I found employment and was able to save enough after several months. And how are your parents?" She already knew since Christina, newly married and living in New York, had filled her in on much of the small town's gossip a week ago. But her question had the desired affect of changing the subject and giving Justin something to talk about while she concentrated on studying her surroundings.

Compared to London, which she'd at once admired and despised, Lewiston was new as a green sapling to an aged oak. But because many of the homes and businesses that graced the center of town stood long before her own birth, to Kelsey they were ancient. More than one cornerstone bore the date 1815, which had been the year of rebuilding after the town was razed by the British. Forty years had passed since then, time had long since softened their raw edges, and now Lewiston bore an air of staid gentility that became her well.

Except that for a lady of elegant middle-age, she was beginning to look and sound like an excited schoolgirl preparing for her first social!

"Aren't there a lot of people out for a Tuesday afternoon?"

Kelsey's question was met with a frown from Justin. "Yes, I'd forgotten about the hearing, but once we get past the Frontier House, the crowd'll thin out."

"Hearing? For the first time during the long ride from Lockport something in Justin's tone piqued her interest. She glanced upward, noting the open glower that darkened his olive complexion. "What kind of hearing?"

Justin flicked the reins with obvious annoyance, the sudden motion sending a lock of tightly curled dark hair falling across his forehead. "It's nothing," he said, feigning unconcern. "Just another runaway."

"Another run—? Oh!" Kelsey's dark eyes widened as she swung her head around to get a better view of the unfolding scene. The three-storied Frontier House was surrounded by townsfolk, men and women, all staring with various expressions of fascination and alarm at the four figures standing on the front porch. Or rather, three of them were standing. One was leaning against a stone pillar, stooped from the waist as if he were about to drop. It was that man, Kelsey noted with horror, who was the center of attention.

His skin was the color of the rich, dark earth, and because his shirt hung in tattered strips from his shoulders, she could see the welts that crisscrossed his back like some horrible, bloodied web. She choked back a cry as the tallest of the other three men jerked him upright with a savage grip and she caught a look at his face.

"Why, that's Micah!" Her strangled whisper was lost among the grumbling murmurs of the crowd, which now surged forward angrily. "Stop, Justin! Can't you see that's Micah Ramsey?"

Despite the dainty hand clutching at his sleeve, Justin chucked the reins smartly, hurrying the buggy past the muttering throng and well away from danger. He ignored

Kelsey's irritated look long enough to steer them up a deserted side alley before turning west again down Onandaga Street. Here, where not a soul was in sight, he turned to face her snapping eyes. ''It *was* Micah,'' he confirmed gravely. ''But there's not a thing we can do about it now.''

Kelsey gasped as anger surged through her, both at the ominous scene they'd just witnessed and at Justin's complacent attitude. ''Do about what? Just what is going on here?''

''You've heard of the Fugitive Slave Act, haven't you?''

Even as far away as England, society had been rife with talk about the unpopular legislation. At least it was unpopular in Europe and, from what she'd heard, also in the northern states, where abolitionists gathered support. Congress had adopted the act in 1850 as a means of appeasing the furious southern slaveholders who demanded more effective laws to assist them in recovering their ''property.'' Under the new law, slaves who escaped from their owners could be hunted down like animals anywhere in the United States, and heavy penalties were sentenced to any person aiding them in their flight. If they were caught, the fugitive slaves were forbidden to testify on their own behalf.

''Of course,'' she said and nodded. ''But what does that have to do with Micah? He's a freeman.'' As a girl, Kelsey had delighted in gathering on the front stoop of his cobbler shop with her friends to listen to the powerful baritone voice that erupted spontaneously as he pounded leather into shiny new shoes. To Kelsey's childish eyes his gentleness had made him seem old, but she realized now that he'd been a young man then and was now in his prime. ''What precisely has Micah done?'' she asked again.

''He's a runaway.'' With a negligent shrug, Justin continued to stare straight ahead as he spoke. ''It's been ten years, but that doesn't matter now. Bart Ogden, that's the tall man you saw next to Micah, claims he's been hired by Micah's owner to catch him and take him back to Kentucky."

"Can they do that?"

Justin gazed down at her with a crooked smile, and Kelsey fumed inwardly at the patronizing look on his face. "They can, and they have," he admitted. "But don't get yourself upset, Kelsey dear. Many things have changed in the years since you went away. And believe me, some will be more disturbing to you than the fate of a simple darkie."

Swallowing back an angry retort, Kelsey forced her eyes straight ahead. Inwardly, she continued to fret over Micah's fate, but her brief glimpse of the scene was all jumbled together with vague impressions of conversations lost long ago. And the closer they came to Riverview, the more her thoughts were drawn toward her own uncertain future.

They'd already made the northward turn onto Second Street that would take her home, and from here she could detect the rushing sound of the river as it swept past Lewiston toward the lake. That constant din had rumbled like background music all her life, and now more than ever before, she felt the pang of homesickness she'd fought off for years.

Gazing steadily ahead, Kelsey struggled against the tears constricting her throat. When the road widened enough to reveal a glimpse of the line of poplars in the distance, she could bear no more. "Let me out here," she cried, gathering her skirts and reticule to descend from the buggy.

"My dear," Justin protested. "It's nearly half a mile."

"I want to walk."

"But . . ." One look at the determined set of her chin was all he needed to convince him there'd be no changing her mind. Drawing the buggy to a halt, Justin eyed the muddy road skeptically. "I see you're still as headstrong as ever, but if you insist . . ."

Kelsey didn't answer as she climbed down unassisted. By pretending to brush dust off her skirt, she managed to hide the tears stinging her eyes. "Thank you for bringing me home. I'll call on your mother as soon as I get settled. Perhaps we'll see one another then."

"I'll just take your trunk to the house now."

She knew the polite thing to do would be to invite him to dinner, but the thought of a few more hours of his well-intended conversation made her head ache. "That's fine. Is Hannah still there? Before you go, please tell her I'll be in shortly."

The sound of the buggy continuing on down the road finally roused Kelsey from her spot. Turning slowly, she studied the expanse of trees and underbrush between her and the sound of the river, then hiked up her skirt in one hand and wrapped the silk thongs of her purse around her wrist. Luckily, she'd opted to wear a pair of low-heeled, serviceable shoes for traveling. Her usual kid slippers would never have done for the cross-country trek she intended.

Using the Niagara's incessant rumble as a guide, she stepped off the road and into the brush. The land here was her father's—now her own, she thought glumly—and she pushed unerringly toward the river's edge. If she bore due west across the narrow stretch of trees, she could then take the little-used path beside the river as her approach to the house. And on the way, she knew, she would pass the tiny cemetery overlooking the Niagara.

Listening intently to the river and glancing occasionally at the gray sky, Kelsey gauged the distance. It would probably start to rain before she reached the safety of Riverview, but that mattered little to her now. What point was there in hurrying toward a house that would only echo her loneliness?

A surge of grief nearly overwhelmed her, causing her to pause and lean against a large boulder overlooking the river. Was it her lot in life to always grieve alone? She already knew what it was to bear the pain of loss in solitude, but then there'd been the knowledge that Papa was here on his rooftop hideaway high above the trees. Many times she had wanted to talk to him, to send a message across the verdant waves, but it was more than her own shame that forced her to hide her troubles from him. He had sent her away with her mother, never asking if she wanted to go. Then, when Mabelle no longer stood in the way, other matters had prevented her return.

Now Sheldon was gone and no one could take his place in her heart. Not even Garrett.

Pulling herself upright, she brushed a wisp of dark hair from her cheek. She wouldn't allow herself to think of *him*, she vowed inwardly. Christina had warned her that Garrett O'Neill had become an important part of her father's life in her absence, but Kelsey could not let him become a part of hers.

Regret pulsed through her heart. Once, she could have poured out her troubles to Garrett, confident that he would listen, would understand. Maybe he still would. . . .

But no! she warned herself harshly. Not now. Not this. What had been improbable five years earlier was now impossible. The sooner she convinced herself—and Garrett, if necessary—of that, the better off they'd both be.

The rain had been drumming against the casement windows for nearly an hour before he finally gave in to the clamoring voice in his head. Without bothering to don a cape, Garrett headed across the south lawn, instinct guiding him to the place where he would find her.

The going was muddy but he never altered his strides until he came within sight of the iron fence that surrounded the tiny clearing on the precipice of the river. It looked like a natural break in the treeline, but was probably made years ago by the Indians who once plied their trade along this route. The grassy slope spread for a hundred feet from the path, marked only by an occasional bush of fragrant lilac, just beginning to bloom. Birch trees bent protectively over the black wrought-iron, lending a look of utter seclusion to the scene. The misty rain provided an additional veil of privacy so that Garrett had to squint to make out any details from this distance.

Inside the fence were a dozen or so small stone markers. Each bore just a name and two dates, but considering that only three belonged to men who could claim Riverview as home, Garrett counted the others lucky to be resting in such a peaceful spot. It was at the front of the tiny cemetery, closest to the river, that Sheldon Tremayne had wished to be buried. The tall monument ordered from Buffalo had not yet arrived, leaving the grave unmarked, but it was easily discerned from the rest because the fresh mound was still bare of grass.

And seated nearby, as dark and bleak as the day, was Kelsey.

Garrett stopped short before the open gate, struggling to control the urge to order her away. A pulse thumped wildly in his jaw, which was clenched so tight he felt as if it might snap at any moment. Almost simultaneously, two thoughts struck his mind like exploding rockets, shattering his self-control. One was that she was more beautiful than he remembered.

The other was that he loved her still.

Immersed in her own grief, Kelsey didn't hear him approach until he stood less than a foot away. Startled, she peered up through tear-swollen eyes to see a look so full of disdain she gasped out loud.

"Welcome home, Miss Tremayne," he drawled mockingly.

Breathless from the way her heart raced the moment she recognized him, she could only whisper in answer. "Garrett."

Rain dripped from her bare head, mingling with the tears that washed her cheeks and stained her serge mourning dress. Despite her appearance, or perhaps because of it, Garrett felt as if he were seeing her for the very first time. No artificial color to cover up her clear porcelain skin, no fancy coiffure to hide the perfect shape of her face. Coal black eyes questioned him openly and he caught a glimpse of her pain and confusion just an instant before she lowered her head once more.

"Oh, Garrett," she breathed. "He's gone."

This heartrending whisper was nearly his undoing, but he managed to walk around to the other side of Sheldon's grave. He didn't see the trembling hand reaching out to smooth a lump from the muddy earth. "Did you expect him to linger forever, or just until you got here?"

Unsure whether her numbed senses were hearing him correctly, Kelsey stammered, "I . . . I don't know what you mean."

"Come in out of the rain before you make yourself ill."

Too chilled to respond even to his unexplained rudeness, she obeyed automatically, taking his hand when he offered it. He was taller than she remembered, or maybe it was just the way his shoulders had broadened to an imposing width. His hair lay flattened against his brow by the rain, darkened to the color of brown autumn leaves, and it gave his features a rather grim look. But it was the coldness in his azure eyes that drew her gaze and then turned it away again. *Why does he look at me like that?* she wondered dismally.

Garrett's heart wrenched at the aching expression on her lovely face, but he peered instead at the oblong mound of earth at his feet, pondering one bitter question. Had either of them truly mattered to her at all?

Kelsey was alone in her old room before awareness finally crept back over her shocked senses. Rainwater dripped from her hair, snaking down her back in icy rivulets, and she stared at the sodden dress lying at her feet, not even remembering when she'd taken it off. Her equally soaked chemise stuck to her, raising gooseflesh beneath the sheer fabric. She crossed her arms and rubbed her hands briskly up and down, warming herself. It did little good except to wake her further from the lethargy that seemed to have paralyzed her from the moment she'd spotted her father's grave.

Shuddering, she forced her attention toward the stone hearth. A fire had been laid, but not lit. Even if she started it now, it would be several minutes before the blaze grew hot enough to take the chill from the room. Kelsey didn't want to wait that long.

Stepping over the wet pile of clothing and moving toward her trunk, she pried open the lid and searched for dry underthings. From the bottom of the trunk she shook out her only warm dress, glad to see it was not too badly wrinkled. Other than the gown she had just discarded, none of her outfits were appropriate for mourning. But there was nothing to be done about that.

As she peeled off her wet chemise, her glance took in the condition of the room around her for the first time. While spotlessly clean, it bore none of the signs of care that would have been attended to during her mother's reign. The draperies were faded and worn, the wood furniture showed signs of age. Clean towels were waiting for her on top of the Chippendale commode, but the blue china vase beside them, sitting exactly where it had for five years, was empty of the spring flowers that abounded in the fields surrounding Riverview.

Kelsey quickly assessed the situation. There must be a shortage of servants at Riverview and the few that remained had been allowed to grow lax in their duties. It was just as well, she thought as she toweled her hair dry, that she had learned in the past year how to fend for herself. Judging from the condition of her home and from Garrett's reception, she'd be fending for herself quite a lot in the future.

Thoughts of Garrett brought her to a standstill, her hands posed above her head. Whatever she had expected, it wasn't the contempt she had seen in his glowering blue eyes nor the odd tremor that had shaken her when he took her hand in his.

Resuming her task with rough vigor, Kelsey thrust her mind away from the turn it was taking. A lady, her mother had admonished repeatedly, did not reveal her emotions to a gentleman. That was a lesson Kelsey had learned the hard way, and did not intend to forget again.

Besides, whatever position Garrett held in her father's business—and Christina had been strangely vague about exactly what that was—it had no bearing on her. Except that Garrett was likely the one who could tell her about Sheldon's last days.

When Kelsey had arrived in New York, weary after a lengthy ocean voyage, she'd been surprised to find Christina Delbert waiting for her at the dock. The telegram she'd sent to her father, Kelsey learned, had been passed on to George Delbert, Christina's father and Sheldon's attorney. Christina then had been assigned the dreadful task of telling Kelsey that her father had died several weeks earlier.

In the days that followed, during which Christina had comforted her friend through her shock and had helped her book passage on a westbound train, she had not shared with Kelsey the details of Sheldon Tremayne's death or the particulars of Garrett O'Neill's involvement.

But Kelsey planned to find out soon.

After she had donned a dry gown, she hung the rest of her dresses in the cedar wardrobe and turned to the cold fireplace, wishing again that someone had thought to light the stacked logs. An uncontrollable shiver made her tremble, reminding her that the merriest of blazes would not revive her frozen heart.

It was time, however, to carry on. Kelsey pondered over the task she was about to face, not looking forward to questioning Garrett when he was in such a foul mood. He had escorted her home from the cemetery in silence, but when she'd turned at the door to thank him, he'd stepped inside behind her and entered her father's study without comment, closing off the chance for further conversation.

Patting her hair quickly to make sure it was secure in its net snood, Kelsey made her way down the stairs until she was standing in front of the closed study door, which looked far more forbidding than it had when her father had occupied it.

Garrett answered her tentative knock with an abrupt "Come in." Bolstering herself for a confrontation, she turned the knob and thrust the door open with far more bravado than she felt.

Her knees turned to jelly almost immediately.

At some point while she'd been upstairs, Garrett had also changed his wet clothing. He stood behind the desk, resplendent in a perfectly tailored wool jacket over a snowy white silk shirt. The midnight blue of his coat only accentuated the lighter hue of his eyes, which stared unwaveringly as she paused in the open doorway. To her surprise, he showed his own trepidation by raking a hand through his thick, golden hair in a gesture so poignantly familiar she nearly forgot what she'd come to say.

The bitterness in his ice blue eyes made her remember. They glittered as cold and hard as the crystal tumbler he clenched in one hand, nearly piercing her resolve.

But not for nothing had she spent five years with the British. Summoning her best imitation of Mrs. Higbee, the woman with whom she had boarded last year, Kelsey lifted her chin a notch. "I'd like to thank you for keeping Riverview in hand until I arrived," she began haltingly, stepping forward. "When I learned of Papa's death, I'd no idea how I'd find things here."

Garrett nodded. He ought to have been prepared for this, but now that she stood before him, he wasn't sure he could trust his voice. His first thought was that she was not wearing mourning garb, but his thoroughly male reaction was that he was glad. She'd changed the unflattering black gown for one of rose wool that hugged her slender waist and full breasts. Though the neckline was modestly high and trimmed with a worn lace collar, there was no disguising her womanly curves.

His gaze, however, was riveted on her face. She's matured, he thought distractedly. Though she'd tried to tame her hair back into a sedate chignon, unruly wisps already curled freely around her face, and Garrett couldn't help recalling the glorious mane that she'd worn free years ago. What had once been youthful prettiness had turned to stunning beauty, made more intriguing by the undisguised sorrow in her dark eyes.

It almost made him weaken, but not quite.

"I did nothing beyond my duty," he answered evenly. "Sheldon Tremayne was a man much admired. His loss will be deeply felt by many who loved him—and by you, no doubt."

Confused by his thinly veiled sarcasm, Kelsey murmured her thanks and seated herself at one of the wing chairs angled toward the center of the room. To her unease, instead of taking a seat across from her, Garrett came around to sit on the front of the desk, hitching one leg up to dangle casually. She had to crane her neck up to look at him.

"I'll ask George Delbert to stop over tomorrow," he began without preamble. "He'll explain the terms of the will to you."

"So soon? I mean, can't the reading wait a few days."

"The reading," Garrett stated dryly, "took place eight weeks ago, shortly after Sheldon's death. The purpose of Delbert's visit is merely to help you understand the terms."

Kelsey's brow furrowed as she peered at Garrett questioningly. She had come down here to ask him about her father's last days. But now, for the first time since Christina had broken the tragic news to her a week ago, Kelsey wondered about the disposition of Riverview. There was more than a hint of challenge in Garrett's set expression. A niggling fear worked at her mind. "And what *are* the terms?"

"Perhaps you should wait for George Delbert to explain."

"But you know, don't you? I'd rather you tell me now and be done with it."

He couldn't help admiring her candidness, but then it was the same forthright manner that would surely turn against him once he told her the truth. Strangely enough, now that the time had come to put her in her place, he took no satisfaction in the deed. He had to summon back his anger toward her. She'd get neither more nor less than she deserved from him. "Sheldon told me of his plans long ago. Shortly after your mother died. When you didn't come home then . . . ,'' accusation made his voice cut like steel, ''. . . he feared you never would. He didn't want Riverview to fall into the wrong hands.''

Kelsey pondered this news carefully, the reason for Garrett's animosity slowly dawning on her. ''Did *you* think I would never come home?'' she asked.

He held her gaze with a steady one of his own. There'd been a time when he'd dreamed . . . No! He wouldn't let her get under his skin again. He had been young then, and she'd been nothing more than a spoiled child. That she'd grown into a selfish, uncaring woman should be no surprise to him. Shrugging, he replied, ''It made no difference to me.''

Pain gnawed at Kelsey's heart, but for his sake she kept her features composed. He *had* missed her. Perhaps not as badly as she'd missed him, but enough that her long absence had wounded his pride. And the best thing she could do for him now was to act as if she believed him. If he refused to acknowledge his disappointment, she would do no less. ''What, then,'' she inquired softly, ''were Papa's wishes?''

He hesitated. ''Sheldon and I had just begun breeding thoroughbreds as a joint venture, so half of that is yours. You'll also inherit a 20 percent share in my shipping company when you turn twenty-one.''

''*Your* shipping company?'' Her voice rose uncertainly. Five years ago it had been her father's. As a former officer in the British Navy, Sheldon had naturally turned to the water for his livelihood, even if it was only the lakefront trade, instead of the vast oceans that he had previously sailed. The fortune he had made with his thriving business had been the one aspect of Sheldon's life with which Mabelle never found fault. Now, however, it appeared things had changed—drastically.

Garrett's lips twisted into a half-smile. ''I realize how little the business concerns you, but you did ask. Sheldon lost interest years ago and he allowed me to purchase his share gradually, in bits and pieces.''

"Only 20 percent!" Kelsey couldn't hold back her dismay. Now the ramshackle condition of Riverview made sense. But why had her father given up the ships he loved so well?

When she voiced her question out loud, Garrett shrugged enigmatically. "He had other interests."

And she thought she knew exactly what those interests were! Pursing her lips to keep them from trembling, she met his narrowed gaze. "Indeed. But how, may I ask, am I to live now that Riverview has no source of income?"

His eyes never moved, but she could have sworn the light in them changed somehow. "You could always return to Europe."

She couldn't tell if he was hoping she'd say yes, but the disdain in his voice brought anger bubbling to the surface and Kelsey shot back quickly, "I have no intention of leaving now. This is my home."

"Indeed." His hollow tone echoed hers.

"I can always make Riverview pay somehow. There's still the land." Kelsey hadn't an inkling how to do such a thing, but at least her bold declaration elicited a reaction from Garrett. His brilliant blue eyes narrowed and his lips grew thin.

"You'd sell it?"

"Yes . . . no . . . I don't know! Maybe I'll farm it."

"Sheldon never intended for the land to support this estate. The farm was a hobby to him. Besides," Garrett said dryly, "you don't know the first thing about farming."

"I can learn."

"It'll take years."

"Time," she replied pointedly, "is something I've got plenty of."

"We'll see." Garrett stifled the urge to continue arguing and instead rose and circled the desk. He noted with rueful pleasure the look of dismay that crossed Kelsey's face when he seated himself in Sheldon's worn leather chair. "A lot has changed in five years."

That was the same thing Justin had told her, Kelsey remembered. Had he been referring to Garrett when he said some of the new developments would be disturbing?

"It seems," she said icily, "that one of the changes has been your status in this household. Papa may have welcomed you to make free with his things," she gestured toward the papers piled neatly on the desk, "but I'm afraid you'll have to find some place else to take your work now. There's a lot to be done here and I can't have you in my way."

To his chagrin, Garrett felt a resurgence of the long buried resentment he had harbored years before. As the son of immigrants, he'd been held in contempt by many who had long forgotten that the country's foundation was made up of 'imported' souls. Mabelle had been one of those self-righteous people. Was Kelsey now as much of a snob as her mother had been? "I have as much right to this house as you do," he growled. "Maybe more."

Springing to her feet, Kelsey glared at him. "There should be laws against people like you, preying on the vulnerabilities of an old man—"

"A *lonely* old man," he emphasized. "And before you start accusing me of avarice, you'd better examine your own actions. Do you think people will take kindly to a daughter who can't tear herself away from London society to visit her father's deathbed, but shows up in time to claim the inheritance?"

Shock washed over Kelsey in pounding waves that nearly rocked her off her feet. She had never thought of it that way, but it *was* possible that it might appear to be true. The problem was she couldn't defend herself without revealing her own shame. Not now, not ever.

Garrett witnessed the battle for control that raged across her lovely face, though when it was clear she had won, he wasn't certain whether it was relief or disappointment he felt. "I don't want to argue with you about this, Kelsey," he said regretfully. "There's no point in it." He watched as she thrust her chin at him, her expression frozen to a blank mask.

"Is there anything else then?"

"There is." He paused, but since she would find out soon enough, there was no use denying her. "According to Sheldon's will, this house is half mine. For propriety's sake I'll move into the caretaker's cottage immediately, but I have no intention of relinquishing ownership. I'd prefer to buy your share outright. You can do whatever you want with the money; you can go back to England if you wish."

Kelsey's first impulse to lash out that she would never leave Riverview. She wanted to scream her frustration and anger, both at Garrett's arrogance and at the knowledge that her father truly had forsaken her. Her mother's training, however, prevailed. Though her insides were churning at this startling news, she managed to pin him with a regal stare. "I'll take your offer into consideration. But not until I consult with my attorney."

By *God,* she was coolheaded bitch, Garrett thought grimly as she walked to the door, her back as straight as one of Sheldon's poplar trees. She hadn't batted an eye at the thought of handing over her birthright. And it galled him to know that Justin Delbert had apparently insinuated himself into her confidence already.

He wanted nothing more than to tear his eyes from the sight of her retreating figure, but when she turned with her hand on the doorknob, faltering, he was compelled to meet her eyes.

"Is . . . is Bridget still here?" She could no longer voice the questions she had come to ask, but this she could manage.

Garrett nodded. The look of relief and anticipation filling her gaze took him by surprise. It was the most emotion she had shown so far. "Shall I send her up to you?"

"Yes, thank you."

A sad smile touched her lips, piercing Garrett's heart with a bittersweet shaft of longing. Then, just as quickly, she left the room, closing the door softly behind her.

* * *

Kelsey sat stiffly in the Windsor chair by the window, her muscles so tense, her senses so acute, she could feel every rung pressing into her back, could feel the hard edges of the seat as she clutched it with both hands at her hips. Even the numbness had been better than the wrenching pain tearing at her heart.

Riverview was not hers.

At least not completely, and the fact that it was Garrett who benefited from her father's decision only clarified the truth. Sheldon Tremayne had cared as much for Garrett as he had his own daughter. Perhaps more, she moaned inwardly, since he'd probably felt obligated to honor the blood tie, if nothing else.

But could she blame him? All through the difficult days of the past year she had ached for her home, for the familiar places and people that she associated with her carefree childhood. Now they were gone, or at least changed so much that she hardly recognized them. Riverview was practically lost to her, and Garrett was acting like a stranger.

A single tear rolled down her cheek, and Kelsey brushed it away angrily. It was better that way, she reminded herself. She had known it would be difficult to be simply friends with him. After today's conversation even friendship appeared to be out of the question.

A shuffling noise sounded from the hallway, followed by a soft click as someone released the latch Kelsey had purposely left unbolted. Hinges creaked as the door to her room inched open, then swung wider as a gray snout and shaggy head appeared.

"Bridget?" Kelsey whispered tearfully as a large Irish wolfhound bounded into the room, coming to a halt with its huge head just inches away from her face. The dog panted happily, appearing to be grinning ear to ear.

"Oh, Bridget! You remembered me." Suddenly, Kelsey was thirteen again, pouring out her heart to the puppy who never laughed at her fears or dashed her hopes to the ground. Wrapping her arms around the friendly beast, she allowed tears of sorrow and gladness to spill freely.

Now, however, instead of numbing her heart they began to cleanse it.

Bridget whined fretfully, but didn't move. The dog seemed to recognize her mistress's need to cling to the one friend who had welcomed her with unwavering devotion. She stood loyally, perhaps not putting the thoughts to words, but able to sense them just the same.

At last, Kelsey was home.

3

The sky over the river gorge resembled the thick black of India ink, and Kelsey felt the sting of bitter wind that meant another spring storm was brewing on the lake. Though the rain had ceased its dreary descent for the time being, heavy clouds still hovered threateningly. Bridget nosed the air and bumped against her leg, signaling a decided preference for a warm hearth, and Kelsey patted the dog's head in agreement. There was little here, she thought resignedly, to remind her of the last time she stood on this very spot, gazing at the water.

But she couldn't help remembering. Five years of confusion and pain hung behind her, burdening her with its weight, and yet simply by closing her eyes and inhaling the scent of the river, by allowing its hushed roar to thrum through her soul, she could almost believe those years had never existed.

Almost, but not quite.

Sighing heavily, Kelsey blinked back sudden tears. Of course everything was different, she scolded herself. Why shouldn't it be? Only the river remained the same.

Drawn to the edge of the precipice by that thought, Kelsey halted unerringly a few feet from the brink. There was just enough light falling from the upper windows of the house to outline the scraggly hedges that had once guarded the path with tidy precision. The rosebushes remained too, their sweet fragrance pervading the air even though it was too early in the year for blooms. The only thing lacking, Kelsey decided, was youth. Youth . . . and innocence.

She had been innocent enough when her mother took her from Riverview, and not only of the ways of men. She had believed, with childish naivete, that whatever troubles existed between her parents would be magically solved by a brief separation. It was not until she and her mother had taken up residence in London with a distant relative that Kelsey was informed, quite bluntly, that her father did not want them to return.

Of course, Kelsey had not believed her mother at first. Even at fifteen she recognized Mabelle's tendency to overreact in almost any situation. Kelsey had immediately written to Sheldon, asking him to do what he could to soothe her mother's state of mind. That she had wished the same consolation for herself she had not realized until months passed with no response. She continued to write, each letter more beseeching than the previous one, until finally she had been forced to accept the truth. Mabelle must have been right. Her father wanted her to stay far away.

For the first year or so Kelsey had been consumed with despair over her father's treatment. She had struggled alone—for Mabelle refused to discuss the matter beyond making cryptic statements about Sheldon's *obsession*—to understand what had caused her to lose her father's love. In one desperate attempt she had even written a letter to Garrett, hoping he was still working for her father and could shed some light on the situation. That letter, too, had remained unanswered. She had hopelessly decided that she would never know the truth.

And now her father was dead. With an unsteady hand, Kelsey felt for the break in the hedges that opened into the secluded garden she had often sought when she was a child. How many nights had she dreamed of this secret haven? And how many of those dreams had ended just the way that long-ago day had ended—with a kiss and a question? How *did* Garrett feel about her?

"Oh, hush!" she said out loud, angry with herself for both the turn her thoughts were taking and for so losing the tenuous control she had kept over her emotions when facing Garrett. So now she knew the meaning behind Christina's sly hints and Justin's veiled references. They had wondered at the bond between Garrett and her father, and pitied her for having been slighted. An ache began to throb deep in her breast, despised, and yet familiar. She had only wanted to come home to her father in the hope of finding some peace and security. Instead, there were only more questions, more hardships to face.

Locating the breach in the overgrown hedges at last, Kelsey pushed her way into the clearing, heedless of the twigs tugging at her dress and at the shawl tossed carelessly over her shoulders. Bridget followed close behind.

With her hands lowered, palms outstretched, she groped for the small granite bench her father had set here long ago before she was born. He had told her it was once his favorite place to watch the river, until the house was finished and his balcony rail had superseded this spot.

A chill danced along her spine and she glanced up quickly toward the stately mansion. Normally a welcoming sight, with its light-colored stone from the local quarry and worn red brick, in the darkness it loomed forbiddingly, as if to remind her that she didn't belong here anymore. She could barely make out the balustrade jutting up from the hipped roof, which could be reached through a trap door from her father's old rooms. Was someone watching her now or were the ghosts of her own memory conjuring up this feeling that she was not alone?

Shuddering, more to cast away the eerie sensation of having been watched than out of fear, Kelsey lowered herself to the damp bench and motioned for Bridget to sit at her feet. If one of the servants were spying on her for Garrett, who had presumedly moved his personal belongings to the caretaker's house during the time Kelsey was picking over a dinner tray in her bedroom, then she could only be amused. And if it was not one of the servants . . . well, it was her father's balcony, after all. There was no need to be afraid. He had loved her—hadn't he?

Like a canker that cannot be ignored, Kelsey's thoughts returned to the past, to the first few years of her exile. Despite her mother's insistence that Sheldon had been at fault, Kelsey could never summon feelings of anger toward her father. Instead, she had reasoned that somehow *she* had come up short of her father's expectations. If she had been more attentive to her lessons, if she had deported herself in a manner more becoming to her station: Such were the doubts Mabelle had planted in her mind. But these were only minor sins. They were nothing when compared with the tragic mistake she had brought upon herself.

Mabelle's tirade recalled itself to her mind, and Kelsey's heart wrenched at the memory of her mother's words. "You have brought shame to yourself and your family. I dare not tell your father; he would disown you in a second."

She wound her fingers through Bridget's shaggy coat, seeking strength from the contact. The dog shifted closer and laid its head on her lap. She would not feel sorry for herself! Closing her eyes tightly to ward off tears, Kelsey lifted her face into the wind. She would stand up to the consequences; not hide away, as her mother had once made her do, or run away, as Garrett seemed to want.

Riverview—at least half of it—was hers. Here was her home. Here she could heal.

A sense of peace slowly filled her, the same peace she had once believed to be an assurance that she and Garrett would come together again. Well, they were together now, she thought wryly. Unwilling partners, bound by legal ties now that the emotional ones no longer existed.

The wind now stung bitterly and carried the scent of rain, making Kelsey wish she had grabbed up her cloak on the way out, though she still did not move to go inside. She loved the fierce lake storms that gathered slowly, then spent themselves in a furious downpour of moisture and noise. They reminded her of her own capricious temper and she hugged her shawl tighter, unwilling to leave this spot just yet. Several hundred feet below, the pounding of the river mingled with the wind's persistent sigh. She tried to empty her mind of everything but the primal call of the rising storm.

A twig snapped behind them, and Kelsey felt Bridget grow tense just a moment before the dog sat upright. She dropped her hands to clutch the ice-cold sides of the bench, her indrawn breath rammed into her throat by a forceful draft. This time there was no question someone was watching her, and not from the safe distance of the balcony. It was more than wind that rattled the bare branches so insistently, and besides, the wind couldn't smother the sound of a rasping cough, though it was clear whoever hid in the bushes had tried to do just that.

Bridget began to growl deep in her throat, though the sound wasn't quite as menacing as Kelsey would have liked.

"Who's there! Who's there, I say!" Glad that her voice did not reflect the tremors coursing through her body, Kelsey released her grip on the stone bench, standing quickly. "Show yourself this instant!"

A movement from behind startled her, and before she could spin away a hand clamped around her mouth, pulling her backward against unyielding hardness. Panic flared within her and all she could think was that she must call to Garrett for help. Her voice, however, was muffled by her captor's large hand.

"Don' holler, Miss Kelsey. Be still."

Despite the impulse to jerk herself free and run, Kelsey willed her mind to think. The man holding her was doing so with gentle restraint, and there was a pleading note in his voice that belied the order given. Though Bridget stood tense and alert, she had not made a move to stop the attacker.

"Please, Miss Kelsey. I don' want to hurt you. Will you be quiet if I let you go?"

She nodded hesitantly, her fear abating as she struggled to place the familiar voice. The man dropped his hand from her face, though Kelsey noticed at once that the dark, muscular arm clutching her waist retained its iron hold. Now she remembered.

"Micah?" Kelsey twisted her head around to confirm his identity, and the tall negro released his grasp as she stared at him with a mixture of shock and relief. Micah Ramsey had always appeared to her to be as indestructible—and as comforting—as a brick house. His eyes had never failed to light up at the sight of a child or a friendly face, but now they were filled with a quiet desperation that shook her to the core.

"It's me all right, Miss Kelsey. Sorry to give you a start, but I was afraid you'd set up a ruckus."

As relieved as she was, Kelsey also felt immediate shame. With all that had happened today, she had completely forgotten about the scene she and Justin witnessed that afternoon, and her intention then of learning more about Micah's plight. "What are you doing here?" she asked. "I saw you at the Frontier House. How on earth did you escape?"

"Had to," he explained tersely.

"Where are you going?"

"Canada."

That single word conveyed the complete extent of his will. Though he no longer held her captive, Micah Ramsey stood in a half-crouch, prepared to lunge at a moment's notice—whether toward her or away she could not be certain. She remembered him as a gentle man, but now his eyes gleamed with a feral intensity that matched the determined angle of his jaw. Though his mahogany skin was glazed with a fine sheen of sweat that could be caused only by fear, Kelsey had no doubt he would do whatever was necessary to reach the safety of the opposite riverbank.

"Oh, Micah . . . I'm so sorry. How can I help?"

As if uncertain that she meant it, Micah cocked his head to one side and studied her carefully. "Don't need your help," he said with a suspicious tone. "I'll make my own way now."

She started to speak but Micah cut her off, his hand slicing through the air in warning.

"Don't try to stop me," he whispered fiercely. "I been free for ten years and I won't let 'em take me back now."

Kelsey was stunned by the vehemence in his voice and appalled by his lack of trust in her, until she remembered what Justin had told her about the Fugitive Slave Act. It was no wonder Micah was bound for Canada. Apparently he wasn't even safe in the town that had sheltered him most of his adult life!

"I won't stop you," Kelsey assured him breathlessly. "But there must be something you need. Food? Money?" Micah shook his head, and Kelsey saw him relax slightly as a grim smile surfaced on his face.

"Unless you got it with you now, I'll have to do without," he said. "I can't wait long enough for you to go back to the house. Storm's about ready to break. I best be goin'."

"But how—?"

"Don't ask. That way you can tell the truth when the slave catchers come through lookin' for ol' Micah Ramsey. Tell 'em I'm nothing more than a shadow in the dark."

Now it was Kelsey's turn to smile, though a hundred questions raced through her mind. "All right, then," she agreed. "But how will I know if you've made it safely?"

Micah's grin faded and he took a step closer, looming over her with a foreboding expression. "You'll know it if I don't. Them slave catchers'll march me through town in chains if they get the chance, and likely they'll lay a few more lashes on for good measure. Providin'," he added in a low voice, "they can take me alive."

Kelsey drew in a startled breath, overwhelmed by the seriousness of Micah's situation. She recalled the evil smirk on the face of the man whom Justin pointed out that afternoon, the one named Bart Ogden. He looked the kind of person who would not take kindly to having been fooled, and she was suddenly sure that Micah's escape had sealed his own fate.

If he were caught, she reminded herself.

"Go on then," she urged quietly. "I'll pray for your safety, and if there's ever anything—"

The sound of squelching footsteps coming toward them stopped her from completing the sentence. Micah tensed immediately, his fists clenching and unclenching as he froze with indecision. He looked at Kelsey, gauging her reaction.

"Hurry," she whispered. "I'll try to cover for you."

Micah hesitated only a moment, peering at her through eyes as deep and searching as the night sky. He seemed to find what he sought, however, for he nodded once before turning away.

It was then that Kelsey got a glimpse of his back, and she stifled a gasp at the sight of the torn cloth and dried blood, evidence of the flogging he'd already received. He paused, glancing over his shoulder at her, but when she waved him onward with one hand, the other covering her mouth, he turned again. The last she saw of him was the faded blue of what remained of his shirt as he disappeared into the darkness. Then she heard her name called out from behind her.

"Kelsey?"

"Who's there?" It was an unnecessary question, for she recognized Garrett's gruff tone immediately, but she raised her voice in order to cover any telltale sound of Micah's departure. "Garrett? Is that you?"

"Who else were you expecting?" he asked, pushing his way through the overgrown entrance to the clearing. "What are you doing out here?"

Kelsey's mind refused to settle upon an answer, so surprised was she by his appearance. He had changed clothes again, and was now clad in dark trousers and a similarly colored wool jersey of the kind she'd seen used by sailors. With his blond hair wind-tousled, he no longer looked the elegant gentleman of the manor. Kelsey was sharply reminded of the Garrett she remembered from years ago.

"You're dressed like a river man!" she blurted carelessly, too taken aback to think of a more intelligent reply.

Garrett was aware of her scrutiny, and of her shocked response, but was too surprised himself to trouble with wondering why it mattered to her. He hadn't expected to find her here above the river's edge but he had to get her away somehow. "Much more practical, wouldn't you say, than what you're wearing? Are you determined today to catch your death?"

Kelsey struggled to control the tremor that raced through her at the solicitous note in his voice. "You forget," she said lightly, "I'm used to London weather, which is worse than this most of the time. Besides, I wanted to wait for the storm."

Stepping closer, Garrett saw her violent shudder and mistook it for one of cold. "You can watch from inside. You're freezing, Kelsey. I won't have you getting sick."

"I don't know why not! It would make things much simpler for you, wouldn't it?" As soon as she said them, Kelsey wished she could recall the words, but once again her impetuousness would stand in the way of good sense. He'd given her the perfect opportunity to steer them both toward the house and away from Micah, but her sharp tongue had spoiled everything. Again.

Garrett felt his muscles grow taut at her scathing retort, but it was nothing compared to the way his chest contracted when she took a step toward him, placing her hand on his arm.

"I didn't mean that," she said contritely. "Of course I'm going inside now. Will you walk with me?"

He was at war with himself, torn between wanting to acquiesce and wanting to keep himself at a safe distance from her. Forgotten for the moment were his own reasons for braving the elements this night, but the howl of baying dogs in the distance brought his mind to full attention.

"What was that?" Kelsey cried.

She whipped her head around, and Garrett could see the fear in her dark eyes, though he incorrectly assumed it was for her own self. Bridget whined and pressed closer to Kelsey's side. "They won't hurt us," he said quickly. "In fact, I'm surprised they can follow a scent at all in this weather. They're tracking an escaped slave."

Kelsey stopped herself just short of saying, "I know," and instead let her eyes widen with pretended ignorance. "An escaped slave? Here at Riverview?" She moved close to Garrett again, as if frightened by the very prospect, and was gratified when his arm closed around her protectively. If he thought she was afraid, he might take her to the house immediately.

Garrett assessed her reaction grimly, then nodded. "Unfortunately, Lewiston has become a sort of gathering point for the men who make catching slaves their living. This is one of the few places where the Niagara River is navigable, so the people fleeing for Canada often come this way."

Kelsey shivered as the cry of the hounds grew more distinct, even with the wind distorting their soul-wrenching voices. *Dear God,* she prayed. *Let Micah be safely away!*

Garrett felt her tremble, his embrace tightening automatically as he spun her toward the opening of the hedge. "Come on," he muttered, his ear tuned to the sound of the dogs.

Before they had taken more than a few rapid steps, a deep rattle of thunder unleashed a torrent of rain, pelting them with freezing drops. Almost simultaneously lightning traced the the sky with a spidery flash, illuminating the high bank in brilliant light. Unable to stop herself, Kelsey looked over her shoulder, hoping that Micah had been able to hide himself well. Garrett, too, stared in the same direction, then caught her bewildered look as he turned his head back. For a long moment they gazed at one another, each wondering what the other had expected to see.

Kelsey was the first to break away. "The dogs have stopped," she said quizzically, cocking her head.

"They've lost the scent."

Relief surged through her, and with it a measure of triumph. She was glad she had been of some small help to Micah. Perhaps by distracting Garrett she had allowed him a few precious seconds to get away. Kelsey shrugged deeper into her shawl, averting her face so that Garrett could not see the satisfaction in her expression as they trudged toward the house through the pouring rain, Bridget following.

Once they had reached the shelter of the wide portico, Garrett removed his arm from around her shoulders as if he had only just realized he had been touching her. "There's some whiskey in my study, if you've a mind to make a toddy. Hannah will have gone to bed by now, so you'll be on your own."

He turned then, but Kelsey's voice, hesitant and appealing, stopped him. "Where . . . where are you going?"

"To the cottage, of course," he said ruefully. "After I check the grounds again."

"In the rain?" She did not pause to wonder that he would think her concern odd, nor was she thinking of Micah's safety at that moment. Suddenly, the idea of sending Garrett off into the cold seemed a heartless thing to do, but she was unable to prevent his departure now.

Garrett peered at her questioningly, then for the first time that day let a smile tug on the creases at the side of his mouth. With damp curls clinging to her cheeks she looked not a day over fifteen, as if the years had been washed away by the spring storm. His anger toward her softened inexplicably, and with its lessening, he felt the return of other, more confusing emotions.

Emotions he would not give in to. "Get some sleep, Kelsey," he said gruffly. "It's been a long day."

He spun on his heel, moving away so rapidly she couldn't guard against a pang of disappointment. And like a traitor, Bridget followed him into the dark.

Stretching her hands over the cheerful blaze, Kelsey let the warmth seep into her chilled bones, grateful that at least one fire had been left banked. The small stone hearth in her own room had still been cold when she returned, so after shedding her wet clothing and donning a warm velvet wrapper, she had sought the kitchen fireplace and had quickly stoked the glowing embers into crackling flames. Not wanting to wait long enough to heat the stove for tea, she had swung a kettle of water over the fire on a little used crane. Garrett's bottle of scotch whiskey waited on the large oak worktable.

Outside, the storm had abated somewhat, the thunder and lightning spending itself quickly, leaving a steady drizzle in its wake. In spite of herself, Kelsey's gaze kept returning to the window over the stone sink.

What was she to do now? she wondered. In the aftermath of the evening's excitement, her earlier discussion with Garrett seemed distant and unclear. She had accused him of taking advantage of Sheldon, and certainly all evidence pointed to that, and yet he must understand that she had no intention of relinquishing her own claim to him, as he appeared to expect.

To add to that, his implication of greed on her part still burned in her mind, filling her with frustration. She could see why it looked that way to him. Maybe, if she took the time to explain calmly and rationally, she could tell him part of what had happened—enough that he would stop looking at her as if she were an intruder.

But why should she care how he saw her? Kelsey upbraided herself. So long as he allowed her to live in peace, it didn't matter if she never saw him again. In fact, it would be for the best!

The rattle of the kettle coming to a boil spurred her out of her thoughts, and Kelsey carefully swung the small pot out and used a folded towel to lift it from the crane.

When she was halfway to the table, the kitchen door swung open, allowing a gust of wind to sweep through the room. Startled, Kelsey nearly dropped the boiling water.

"Garrett!" she cried breathlessly, heat rushing, unbidden, to fill her cheeks. Dismayed at the effect he had on her, she tried to cover the pounding in her heart. ''What do you think you're doing, frightening me like that?'' She clunked the kettle down to the table, sloshing water over the sides. ''You have no right barging in here like this.''

Flicking the rain out of his hair with one hand, Garrett ignored her and moved into the room, kicking the door shut behind him. He strode toward the hearth determinedly. ''Considering there wasn't time to stock the cottage with dry wood before I moved in, I think I have every right to share your fire. Damn, but it's cold outside.''

Kelsey had no time to react beyond placing her hands on her hips when Garrett unceremoniously stripped the soaked jersey over his head, flinging it to a chair. For a moment she wondered if he would remove his trousers as well, but then she roused herself enough to turn her gaze away from his bare torso. ''There was no fire in my room, either,'' she choked, her hands moving automatically to prepare the tea. It was clear Garrett felt completely at home in this kitchen, and he seemed unaware of her embarrassment as he snatched up another clean towel from a sideboard and proceeded to run it over his chest and face. Kelsey stole a glance and swallowed hard as she watched the firelight play over his glistening skin, rippling smooth and supple over the firm muscles of his back. He leaned closer to the fire, drying his hair with brisk motions, then hung the towel around his neck as he combed his fingers through his sun-streaked hair.

''Is there enough of that for me?''

The teasing note in his voice made her gaze fly to his eyes, and she blushed furiously when she realized he had caught her staring. Lowering her head, she fussed unnecessarily over the teakettle. ''Do you want honey, too?'' she chattered, sliding the covered jar from the center of the table. After spooning a generous amount into her own cup, she reached for another.

''A double measure of whiskey will do,'' Garrett answered. ''And forget the tea.''

In a second he was at her side, reaching for the whiskey bottle and tipping it toward the china teacup Kelsey had indicated was his. He paused with the neck over her cup, one eyebrow quirked high. When she nodded, he poured a small amount into her tea, then added another quick shot and grinned. "This won't make you tipsy, will it?"

To his surprise, Kelsey paled at his teasing comment, and her chin jerked as if pulled upward by a string. For a moment her eyes held an unfocused gaze, fraught with painful memory, but then quickly her expression cleared, leaving her face as smooth and emotionless as ever. She took a long time responding, and did so only after taking a generous gulp of her whiskey-laden tea.

"Not likely," she replied. "It takes far more liquor than this to intoxicate me."

"You speak from experience?" Garrett watched her carefully, puzzled, yet half amused by her odd behavior. She shrugged noncommittally, like a world-wise courtesan, then turned to the hearth, where she seated herself in a Windsor chair angled toward the fire.

The bitter drink brought choking tears to Kelsey's eyes, but she took yet another swallow before clutching the cup on her lap between both hands. Garrett would laugh if he knew just how far her "experience" had taken her, she thought dismally. He had even warned her once, though she doubted if he would remember. As if the whiskey and the memories had combined to tear down her resistance, Kelsey shivered violently, reacting, finally, to the stresses of that day and the anxieties of this night. She struggled to bring the cup to her lips once more, but her hands trembled so that she splashed tea onto her wrapper.

Garrett was struggling too, but within himself. It was all he could do to keep from kneeling at her side and drawing her into his arms to still her shuddering form. Except it was probably, he reminded himself harshly, a very practiced act. She wasn't so delicate that a little rain and the distant howling of dogs should send her into hysterics.

"What is it that upsets you most, Miss Tremayne," he drawled, "the fact that your inheritance fell short of your expectations, or that the rain ruined your dress?"

Anger flowed through Kelsey's veins, reviving her somewhat from her numb shock. That she had begun to think Garrett might not be as heartless as he appeared only made her ire more intense. "Neither!" she spat. "But I hardly supposed you would understand."

"I understand quite enough," Garrett replied evenly. "But don't expect sympathy from me, or anyone else. There'll be no playing the English "lady" around here. I have neither the time, nor the inclination to cater to your whims. You'd be better off returning to your high-born friends."

Stunned, Kelsey stared at him openmouthed before her jaw clamped shut stubbornly. "I've already decided I'm not leaving Riverview, and if you think lack of sympathy will drive me away then I'm afraid you're sadly mistaken. And it seems," she added, her voice rising with emotion, "that *I* was mistaken, too. I had the foolish notion that you *cared* for my father. I'm glad he died quickly, do you hear me? Glad!"

"What in hell are you talking about?" Garrett strode forward, standing over her with his fists jammed against his hips, his legs planted wide. "How can you say that?"

Kelsey forced her ragged breathing back to normal, aware that it was Garrett's nearness causing the air to leave her lungs as much as it was their heated conversation. Towering above her, he looked like a fierce bronze god. And not a benevolent one. She lifted her face to him with a bravado she did not feel. "I meant that it would have hurt him to see you trying to take everything over this way, before he's even cold in his grave. When Christina told me last week that my father was dead it was a terrible shock, but I won't stand for you—"

"Christina told you?" Disbelief washed over Garrett, and now it was his turn to stare at Kelsey.

Her scathing rejoinder died on her lips at the incredulous tone in his voice. "Y-yes."

"You didn't get my letter?" Garrett shoved his fingers through his thick hair when she shook her head. Angry as he had been, he had taken care to break the news of Sheldon's death as kindly as possible. Writing that letter had been agonizing, and now she said she had never even seen it.

"So you did decide to come home on your own," he sighed heavily. "At least you had the decency to *try* to see your father before he died. A few years sooner would have been more appropriate, however."

"A few years . . . ?" Kelsey bit back a retort, tears filling her eyes as she realized what Garrett was saying. "You mean he was ill before . . . ? Oh, God, why didn't he tell me?"

This time Garrett didn't doubt her reaction. The china cup slid from her lap, shattering at her feet upon the stone hearth. She made no move to stop it. Her shoulders slumped forward, her sable hair flowing forward to shield her face even as her delicate hands moved to cover her eyes.

All the anguish he had held inside since Sheldon's death now rose within him, jumbling up in Garrett's throat with a strangling hold. "Kelsey . . ." His voice broke off, unable to offer comfort where comfort was needed.

She raised her head, her despairing gaze meeting his, her mind finally comprehending the extent of his own sorrow. "You loved him, too . . . didn't you?"

Hesitantly, Kelsey stood, reaching one hand to his, the need to connect, to share her grief overwhelming her. His flesh was warm to her cold hands, but the feel of it tingled through her fingers . . . vibrant . . . alive, and when he clasped her hand, drawing her forward, she went willingly.

Holding her close, he lowered his cheek to the top of her damp hair and inhaled shakily. Her slender curves pressed against the length of him, her sobbing breath fluttered across his chest like a teasing wind. As suddenly as he realized that he had misjudged her about this, Garrett also knew that she had held her grief in check until this moment, as had he.

The strength in his arms bolstered Kelsey, his warmth flowed into her veins, easing away the aching sadness that had claimed her for so long. Gradually she became aware, not only of the intangible support he offered, but of his physical nearness. The skin beneath her cheek blazed with smooth heat, softness over hardness, silk over stone. Her hands moved of their own volition, exploring the same contrast of textures on his back, feeling the muscles tense and pulse beneath her questioning touch. Her back arched slightly as his grip tightened at her waist, and she felt a tremor of anticipation waltz up her spine when he raised one hand to tangle his fingers through her hair.

Her scent, sweet and womanly, filled his head until there was no room left for sorrow—only Kelsey. Slowly he cupped her cheek, lifting her face until her breath whispered against his chin. Her eyes, dark and wide with wonder, searched his, seeking answers; finding only more questions. Quickly, before they saw what he wanted to keep hidden, he lowered his mouth to hers.

A fiery jolt shot through Kelsey, and she instinctively parted her lips to emit a stifled moan. All the loneliness of the past five years fell away as the pressure of his mouth increased, and her response came from deep within, from every secret corner of her soul. Unthinkingly, she leaned closer to him, molding herself against his protective strength.

"Sweet . . . ," Garrett murmured against her lips, before tasting once more. With the tip of his tongue he traced the soft fullness of her mouth until she met his tender foray with a tentative one of her own. Unprepared for his own body's response, Garrett groaned, every muscle tensing against the onslaught of desire pouring through him.

Kelsey felt his subtle resistance, and it was enough to draw her out of the haze that fogged her senses. She lowered her face, though she remained within the circle of his embrace, reluctant to step from beyond its secure bounds.

Aware of her withdrawal, Garrett exhaled slowly, forcing himself to relax. He continued to stroke her hair and the small of her back, as if his hands refused to heed the voice in his brain telling him to walk away now, before it was too late.

"Kelsey—," he began again, his voice rough, grating.

"Oh, Garrett," she breathed, not wanting to hear his words of denial. Her mind shifted to safer territory, back to where they had begun. "Papa never wrote that he was sick. He never wrote at all! How . . . ? Was it very bad?"

It occurred to him that he had once intended to tell her Sheldon had died of a broken heart, but now that explanation seemed too cruel, though Garrett believed it to be partially true. "The doctor warned him of overtaxing himself. His heart had been troubling him since shortly after you left, but he refused to slow down. He was committed—"

Kelsey waited. Did Garrett know that it had been more than his work that had been her father's obsession? That this commitment he spoke of had taken her place in her father's heart. Sheldon had asked her to come home after her mother had died, but only once, and probably out of a sense of duty. "He should have written to me that he was ill," she insisted quietly.

Garrett's hold tightened imperceptibly, knowing his next question would likely force an end to the comforting intimacy they now shared. "Would you have come home if you had known?" He felt her frame grow stiff within his arms, answering him before she had uttered a word. Soundlessly, he released her, stepping back so he could see her gaze grow dull and expressionless. "Would you?" he demanded softly.

For just a moment something flickered behind the darkness of her eyes—remorse?—but it was gone as quickly as a burning star. She shook her head, the regal lift of her chin somehow renewing his anger.

"No," she whispered flatly. "I couldn't."

He wished he could reply with words that were sharp and scathing, but the disappointment pierced his resentment, leaving him drained and weary. Was he so easily swayed by her feminine wiles that he had forgotten what a heartless woman she had become? He had believed her sorrow was genuine, but who was she grieving for? Sheldon, or herself?

He donned his wet jersey as she watched him wordlessly. She looked as if she were frozen in place, and something in him wanted to reach out to her, to shake life back into the limbs that had moments ago melted against him, but his resolve forced him away.

Garrett opened the door and strode out into the rainy night.

Hands clutched at her; tearing, ripping claws that tore the very life from her soul. Helpless terror, all too familiar, threatened to overwhelm her once again, though she tried with all her might to fight the feelings that threatened her sanity. She cried out at her faceless assailants, but as she had once screamed in vain for release from the horror of reality, so did her nightmare screams fall unheeded. And, as always, they were drowned out by the frail cries of an infant—a child who now existed only in her dreams. . . .

Her own thrashing finally woke Kelsey up. For a long moment she lay in her bed, allowing the shadows of her nightmare to fade, though the darkness of the room did not help to dispel her fear. Shuddering, she looked around her. The room, ordinary by day, was now filled with an eerie half-light produced by the pale moon filtering through rapidly dispersing clouds. Other than her own rapid breaths, no other sound invaded the stillness, though Bridget eyed her watchfully from the floor in front of the hearth.

"Oh, God." She sat up, burying her face in her hands as she wiped lingering tears from her eyes. Deep in her heart, she had hoped the dreams would stop once she came home. Now, it seemed they would not.

Bridget rose slowly from her sleeping place, whining softly as she approached her mistress. Kelsey lifted her face, tear-streaked and swollen, when a wet nose nudged at her hands insistently. "Dear Bridget," she whispered. "What shall I do?"

It was a question she had asked herself often in the past two years, and one that had no easy answer. Once she had believed she could count on her own instincts, but when her instincts proved false, she had allowed Mabelle's already rigid hold on her to tighten unbearably. And then the tragedy of her mother's death—and the guilt that came with it—was eclipsed by both Kelsey's greatest joy—and her greatest sorrow.

The only way she could protect herself from her bruised emotions was to deny them, though sometimes they welled huge inside her, aching for recognition, demanding release. She had prayed that the security of home would bring comfort.

An image assailed her, that of Garrett's strong features as he bent low toward her. It was more than comfort she had felt in his arms. It was life itself. And for the first time in months, life had poured through her veins.

With an impatient sigh, Kelsey stretched her hand to ruffle the fur on Bridget's neck, unwilling to consider the consequences of letting him kiss her tonight, nor how badly she wished she could go to him now.

With her fingertips plunged deep into the dog's thick coat, she paused, frowning. That would be foolish, and foolishness was something she had long since given up. Garrett represented a dilemma to her, a puzzle, and nothing else. The fact that his very presence awakened her to feelings she thought dead, she would work to her advantage. She would simply concentrate all her energies on figuring out how to survive and keep Riverview at the same time, and in doing so would solve two problems. She would redeem herself for all the shortcomings that had robbed her of Sheldon's love, and would keep her mind away from the sorrows that haunted her still.

Her decision made, Kelsey gave Bridget one final hug and lay back, drawing the covers around her chin.

But sleep, however badly needed, would not come, and she realized it was not fear of the nightmare that kept her staring at the plastered ceiling, nor was it sorrow haunting her.

It was a pair of bright blue eyes.

4

An easterly wind scourged the dunes of Carolina, drying out the spring earth quickly. Soon, the young woman pondered as she peered over the ever-changing landscape, the rains would stop altogether, the green pines would grow brown and dusty, and the sand would lie hard and silver-white beneath the scorching summer sun.

And, if she was very lucky, she would not be here to see it.

Bending over the row of tobacco seedlings, Dacia gasped as pain stabbed through her lower back, drawing beads of sweat to her brow. She paused long enough to press her palm against her belly protectively. Though she was nearing her seventh month, the bulge was barely discernable beneath her shabby, over-large dress. Lately, however, she had been unable to think of anything else but the life that twisted and surged within her.

"Git on, girl. Cain't let McCready see you laggin'."

The low voice behind her enveloped Dacia with warmth. Ever since her mother died, Trudy had watched over her with maternal care, probably because all Trudy's own children were either sold off or dead.

"I'm all right," Dacia replied without turning around. She stooped to her task once more, handling the tiny plants with practiced ease. For all of her eighteen summers—or at least for the fifteen she remembered clearly—Dacia had labored in the tobacco fields. She was as familiar with the various stages of the crop as she was with her own body, and though she'd been shunted from one plantation to another over the years, the work had remained the same.

Except, she reminded herself, for this past autumn. After harvest, several of the slaves from Bennington Plantation had been hired out to a supply company in Roanoke. Dacia had been included, purportedly to cook for the extra hands, but she had soon learned the warehouse manager had another use for her in mind.

"You ain't worryin' 'bout what Eli said, is you?"

Dacia drew her thoughts back to the present and considered Trudy's question. She was concerned, yes, but not in the way her friend would have expected. Eli, Trudy's twelve-year-old nephew, worked and lived in the big house. On the rare occasion when he was allowed to visit with his family in the quarters, he brought all manner of news and gossip. This last time he had told them he'd overheard Asa Bennington telling the overseer, McCready, that Dacia's baby would be sold as soon as it was weaned.

This did not come as much of a surprise. Dacia herself had been the only child of her mother's not sold before the age of four, and that only because she had been considered too sickly to bring a decent price. She had been thin and yellow-complected as a young girl, and though fair-colored negroes were usually in high demand, especially as house servants, she had been fortunate to be allowed to remain with her mother as long as she had.

In recent years, however, her appearance had caused her more trouble than she would have liked. As she grew older, her skinny frame had developed into slender curves, and her once sallow skin now glowed a golden hue, set off by glossy black curls that grew to her shoulders in gentle waves. She had high cheekbones and a straight nose—the blood of a Seminole trader ran through their veins, her mother had once told her—giving her an exotic, foreign look.

Dacia had learned early on to separate herself from people, which hadn't been all that difficult; with her unusual looks, the other children shunned her. She maintained a distant, dreamy air that sometimes led her co-workers to accuse her of being stupid. Dacia knew she wasn't stupid. Once, when she was little, she had heard the master say she was as alert as a whippet, and though she did not know exactly what a whippet was, she knew herself to be canny and shrewd, and she often had a sense about events that had not yet occurred.

That very sense led her thoughts to her current dilemma. Even before Eli had warned her of her unborn infant's fate, Dacia had instinctively known what would happen, just as she had known what she would do when the right moment came.

It was time, she decided, unconsciously straightening her back, to seek her angel.

As if on cue, the voices around her began a gentle humming, and the tune that followed swirled through her like a healing balm, easing her pain, lifting her spirits as she struggled to complete her task.

Angels watchin' over me, my Lord.

Dacia knew all about angels. From the time she was a baby, her mother had whispered to her at night of the beautiful creatures. There were angels of the Lord, and angels of wrath, and even an angel of mercy, as her mother had called the kind mistress who nursed Dacia through two long nights after she'd been bitten by a snake in the tobacco barn. Dacia could still remember the woman hovering over the bed, her dark hair streaked with white, her smile gentle and loving. Like an angel's.

And so the mental image Dacia carried was a combination of stories and songs and feelings, all jumbled together like colored stones in a jar. But as sure as she was that sweet Jesus was in Heaven, she knew that somewhere there was an angel of her own.

A band of angels, comin' after me.

The song swelled around her, and she contemplated the words long and hard. For all her beliefs, Dacia was realistic enough to see that no one had ever been carried away from misery by an angel, except maybe when they died. No, if a body wanted to see her angel, Dacia knew, she had to find her for herself.

That was just what she intended to do, first chance she got. Already there were whispers about folks who would show her the way. If anyone really could.

Comin' for ta carry me home.

The final stanza of the song eased into her troubled mind, and she found herself humming it over and over as she resisted the pangs tearing at her belly. It represented her hope. It represented her salvation.

Her angel, she knew, was one of freedom, and she was bound and determined to find her, if not to save herself, then for the sake of her unborn child.

She would have freedom, or she would die trying.

5

"But you agree it is not proper, *oui?*"

Kelsey had wondered how long it would take for the conversation to reach the subject of Garrett's remaining at Riverview, and now she knew. Antoinette Delbert had breezed past the greetings, deftly skimmed by condolences, and had settled quickly and happily upon the only topic that truly concerned her—the possibility of another scandal to dissect.

"She said O'Neill is staying in that old caretaker's house, Annie," George Delbert interceded on Kelsey's behalf. "Once this is all settled—and we really should get on with business, my dear—I'm sure the boy will find lodgings in town."

Kelsey smiled gratefully as the older man rose and extended one hand toward her, extricating her from the disconcerting, but quite necessary, social visit. Though Kelsey was fond of all the Delbert family, she had never been completely comfortable in Antoinette's presence. And even less so today. With her exceedingly correct Creole heritage, Mrs. Delbert reminded Kelsey too much of her own mother.

George Delbert, on the other hand, was as blustery and cheerful as a character from a novel by Mr. Dickens, though hopelessly old-fashioned. She prayed her father's attorney would give her the answers she sought.

"Perhaps you should have stayed at home until Father and I came to you," Justin Delbert suggested. "A young lady shouldn't be expected to make business calls. . . ."

Kelsey smiled frigidly at Justin as she followed him

down the hallway into the law office. He hadn't changed much. When they were children he had adopted a boastful, swaggering manner to cover up his own feelings of inadequacy. That habit was readily apparent to anyone who knew him well, and yet those same friends recognized his extraordinary ability when it came to grasping matters of law. If only her friend could see his talents for himself, Kelsey thought, he might leave off trying to impress others.

"I'm sorry I couldn't say anything yesterday," he continued immediately after they were seated. "Father was Sheldon's attorney, and though I'm aware of the contents of his will, we didn't feel it was proper for me to discuss it with you alone."

Kelsey nodded. "I understand that. What I don't understand is how Garrett O'Neill gained so much control over my father!"

"I wouldn't exactly call it control, my dear," George soothed. "Influence, surely, but not an inordinate amount, under the circumstances. Perhaps we should review his background."

"My father's?"

"No," George said, shuffling through the papers on his desk. "Garrett O'Neill's. You've probably heard bits and pieces over the years. His father was an Irish immigrant, working on the Erie canal. His mother a German girl from Albany. Young Garrett was born in '31, but by then his father was no better than a drunkard. I doubt the boy saw him more than half a dozen times in his life."

Kelsey *had* known much of this information, but hearing it now in George Delbert's sympathetic words left a far different impression than her mother's critical tones. Her heart ached for the boy Garrett had been, though she forced herself to remember that, despite his unfortunate childhood, he now represented a threat to her security. She listened intently as George went on.

"Garrett O'Neill began as an errand boy at the age of nine. Sheldon saw his potential early on and proceeded to take particular interest in his progress. But I daresay there was more to it than business,'' George Delbert added, pausing as he glanced at his son. His gaze returned to Kelsey, softening in remembrance.

''Sheldon Tremayne was an affectionate man, and loyal to a fault. I believe he recognized in young Garrett the same characteristics, in addition to a need for constancy that had been lacking in the boy's life before.''

Kelsey blinked back the tears that sprang to her eyes at George's words. It was true her father had been an affectionate man, but it hurt to think he'd not been satisfied with a mere daughter to care for. *She* loved Riverview as much as anyone, but except for that one summer long ago, her father had not seen fit to share his knowledge with her. Though that was not Garrett's fault, her disappointment was tinged with resentment.

''And so am I, too, bound to Garrett O'Neill?'' she asked.

''In a manner of speaking,'' George nodded, ''you are.''

Kelsey stared wordlessly at her hands clenched in her lap until a sound from Justin caused her to look up. Her friend was gazing at her with a mixed expression of pity and anger.

''Isn't there something we can do to break the will?'' he asked his father.

George smiled. ''It's ironclad, I'm afraid. After all, I helped Sheldon draft it.'' He turned to Kelsey. ''Despite appearances, your father had your best interests at heart. No one is more capable of managing your business affairs than O'Neill, and except for the part about his sharing your home, I was in complete agreement with everything Sheldon intended. For all intents and purposes it was O'Neill who kept your father from going completely bankrupt.''

''But Father always had plenty of money!'' At least, that's what she'd thought. It occurred to Kelsey that Mabelle might have exaggerated their financial status when boasting to potential suitors while in Europe. Still, she was dismayed at the thought that the entire estate might have been lost, even if it wasn't as large or prosperous as she'd been led to believe.

George looked at her sympathetically, clearly unhappy to be the bearer of bad news. "Your father bought his first fleet of trading ships with an inheritance, and completed the building of Riverview from that same capital. His income from the business should have been enough to maintain quite an extravagant life-style, had he not been beset with a series of unfortunate events that caused him to lose interest in his work."

"What events?"

"Stock-market losses, a lull in trade . . ." There was more, but Justin looked at his father, who nodded sagely, before continuing. "But the main reason was that he became more involved with helping runaway slaves than ever before—almost fanatically so. He sold most of his business to Garrett and gave everything else away."

Including me, Kelsey thought despondently. Of course she had always been aware that part of the problem between her parents was Sheldon's antislavery sentiments. But she had no idea how emphatic he had truly been.

"Even his death was caused by his obsession with these people," Justin added, bafflement clearly written on his face. "Apparently he fell in the river two winters ago while rowing a boatload of darkies across to Canada. He caught pneumonia, and after that he never really recovered."

"It was O'Neill who rescued him," George explained gently, "and cared for him for the past few years. Probably at his own expense, I might add."

Kelsey digested this information while fighting the tears that pooled in her eyes. Her father wasting away, dying for a cause that gave him nothing in return, when she would have given anything to be at his side.

She pulled her shoulders straighter and lifted her chin. "There is little we can do about that now. What I need to know is whether there will be enough income from my share in the boatyard"—she could not bring herself to say Garrett's boatyard—"to maintain Riverview."

Justin shuffled his feet and George Delbert took on a pained expression. "Probably not. Business has been slow. That horse-breeding notion hasn't paid off yet either, and likely won't until the foals are old enough to sell in a couple of years."

"Then what can I do?" Kelsey struggled to keep from wailing.

Again, George made clear his very dated outlook on the options available to women. "I wouldn't worry overmuch if I were you," he said placatingly. "You're a pretty girl. You'll be married before you know it. Or you can sell the land."

"What about the farm? Are any of the tenants left? I remember father had hoped to turn it into a profitable venture."

"He did at that," Justin contributed, "but like everything else, he let it go shamefully in the past few years. It'd take far too much work to make it pay now."

He didn't have to say "for a woman." Kelsey could see it in the patronizing expression he sent her way.

"You might consider examining your father's books for a start," George suggested, "they might help make up your mind."

"I fully intend to study my father's book, though I'll certainly depend on you both for advice," Kelsey said determinedly.

"Good. Then there's only one more thing of which I must remind you. Until you reach your majority in August, if you choose not to remain at Riverview, your entire holdings will revert to Garrett. You cannot sell your half of the house, except to O'Neill, nor can you lease it to anyone else without his signature. In fact, his moving to the cottage is really quite gallant, considering that by rights he could insist on staying in the main house."

Kelsey rose half out of her chair with an exclamation of surprise. Knowing she could be forced to share Riverview with Garrett, not just legally, but physically as well, struck her as the height of absurdity. That her father had wished it that way only wounded her pride more.

Behind her, Justin was sputtering, and she could visualize him growing red with frustration. "That's preposterous," he complained. "If O'Neill was any kind of a gentleman he'd *give* Kelsey the house. Don't you agree it should *all* be hers."

"That is not for us to determine," George reminded gruffly. "Our purpose is to see Sheldon Tremayne's wishes carried out, and now Kelsey's, within the constraints of her father's will."

As Kelsey said her good-byes and gathered her gloves and reticule to leave, she briefly wondered if there was some sense of rivalry lingering from years ago, when Justin had continually vied for her attention and Garrett had so easily won it. But thoughts of how she might salvage her home soon replaced such musing. She remembered clearly what Garrett had said yesterday. How could she expect to run her father's farm without experience? Should she try?

She was out the door and nearing the two-seater buggy she'd driven to town that morning before she realized Justin was walking beside her. He hurried to take her elbow as she gathered her skirts to enter the vehicle.

"I'm glad you've come home, Kelsey," he stopped her. His voice dipped low as he bent nearer, gripping her arm possessively. "I only wish you'd found your inheritance intact. It's too bad Garrett has acted as irresponsibly as your father."

She drew herself up with displeasure, then realized, sighing, that Justin was unaware of the insult. "I find it hard to believe—"

"That your precious Garrett could do anything wrong?" His expression grew hard as he tightened his hold on her arm.

Surprised and appalled by his sudden change in demeanor, Kelsey adopted her most proper tone of voice. "He is not *my* Garrett. And I'm certainly capable of judging whether or not either he *or* my father has acted irresponsibly."

With a cool smile, Justin drew back. "I'm certain you are.

Suddenly afraid that she'd been far too sharp with her friend, Kelsey reached her hand toward him, brushing her fingertips over his coat sleeve. "And I know you're trying to help. I appreciate your concern, truly I do, but I need to make these decisions by myself. You can understand that, can't you?"

Having made few decisions on his own, Justin wasn't sure he understood at all, but the appeal in Kelsey's dark eyes made him forget everything except how much she meant to him. "Of course I do. Just remember that you can count on me. I'll stop over tomorrow to see how you're faring."

Kelsey willingly agreed. By tomorrow, she hoped, she would have a much clearer vision of the state of affairs at Riverview and how she would fit into it. And not a small part of her hoped she could also assure Justin that his accusations were groundless.

She allowed him to assist her into the buggy, but her thoughts were already halfway to the shipping office where she would confront Garrett. As she flicked the reins over the horse's rump, setting the buggy into motion, she waved to the dark-haired man who stared after her longingly.

The image she was picturing in her mind, however, was that of another man altogether.

Garrett read over the invoice for perhaps the third time and still the figures made no sense. Savagely, he thrust the offending piece of paper into a leather portfolio, then spread the plans for the new boat house across the desk in the hope that his pet project would hold his attention. All morning his concentration had been scattered, partly due to his being unused to working here at the shipping office at the landing, but mostly due to his own traitorous thoughts. His mind refused to focus on anything . . . anything, that is, except Kelsey.

How in God's name had he let things get out of hand,

he lashed inwardly. Had he been so intent upon getting her away from the riverbank that he forgot his vow to himself? Or had it been a case of what he feared most—that she still had the power to entrap him completely within her spell?

Either way, Garrett fumed, he had shown poor judgment last night, and he would not allow it again.

As he unrolled the carefully drawn diagrams, Garrett recalled the promise he had made to his mentor.

"Take care of my Kelsey," Sheldon had whispered breathlessly, struggling to draw air into his weakened lungs. "Don't let her know . . . she's headstrong, but she needs . . ."

Tremayne's voice had never returned after that, but Garrett thought he understood. Sheldon wanted his daughter to remain the pampered, willful girl she had always been, and as much as it stuck in his craw, it was up to him to see that what remained of her inheritance stayed profitable.

Even if he had to fight her every step of the way.

His determination renewed, Garrett turned his gaze to the drawings before him, adding a penciled note or two to the margin as he studied the architect's renderings. If they had good sailing weather this year and the markets remained firm, he could begin construction of the new facility by next spring. But only, he reminded himself, if he could convince Kelsey to invest her part of the profit, as Sheldon would have done.

Maybe, Garrett mused, Kelsey would not even be here by then.

The likelihood loomed before him, presenting both the answer to more than one tricky issue, and the dilemma which was tearing him apart in the first place. If Kelsey returned to London, his worst suspicions would be confirmed—Riverview meant little to her other than a source of ready cash, and by association, neither did he.

But if she stayed? Now there was an even stickier situation. How could he continue to carry out his and Sheldon's work with Kelsey interfering at every turn? And if she stayed, he would have to face the possibility that he had misjudged her. No matter which, Garrett surmised, there were some difficult times ahead.

A flock of gulls took wing from the wharf behind the office, setting up such a raucous noise that his attention was drawn to the window. A cloud of gray-white wings and fluttering feathers rose to block his vision of the road, but when they cleared, he spotted the cause of their indignation. Turning into the yard at a lazy pace was a scrawny nag, ridden by a man who looked far too large for the poor animal's comfort.

Garrett rose from his desk. His gaze remained fixed on the approaching figure, which was moving so slowly that it took several minutes before he could make out the rider's identity.

And when he did, his first thought was that it was a good thing Kelsey was not here.

Bart Ogden was the kind of man no decent woman should ever have to face. But Garrett knew it was the purpose of this visit that threatened him most. His fists clenched tightly and when his unwelcome visitor disappeared around the other side of the building, Garrett turned toward the door, preparing himself for the confrontation he had half expected.

Ogden didn't even bother to knock. He stepped into the room, his bulky frame made larger by the quilted coat he wore despite the warm spring day. "Well, well," he drawled. "Had a feelin' ah'd be seein' you again."

"Stop right there." Garrett's voice reflected the disgust he felt toward the unsavory man. "Unfortunately, I had the same feeling, much as I hoped it was a bad case of indigestion. What do you want?"

Bart Ogden ignored the question, sidling instead toward a large bookcase to the left of the entrance, which stood with its glass doors opened invitingly. Though his squinted eyes scanned the bound volumes, it was obvious that he was not reading the titles. His voice when he faced Garrett again was as oily as the lank hair falling over his forehead.

"Been a few months since ah been here. Ah heard Tremayne's dead," he said abruptly. "Thought ah'd pay my respects, seein' as how him and me had dealin's, if ya know what ah mean."

Garrett stiffened. "Sheldon Tremayne never had dealings with the likes of you."

Now Ogden's mouth gaped open, revealing a set of extremely crooked teeth and blackened gums. His laugh was a cross between a snort and a belch. "Loyal little pup, ain't ya? Ya know, when the sheriff tole me you was handlin' Tremayne's business, ah kinda wondered 'bout that. Last time ah saw him, the fella was feelin' right poorly. Bet he was glad ta have a fine young upstart like you just waitin' ta step in his shoes. What ah want to know is, are ya takin' over everything?'Cause if ya are, then you and me's got some serious discussin' ta do."

Garrett ignored the slur. He'd been called an upstart by better men than Ogden, and had learned to work around the prejudice his unpretentious birth aroused. What concerned him more was the fact that Bart Ogden seemed intent on forcing him to show his hand. "I have no idea what you're talking about and I don't care. Close the door on your way out."

Unheedful, Ogden approached the edge of Garrett's wide desk, hitching one leg over the corner as he settled his weight onto the polished surface. "Ah only got a few more questions, like, what's in this fer you?"

Garrett stepped around to the front of the desk, planting his feet wide as he braced his fists on his hips. "It's none of your damned business."

"Ah reckon it is, seein' as how every last trail ah've followed in the past two years leads ta Riverview. Includin' one 'at's so fresh ya can still feel the heat." Ogden's gaze narrowed menacingly. "The sheriff and me came by yer place last night. Where were ya?"

"He was with me!"

The sound of a third voice had the identical effect on both men. Ogden froze, his thick neck swiveling to take in the new arrival. Garrett, too, spun toward the door, surprise mingling with alarm at this unexpected appearance.

"Kelsey," he said, his voice grating with a mixture of concern and irritation, "wait for me outside."

To his dismay, she ignored his command, stepping further into the room. Her gaze was riveted on Bart Ogden as if she were trying to drive him from the room with her contempt alone. She was failing.

Ogden's grin broadened, his sunburned cheeks stretching like two pieces of overripe fruit. "Miz Tremayne, ah presume," he cackled, his mocking effort at politeness having the opposite effect. Kelsey's back straightened, and Garrett noticed the arch of her left brow rising slightly.

"You presume correctly," she replied, her tone as smooth—and as cutting—as a sword. "Your business here is finished, I hope."

Garrett would have admired her astounding display of control, apparently mastered during her stay in Europe, had he not been so recently at the pointed end of her verbal barbs.

Bart Ogden, however, seemed immune. He merely shrugged, casting a leering grin toward Garrett. "He was with *you*?" he snickered, responding to Kelsey's initial statement. "Why, that's right noble of ya, little lady, ta protect yer daddy's boy, here. Are ya sure he's worth it?"

Garrett warned himself that to lose his temper now would only worsen matters. He flexed his hands, forcing his muscles to relax, willing his head to remain cool. "As I said before," he enunciated, "Sheldon Tremayne had nothing to say to you, nor do I. Just because the law allows lowlifes like you to exist doesn't mean decent people are forced to put up with your vile attempts to cause trouble."

"Ah wouldn't be carryin' on about trouble, if ah was you," Ogden sneered, his lecherous grin dropping away like rotten apples from a tree. "It won't take me more'n a minute ta get a warrant ta search that stinkin' pile o' rocks out there on the river. Only reason ah ain't done it yet is ah reckon ya ain't stupid enough ta hide the evidence in yer own house. But ah'll tear it apart, if ah have ta. And on this side o' the law, too. We'll see how high-and-mighty you are when yer rottin' in jail."

Kelsey wasn't certain what was going on, but the sight of Bart Ogden had sent a finger of fear slithering down between her shoulder blades. She thought of Micah, and his determination last night to reach the shores of freedom.

With more calm than she felt, she walked closer to Ogden, who was standing again. Though he was taller than she by a head, Kelsey did her level best to peer down her nose at the man. "You'll not step foot on my property or I shall have the sheriff throw *you* in jail for trespassing. Do I make myself clear? Stinking pile of rocks, indeed!"

Silence stretched through the tiny office, emphasized by the creaking sound of a wagon as it rolled by outside and the soft recriminations called by its driver to his team. Ogden stared at Kelsey insolently, but before long his gaze faltered, unable to match her unwavering superiority. He glanced once more at Garrett, his expression more menacing than ever.

"Reckon that's one o' my questions answered," he said. "Now I see what yer gettin' outta this. How long's she been home? A day? Two! Plenty o' folks'll be interested in hearin' about how cozy things is up there in that big ole house."

"How dare you—"

"Kelsey, don't."

Again, Garrett spoke her name softly, but it had the desired effect. Her control regained, she sucked in her breath, holding perfectly still as she watched him step forward. The two men were of equal height, but Bart Ogden outweighed Garrett by fifty pounds. That, coupled with his rough-looking appearance, made her despair of Garrett's ever besting the man if it came to blows. She was not prepared, however, for the sheer force of Garrett's ire as he grasped the filthy man by his frayed lapels.

"If *I* see you anywhere near Riverview, you'll wish you'd never crawled out of that swamp in Mississippi. And you can be sure that I *won't* send for the sheriff."

Ogden's face turned a mottled shade of purple, and for a moment Kelsey was sure he would strike Garrett down. But to her relief, he merely shrugged, pushing at the hands that held him tightly as he backed away.

"Mighty cocksure, ain't ya," he spat, after Garrett had released him. Despite his brave words Ogden was already edging for the door. "One o' these days you'll regret it, ya stinkin' Irish. An ah'll be the one ta see ya go down."

His departure after that was a hasty one, as if he realized just how far he had pushed his opponent and was unprepared to back his threats with a fight he wasn't certain he could win. Garrett watched him go with a mixture of relief and disappointment; just now the idea of a brawl was appealing, and it wouldn't take much to convince him to go after the coward. But Kelsey's delicate hand on his sleeve stopped him.

"What a terrible man," she exclaimed breathlessly, the encounter having robbed her voice of the power it had once known. A violent shudder swept through her.

Impulsively, Garrett covered her hand with his own, drawing her closer to his side. Bound by temporary triumph, they stood together, each loath to break the tenuous threads rewound in those few moments of shared purpose. This was how they had once been—allies, not adversaries—and the memory left him more desolate than had the feeling remained locked forever in the forbidden recesses of his heart.

"You handled him well," Garrett said, his voice quiet. "I've never seen anyone in such a hurry to leave."

"I doubt my threats had quite the same impact as yours. I was afraid . . . I thought he might hurt you."

Masked with calm, Kelsey's face reflected none of the emotions she had almost revealed when Ogden aroused her anger, though they were nothing compared to the knot that had formed in her stomach when the two men stood face-to-face in a silent battle of wills. She struggled still to maintain her composure, because never had the desire to feel Garrett's protective embrace enveloped her to thoroughly. Kelsey was certain that, if it were not for the everyday noises of the town that drifted through the open door, the sound of her knees clacking together would give away the true state of her nerves.

She wasn't sure what caused the incessant pounding in her heart: the indescribable feeling beginning at the point where Garrett's touch burned through her sleeve, or the possibility that Bart Ogden had known more than he let on?

Thank God that beastly man hadn't asked outright about Micah! Though she had no qualms about lying to protect him, she wasn't so confident in her ability to hold up under an interrogation. It took all her willpower just to remain calm now, beneath Garrett's intense scrutiny. She pressed her lips together to keep them from trembling, but that didn't prevent her from blurting the question uppermost in her mind.

"Do you suppose he'll do any real harm?" she asked.

Garrett's chest squeezed tight, disillusionment wrapping its painful arms around him even while he marveled at her resemblance to her mother at that moment, marveled that a simple motion could alter her face so drastically. With her lush lips tense and narrowed, that glorious mane of hair twisted into a tight knot at the nape of her neck—subdued, restrained—there was little of the Kelsey he remembered. Only her eyes flickered with life and spirit, but even they hid their essence from him. She was never more a stranger to him than now.

He raised one mocking brow. "If it's your reputation you're worried about, you needn't bother. Fortunately, few people of intelligence or character will give Bart Ogden the time of day, much less listen to spiteful gossip. So, you and I are safe with our scandalous secret. For now."

He had used this same tone of voice with her so often in the past two days, Kelsey was hardly surprised this time, though her heart plummeted at the way his eyes seemed to search to her very soul, and then reflected disapproval with what he found there.

"Justin told me Micah Ramsey got away," she fibbed, deciding that a strong offensive was her best defense. "Why did Ogden come here?" She felt a resurgent anger toward her father. She had heard what Bart Ogden said about past dealings. Had Justin been right? Was Garrett as foolish?"

"I'd rather know why *you're* here," he hedged. His patience with her was dissolving nearly as fast as his resistance. He stepped past her, turning only when he was safely on the other side of the desk. Not that it made much difference. No distance would be great enough—or small enough—ever again. "I would have thought you'd want to stay at Riverview. You know, reacquaint yourself with the house, walk the grounds," his upper lip quirked high, "say your good-byes?"

Kelsey bristled at the challenge, her shoulders stiffening with a resolve she hadn't fully understood before. She drew a sustaining breath, then plunged ahead. "I've come to a decision about Riverview," she said staunchly. "I'm going to stay."

"There's no need for haste," Garrett replied, unsure what to make of her abrupt announcement. "My offer to buy your share has no time limit. Why don't you think about this for a while longer?" With more nonchalance than he felt, he gestured toward a waiting chair, which Kelsey obstinately ignored.

"I don't need to think anymore, nor do I believe my decision to be hasty. Riverview is my home. You should remember that."

Curbing the sudden anger that surged through him at her lofty tone, Garrett seated himself behind the desk, picking up a pen as if to resume an interrupted task. "I suppose I should consider it fortunate that *you* remembered. At long last."

"And just what is that supposed to mean?" Kelsey demanded impulsively, though she well knew his implication. It was the same spectre come to haunt her again, and she couldn't stop a despondent sigh from escaping into the tense silence.

Garrett glanced up, his own expression masking the sense of defeat—and something else he didn't care to name—he felt as he spoke the words he had given up on long ago. Now they fell from his mouth like bitter seeds he could not bear to swallow.

"It means only this," he said dryly, shrugging aside his own doubts. "Welcome home, Miss Tremayne. Welcome home."

6

Just who did Garrett think he was! Kelsey fumed as she drove toward Riverview. This was *her* home, not his!

Furious at both herself and at Garrett, Kelsey unconsciously took her anger out on the reins gripped tightly in her hands. The result was a brisker ride than the poor, unsuspecting horse was accustomed to. By the time they arrived at the stables at Riverview, the buggy was very nearly out of control.

"Whoa there, chile," Benjamin called as he limped toward the agitated pair. Kelsey hauled back on the reins, the buggy careening around the corner and rattling to a halt before the open barn doors.

Benjamin hobbled to her side, taking the reins from Kelsey's trembling hands. "You all right?" he asked, his expression respectfully concerned, eternally patient.

She nodded, smiling humbly. "All except for my pride." She was ashamed at having lost control of herself so thoroughly, yet realized that she could never hide the fact from Benjamin. He'd been her father's right hand since before she was born, and never had there been a day when the old man hadn't a kind word or a playful grin waiting for her. Today was no exception.

"Never was content with a buggy," he teased, patting the horse's thick neck before moving to help her down. "If you wanted a race, you shoulda took Prince."

"Garrett's Prince?"

"Uh-huh. Had to sell some of the stock last spring, but no way would the master part with that 'un, or any of the colts he sired. One of 'em ought to make you a fine mount. That is, if you're gonna stay."

Kelsey studied his dark-eyed gaze, wondering if it was really hopefulness she saw there. "I want to," she answered. "I want Riverview to be everything it once was, and more. Will you help me?"

His creased face widened into a grin. "Shore would like to, Missy. You know I'd do anything for you an' Mister Garrett."

There it was again! She fought to keep her expression from revealing her disappointment as she thanked him. It seemed Garrett had won Riverview over in every way. But not quite, she vowed silently. Not yet. Holding back a smug grin, Kelsey removed her handbag from the buggy and straightened her skirt. She wondered what Garrett would think if he knew that she planned to look over the estate just as he had suggested, though with a different purpose than he'd had in mind. She needed to see what was available before she could figure out a way to make money, and the quickest way to do that would be to examine every inch of her inheritance.

Taking the opportunity to follow Benjamin, Kelsey quickly assessed the condition of the stables, and was pleasantly surprised. Here, unlike the rest of the grounds, was evidence of some care. The wooden structure sported fresh paint outside, and inside there were sturdy new posts supporting the roof. The tangy fragrance of fresh sawdust mingled with the sweet smell of cut hay and the odor of horses. The stable had been enlarged, with several new stalls and another tack room added to the rear.

"It's so well cared for!"

Benjamin cocked his head, puzzled by her surprise. "Mister Garrett likes things to be kept nice.'Sides, he was hoping these horse'd help ta bring this place back. But it'll be a couple years 'fore these colts can be sold. That's when they'll start to pay."

Kelsey did a poor job of hiding her irritation. "This is all Garrett's doing?"

"Sure is, Missy. An' he's makin' a fine job of it, too!"

So Garrett had begun breeding thoroughbreds! Glancing at the empty stall next to her, she noticed the brass nameplate nailed over the entrance. *Prince,* it read.

Prince is a silly name for a horse.

Unbidden, the childish words danced into her mind, taunting her heart with memories. But Kelsey shrugged them away, determined not to let sentiment get in the way of her goal. Lifting her chin, she wondered if Garrett were paying rent for the half of the stable *she* owned, and if not, how much she could get away with charging him?

After a cursory tour of the rest of the building, she returned to the yard. Emerging into the bright sunlight, she raised her arm to her forehead and peered around. There was no question about it. Aside from the stables, the rest of Riverview was in dismal shape.

Slender maple trees guarded the four corners of the yard, but one had been sheared in half by lightning and another dropped nearly to the ground with overgrown branches. The lawns, once neatly trimmed and lined with flowerbeds, now teemed with weeds of every ilk. What little grass remained was so chopped and uneven, it looked as if a flock of sheep had been brought in to graze and then herded out of the yard before completing the job. The only place where the grass grew thick and green was between the bricks on the path leading to the front porch.

Raising her head, half dreading what she knew she would see, Kelsey studied what had once been Riverview's showplace.

" 'Tain't what it was, is it?"

Benjamin's soft voice came from behind her, and Kelsey shook her head sadly, speaking over her shoulder. "It's not at all like I remembered."

The whitewashed stone of the mansion had weathered the years poorly, patches of gray and brown mottling the facade like age spots. In several places the mortar was crumbling away between the brick quoins, or cornerstones. Four steps led up to a low porch that ran the width of the building, in the manner of a southern plantation house. Kelsey couldn't help remembering the autumn Sheldon had added it on. Mabelle had just returned from her mother's deathbed, and the porch was Sheldon's way of easing her way through that difficult time.

It was also the cause of a fierce argument between them. Kelsey couldn't recall exactly what the fight had been about, but the result was that her mother began using one of the side doors, never once setting foot on the verandah her husband had built for her. Now the paint on the wide planks was peeling, the wood railings cracked and splintered.

"I just don't understand," Kelsey sighed, wagging her head. "Didn't Papa care at all?"

Benjamin shifted his weight to his other leg silently. *He* knew the answer to that question, but she wouldn't believe him even if he tried to tell her. Some things a body just had to learn for herself. "Looks ain't everything," he offered sagely. "It's a sound house, 'n the land is prime, even if it ain't been worked for a while. Ain't nothin' to be 'shamed of here."

"I'm not ashamed!" Turning, Kelsey saw his eyes widen knowingly at her outburst, then crinkle shut as he smiled and nodded. She softened her voice. "I'm not ashamed at all, just overwhelmed. There's so much work to do."

Benjamin hesitated only a moment. "Then it's best to get on with it. Got two young lads helpin' with the horses now, but they can just as well swing a paintbrush 'round as a pitchfork. You say what you want 'n it'll be done."

"I will," Kelsey promised. "Just as soon as I figure out where to start."

It probably wouldn't be with paint, she decided. He was right about looks not being everything. As much as she wanted to see the house restored to its former majesty, raising money was her first priority. Besides, she still hadn't explored the interior of the house thoroughly. And from what she had already seen, the inside might need more work than the outside!

"Hannah's makin' gingerbread," Benjamin called good-naturedly as Kelsey started for the house. "Don't you go eatin' it all before this old man gets his."

Gingerbread? Pausing in her tracks, she allowed a smile to surface. She'd been concentrating so hard on the difficulties ahead of her, she had almost forgotten about Hannah. Kelsey's step quickened perceptibly, and the foul mood surrounding her loosened its grim hold. Hannah's gingerbread was a treat reserved for special occasions, for birthdays and picnics . . . and homecomings.

Long after she had gone, Garrett remained standing, staring at the empty doorway as if trying to conjure a ghost. Maybe he was, in a way, he thought disparagingly, thrusting his fingers through his hair as he turned back to the desk. Ghosts were reminders of people and places long dead, and he was honest enough to admit that he was still searching for something of the Kelsey he once knew. Where had she gone? he wondered idly. And why?

Seating himself on the desk chair, he leaned back, stretching his long legs before him as he searched the ceiling for elusive answers. Of course he knew where she had been all this time—at least, he knew as much as Sheldon had. Mabelle and her daughter had departed from Riverview five and a half years ago, taking up residence with Mabelle's cousins, Lord and Lady St. John Kelsey in England. From there, according to the requests for money Mabelle sent frequently to Sheldon, they had made excursions to the continent, purportedly to visit yet more relatives, and had even spent a year in Paris.

Sheldon had attempted to correspond with his daughter, but when no return letters ever reached him, he made the excuse that the constant traveling had prevented Kelsey's mail from catching up with her. What Sheldon chose to ignore, but Garrett couldn't help noticing, was that the problem never occurred when it came to his generous bank checks.

Garrett slammed his feet to the floor, the chair creaking loudly in protest as he swung his weight forward, planting his elbows on the desk and cradling his head. Kelsey had not bothered to answer any of *his* letters, either, and it did no good to pretend that his indignation was all for Sheldon's sake. Of all the people who had snubbed him, it was Kelsey's cut that wounded him most deeply, that pained him still.

What the hell had happened to her over there? Garrett frowned, trying to study the changes objectively. Mabelle's influence, for one thing, had probably accounted for much. Had she finally convinced Kelsey that life outside the proper social circles was not worthwhile, even if that stigma included her own father?

Thank God Sheldon had never felt such differences of class. A year after Kelsey and Mabelle left, Garrett, too, had found himself alone. When his father had been found dead in an alley in Buffalo, his mother had finally made the decision to return to her people in Albany. It seemed only natural that Sheldon would then open his home to his young friend and eventual partner. Two bachelors could fare better together than apart. Looking back now, Garrett realized those short years were the closest thing to a family life he had ever known.

At Sheldon's side he had learned the business from top to bottom, contributing his own ideas and his willing back to running the boatyard. And before long, his mentor had also included Garrett in other, more secret aspects of his life.

He paused, remembering how Sheldon had once exonerated his wife from blame by claiming that it was he who had chosen a path far from the one she had been raised to follow. If that was true, and if Kelsey had merely heeded her mother's teachings, then perhaps she was no more to blame than Mabelle?

But no! He pushed himself away from the desk angrily. About that one thing, Sheldon had been too forgiving. And he'd been repaid with nothing but heartache.

Garrett, however, would not forgive so easily. If Kelsey wanted to claim her share of Sheldon's earthly belongings, then she would have to prove herself worthy of them. He would give her that chance, but only that. The rest would be up to her.

But there was more here at stake than his own pride. He would have to tread his ground with her carefully, or much of what he worked for could be ruined. He would do well to consider that.

Recalling the sarcastic flavor of his last conversation with Kelsey made him remember the expression that had crossed her face in that brief moment before she drew her features into a tight, unbreakable plane. For just a second she had appeared hurt, wounded. It was the same look he'd seen on her face yesterday at the cemetery, and then again last night. He'd assumed it was grief, but now he wasn't certain. She wore it too often, and too well, as if pain was a familiar companion.

Garrett paused, then strode to the door. There were questions to be asked on both sides, he realized now. And secrets to be brought to light. Just how many, and how soon, only Kelsey could answer.

"Mmmm. These are even better than I remembered." Kelsey wiped a crumb from the corner of her mouth and slipped it between her lips for one last taste of the spicy cake. From her place before the stove, Hannah watched approvingly, her turbanned head nodding like a huge sunflower on a spindly stem as she waved a wooden spoon through the air.

"Skinny, you is," she berated lovingly, her black eyes glowing soft as she studied the young woman seated at her kitchen work table. "but not too skinny. You filled out more'n I expected, I'll say that. Top and bottom."

Not given to withholding her opinions, Hannah continued to examine her charge from head to toe. She missed nothing, not even Kelsey's deep sigh—was it content, or discontent?—nor the slight flush to her cheeks at the mention of her figure.

"Of course I've changed," Kelsey replied, leaning

against the railback chair. "Why does that surprise everyone so?"

"Don't surprise me," Hannah grunted, turning back to the batter she had been stirring. She continued to dig small mounds of dough out of a clay bowl, plunking them onto a metal baking pan with concentrated regularity. "What you gonna do now, child?" she asked, her bony shoulders bobbing up and down with the task.

"I want to explore the house first," Kelsey announced tentatively, not wishing to offend by adding that she intended to follow that up with a good spring cleaning. She was surprised by how much Hannah had aged, or maybe Kelsey just hadn't paid attention to such things before. When she thought about it, it was amazing the house wasn't in worse condition, with only the cook and Benjamin remaining.

"This place could use a little polishin' up," Hannah confirmed, as if reading her mind.

"Then I'll start with Papa's rooms on the third floor and work my way down. Then I should have a pretty good idea what needs to be done. By the way, do you know where Papa kept his account books and personal papers?"

She watched while Hannah's already stiff form grew tense, then a moment later resumed her baking, as if she'd had to stop only long enough to think of an answer. Kelsey's interest was immediately piqued.

"I 'spect up there." Her gaze flicked to the ceiling, then back to the bowl in her hands. "This last year your daddy didn't let no one near his things, 'cept Mistah Garrett. You'd best ask him."

"I'll do just that." Kelsey answered with more firmness than was necessary. She should have known, of course. So much for taking charge herself! Was there anything about Riverview Garrett didn't control?

In the relatively unaltered confines of Hannah's kitchen, she considered all she had learned in the past two days. First—and worst—was that it would be more difficult to make her home here at Riverview than she'd ever anticipated.

There was the question of money. There must be some explanation for her father's sudden loss of funds. And what of Micah, and Bart Ogden? The fleeing man's terror-filled eyes still haunted her, and she'd not easily forget the confrontation with Ogden that afternoon. Was that beastly man just another unwanted legacy left to her by Sheldon?

And yet, even as she considered them, none of these problems tormented her like the one to which her thoughts kept returning. She was bound to Garrett by her father's will, and yet her own sense of reason demanded she stay away from him. Her heart, however, clamored for something else entirely. It was a dilemma made more complex because she could no longer determine what were her true feelings, and what she had only allowed herself to feel.

How, she wondered dismally, had everything got so complicated?

Hannah busied herself around the stove, casting worried frowns in Kelsey's direction as the young woman stared pensively into an empty teacup. As usual, she found no use for hedging her words. "England ain't all it's talked of, is it?"

Looking up, Kelsey gave a lopsided smile. "It's not so bad, I guess. But it's not home. I did meet some very interesting people and saw places I'd only read about before. I suppose that should count for something."

"What 'bout your kinfolk? Ah remember that AnnaMarie from when she was a young gal like you. She ever grow outta that pout?"

"Hardly." Kelsey recalled her mother's cousin with a grimace. The woman's mouth bore a remarkable resemblance to a dried plum, and Kelsey had often been a victim of her sneering countenance. Her children, a girl Kelsey's age and a boy two years younger, regularly wore expressions even more sour, if that were possible. "Lady Kelsey kept assuring Mother and me that we were welcome, but I don't think she truly meant it. Yet Mother wouldn't even consider coming home.''

''Hmmph.'' Hannah paused at her work, her mind sifting over the events of the past. Out of the corner of her eye she glanced at Kelsey, who waited expectantly. Not a child anymore, the old woman decided to herself.

''Your mama weren't never a cheerful one. Even when she was a babe—an' ah held her in my own arms not two minutes after she was born—she was always lookin' for somethin' to make her happy, 'stead of makin' herself happy with what she had. Folks that think that way got a tendency to make ever'one around 'em unhappy, too.''

Kelsey's head shot up higher. ''Are you saying my mother was always—? You mean it wasn't just the fighting with Papa that made her sad?''

Hannah nodded slowly, turning back to her cooking. Sad hardly covered it. The woman had been right disturbed. And poor Kelsey, despite her brave words, showed all the signs of someone who'd been asked for too much. She weren't nearly as confident as before. Where was that exuberance for life that had once filled this house with laughter and joy? Hannah only hoped that her baby wasn't hurt so bad. She couldn't see that everything she needed to get herself back was right here in this house—or close enough, at least.

Pondering over this new bit of information about her mother, Kelsey refrained from asking Hannah for details of her parents' relationship. She wasn't sure she wanted to know anymore. Talking about them just brought back all the feelings of inadequacy and guilt, and it was all she could do to keep from weeping into her teacup.

Determinedly, she pressed her lips together. She was wasting time by sitting here, mulling over her problems. No longer was she a girl, coddled and protected, waiting for someone else to help her out of trouble. Nor was she the confused, panicked young woman of a few months ago, hoping for a miracle long after miracles had gone out of fashion.

She had grown up, and if it took every ounce of her

strength to convince Garrett O'Neill she could turn Riverview around, then so be it. After all, what else was there for her now.

"Thank you for the cookies, Hannah. I missed them while I was gone." Rising from her chair to leave, Kelsey's gaze passed over the familiar kitchen once more, and she was surprised to find herself hesitating. It was as if there was more she was supposed to do, some forgotten ritual waiting to be completed.

At that moment, her resolutions dissolved before the face of something more compelling than the future, more substantial than the past, and she stood frozen, not knowing what was expected of her.

Hannah sensed her uncertainty and turned from the stove, her wizened features growing slack as she saw the aching need in Kelsey's eloquent eyes. "Come here, child," she said gruffly, spreading her thin arms wide.

Kelsey took one step forward, then another, and suddenly found herself moving toward Hannah unquestionably. She had been wrong to think she was different now, she told herself, blinking back tears as Hannah's hug drew her close to her heart.

"You been through a lot of changes," the old cook said brusquely, though her voice was warm with affection. "Probably see a lot more 'fore you're done. But way inside, you're still my little Kelsey-girl."

The wind had picked up during the course of the day, and thankful for its refreshing coolness, Kelsey turned toward the easterly breeze. She closed her eyes, allowing the air currents to caress her face and bared neck. Wisps of hair curled around her cheeks and brow, loosened by the exertion of sorting through her father's cluttered rooms. Lifting one hand to the knot at the back of her head, she released the pins there, thick curls cascading freely around her shoulders. Kelsey gave her head a little shake.

At least she could be grateful to Garrett for two things: It was he who had given her the idea to explore the house, and it was he who had roused her from the lethargy of grief enough to want to do it. She wasn't sure she could have faced the task a week ago, or even a day ago.

But at least she hadn't done so alone. Bridget had greeted her the moment she left Hannah's kitchen and had been her constant companion for the rest of the afternoon.

Now the sun was a ball of fire hovering over the treeline, as if reluctant to depart from such a fine day. Kelsey scanned the horizon. As a child she had rarely been allowed on Sheldon's balcony, for her mother had deemed the wooden structure unsafe. She could see now, however, why her father had loved to stand up here for hours on end.

The rectangular platform was flanked by double chimneys on each end, but one could walk all the way around. To the north, Lake Ontario sparkled in the fading sunlight, a brilliant jewel reflecting the azure sky. Directly to the east, Kelsey could see the fields and orchards. They lay fallow now, but once they had rippled green and gold beneath the summer sun. If she was lucky, they would be that way again.

Lewiston lay to the south and east, and from here Kelsey could just make out the familiar pattern of streets by the rooftops of the most prominent buildings. And to the west . . .

She approached that side of the parapet slowly, studying the distant shore with a new eye. Many times she had traveled across the Niagara River with her father, and though always aware that Canada was a country different from her own, she had never stopped to consider just how much. The people she met had seemed the same as the townsfolk of Lewiston: they spoke the same language, wore the same clothes. But now the British-owned colony held a new fascination. Was Micah there? she wondered. Had he made it to safety?

"I thought I might find you here."

At the unexpected sound of his voice, Kelsey spun around, raising her hand to the unfastened row of buttons at her throat. ''Garrett, you startled me. I didn't hear you come up.''

''Bridget did.'' He gestured down toward the dog, who was seated beside Kelsey, tail wagging madly. Garrett's smile was rueful. ''Some protection you are,'' he accused the animal. ''You're supposed to warn your mistress when an enemy approaches.''

Uncertain whether he was teasing her or the dog, Kelsey asked abruptly, ''Are you my enemy?''

''I suppose that depends on you.'' Stepping out onto the balcony, he let his gaze flick over her disheveled appearance, taking in the rumpled state of her dress and the fall of dark hair swirling around her shoulders in the evening breeze. He liked seeing her this way. She looked more natural, more approachable, and the thought gave him confidence even while forbidden desires filled his chest with their rising flame. ''It seems . . . we've started off badly, you and I,'' he began haltingly. ''And I came to apologize, and perhaps to explain. If you're truly determined to stay here at Riverview, then it's best for both of us if we can remain civil with one another, at the very least.''

''At the very least,'' she repeated vacantly, her mind already speculating over the possibility for more. His sudden appearance had allowed her no time to prepare, to defend, and she was finding it hard to focus on his words when he was standing so close. Unthinkingly, she took a step backward, and felt the hard railing press against the backs of her thighs at the same moment Garrett's arm shot out to clasp her wrist.

''Be careful,'' he growled, pulling her toward him so quickly, she stumbled and fell against his chest. ''These supports aren't safe. It's been too long since they were last checked.'' As if waiting for a cue, a chunk of loose slate bounced across the sloping roof, clattering down the side of the house until it dropped clear of the building and fell unobstructed to the ground far below.

Kelsey gasped as she watched its descent, then turned questioningly to Garrett. This close, his features had lost none of their imposing strength, but were magnified by his momentary power over her. But with his own gaze focused on the offending rail, she was free to study him.

He was wearing the same dark trousers and shirt he'd had on at the shipping office, though he had removed his coat and had unfastened the top three buttons of his shirt. Much the way a man would when arriving home, Kelsey thought, before she remembered that for Garrett, this was home. His gold-streaked hair looked tousled, and she knew it was more than the wind that had worked its effect on him; he apparently hadn't broken the boyhood habit of running his hands through his hair whenever he was stumped or irritated. Now his expression looked a little of both.

"You shouldn't be up here alone."

"I'm not," Kelsey retorted, withdrawing from his unwilling embrace with as much dignity as she could muster. "You came up here to apologize."

Garrett let her back away from him again, though this time she was careful to stay clear of the railing. When her mincing steps inched her closer to the open trapdoor, a grim smile tugged at the corner of his mouth. "You don't need to run away. The balcony itself is safe enough, I expect."

She hadn't realized she was running until Garrett's challenge stopped her short. And it wasn't the sturdiness of the balcony she was concerned for, but her own shaky limbs. If she only had a moment to gather herself. . . .

"Don't do that."

Again, Garrett's words halted her, this time with her hands in midair, attempting to bring some order back to her tumbling curls. It had been an automatic gesture, which now seemed foolish when caught with her arms lifted above her head, her elbows thrust forward. "What . . . ?" she faltered.

At that instant her expression was so innocently puzzled, so completely guileless, that Garrett wished he had kept his mouth shut and left well enough alone. Angrily, he forced himself to shrug. "Never mind," he said, sighting his gaze on the treeline across the river. "I just meant you shouldn't bother primping for me. Not if we're going to be working together. I'll have to get used to seeing you dirty and unkempt."

Kelsey's hand dropped to the open V of her dress while the other brushed a recalcitrant curl from her brow. Garrett turned back just in time to see her fumble with the stubborn buttons at her throat, then abandon them with a surrendering sigh.

It was no use. Her cheeks felt like hot flames and she wanted more than anything in the world to extinguish their blaze with the icy palms of her hands. Instead she raised her eyes just enough to view the sardonic smile curling Garrett's lips.

"You're right, of course," she managed to say, letting her hands fall to her sides. "I remember how Papa would come in from the docks, his trousers splattered with mud and his shirt sweat-soaked and stained. Mother used to say . . . well, never mind what she said."

Garrett already had an idea just what Mabelle's attitude had been, and it reminded him why he had come in search of Kelsey in the first place—to learn just how much *she* was willing to do to keep Riverview. He leaned against a sturdier portion of the railing, pulling a cheroot from his pocket and rolling it between his thumb and forefinger as he studied her. She had absolutely no idea how difficult the job was, but maybe once she found out, she would change her mind about staying here.

"You don't think I can do it, do you?" Kelsey asked, correctly guessing the direction of his thoughts.

"It's not important what I think. What matters is that you don't know what you're getting into. Farming is hard work. A lot of it's physically strenuous. Even with foremen in the fields and orchards, you can't expect a man to do thing you wouldn't—or couldn't—handle yourself."

"I'm stronger than I look," she retorted, not doubting the truth of his words for a minute, but knowing how most men underestimated women.

As if to prove his point, Garrett let his gaze wander over her skeptically.

"And then there're the people you'll have to deal with," he continued, waving the unlit cigar for emphasis. "Like today. Bart Ogden may be one of the worst, but you'll never know when another like him'll be sent to deal with you."

Kelsey summoned a mitigating defense. "You said yourself I handled him well."

"And *you* said it was my threat of bodily harm that finally worked." Garrett lounged against the wall, for all purposes looking as if the discussion were over. Kelsey, however, had no intention of letting it end here.

"You have no idea what I'm capable of handling. I've done more—" She stopped herself, unable to think of anything sufficiently impressive, but realizing almost as soon as she did exactly how he would choose to interpret the statement. He did not disappoint her.

"I'm sure you have," he drawled, turning his attention to his cigar.

Kelsey watched him twist the end and then raise the cheroot to his firm, smiling lips. She'd never seen him smoke before, and she watched in fascination as he wet the tip with his tongue, then held it between his teeth while he cupped his hands around a flickering match. The ritual was somehow personal, even intimate, and she felt her breath catch again as he puffed smoke through his open mouth, then switched his gaze to her. She bristled immediately. "When did you take up cigars?"

Garrett squinted through the smoke. "About the same time you took up kissing."

"Well, I don't like it."

"That's your problem."

"It's a vulgar habit."

"That all depends on whether you're using the correct technique."

It took a moment—but only a moment—for Kelsey to realize he was not referring to the cigar anymore, and that this conversation was rapidly going the way of the previous ones. "If this is your idea of an apology, I hope I'm not around when you decide to get nasty. I *would* like to know what it is that I've done to deserve your spite—other than existing, I mean."

Garrett blew a ring of smoke toward the sky, then ground the cigar against the rock wall. "I suppose I'm no better at apologies than I am at anything else, but I did promise you an explanation." He straightened, then, thinking better of it, resumed his stance against the solid rail, his eyes searching the horizon for some safe place to rest.

"When I was a boy, my mother tried to keep from wandering off by telling me there was an invisible wall surrounding our house. The reason I could see through it, she said, was that it was only as high as my eyes. It must have worked, I guess. I remember wishing I was tall enough to step over it, and wondering if the wall would stay little as I grew bigger."

Mesmerized by his rough voice, Kelsey unwittingly moved closer, leaning toward the rail herself. "Did it?" she asked, unsure where the story was leading, but not caring so long as he continued to speak in the gentle, rasping tone she remembered.

"No, nor did it stay in place. Once I was allowed more freedom, it seemed the wall moved. Instead of keeping me inside, I found it was keeping me out. It remained just low enough for me to see what was on the other side, though. But was still far too high to climb over."

Now Garrett turned to her again, his eyes searching, his expression bleak. "You don't know what it's like, to want something so badly that every day seems like an endless quest for an impossible dream."

Kelsey stirred, compelled by his gaze to answer, yet knowing there was no answer she could give that would satisfy him. "Tell me," she whispered instead.

He sighed heavily. "You know about my father. My mother, though she tried, never was one to show her feelings. I think Sean O'Neill had robbed her of whatever kindness she ever had. She fed me and clothed me, but she was never anything but a tired, bitter old woman. Maybe I could have lived with that, if there hadn't always been the other side of the wall, tempting me with so much more.

"And then Sheldon Tremayne showed me the other side. Did you know that, Kelsey? Only two people ever made me forget the wall existed. Your father started knocking it down the day he took me off the street and taught me how to tell a scow from a river sloop. I owe him a debt that'll never be repaid."

Kelsey almost asked who the other person was, but something in the way he was looking at her prevented the words from forming. His eyes were haunted, despairing, and it hit her with the force of a thunderbolt that he was waiting for some kind of response from her. She felt tears hovering close behind her eyelids—tears for his pain, tears for hers—but to let them fall now would be an admission she was not prepared to make.

And so she closed her eyes, and her heart, and summoned the defenses that had protected her for so long. Then, safe behind a barrier of her own device, she opened her eyes once more.

"It's a touching story," she said in a low voice, steadied by willpower alone. "But what does it have to do with me?"

Garrett looked up, shocked more by the emptiness in her tone than by the pretended ignorance she displayed. His expression turned to granite. "Until yesterday, I thought that wall was gone forever. I won't let you build it up again."

And now Kelsey thought she understood. In her absence, Sheldon had given him everything, or if one were fair about it, he had helped Garrett to earn it for himself. But now she was home, claiming back what he thought would be his by default.

She didn't doubt his affection for her father anymore, but that didn't make up for the way he was treating her. "I don't intend to create more problems for you," she insisted gently, "but you can't blame me for things I had nothing to do with.'' Rather than take a chance on revealing too much, she turned toward the door again, only to have her arm grabbed roughly above the elbow. Holding her in place, Garrett pitched the dead cigar over the balcony rail. In the silence that followed she thought she could hear it hit the flagstone terrace far below.

''Let me go,'' she hissed. He only pulled her closer. Kelsey managed to keep her body angled away from him, but only just. His hand wound around her arm, pressing her shoulder against his hard chest.

''You can't walk away from everything and everyone who doesn't meet your standards, Kelsey. It's about time someone taught you that.''

''I don't know what you're talking about.''

''I think you do.''

Before she could react beyond uttering a startled cry, Garrett reached around to grasp her with his other arm, his hand still clutching her shoulder painfully. ''No more walls, Kelsey,'' he ground out the instant before he lowered his head. ''No more walls.''

When his mouth touched hers she thought at first that his intent was to gentle her into compliance. His lips and tongue moved over hers reverently, beckoning with a seductive power unlike any she had ever experienced. That power worked its magic well, for she felt her unbidden response surge and blossom in the instant before her own lips parted in welcome surrender.

And then it changed. No longer gentle, his mouth scourged hers with relentless purpose, claiming her, punishing her. She tried to fight, but his will was too strong, hers too weak. And because she had no defense against him, she could do nothing but release herself into his fiery spell.

It was like a well had opened up beneath her, plunging her down into depths both frightening and without end. He was a stranger to her, and yet—though this kiss bore little resemblance to the one she'd cherished in her memory—it was as if she had known the feel, the taste, the texture of his mouth for all her life, and was only now remembering it again. Her consciousness seemed to spread outward and she was aware, also, of the solid strength of his arms, of the unsteady beat of his heart. All wonderfully new. All achingly familiar.

And too soon gone.

The emptiness when he pushed her away was nothing compared to the hollow thump of her heart when he turned from her dispassionately. With a soundless cry, Kelsey covered her mouth with her hands.

Garrett thought for a moment his mind must be playing tricks on him. He hadn't noticed before that the sun had fallen low, or that the birds had ceased their ritual evensong. But they had, and he knew that the only trick here had been the one he'd played on himself.

Slowly, he forced his gaze back to her. He grimaced at her stunned expression, lashing himself inwardly when he saw her bruised and swollen mouth. But nothing prepared him for the pure, unadulterated pain radiating from eyes that had darkened to midnight in the wake of the sun's fading light.

Then, as quickly as the far horizon blanketed that final glimmering ray, her eyes closed and the anguish disappeared.

Kelsey drew herself up, willing her spine to straighten though she felt as if every bone had fled from her body. Jutting her chin high, she peered at Garrett. "Now you've shown us we're both human, I hope you won't find it necessary to prove it again."

With that she turned and fled, leaving him to contemplate his deeds, and the darkness, alone.

7

Oh, God! What a mess!

Kelsey took one more look at the dusty pile of books she had just carried from one side of her father's suite to the other. The corner desk was stacked high with ledgers she would have to go through, and the prospect was daunting.

She sighed. Perhaps she had been too hasty to assume she could make sense of her father's account books just because her brief work experience had included keeping the ledgers for a milliner's shop. Though she had a head for figures, these were far more complex then she had expected.

That, however, was one confession she would never breathe out loud, just on the off chance that Garrett might be around to hear it. She would never admit defeat to him. Never.

Irritably, she brushed a cloud of dust off the nearest stack of books. After spending a near sleepless night, Kelsey had descended the stairs that morning with righteous indignation her only weapon and resolution her shield. It turned out she needed neither, for Garrett greeted her with an expression as blank as the smooth rocks lining the river bluff, as if the exchange of last night had never occurred.

"Good morning, Kelsey," he had stated effortlessly, pointing the way to the dining room where Hannah had already set out a prodigious breakfast. Kelsey had no choice but to follow his lead. Once seated, he ignored her completely, directing all his attention instead to the mounds of steaming food heaped upon his plate. She kept stealing glances in his direction, waiting for him to make some comment to which she could respond with an exceptionally scathing retort, but he never spoke to her, never even looked at her. He just ate.

And then, when Kelsey had finally calmed her own ire enough to attempt a mouthful, he tossed his napkin to his plate and rose, looking down at her with that arrogant half-smile she had come to know—and despise.

"If you're serious about staying at Riverview, you might want to look over the books I left on the study desk," he instructed her in an excruciatingly patronizing tone. "Then you'd best do something about your father's personal papers."

Kelsey had struggled to form an intelligent reply—namely, a demand for the shipping firm's accounts, which Justin had advised she review—but short of choking on her eggs, she had been unable to respond before Garrett strode from the room, looking disgustingly dashing in riding breeches and a tan open-necked shirt. She would have dearly loved to toss the entire platter of eggs at his broad back, but her own sense of decorum, plus Hannah's curious gaze, kept that particular reaction in check. She had forced herself to eat a few more bites, mostly to give Garrett plenty of time to be clear of the house, and then had risen from her place, saying to Hannah, quite unnecessarily, "I'll be in the study if you need me."

Much to her surprise, and consternation, she found that Garrett had provided exactly the information she wished to see, and without her ever having requested it. Not the actions of a man with something to hide, she admitted to herself.

But then, who could tell for sure? Garrett could have been embezzling thousands from her father and she would never know.

Good Lord! Kelsey's internal wail was tempered only by the knowledge that, if Sheldon's personal accounts were in a serious state of disorder, at least the company's finances were not. Clearly written in Garrett's hand—at least she presumed it was his, since it was certainly not Sheldon's—the business ledgers were easy to read and just as easy to comprehend.

Not so her father's papers. Once she was finished poring over the shipping ledgers, Kelsey had come up to the large, third-floor suite that had been Sheldon's private retreat.

It took a few minutes to separate the accounting ledgers from the others, but that was the only easy part of her chore. After several hours attempting to decipher the scrawled figures and disorderly notations, Kelsey was on the verge of screaming. Flinging the graphite pencil she had been using to the desk, she pushed away with both hands and stood slowly, wiping an escaped strand of hair from her brow with the back of her wrist.

"So much for that," she said dejectedly, glaring down at the mound of papers and leather-bound books spread over the surface of her father's desk. The handwriting in the books told a sad tale, and not the one she had wished to hear.

Sheldon Tremayne, once a respected businessman and wealthy entrepreneur, had died almost penniless. His income from the shipping company might have been enough to maintain Riverview if he had been frugal, but there were too many unexplained entries in the debit column for that, most of them barely legible, not to mention illogical.

"Tea's ready," Hannah announced from the open doorway. She moved inside cautiously, sidestepping a pile of books on the floor as Kelsey cleared a spot on the desk for the pewter tray.

"How did you know I could use a rest?"

"Been up here before," Hannah grunted. "Figured it'd be a mighty big job, sortin' through these rooms." When Kelsey pulled a second chair to the desk, Hannah sank into it gratefully. "Don't get up these stairs much." She looked around her meaningfully. "Shoulda come sooner. Place is worse 'n a straw byre after a windstorm."

Kelsey was torn between a smile at the vivid description and genuine distress that Riverview had fallen to such straits. "It's not your fault. I'm sure Papa would have hired more help if he'd been able."

Hannah grunted in reply. "More help wasn't what he wanted round here. Most o' the house been closed up for years, and he didn't let no one up these stairs 'cept Mister Garrett."

"Why not?"

"Don't know. You'd best ask him."

Kelsey sighed impatiently, pressing her temples with the tips of her fingers. The very idea of speaking to Garrett about anything left her palms clammy, a reaction she could only attribute to panic. *Why* he made her feel that way, she wouldn't begin to examine. "How could Papa have let things get so bad? What happened to change him so?" It was true that Sheldon had never been a fastidious man, but this was beyond the acceptable amount of clutter, even for an all-male household.

"I 'spect since you'll hear it in town, I might 's well tell it myself. Folks said your papa was goin' queer in the head."

Stunned by this abrupt news, Kelsey could only sit with her mouth grown slack. Hannah managed to look at her with a mixture of concern and amusement before she continued.

"Ah don't hold with that, mahself. Seems to me if wantin' to mind your own business meant you was crazy, this world could do with a little more craziness. 'Tweren't nothin' wrong with the master's head. 'Twas his heart that was broke."

It was all Kelsey could do to prevent tears from pooling in her eyes, but she struggled to keep her face expressionless. "By me?" she asked hoarsely. Taking Hannah's silence as an answer, she lowered her teacup to the desk and rose to stand near the windows overlooking the broad lawn and stables. Her hands trembled even more than her voice. "I would've come back if I could. I know Garrett doesn't think so, but I missed Papa terribly. I *wanted* to come home, but he didn't want me here."

The sun shining through the window bathed Kelsey's head and shoulders with brilliant light, revealing every line of pain and sorrow on her lovely face. Hannah squinted a little against the brightness. "What makes you think that?"

"It's what Mother told me. It must be true, because he never answered my letters until the one I wrote after she died."

Now it was Hannah's turn to sigh, and the sound fluttered through the dim room like a wary moth. "I was afraid somethin' like that was happenin'," she said gruffly. "Your mama and daddy was as different from each other as a bird is from a fish. They shoulda never let you get caught up in their troubles. Plain stubborn, they was."

"Then at least I come by it honestly," Kelsey observed with wry humor. She fingered the dust-coated draperies idly as her thoughts tumbled. Hannah believed her father had cared for her. Her mother had said he did not. Yet neither explained his unusual behavior. "Hannah, you've been here forever—"

"Ever since your mama came from Alabama."

"Was their relationship always so . . . unpleasant?"

The old woman searched Kelsey's face worriedly. What good would it do to tell things that were better left in the past? On the other hand, it was obvious that her beloved charge was troubled by many unanswered questions. "Not at first," she replied tiredly. "Sheldon Tremayne cut a fine figure and he weren't a stingy many. Mabelle was right pleased when he asked for her hand. She was already past the age when most gals marry, so ah 'spect she had cause to be happy with him. 'Least her daddy was. Me an' Benjamin was part of her dowry."

Kelsey turned enough to study the servant's wrinkled face. This was the first time Hannah had mentioned that she was once a slave, though Kelsey had always known that her father had freed the two servants as soon as they had arrived in New York state. "Why didn't you leave when Papa signed your manumission papers?"

Hannah chuckled deeply. "Didn't have nowhere to go, chile. Besides, ah'd cared for your mama since she was a tiny thing. An' then there was you." She paused for a deep breath before continuing. "You gotta understand that things were different here than in Alabama. Your mama never did adjust herself to the changes. It wasn't long 'fore she started pinin' for the old ways. And pretty quick she forgot that your daddy was her last chance at marryin', an' only remembered that her family name was one of the finest in the South. You can't blame her much though; that was how she was raised."

The woman glanced over at Kelsey, seeing that her head had dropped lower, as if in shame for her mother's faults. Hannah's loyalties shifted effortlessly. "Your daddy tried to make her happy. He thought sendin' you both off to England would work."

"Did he know then that Mother never intended to come back? Kelsey asked suspiciously, when the cook's gaze darted around the room, avoiding hers. "Did Mother say anything to you?"

Hannah shrugged. "Cain't rightly remember."

Coming from someone who could name every single meal she'd served for the last ten years, Kelsey found that hard to believe. There was no point in pursuing the subject, however. Hannah's jaw was clamped tight as she gathered the tea things together before returning downstairs.

The rift between her parents now seemed wider than ever, but who had caused it. Her mother or her father—or both? And how would she ever know for sure? Kelsey turned away from the window, her glance encompassing the disorganized room. Were there more secrets to be revealed here, or were the answers buried in a grave overlooking the Niagara River, surrounded by beech trees and mystery?

There were only two ways to find out, she sighed reluctantly. One was to struggle to make sense of her father's paperwork. The other was to question Garrett outright.

And just now, either solution was about as appealing as diving from the cliff outside to the river below.

Kelsey continued to sort through the mountain of books for the next two hours, and she had just thrust aside another fruitless fistful of papers when her thoughts were interrupted by the sound of Bridget's very strident barking. She brushed away the curls that fell across her forehead as she moved once again to look out the wind. Even as a pup, Bridget rarely roused herself from her usual lazy contentment, so Kelsey's curiosity was immediately piqued.

The sight that greeted her brought a much-needed smile to her lips. From her place within the high dormer she could see the entire expanse of the front lawn, as well as the red-brick drive that ended in a large circle in front of the house. Justin Delbert, his buggy drawn all the way up to the porch steps, was leaning sideways in his seat in an effort to stay clear of Bridget's massive jaws. That he didn't recognize the dog's attempt to offer a friendly greeting was obvious to Kelsey; Justin's frantic expression was clear, even if the words he was shouting were muffled by the thick panes of glass.

Struggling to crank open the heavy casement window, she increased her effort when she saw that Bridget had managed to hoist herself onto the buggy, and that Justin now lay prostrate across the leather seat with the dog slavering over top of him, having never let up on that ferocious-sounding—though utterly harmless—bark. When the seldom-used window refused to budge, Kelsey knew she should hurry to Justin's rescue.

By the time she made it downstairs, flinging open the wide front door and hurrying to the edge of the porch, her smile had grown to laughter, which she choked back for her friend's sake.

"Bridget! Come!" she called, amusement taking the sharpness from her voice. Ever responsive—if not extremely selective—to a loving command, Bridget jumped from the buggy and loped to Kelsey's side, where she nuzzled her mistress's skirts fondly.

"Damned hound! Look what he did to my shirt."

"She," Kelsey corrected, unconsciously patting Bridget's head as she glanced over Justin's apparrel.

Meticulously groomed as always, he looked extremely uncomfortable in a dark frock coat and white trousers and high-necked cravat. His satin lapels and snowy shirt bore several wet splotches, proof of Bridget's exuberant welcome. "Damned dog!" he repeated.

"She was only being friendly," Kelsey admonished lightly, taking Justin's arm as he joined her on the porch. "I thought you liked dogs."

He eyed the grinning wolfhound warily. "I do when they know how to behave. Where did you get this monstrous beast?"

"Don't you remember Bridget?" Kelsey's tone was incredulous. It had only been a few months before she went to Europe that Garrett had given her the deceptively small puppy, but the argument it caused between him and Justin had seemed at the time to have taken on greater proportions. Or had it mattered only to her?

"I do remember," Justin replied nonchalantly. "I just thought you would have been rid of the pest by now, or that your father would have seen to it himself.

For a moment, Kelsey wasn't sure whether he was referring to the dog or to Garrett. Before she could respond, however, Justin hurried to state the purpose of his visit.

"I told you I would stop by today. Have you found everything we'll need?"

"Everything we'll need?"

"To assess your financial position. Your father's account books. Did you find them all right?"

She had nearly forgotten Justin's offer to help her, primarily because she had no intention of taking him up on it. "I've already been through them, and you and your father were right. It appears there's very little money left. But I'll manage."

"Then you've not spoken yet to Mr. Snowden?"

"Should I have?" Escorting Justin into the dark-panelled study, she noted at once his reaction to the inside of the house. He eyed the velvet draperies with a frown, then examined the worn brocade of an armchair carefully before seating himself. Since she'd been sitting in the very same chair just that morning and had not found it quite so disgusting, Kelsey felt herself growing irritated with Justin's show of snobbishness. And defensive.

"As you can see, the servants haven't touched this room out of deference to my father's belongings," she fibbed, gesturing toward the paper-laden desk. She could only hope that Justin, being a man, would not recognize that the worn-out furniture and decor spoke of years of neglect, not mere weeks. Wishing to put an end to his perusal of the room, she continued hurriedly, "What would Mr. Snowden want with me? You said you checked on my father's bank accounts and that they had all been closed for months." Justin's overly patient expression sent a shaft of foreboding straight into her heart. "Isn't that true?"

"It's true. But unfortunately, the situation is even worse than that. It seems that Sheldon took out a loan from Snowden's bank nearly a year ago, using Riverview as collateral."

"What . . . what does that mean?" Kelsey did her best to hide the dread that threatened to overwhelm her.

"It means, if you don't pay off the loan according to the original terms, the bank can seize your property. Snowden informed me that the first installment is due in two months, with the remainder payable a year from now."

Stunned by this new information, she jumped from her chair and paced to the window. "Lose Riverview?" Outside, the weather had turned fine, the kind of spring day made for picnics and leisurely walks along country lanes. In the distance, Benjamin directed his two young charges in the task of pitching a wagon full of cut grass into the hay loft. How tranquil it all looks, Kelsey thought miserably. The peaceful scene reflected none of the turmoil in her heart.

She knew exactly what the loan had been for. Shortly after her mother's death, and after she had written to her father that she planned to stay abroad, he had sent her a very large bank draft with a note stating that he hoped it was enough to see her established for several years. Unfortunately, Lord and Lady Kelsey had claimed that her mother owed them money, and demanded that she turn over the entire amount in return for their hospitality—and their silence. Distraught and entirely alone, Kelsey had had no choice but to comply.

So her father had borrowed money to send to her, only she had never had the use of it.

Behind her, Justin shifted uncomfortably. "I know it all sounds quite melodramatic, but there are actually several courses of action you might consider taking."

"Will any of them save my home?"

Bitterness spilled from her, surprising him with its strength. "My dear, this hasn't been your home for years. Now is not the time for undue sentimentality. Cold reason will serve you far better."

Cold reason. Kelsey closed her eyes, leaning her head against the lead windowpane, warm from the sun. Somehow, that term made her think of her mother, even though reasonable was not an apt description of her last few years. Cold, however, was. "Tell me then," she asked Justin, "exactly what you think my options are."

He cleared his throat with a squeaky grunt. "Sell everything to Garrett. If he's unable to come up with the funds, it would give you a legal avenue of escape from that clause and you could sell to someone else. Either way, the house and surrounding land should bring enough to keep you comfortably for two or three years. By then . . . well, perhaps by then you'll have a better idea what you wish to do."

Even as he said the words, Kelsey knew that in his mind, as in the minds of everyone else, there was only one satisfactory thing for her to do. What none of them realized was that marriage was the one course of action she could never take.

"Would Mr. Snowden consider extending the loan?"

"He might, but that would only postpone the inevitable, my dear. You'd end up paying him interest for the delay, and have less for yourself."

"But I need time!" she said insistently, as much as to herself as to Justin. "I need time to find a way to make money."

You can't mean that you're thinking about staying here! My God, Kelsey, why?"

"I should think the reasons would be clear. Riverview is my home." After the previous day's interview, she hadn't figured on getting much backing from George Delbert, but she had expected a little more show of support from Justin. Hadn't he hinted that he wanted her to stay? "I have no intention of leaving Riverview now," she repeated firmly.

Justin looked taken aback by her directness, though he recovered quickly, a broad smile replacing the scowl on his face. It reminded Kelsey how good-looking he could be when he let his mask of high-handedness slip.

It can't hurt to humor her, he thought to himself, studying the proud lift of her shoulders as she returned to her seat. Glancing around the musty room, he let a smile slip through his careful facade. A few days of dealing with conditions here and he had no doubt she'd change her mind about staying at Riverview. His second reason for coming here might just provide her with a model with which to compare her circumstances.

"Mother has decided to give a small dinner party in honor of your return," he said, noticing that she seemed as relieved at the change of subject as he.

"I'm not certain—"

"An intimate affair," he continued, "keeping in mind your recent loss."

His expression was so earnest, Kelsey couldn't help but relax her guard. "Tell Antoinette I'd be pleased to attend.'' Secretly, she hoped she could use the occasion to announce her plan to stay at Riverview—if she had one by then!

The remainder of Justin's visit passed unremarkably, Kelsey having too much on her mind to wish for an extended chat, and Justin appearing unaccountably eager to escape. It was not until he was preparing to leave that he made a remark which garnered Kelsey's complete attention.

''It's a shame Sheldon's politics brought this down on you, but perhaps it's for the best.''

Kelsey had been admiring the rosebushes lining the porch while he busied himself with the horse, but now he stood beside her, the breeze from the lake ruffling his wavy dark hair. She glanced up to find him studying her intently.

''For the best?''

He nodded imperiously. ''At least now you won't let O'Neill persuade you to take part in his schemes. In this case, you'd do well *not* to follow in your father's footsteps.''

Justin placed a patronizing arm around her shoulders. Kelsey was inclined to jerk away, but his tone was so brotherly, so protective, she decided to allow it.

''I know how anxious you are to get on with your life, my dear. You have more to look forward to than struggling with an uncouth Irishman and a ramshackle old house. Trust me to help you out of this mess.''

It occurred to her that he'd just a soon help her right out of her home, but Kelsey knew his intentions were good. ''I won't make the same mistakes my father did. You can count on that.''

As she watched Justin's buggy drive away, Kelsey hugged her arms around her waist and leaned against one of the columns on the broad porch. She was a fine one to cast blame for mistakes, she thought scornfully. Sheldon's may have cost a great deal, but hers had destroyed human lives, and might now cost her home!

Shaking herself mentally from the turn her thoughts

were taking, she straightened. She hadn't lost everything yet. Riverview was all she had left to remind her of happier days, and she would summon every ounce of strength she had to fight for it. She could fight Mr. Snowden. She could fight Justin Delbert. She could fight even Garrett, if necessary.

A wry smile tugged at her lips as she pictured the way he had looked at her last night, eyes blazing with need and desire. She could fight him, she had no doubt.

The question was, how well could she fight herself?

8

After Justin's buggy disappeared from sight beyond the row of poplar trees, Kelsey returned to the study, but sunshine and sweet air were a potent lure, and before long she was gathering her skirts up on either side and striding across the lawn toward the stables, with Bridget bounding ahead her.

When she entered the cool building, Kelsey glanced down at her dark brown skirt and bodice, trimmed with cream-colored ruching at the throat and cuffs. It wasn't a very flattering garment, but since she didn't own a riding habit anymore, this outfit would just have to do. At least the skirt was full enough to allow her to ride comfortably. Besides, no one would see her besides Bridget.

"Come on, girl," she called. Benjamin was not in the stables, so Kelsey quickly perused the available stock and settled on a spirited stallion tethered in the far stall. "You're not one of Prince's sons," she murmured gently, noting that he bore no resemblance to Garrett's horse. "I thought Benjamin said there were no others left?"

She had some difficulty locating her old sidesaddle, and then discovered the leather straps were cracked and in dangerously poor condition. Usually stallions weren't trained to take the sidesaddle anyway, she rationalized as she fitted the horse with one of the sleek newer saddles available in the tack room and led him out into the yard. Besides, she much preferred riding astride, though it had been many years since she had been allowed such freedom.

Awkward from lack of practice, she swung her right

leg over the saddle. After a few minutes, however, she found that she had not lost what Garrett once called "her good seat."

That thought sent a wash of hot color straight to her cheeks, and with her free hand she worked at arranging her skirt better. Full as it was, there was still an inordinate amount of leg showing, and Kelsey prayed fervently that she would not come across anyone else along the way.

Guiding the horse toward the river, she soon found the path she and Garrett had followed back to the house on her first day, the same one that led past the cemetery. On that dreary day she hadn't noticed the abundance of spring wildflowers lining the lane, nor the barely opening buds on the trees. Two days of sunshine had done wonders for the ground as well, and instead of mud, the path was firm and easy to traverse.

The horse responded easily to Kelsey's light touch with a wonderfully smooth gait, Bridget loping happily alongside. At one point where the path widened, she urged her mount to a canter, slowing only when the trees on either side drew in too close for safety. She leaned forward and patted the horse's neck appreciatively, then dismounted and led the animal by the reins the final yards.

It had not been her plan to come here, yet now that she had arrived, it seemed more than fitting. Bridget obviously thought so too, for she immediately trotted toward the bare mound that was Sheldon's grave and settled herself on the ground beside it, her huge head resting on her outstretched paws. For a moment Kelsey wondered if it was instinct that led the dog to just the right spot, then she realized that Bridget had probably been here many times before, with Garrett.

Kelsey tied the reins to the wrought-iron fence before entering the tiny cemetery, her mind filled with the image of Garrett sitting alone, keeping silent vigil over the man he had admired and loved. Two days ago she might have been angered by that thought, but after what Garrett had said last night she couldn't find it in her to begrudge him his right to mourn. Perhaps he had more right; she had yet to prove worthy.

Drawn to the same spot she had occupied just a few days ago, she sank to her knees. "Oh, Papa," she whispered dismally. "I wish you were here. I want to show you that I love you, but I don't know if I can do it by myself."

Kelsey found herself straining to hear an answer, but the silence in the small enclosure was disturbed only by the distant rumble of the river coursing far below. Even the birds, normally twittering as they performed their spring rituals, had fallen hushed, as if extending an offering of peace.

Peace and quiet, yes, she thought wryly. But no easy answers. Only the river, incessant in its journey from lake to lake, an endless flow of water that never stopped, unmindful of the heartaches and heroics enacted within sight of its banks. Kelsey lifted her head, all senses suddenly tuned to the river.

Was that the answer? Nothing she or anyone could do would ever change the course or halt its mighty flow, so perhaps there was no use in trying. That idea was even more depressing than the thought of what she had yet to conquer, and deep within her a sense of the old rebellion flared.

Perhaps in some aspects of her life she had already accepted defeat. But not all. She would face up to whatever lay ahead, beginning with Antoinette Delbert's party Friday night. Despite their doubts, she would show the people of Lewiston once and for all that she was Sheldon Tremayne's daughter.

And if loneliness were her constant companion, at least she could take comfort in knowing she had once reached the bottom, and had climbed back out of despair on her own.

"Whoa there, boy," Garrett crooned soothingly, tightening his grasp on the reins as Prince tossed his head and danced sideways. Sliding from the saddle, Garrett hooked his right hand under the animal's bridle for a better hold, then waited patiently until Prince calmed down. It was probably an animal, he thought, peering at the underbrush alongside the path.

Too early in the year for snakes, but Prince had been known to shy at the most unlikely creatures, from chipmunks to kittens. He should have known better than to take this road anyway, seeing as how the horse had already proved himself to be in a temperamental mood once today.

Garrett grinned in remembrance at the look on Justin Delbert's face as his buggy careened out of control through the rutted field. It served him right. Only a fool would try to harness a mare in heat, and who could blame Prince for responding at the first scent. And it wasn't as if Garrett hadn't tried to control his own horse, either. His mud-splattered attire was proof of that.

Prince threw his head high, nearly jerking out of Garrett's grasp, reminding him to attend to the present situation. Whatever was making the horse nervous was still around, so Garrett decided the best course was to move on as quickly as possible. With a firm pat on Prince's thick neck, he eased himself up onto the saddle, urging the animal into a fast trot.

They had advanced only a few yards, however, when Prince nickered wildly again. This time Garrett heard an answering whinny and knew at once what was causing his mount's agitation. Since Prince's angry response bore no resemblance to passion, he presumed it was a stallion tethered nearby. And he knew without a doubt where it would be, and with whom.

Angrily, he spurred his mount forward.

Bridget was the only one to notice when the horse neighed quietly, for Kelsey was too immersed in her thoughts to pay attention. Neither when her mount began to pull against the loosely tied rein, nor at the moment at which he broke completely free was she aware that anything was amiss. It was not until Garrett rode into the clearing looking like an angry centaur that Kelsey sat up, glancing around dazedly.

"I thought it must be you," Garrett said grimly, peering in the direction of the house. "Did it occur to you that you might have asked before taking a horse that doesn't even belong to us? It took weeks of negotiating to get him here in the first place. If that stallion breaks a leg, there'll be hell to pay. And it won't come out of my pocket."

Stunned not only by his sudden arrival, but by his barely concealed anger, Kelsey stood, placing her hands on her hips. "I didn't realize I had to ask your permission to take a horse out of my own stable. And why shouldn't it come out of your pocket, since you seem to control all the money around here?"

Garrett appeared startled at that last statement but recovered quickly enough. "Is that all you managed to learn after spending the best part of the day holed up in the house?" He wanted to add, "with Delbert," but thought better of it. He had enough problems without crediting jealousy to the list.

Kelsey bit back another cutting answer, remembering in time her vow to keep Riverview. The one thing that remained painfully obvious was that she needed Garrett's help, at least until such time as she had the situation under control. Antagonizing him wouldn't further her own aims. "If you're so worried about the horse, why don't you go after him?"

She watched Garrett dismount smoothly, his thighs and calves taut beneath buff-colored trousers. His powerful muscles rippled beneath his tan shirt as he secured Prince's reins to a sapling outside the cemetery fence, then strode toward her.

"Has no one ever told you it's not polite to answer a question with a question?"

"You mean the way you just did?"

"Did I?" Garrett appeared taken aback, but then his face relaxed, erasing the lines of tension drawn around his mouth.

At least, Kelsey thought, he had the good grace to smile at himself. It changed the way he looked entirely, and her own anger slipped away, her mouth curving upward unconsciously as his grin worked its charm on her, much as it always had. She allowed her gaze to linger over him, taking in the muddy state of his trousers and his mussed-up shirt. She could even see streaks of dirt where he had ploughed his fingers through his blond hair, unknowingly spreading the dark mud, literally from head to toe. "What happened to you?"

He grimaced, but the smile never left his eyes as he watched her gather her skirts to sit again. He hunched down beside her. "Prince threw me. I managed to hold on to the reins, but he dragged me across the east pasture before I could stop him."

"Are you hurt?"

"No, I'm fine." Her wide-eyed concern drove straight for his heart, and Garrett felt his chest thump wildly. She looked so innocent, sitting here among the stark gray tombstones, and he was reminded of another time. Despite his resolve to forget the past, he could not stop this particular scene from materializing before his eyes.

"Do you remember when we met?" he asked softly, surprising himself as much as her. She raised her head slowly, her dark eyes focused in the distance as she summoned the memory.

"It was here," she answered, recalling the day easily, for it had been fraught with much that had symbolized the best and the worst of her childhood. "I was six years old, I think, and I was trying to run away."

Garrett nodded. "But not far enough. When your father came to the dock looking for you and recruited some of us to help search, all the men took horses and fanned out. I wanted to help, but since I was on foot I could only check the grounds nearest the house. That's how I found you here." What Garrett didn't tell her was the sense that he had been drawn to the spot inexplicably, or that upon finding her, his heart had been lost forever. "You were sound asleep under that very tree. When I woke you, you never even asked my name. You just let me take you home without making a sound.''

''I already knew who you were,'' Kelsey explained uneasily, not sure herself the reason why. ''I guess I'd heard Papa speak of you at some point. And by that time I was more than ready to go home. It was getting cold, and I was hungry.'' She smiled uncertainly. ''I didn't really want to leave home.''

''Then why did you run away? You never would tell me.''

Silence hung over them for a long moment as he waited for an answer that Kelsey wasn't sure she could give. She sensed that they were no longer talking only about the time when she was six, and the need to make her reasons clear to him had become an insistent ache in her heart. It welled uncomfortably within her throat, making her voice sound scratchy and faltering. ''They were fighting about me again. Papa used to call me kitten, or Kit. It was just a nickname, made from my initials, but Mother said it sounded like I was an animal and she wouldn't allow it. I remember her claiming that he was turning me into a wild little thing anyway.''

Kelsey drew a shattered breath and continued. ''I hated it when they argued like that. I suppose I thought if I wasn't around, they wouldn't have anything to fight about anymore. So I ran away.''

Only a deep-seated belief that one should never speak ill of the dead kept Garrett from cursing out loud. Instead, he merely grunted and said, ''I always thought of nicknames as terms of endearment, not signs of rebellion.''

''That's what Papa said,'' Kelsey sighed. ''But he gave in to her, nevertheless. Just like he always did.''

Garrett's head snapped up, until he realized that Kelsey had not meant that last comment as a slight to Sheldon, but was merely stating a fact. ''Not always,'' he said, as much to comfort her as to defend his mentor. Her gaze had dropped to her lap, and all he could see was the top of her shining dark hair as she bowed her head sadly.

"Perhaps not."

To say any more, Garrett realized, would put him in the awkward position of having to explain his meaning, and so he remained silent for a while longer, in the hope that she would trust his word as she had that day so long ago.

In the ensuing quiet, he took the opportunity to study her candidly. Though still thin and pale, her face had lost some of the tension she had worn these past days like a painful mask, as if she had come, if not to welcome what was inevitable, at least to accept it. That newfound serenity made her seem at once more mature and more vulnerable, though maybe it was the setting that lent an air of youthfulness to her appearance. Her hair had come loose from the tight coil she had worn that morning, spilling softly over her shoulders in a cascade of rich sable that shimmered with red-gold in the sunlight. Though her somber dress did not suit her, its well-tailored lines emphasized her womanly curves, and Garrett was reminded intensely of the feel of her breasts pressed hard against him.

That thought brought another to his mind, and since their conversation so far had been comparatively peaceful, he decided the time was right to make further amends. "I didn't mean to shout at you about the horse. I suppose you couldn't have known that he was loaned to me for stud purposes only."

"Then you really are serious about raising thoroughbreds?"

"Absolutely." Relaxing against the wrought-iron fence, Garrett crossed his long legs and picked a piece of grass from the ground, pretending to study it intently. "It's something I always wanted to do, even before it became necessary to come up with another source of income—" He stopped just short of saying "for Sheldon," but she caught his meaning anyway.

Kelsey's fluttering sigh danced away in the same breeze that lifted the curls from her face. "And I shouldn't have turned on you like that about the money. According to

Hannah, you'd been paying for the upkeep of the house even before it belonged to you. She said Papa probably didn't even realize how little money he had left."

Garrett paused thoughtfully. "I believe he knew; he just didn't care. To him Riverview had become only a building made of bricks and stone, and money a necessary nuisance. I tried to discourage him from reckless spending, but he wouldn't listen."

"And then he went into debt borrowing money from the bank." Garrett's show of surprise made her think at first that he hadn't known, but she quickly found out that wasn't the case.

"I intended to pay that off myself after the next shipment comes in from Cleveland."

"To have me in your debt?" A measure of defiance had crept back into Kelsey's voice.

He shrugged noncommittally. "Hardly. I'm half responsible for that note, remember. I don't want to lose my share of Riverview either."

It hadn't dawned on her before that her father's disposition of the house would make Garrett just as liable for his debts as she. The idea brought her a liberating sense of relief, even if it was only temporary. "But sooner or later I'd have to pay my half, right?"

"To me, or to the bank," Garrett agreed. "But have you given much thought yet as to how you'll raise the money?"

She couldn't help noticing that, though he asked the question as easily as before, his hands were now clenched at his sides in a manner that was anything but casual. What was he worried about? Or was he still hoping she'd sell out to him and leave?

"I'd like to check out the orchards and the rest of the fields. It's still early enough in the year to plant a crop."

"What crop?"

Now it was Kelsey's turn to shrug. "I don't know. Whatever is easiest,and will bring the quickest profit. Do you know of an overseer for hire?"

Garrett threw back his head, rich laughter pouring from

his throat like a song. "By God, you're optimistic," he chuckled. "As if that's all there is to it."

"Isn't it?" Kelsey wasn't sure whether to be angry at him for laughing, or pleased that he was no longer honing his sarcastic wit on her. She drew her knees up under her chin and frowned. "The land is already there. All I'll need is some seed, and someone to plant it."

Shaking his head, Garrett leaned forward and clasped her hand impulsively, giving it a tight squeeze. "Seed costs money and workers expect to be paid monthly, but if you're set on doing this, I'll advance you the funds to get started."

She withdrew her hand slowly, suspiciously. "Why? What's in it for you?"

The question was the same one Bart Ogden had asked, and apparently the coincidence was not lost on Garrett either, for his smile turned into a grim frown. Kelsey remembered what Ogden had assumed his motive was. Garrett wouldn't ask that of her, would he?

"All right then. I'll make a deal with you . . ."

Kelsey's breath grew tight in her chest.

". . . if you promise to hold to your end of the bargain. I'll pay the first installment of the bank loan next month, and foot the bill for equipment to start planting. In return I want one-third of the profit at harvest, plus your word that you won't go up on that balcony until I've had it fixed."

"That's all?"

Disbelief, along with the same intriguing naivete he had seen before, was so apparent in her dark eyes that Garrett almost lost himself in their depths. With an effort, he forced himself to respond to her question. "No, that's not all. It's quite possible that Bart Ogden will come snooping around here again. I want you to promise you won't speak to him about anything you may see or hear."

Kelsey's heart sank when she realized what he was telling her, but she hardened her resolve. "You can't ask me to do something that's illegal. Don't you think I know the reason my father let everything slip away. How can you expect me to take the same risk with Riverview?''

''I'm not asking you to do anything but remain quiet. Just stay out of the way, and you won't even have to lie to Ogden.'' His eyes narrowed slyly. ''Except about Micah.''

Sitting up straighter, she gasped. ''How did you . . . ?''

''You mentioned him yourself yesterday. Are you denying that you knew he was here that night? You're not as immune to the problem as you think, Kelsey.''

''Micah was different.'' She barely kept herself from sputtering. With her chin thrust out stubbornly, she peered at him through blazing eyes. ''I mean what I say, Garrett O'Neill. I refuse to see Riverview bartered away to nothing. There's little enough left as it is. I thought you loved this place.''

She didn't realize how very vulnerable she appeared, just by trying so hard to be strong. His gaze softened as he stood over her. ''I do, Kelsey. But it's not as simple as all that.''

''It is to me.'' Even to her own ears her words sounded childish just then, so she forced herself to draw a calming breath. After all, what he had asked of her wasn't so bad. Not when she thought of what he might have demanded! Her cheeks flooded with heat and she lowered her head quickly, making a show at picking bits of grass off her skirt.

''Don't think I don't appreciate your offer, Garrett. I do.''

''Then you'll accept?'' A long moment passed in which he stared down at the top of her head, wanting for all the world to run his hands through her silky hair.

''I accept,'' she said, lifting her face to the sun, and to the warmth of Garrett's smile.

''Last night . . . ,'' he halted, more aware now of her waiting stillness than ever before. ''You won't have to worry about a repeat performance of last night. It won't happen again.''

Though they were separated by a good five feet he could feel her tremble, and he knew that she, too, was recalling every nuance of that kiss. The air between them was suddenly void of any calm, was filled instead with a tension that crackled and vibrated with longing. Compelled by some unknown force to touch her, he reached down, one hand extended. The next few moments stretched to time immeasurable as he waited for her response, his heart pounding in its demand that she meet him halfway, even while he berated himself for caring so much.

But that, he admitted grudgingly, was his own compromise. He did care. This was unchangeable; this he would concede. He would not, however, let her know how much.

Kelsey stared at his hand mutely, knowing that by taking it she would forever seal her heart, yet unable, by all the power within her, to do otherwise. Her own fingers quivered as she stretched forward, knowing even before she touched him the strength of his grip, the roughness of his callused palm.

Still, she was not prepared for the jolt of electricity that coursed through her when their hands made contact. She felt its heat pour into her veins, suffusing her flesh with warm color. She tried to hide her reaction by summoning her most businesslike tone, but even so feared her voice gave her away.

"We'll work together then," she agreed, acknowledging his offer of help and ignoring the rest. "Papa would have wanted it that way."

9

That night the winds howled down from across the lake, rattling the windowpanes as a bitter reminder that winter was only a short time gone. But the next morning the sun was nearly white with brightness, sending clouds scuttling away like chastised pups. Spring had arrived, and would brook no mischief from any lingering suggestions of the season past.

Kelsey paused to lift her face to the sunlight, then made her way across the yard quickly, hastened by Hannah's warning that Garrett had been up and about an hour ago. She did not want to miss him this morning, for he had promised to take her to see a man who might be persuaded to hire on as overseer.

Hitching her skirt, the same one she had worn yesterday, a little higher, Kelsey sped across the lawn toward the stables. The rain-soaked grass was cold, and by the time she reached the cobbled lane in front of the stables her shoes were completely saturated and her feet frozen. Yesterday she hadn't suffered for the lack of riding boots, but wet grass was something she hadn't counted on.

Kelsey slipped inside the wide stable doors and stopped, squinting as she waited for her eyes to adjust to the dim light. There was no movement inside, and no sounds other than softly snorted greetings from the nearby stalls. Deciding that Garrett must have gone on without her, she headed for the tack room, intent upon finding a clean rag to dry her feet.

Just as her hand touched the cold metal handle of the tack-room door, voices from the other side rose to surround her. She nearly jumped at the unexpected sound. Their words came clearly to her through several large cracks in the wooden door, and she nibbled her lower lip with indecision. Should she leave? Or knock to make her presence known? Raising her hand in a fist, she paused just before rapping her knuckles on the door. But the sentence she heard next caused her to freeze once more.

"Does she know yet?" someone asked in a hushed tone.

"She's suspicious. We'll have to be extra careful, though, so nothing certain can be pinned on us."

"What do you plan to do?"

The question was met with silence, and Kelsey held her own breath, fear of being caught eavesdropping overwhelmed by her need to hear the answer. Gone was any thought of moving away now. The first voice she had been unable to place, but the second speaker she easily recognized as Garrett. Straining to hear better, Kelsey leaned toward the door.

"There's nothing I can do. She's determined to stay on so we'll have to make the best of it. It may work out better than we expected, you know."

"You mean you'll tell her everything?"

"No. At least not until I know where she stands. But maybe her being here will cause a distraction, enough to give the people of Lewiston something else to talk about for a while."

The unidentified man chuckled softly, a rich, warm sound that struck a chord in Kelsey's memory, then faded just beyond her grasp. Then the next words sent her heart racing.

"When do you expect the next shipment?"

"Not for a week. I'll send you the signal we discussed and we can work out details for a crossing then. In the meantime, keep your head low and take carc."

Of course, Kelsey's mind immediately rationalized, the words "shipments" and "crossings" might simply refer to the normal business transactions Garrett performed daily. But other parts, significant parts, of the conversation did not fit. For example, why was this discussion not taking place in the office at the landing? Why the extra caution to "take care"?

And most of all, she thought, biting her lip hard to stifle the disappointment seething through her, why should she be kept in the dark about the entire matter?

There was only one explanation, and it made her stomach roll with a sickening lurch. Garrett *was* involved with helping escaped slaves, and whether it was illegal or not was only another factor to consider. Right now, it was the sting of his deceit that worked its poison into her soul.

A rustling sound from the other side of the door indicated that the men were moving around. Kelsey snatched her hand away from the handle as if it were red-hot, then spun frantically, searching for a place to hide before she was caught listening. The stable doors, which she had left open, beckoned to her.

She had nearly reached them when she felt herself skidding across the slick cobbled floor, and Kelsey remembered, too late, that her wet slippers offered no traction whatsoever. Arms pinwheeling wildly, she fought to regain her footing, to no avail. She landed hard on her bottom before she could do more than utter a startled cry.

The sound of her fall brought Garrett out of the tack room in a flash, and when she saw him hurry toward her, she dipped her head low, praying fervently that he would assume her fall had occurred as she entered the stable and not the other way around. To her relief, he seemed not to notice that she was pointed in the wrong direction as he stooped to her side.

"Are you all right?"

"Does it look like I'm all right?" she replied caustically, grimacing as she pushed herself up with her hands. Her palms bore scratches from the stone floor and her arms ached from bearing part of the force of her fall. Garrett steadied her by the shoulders and helped her to her feet. Kelsey tried not to meet his look, but found it impossible when he did not let her go immediately. His blue eyes impaled her with their insistent gaze and she faltered for a moment, uncertain whether it was concern or contempt that glimmered there.

"What happened?" he asked, his firm lips curving into an amused smile.

"What do you think happened?" she shot back.

Garrett paused as if to consider this, dropping his hands from her shoulders as he took a step backward and grinned. "I think you're doing it again . . . answering my questions with more questions, that is. As for sprawling yourself across the stable floor, I can only guess. Checking for mice?"

Kelsey forced her lips into an uneasy smile, grateful, at least, that he hadn't guessed that she had overheard him and his mysterious consort. The same man who must still be in the tack room, she realized suddenly. She averted her gaze from Garrett, lifting one foot as if to inspect it.

"My shoes are wet and I slipped. Have you something in there to dry them off?" She gestured toward the room Garrett had just exited, pretending a casualness she did not feel. If he had nothing to hide, she reasoned, let him show himself now.

To her surprise, Garrett did just that, clasping her arm above the elbow in a gentle grip and guiding her toward the tack room. Something akin to relief bubbled through Kelsey. Even though Garrett obviously did not know she had listened in on part of their conversation, the fact that he showed no reluctance to introduce her to the man made her secretly elated.

And just as quickly, her elation evaporated. Garrett reached ahead of her to thrust open the door, revealing the entire room, empty except for the row of saddles straddling their blocks and the many bridles and harnesses hanging neatly from the walls. Everything was, Kelsey noted, exactly as it had been yesterday, right down to the tangy odor of old leather and saddle soap. Her gaze shifted to the single window, a narrow affair, designed to allow a minimum of sunlight and dampness into the room. Too small for a man to pass through.

"There should be a rag right over here," Garrett said, moving toward a large wooden box situated in one corner. He lifted the hinged lid with both hands as if it were heavy, then flung it toward the wall. "I think there may even be a pair of your old riding boots in here as well. They might still fit, unless your feet have grown as much as the rest of you."

Again, she dredged up a smile, trying to match, at least on the surface, his playful mood. "I shouldn't think so," she responded lightly. "I'll try to force my way into them anyway." With that, Garrett turned back to face her, his smile closer now to the familiar grin he had worn so often years ago. Kelsey felt her heart lurch, both at the poignant ache that seeped through her at his teasing expression, and at the sense of mistrust that grew with each passing moment. She was *certain* there had been another man in here just a minute ago. Where was he now?

"That's the spirit. Ah, here they are." Garrett dragged the boots out from under a pile of saddle blankets, snatching a clean cloth from a folded stack on a shelf beneath the window. He motioned toward a chair in one corner, then scooted a low stool closer with one foot. "Sit down and we'll try these on."

Kelsey blushed furiously when she realized that he meant to help her change her shoes, but when he busied himself with brushing dust off the boots rather matter-of-factly, she decided to go along. If the task meant so little to him, far be it from her to say otherwise.

She lowered herself gingerly, wincing as her tender derriere made contact with the rush-bottomed chair. She'd be bruised tomorrow, Kelsey was certain. Between the fall and the prospect of several hours in the saddle, she'd be lucky if she didn't cripple herself before the day was out.

Then Garrett lifted her foot, and all thoughts of various other parts of her anatomy fled from her mind. His hand cupped her heel tenderly, his long fingers branding her ankle with their warm strength, burning right through her lisle stocking as if it were made of the sheerest silk. With the other hand he slipped her soaked shoe from her foot. Kelsey shivered lightly.

"You may as well have gone barefoot," Garrett said, frowning as he held the shoe up to the light coming in from the window. "This leather's so thin I can practically see through it. Is this what you've been wearing to ride in England?"

Kelsey tried to jerk her foot out of his hand, but he held tight. "Of course it isn't!" she protested, her cheeks growing hot. "I just didn't want to wear my best shoes today."

"And I suppose you left your riding boots in London."

"Yes . . . no! It's none of your concern whether I own boots or not. Let go of my foot!"

"That's odd," Garrett drawled, not relaxing his grip on her ankle one bit. "I had the impression the British gentry were keen on riding. With the proper attire, of course. Don't tell me you weren't giving them a good show for the American cause."

"Believe it or not," Kelsey huffed, "I never gave a good goddamn for most of the so-called gentry I came in contact with. And how did you get to be such an expert on the British?"

She could have sworn she saw the pulse jump in his throat before he bent his head again, but she could no longer read the expression in his eyes as he uttered a cryptic answer.

"You know very well how." With one casual motion, he reached beneath the hem of her skirt and slid her garter up over the top of her stocking, stripping the cotton garment from her foot with practiced ease. Kelsey's shocked gasp seemed to go unnoticed, for he quickly lifted her foot and placed it on his own knee. "You said *most* of the gentry you met. But not all?"

Her response stuck in her throat as he wrapped the

towel around her slender foot, massaging it dry with both hands. Waves of pleasure flowed upward from the source of contact and she nearly sighed out loud from the sheer bliss of it. Instead, she forced her attention back to his question, for he was peering at her intently, waiting for a reply.

"No, not all," she said quietly, thinking of the few friendly faces who had looked upon her—not with snobbish resentfulness or scandalized glee—but with kindness. Mrs. Higbee . . . Martha Shallcross, the kind woman who had employed her . . . but no others.

Garrett watched her expression soften, then grow shuttered again. There was pain in her memories, and something much worse hidden behind the shadows in her deep brown eyes. Obviously, he had been wrong to assume she had been completely happy in England. But why, then, had she not come home long ago?

It was several moments before Garrett realized he was still holding her foot in his lap, one hand wrapped protectively around the delicate arch of her instep, the other resting lightly on her ankle. His blood surged hot and fast through his loins, as within himself he waged a violent battle for control. Kelsey seemed unaware of the intimacy of their position, her gaze becoming gradually more focused as her mind returned to the present. Quickly, as much to hide the trembling in his hands as to hurry through the ordeal, Garrett placed her foot back on the cobbled floor and reached for the other.

"I'll do that."

He looked up to see Kelsey, face flushed, bending to the task of removing her other shoe and stocking. Handing her the towel so she could dry her foot, he then passed her the boots he had found in the tack box. Despite their age, the leather had been well treated, remaining supple and firm. Kelsey yanked one onto each foot and stood, brushing off her dress as she did. "They fit well enough. Shall we go?"

"You're not too sore, are you?" Garrett glanced pointedly at the back of her skirt and picked a piece of straw from the dark fabric. "I mean, are you sure you want to try this?"

"We'll find out soon enough, won't we?" Kelsey looked over her shoulder on the way out the door, a rueful smile lifting one corner of her mouth. Whether Garrett knew it or not, she had more to overcome than mere bruises, and only he could give her the knowledge she needed in order to win—willingly or not.

Her glance swept the tiny confines of the room once more. She had promised Garrett to turn a blind eye to his activities in return for his help. Though his lack of trust stung her, she would keep her word until she didn't need him any longer.

That day, she admitted reluctantly, couldn't come too soon.

An hour later she had begun to have doubts about her plan to revive Riverview. After two hours, she was certain it would never work. And by the time they returned to the house for lunch, Kelsey was convinced that only a miracle would help her turn the land her father loved so well into something more than a liability.

It was not, she decided, that she wouldn't give it an honest effort. It was just that for the time being she was completely overwhelmed by the magnitude of what lay ahead. Riverview, she now understood, was at once more and less than she had imagined.

It was ironic, after her wish to be free of him, that the miracle she required was present in the form of Garrett O'Neill. He surprised her by knowing more about agriculture than she ever imagined, not to mention having more than a passing acquaintance with the other farmers in the county.

Riding astride Ladyfair, the filly Benjamin brought out for her, she had followed Garrett across hundreds of acres of prime land, entranced by the stark beauty of the spring earth, barren for now but teeming with potential.

"I remember coming here once," she shouted gleefully, spurring Ladyfair to a gallop across a flowering meadow. Garrett followed on Prince, reining his mount beside her after she stopped to scan the next field. Instead of the freshly turned soil she half-expected to find, the large plot was choked with weeds and undergrowth. She cast him a puzzled frown. "I thought this was it. Wasn't there a cottage over there, and a stream on the other side? Or am I confusing this place with another?"

"No, you're right. Sheldon let the tenants go years ago, and the building was torn down so the materials could be used elsewhere. There are three more sections of land like this farther north, and another two on the far side of the orchard."

"All this lying fallow?"

Prince tossed his powerful head as Garrett urged him forward. "Come on. There's something else I want to show you. I'll explain as we go along."

Kelsey cantered Ladyfair to catch up with him, eager for an explanation. It seemed a shame to let so much land go to waste and she couldn't understand why her father had allowed it.

"How much do you know of Sheldon's background?" Garrett asked as they slowed the horses to an easy walk.

Kelsey opened her mouth to answer, then snapped it shut again with a bemused expression on her face. "Not much, I guess," she admitted. "He never mentioned having a family, and Mother only talked about her own relations."

Garrett nodded. "Your ancestors were largely a seafaring lot, according to Sheldon, and in the family tradition he joined the British navy, though he claimed he'd always had a hankering to keep his feet firmly on the ground. Despite that, he might have stayed with the sea except for three events that occurred the year he turned twenty-six: His parents died, freeing him of his honor bound obligation to remain in the navy; he inherited a large amount of money from an uncle he barely knew; and he spent part of the money touring the United States, where he met and fell in love with your mother."

Something in Garrett's tone made Kelsey look over at

him, but his feelings were carefully guarded behind a rugged mask of concentration.

"He heard about the great northern lakes from tars who had sailed there during the last war with England, and so this part of the country was one that he intended to visit all along. When he arrived, however, it was a case of instant love. He spent every last dime of his inheritance starting the shipping business, building the house for his new bride, and buying up all the surrounding farmland that was for sale. He named his home Riverview, then brought Mabelle here to live."

"And she hated it," Kelsey interjected, half to herself. "She hated the house and the trees, and especially the river. She used to say everything about this place was uncivilized."

There was no use in denying it, especially since Kelsey herself had made the statement. Until now, Garrett hadn't been sure that she was aware of her mother's bitterness, or of its effect on Sheldon.

Now Kelsey began to wonder if Garrett were telling her everything, for his silence was weighing heavily in the morning air. "Is that the only reason she was so unhappy?"

"Not quite." Garrett paused. He'd known before he started that this question was inevitable, but that didn't help him when it came to devising an acceptable answer—at least one which would appease Kelsey for now. "There were other disagreements. I don't know all of them, but I do know that Sheldon was committed to his work, and that Mabelle resented that."

"So did I," Kelsey blurted, then quickly explained when Garrett's head snapped around with surprise. "I mean, I wish Papa had spent more time with us. He was always so busy, so preoccupied. When I was little, I wished he would just stay home once in a while."

"He did what he could."

Now it was Kelsey's turn to peer at Garrett intently. It was clear from his set expression that he would not listen to any arguments against Sheldon—not that she was planning to try—so she focused her attention on the buildings huddled together a short distance away.

"This is what I wanted to show you," he said. "These are some of the tenant farmers who used to work your father's land. Most of them have managed to make a living hiring out as day laborers. Even though Sheldon stopped production, he allowed them to stay in their cottages. Tie your horse to that tree."

Kelsey could see at once that there were ten or twelve cottages, newer than the ones she remembered from years ago, and arranged along a wide, grassy common with a large covered well in the center. A few women stood outside, apparently stopping to chat on the way to attending to their chores. One carried a basket of wet clothing, a second woman clutched a parcel beneath one arm, her other wrapped securely around the baby straddling her hip. A third female figure carried two squawking chickens by the feet, holding them just far enough from her that their flapping wings barely touched her skirts as she conversed with her neighbors.

And surrounding them all, Kelsey saw, her throat growing thick with emotion, were the children.

They came in various sizes, perhaps twenty in all, but each and every one stopped in mid-play when they spotted Garrett dismounting. For a few scant moments they stared at her, too, and Kelsey could only stare back, unable to summon a proper reaction. But within seconds the children scampered forward, swarming toward them with gleeful cries and outstretched hands.

Garrett took a step away from the horses, his rugged face softened by a welcoming smile. As Kelsey hung back, overwhelmed by the children's exuberance, he greeted each one by name and reached deep into his pockets, withdrawing double handfuls of rock candy. "I'd like you to meet someone," he said, standing and drawing Kelsey to his side.

Her smile was shaky as she took in the enormous number of upturned faces. Some were scrubbed pink; others were already streaked with dirt though the morning had barely begun. All were beautiful and innocent—and far, far too thin.

"Pleased ta meet ya, Miz Kelsey," one boy said, stepping boldly ahead of the others. He appeared to be about eight years old, with hair so blond it was nearly white and a wide grin that bespoke a cunning knowledge beyond his years.

"How do you do," she replied, aware immediately that her voice was high-pitched and quavering. She cleared her throat and tried again, searching the throng of children for a less intimidating face she could focus on. She found one directly below, a tiny girl who gazed up at her with a delightful, toothless grin. "What's your name?" Kelsey asked.

Ethter," the girl replied. "What'th yourth?"

The towheaded boy laughed loudly. "Ya know her name, stupid. Miz Kelsey Tremayne. Garrett told us yesterday."

"I believe I also mentioned something about manners, James Brady. So you'd better watch yours. Did you finish the job I assigned you?"

James looked sheepish, but only for a split second before his eyes lit up like firecrackers. "I finished, all right. You gonna come and check?"

Garrett glanced sideways at Kelsey, then shook his head. "If you say it's done, your word's good enough for me." He fished a coin from his pocket and flipped it toward the boy. Kelsey could not see what it was, but she caught a flash of silver before James reached out and snatched it deftly from the air. And from the oohs of the other children, she imagined it represented more money than they had ever seen before.

Something tugged at her skirt and Kelsey looked down. Esther, now solemn in her regard, slipped a thin hand into hers.

"I'm thorry. I didn't really forget your name. I jutht didn't wanna thay it wrong."

The bubble inside Kelsey's chest grew larger, but somehow what had begun as pain now pulsed with a different feeling altogether. She dropped to her knees before the little girl, her hand clasping tighter around her tiny fingers. "That's all right, Esther. When my front teeth fell out, I sounded just like you, but they grew back soon. You just wait."

Her only answer was a smile, revealing again the wide gap where several teeth were missing, but it was more than enough for Kelsey. Suddenly, all the children were clamoring for an equal share of her attention. And strangely enough, the fear that had nearly paralyzed her when she first saw them evaporated rapidly, allowing her to enjoy the next half-hour more than she would have imagined possible.

The women, too, came over one by one, encouraged by Garrett's beckoning waves. Each of them greeted Kelsey politely before returning to her task, obviously uncomfortable meeting her. It made her wonder why. That was the first thing she asked Garrett when they finally remounted and rode away.

"I suppose they aren't used to talking to strangers," he hedged. "Anyway, they were no more nervous than you were with the children . . . at first."

His voice rose questioningly, but Kelsey was unprepared to give him the answer he sought. She wasn't even sure herself why she had reacted so strangely, though at least she could summon a guess. And it was more than the fact that she wasn't used to children. When she continued to ride along in silence, Garrett eventually raised another issue.

"We'll go now to meet Stocker Fulton, the man I have in mind for overseer. Last I heard he was just about finished with a job for Matt Ruther."

"What about the families we just met? Can we hire back some of the same people who used to work here before?" she asked, her brow furrowing. "I hate to see them living like that."

Garrett cast her a puzzled glance. "You're right, of course. But not everyone is accustomed to the easy life. I expect they're happy to have a dry place to sleep. Not having any money puts quite a different value on it, doesn't it?

"There *is* something that can be done, but you may not like it," Garrett cautioned, pulling back on the reins to bring Prince to a complete stop. He urged his horse around beside hers, so that their thighs nearly touched, leaning so close she could see the flecks of dark silver sparkling in his eyes and the tense line of his jaw as he spoke in clipped tones.

"We can provide them with tools, a share of the crop, education. But all those thing cost money, Miss Tremayne. Are you willing to make that commitment, or is reviving Riverview merely a whim?"

"I don't have the money and you know it," Kelsey responded dryly. "Though you can hardly blame me. What did happen to my father's wealth?"

"A number of things, including a bad investment and poor crops several years in a row. Not to mention the expense of supporting an absentee family. I could ask you the same thing. The money from the bank loan was sent to England shortly after your mother's death. Sheldon never went into great detail, but I think he believed it was to pay for a trousseau—yours."

At that he moved on ahead, leaving Kelsey to follow in the relative privacy of her own thoughts. She hated to let him go on thinking she had spent the money on herself, but if she confessed that her greedy relatives had taken it, she would also have to explain why. And that she could not do.

Before long, Garrett slowed and pointed out the orchard they were nearing.

Neat rows of apple trees striped the low-lying section, but as they drew closer Kelsey could see the signs that this project, too, had been abandoned. Many of the trees were overgrown and drooping, and rotted apples littered the ground beneath the branches, last year's crop gone to waste.

"The orchard is probably your safest bet," Garrett said, riding just beneath a bough so that he could hold it down for her to see. The branch was dotted with tiny buds, some of them so small they were little more than slight discolorations on the smooth brown surface.

"This section is in it's prime. All it needs is a little cleaning and someone to go through and cut out the branches that aren't producing, so as not to take away vital nutrients from the ones that are bearing well."

"Pruning," Kelsey responded automatically, then flushed when Garrett glanced sideways at her. "I do the same with roses."

"More or less." He released the branch, urging Prince toward the next stand of trees. "The only problem is that apples are a late harvest, and with so many orchards in this county, the market is soft. But on the other hand, it's almost a sure thing, requiring a relatively small investment."

"Almost a sure thing?"

"Short of a blizzard, nothing will stop these buds from turning into juicy red apples."

Kelsey dismounted, wrapping Ladyfair's reins around her wrist as she stepped closer to one of the sprawling apple trees for a better look. Peering up into the new foliage above, she tried to determine if the trees looked healthy enough, but it was so early in the spring—or her eye so inexperienced—she just couldn't tell.

"I have a lot to learn," she sighed, then looked up when she realized she had spoken out loud.

Garrett leaned forward in the saddle to pat Prince on the neck. The horse was stomping restlessly at the delay. "That's true. These next few weeks will be the most important, because the success of any crop depends on how good a start it gets. You'll have to begin with at least one other cash crop this year. Stocker will know best, and can help decide which of the fields can be cleared fastest."

"Then it looks like I'm going to be a farmer after all," Kelsey said wryly. "I suppose I'll have to buy a straw hat."

"And start getting up earlier in the morning. No more lazing in bed like you did today."

She started to protest, but stopped when she caught a glimpse of his teasing expression. She often suffered from insomnia and slept through the late morning hours to make up for lost sleep. But Garrett couldn't know that. Besides, if she was to be a farmer, she supposed she'd have to start acting like one. "Buy me a rooster," she quipped, "and I'll be up before you every day."

"I'll believe that when I see it. But at least you've proven yourself as a rider."

Kelsey had to smile at that, because she had just been thinking how very much she would welcome a rest from the saddle. But since Garrett had unwittingly tossed her the challenge, she walked Ladyfair away from the trees and swung herself onto her back, arranging her skirt primly to cover her legs. "Then I guess I don't take after Mother in *every* way," she said lightly. "She always said I did, but she also made it clear no one in her family ever cared to ride."

"I hardly think riding skills are hereditary," Garrett replied, moving closer. "But if you like to believe you take after someone, you probably will."

Hannah had said almost the same thing, and for a brief moment Kelsey wondered if it could possibly be true. She jumped when Garrett gripped her arm to keep her from moving away, though she couldn't possibly escape when he pinned her with that compelling gaze, his eyes deep blue whirlpools, drawing her into their depths.

As if reading her thoughts, he spoke gently, yet forcefully. "Don't make the mistake of thinking you're bound by what your parents were. The opinions and ideas they taught us might have been their own, but each of us has the choice to follow a new path in life. It's no more fair for us to blame our shortcomings on our heritage than it is to rely on them for our successes. I thank God Sheldon believed that."

Garrett released her arm and offered her a tender smile, but Kelsey could see pain there. She thought she understood his fight to overcome the prejudices of others as well as those of his own heart. "And now you think it's so because my father said it?" She heard the appeal in her own voice, and wondered if he knew how much she needed to feel the truth of his words.

"I believe it," Garrett answered, "because I must."

10

"You can come out now. It's as safe as it'll ever be."

The hushed words were spoken gently, but they woke Dacia with the impact of a gunshot, nevertheless. Her eyes flew open, meeting nothing but blackness, and she breathed in a deep lungful of stale air as she fought against the panic of waking in an unfamiliar place. But it took only a moment for her to realize that the voice had spoken the truth. For now, at least, they were still safe.

Peering around in the darkness, she struggled to regain her bearings. It had been six days since she'd walked away from Bennington Plantation without a backward glance. Her escape had seemed almost too easy that first night, but once she'd joined up with several slaves from a nearby plantation, they'd been followed persistently by hounds and man alike. After two days of travel without rest, they'd met up with a man who brought them to this tiny shack, where at last they could rest their weary bones.

She must have dozed off despite the ever-present fear of capture, and knowing she had done so made Dacia grow hot with shame. It would take all their ears, they had been told, to listen sharp for sounds of pursuit. It wouldn't do for one of them to endanger the others with individual laziness.

That particular statement had been aimed at her, she reminded herself. They had said she should feel lucky they had allowed her to join them. A pregnant woman would slow them down.

Inwardly, Dacia had scoffed at the complaints of the other runaway slaves. Her pregnancy hadn't stopped one from suggesting she share a hayloft with him the day they hid in the relative comfort of an out-of-the-way barn. Nor had it stopped any of the ragtag group from making their way north. In fact, it was she who had prevented their capture on the second night out. Warned by some innate sensitivity to danger, she had urged them all into hiding just in time to avoid notice by a party of travelers.

Yes, she scoffed at their male pride, but only inwardly. If the pale scars imbedded in the backs of each and every one of her companions were any indication, they were just as frightened, and desperate, as she.

Dacia stifled a moan as she uncurled her limbs, her cramped muscles screaming at the sudden movement. Two days. Two days they had been crowded into this little shack, not daring a sound or a movement lest some passerby take note and raise an investigation. Two days without food or water, privacy or relief. Two days sitting in their own stench, wondering over and over again whether freedom would ever come, and if it did, would it be worth it? Dacia had often tried to imagine what Hell was like. Now she knew.

"Hurry, y'all. Not much time." The whispered voice bore a hint of urgency, but it was a sound familiar to them all and therefore no more alarming than any other part of their journey had been. Dacia filed outside the shack between two of her traveling companions. She blinked her eyes. Though the small yard was illuminated only by the bright moon, even that was more light than she was accustomed to. Glancing around cautiously, she surveyed the area.

They had made it on foot as far as this railroad depot in Charlottesville, which was deserted now except for the stationmaster, who could be seen through the window of his lighted office, feet propped on his desk and chin tucked low against his chest.

Between the red-brick depot and the shanty were the tracks themselves, ribbons of cold steel and cinders that represented pathways to distant places. Dacia wondered briefly if any of the tracks led to the north, and her question was answered when the man who had come for them whispered once more. She studied him closely.

Until he stepped forward, Dacia had not been certain whether he was colored or white, for men and women of both races had aided them thus far. But now she could see his copper-colored hair shimmering in the moonlight. He carried himself with an aristocratic air that bespoke the finest southern upbringing; his voice was cultured and as gently rolling as the hills of Virginia, though necessarily cautious. The frown on his clean-shaven face was a sign of the intensity with which he performed this duty.

"There're two crates over here, ready to be loaded into the baggage car. You and you . . . ," he pointed, selecting the two smallest men of the group, ". . . find the barrel of water behind the shack. Clean yourselves as best you can, and see to your other needs as well. It'll be a long trip boxed up like that but you'll make it all right."

He next addressed the largest of the slaves. "You will travel with my friend over there. He'll take you as far as Fredericksburg by wagon. He has ownership papers fitting your general description, in case it becomes necessary to produce them."

Dacia watched the lumbering negro stare at a loaded farm wagon, barely visible at the edge of the yard, and then nod slowly. Sam had been their unofficial leader for the past week, having some knowledge of the terrain they had crossed, but of all the group he was the least trusting, the first to cast suspicion on whomever or whatever lay before them. After knowing him only a week, Dacia thought she understood Sam—she suspected that name was an alias—all too well. If not for her complete faith in her own eventual freedom, she would have acted the same. Now, she was perfectly willing to place her fate in the hands of strangers.

For tonight, at least, it would be this stranger.

She listened closely as he instructed the last two of the

men. From beneath his cape he produced a bundle of clothing and a single railroad ticket, which he handed to the most recent member of the group of runaways, a man who had been thrust into that shack only the previous night. In the blackness of their temporary prison, Dacia had not been able to make out his features, but now she saw that he was as light-skinned as she, and quite good-looking as well.

"With this change of clothing," their benefactor said, "you can pass for white. Speak to as few people as possible on the train. Get off at the Baltimore junction and walk to Franklin Street. A man named Porter will direct you from there."

Now the elegantly dressed man turned toward Dacia, and his concentrated frown deepened as he glanced down at her distended belly, which she clutched protectively with both hands. "When they told me you were fair-complected," he began, "I hoped the two of you could pose as man and wife. That would be impossible now. No white woman would ever travel in such advanced condition. I'm afraid you'll have to come with me."

Dacia stepped forward unhesitantly, the other men having already moved toward their own destinies. Only Sam stopped to give her a long, measuring look, nodding once more as if to send his blessing, and his farewell.

She smiled in answer, then turned her steady regard toward the man who would guide her on the next step of her journey. He glanced up and down over her swollen figure again and his expression softened.

"We'll have to walk several miles." His tone was doubtful. "Can you make it?"

Dacia's response was to lift her chin higher. "We'd best start then," she said firmly. "The night's wastin'."

There were no doubts in her mind. If she had to, she would walk all the way to freedom.

11

Kelsey stared at the age-darkened mirror in the corner of her room and frowned at her reflection. *Dowdy,* she told herself, tugging at the waistband of her paisley skirt. She removed the offensive garment and turned with hands on her hips to face the open wardrobe doors.

A total of six dresses, compared to the twenty or so she had once claimed, hung limply from wooden pegs. One was the brown outfit she had worn four days in a row, another was the black serge traveling gown she hated so. The paisley skirt and two others given to her by Mrs. Higbee were so ill-fitting, she could hardly consider them for wear, which left only the rose wool.

When Justin invited her to his mother's soireé, she had given little thought to what she might wear. Now, however, it was painfully clear that nothing she owned was appropriate. Though made of a soft, finely woven wool that was of good quality, the rose-colored dress was never intended for a social event. The high, rounded neckline and lace collar gave it an innocent appeal, making it more suited to an evening at home with family.

But after all, she reminded herself, she *was* in mourning.

Bridget raised her head from her paws, then settled back to a position of watchful repose. Kelsey began to unfasten the row of hooks running up the back of the dress. "What do you think, girl?" she asked as she raised her arms and slipped the dress over her head. "Will this gown make me look properly somber, or like a little girl fresh out of the schoolroom?"

Neither, she decided, peering once again into the mirror. Perhaps she looked innocent when she had first been fitted for the dress, but the ensuing year had wrought many changes, not the least of which were the changes to her figure. The dress clung to her at every line, emphasizing the fullness of her breasts and the curving indentation of her waist. High neckline or not, the gown was very nearly indecent.

"Oh, bother!" Disgusted with the whole business, Kelsey was about to call Hannah to send her regrets to the Delberts when a soft knock had her striding to the door, ready to fling it open.

"Hannah, I've changed my—" Stopping in mid-pace, Kelsey gaped at Garrett. "What are you doing here?"

"I came to see if you were ready." His gaze slid downward over the front of her dress, taking in every glorious inch of her. He recognized the gown, not because of its style or color, but because of the immediate and unwelcome reaction that slammed through him when he saw her in it. Nevertheless, he gave her one last look to confirm the feeling.

Kelsey was all too cognizant of the direction his eyes were traveling and she spun angrily, searching for the shawl which she remembered tossing into a drawer somewhere. "You should have identified yourself before I opened the door."

"You didn't give me a chance."

"Well then, you shouldn't have knocked in the first place. What if I'd been unclothed?"

When he did not answer, Kelsey stiffened, painfully aware that she had said exactly the wrong thing. Hot flames leapt to her cheeks and she stifled the urge to cover them with her hands. Instead, she snatched the shawl up and whipped it around her shoulders, turning to face Garrett with her chin held high.

He was leaning against the doorjamb, thumbs hooked in his pockets and ankles crossed. He looked, Kelsey fumed, completely at home. "Don't just stand there as if this was the doorway to some . . . some saloon!"

To her utter dismay, he straightened, then sauntered farther into the room, casting around for a place to sit. With discarded pieces of clothing scattered everywhere, none was available. "Are you ready to go?'

Entranced by his maddeningly slow smile, it was a moment before Kelsey noticed that he was wearing a dark frockcoat over fawn-colored trousers, and that his neckcloth was arranged in a froth of snowy white linen. He looked absolutely splendid. "Do you mean to say that you're going too?" she exclaimed.

Garrett's smile froze imperceptibly. "Don't sound so shocked, Kelsey. For a poor Irish lad, I've made huge strides in this town. Not that it makes much difference to some people."

His voice had not changed one bit from the lightly bantering tone he used before, but it didn't have to for Kelsey to know that she had unintentionally hurt him. And for all his claims that social position did not matter, she could tell that he *did* care—and a great deal. "I . . . I was just surprised, that's all. Justin didn't tell me he'd invited you."

"He didn't, George did. We have some business to discuss and thought tonight would be an opportune time. Benjamin has the carriage ready."

"But—" Kelsey stopped, wanting to avoid saying the wrong thing again. She frowned. "I appreciate the offer of a ride, but I think Justin planned to come for me."

Garrett stepped through the door, holding out his arm to Kelsey once they were in the broad upstairs hall. "He did, but I took the liberty of sending a message saying we wouldn't need the ride. I'd rather have my own transportation available. It makes those unscheduled departures so much easier."

Her expression grew puzzled for a moment, then laughter spilled from her throat, bubbling easily into the once tense atmosphere. She took his arm. "Christina vowed never to forgive you for that, but I think she was secretly pleased that her birthday party was turned into a such a memorable occasion. I hope your plans for tonight aren't quite so . . . extraordinary."

"If I remember correctly, it was you who diverted disaster by calling out for more. My only intention was to ride through the garden at breakneck speed and snatch the birthday cake from the trestle table. I wasn't planning to be coerced into performing riding stunts until Antoinette Delbert chased me away with dire threats against my life."

"She would have sent you home anyway, and without all the other guests clapping and cheering for you."

"Then you caught a scolding for riding home behind me." They had reached the buggy and after helping Kelsey up, Garrett pulled himself into the seat beside her. Fingering the reins lightly, he stared straight ahead over the horse's rump. "You should have known better."

Just like she should have known better than to go with him now, Kelsey thought, unaccountably disturbed by the way their bodies were pressed together from hip to shoulder in the narrow buggy. The night air was cool and refreshing, but she felt as if she couldn't draw breath into her lungs. Her heart pounded fractiously when the horse made the turn onto the river road and she was forced to lean into Garrett to keep her balance. She was also finding it increasingly difficult to think of something to say, and the longer the minutes stretched since his last comment, the harder it was to respond.

Garrett took her silence as affirmation, and wondered why it bothered him that she should agree. It was he who should have known better than to expect the same kind of loyalty as when she was a mere child, with a child's expectations.

And just because she had shown herself to be more eager to make a go of managing Riverview than he had reckoned didn't mean he should start counting on anything more. "What did you think of Stocker Fulton?" he asked, settling on a safe topic.

Grateful that Garrett had started the conversation in a new direction, Kelsey responded willingly. "I like him.

He's been terribly patient with me the past few days. I'm afraid I've been asking him a lot of questions, but he does seem to know a lot about farming."

"That's why he used to be field foreman. And he *is* a good man, with a nice family. You already met his daughter."

"Esther?" Kelsey smiled as Garrett nodded. She had been so taken with the little girl, with all the children, that she'd made a point of stopping to see them every day that week. She was getting to know each of the children individually.

"They like you too, you know," Garrett commented.

Was he reading her mind again? Kelsey wondered. She glanced sideways at him, studying his profile by the swaying light of the buggy lantern. His light hair was swept casually back off his brow and behind his ears, curling only slightly where it touched his collar in the back. That unlikely wave somehow softened the hard thrust of his jaw, just as his smile did. It seemed he was smiling more often lately.

And laughing, Kelsey thought, thinking of their visit to the cottages that afternoon. Perhaps the children did like her, but they were truly fond of Garrett, and he of them. It was a side of him she'd never seen before, or more likely had never bothered to notice.

He took an interest in *all* the children, but especially James. The precocious lad was earning pocket money running errands at the shipping office, though Kelsey suspected some of the errands were contrived to keep him busy. It didn't take a genius to see that Garrett was attempting to play the same role Sheldon had taken in his life.

"You should have children of your own, instead of using James Brady to fill the gap," she mused, then fought the blush that stained her cheeks when she realized she'd spoken aloud.

Garrett flicked his wrists, guiding the horse onto Center Street. He answered tersely. "It's not *my* gap that needs filling. The boy's father died three years ago.

Would you rather see him turn into a pickpocket or a thief?''

''Of course not! That's not what I meant at all.''

''Then what did you mean?''

Kelsey wasn't even certain, but somehow she had to try to voice the feelings that had been building inside. ''I think it's a fine thing to want to help other people, but one man can't be responsible for all the woes in this world. In a way that's what my father did, and he ended up hurting his own family.''

''As you've already pointed out, I have no family of my own to hurt. So what I do with my time is of no concern to you.''

''It is if you jeopardize my home!''

They were no longer talking about James Brady, and they both knew it. The tension that had waxed and waned now rose to snap around them like a cracking whip.

Their arrival at the Delbert home was marked by a stable boy's hail, and Garrett managed only a quick ''we'll talk about this later'' before he stopped the buggy and handed the reins over. Kelsey accepted his hand as he helped her over the side, but when she would have taken his arm for him to escort her to the door, Garrett hung back.

''You go on in,'' he said gruffly. ''There's someone I need to talk to before dinner. I'll see if I can catch him out here. It's private.''

With that he turned and disappeared into the darkness behind the row of vehicles parked along Center Street, leaving Kelsey to approach the lighted doorway of the Delbert home alone.

Garrett walked the two blocks down Center Street quickly, thankful that darkness still fell early enough to cover his movements. Reaching his destination, he slipped into an alley between a livery establishment and the now-deserted cobbler shop, casting a glance over his shoulder to make certain he had not been followed.

''Careful as always, I see.'' The cultured voice came

from farther within the narrow gap, guiding Garrett forward.

"And you," he acknowledged. "But we'll have to make this fast." It wasn't necessary to explain to his fellow conspirator the need for haste, since Martin Crandall was a guest at the same party Garrett had just neatly sidestepped. "Any news?"

"Only the same. A shipment from Lockport tomorrow night."

"How many?"

"Three—this time."

Ignoring the question in Crandall's voice, Garrett went over the possible arrangements mentally. Three could be handled by Chesterton easily enough. Thank God there hadn't been more. "I'll get word to Chesterton tomorrow. As far as I can tell, Ogden's not on to him yet."

"That's good to know, since that farmhouse is hardly the ideal location. You'll have to make up your mind soon."

Garrett nodded. He knew as well as Crandall that Riverview offered resources unavailable almost anywhere else in the county, despite Ogden's return. And it was just a matter of time before a shipment arrived that only he could handle. "She stands against us," he murmured grimly. "But not so much that I can't work around her."

"Can you do that without giving yourself away?"

"It looks like I'll have to."

With the discussion ended, Garrett watched Martin Crandall slip through the rear door of the livery where he kept his carriage. No one would question his need to ride to a party held less than four blocks from his home. Respectability brought with it a certain tolerance to unorthodox behavior. And, as a federal judge, Crandall had earned his share of respect.

Turning back the way he had come, Garrett paused at the entrance to the alley long enough to scan the darkened street. With Bart Ogden tenaciously hanging on to Lewiston, caution had become second nature to him.

Maybe he was being too cautious where Kelsey was

concerned, he thought as he began the short walk to George Delbert's house. After all, she had certainly taken him by surprise in every other way.

An image of her stooped over a pile of rotten apples assailed him, and he smiled at the memory of her pert nose wrinkling in distaste. It had not stopped her from carrying out her task diligently, however, as she had done everything in the past few days.

Garrett had spent more time away from the shipping office than he ought in an effort to ease Kelsey's first efforts at farming. Surprisingly enough, she did not question his presence or refuse his help. It seemed she had learned that misplaced pride could put an end to her scheme as surely as her own ignorance. She had stifled the first and was doing her best to eliminate the latter.

Once Stocker Fulton got over his initial resistance to having her work beside him, he hadn't wasted any time singing her praise to Garrett, either. If Kelsey got nothing else out of this, she had earned the gruff man's unflagging respect.

On the other hand, endurance wasn't the same thing as compassion. If tonight's discussion were any indication, she was as stubbornly self-serving as ever, even though her focus had shifted away from her personal wants, such as new dresses, to the more general needs of Riverview.

And that, he understood completely, was the only condition under which she would accept his help. For the sake of Riverview she suffered his presence gladly. As long as there was nothing personal about it, she tolerated his existence.

It was not the first time she had dealt that blow.

A shaft of unadulterated desire coursed through Garrett, causing him to slow to a groaning halt just before the well-lighted doors of the Delbert home. A vision of her face flashed through his mind, upturned to his as he forced a grinding kiss onto her trembling lips.

Never again, he had promised her. Steeling himself against the long-buried needs that surged within, he forced his attention to the other guests greeting him as they arrived for the party. If Kelsey wanted to remain business associates, then he would abide by her wishes.

But business associates didn't interfere with one another's personal affairs, and Garrett was damned if he'd let her interfere with his.

Too much was at stake here. Including his own pride.

Damn him, she thought nearly an hour later when he still had not appeared. She was tiring of making excuses for him, and weary, too, of the curious glances she received every time the subject of their unusual living arrangements came up, as it had each time Antoinette Delbert introduced her to another guest.

Her small dinner party, as Justin had described it, had turned into a crowded affair of over thirty attendees, most of whom were eager to welcome Kelsey back to Lewiston. Many were also eager, she learned quickly, to know what her intentions were when it came to the future of Riverview. *Too* eager.

So when, after one time too many, someone inquired about her plans, Kelsey was fully prepared to answer.

"I have no intention of selling one square foot of my land," she pronounced, perhaps a bit too adamantly. Matthew Ruther, who was unfortunate enough to have been the last person to ask her, nearly bit his cigar in half. The room fell silent and Kelsey's hands grew icy cold, her cheeks flaming as she realized that every head was now turned in her direction.

"But, my dear," Old Lady Gephardt gasped loudly, "how will you live?"

So, not only were they all inordinately interested in her personal affairs, it seemed that everyone present was also aware of the miserable state of her finances. Kelsey's heart beat so heavily she could almost feel it throbbing in the soles of her feet, but she raised her chin stubbornly, her eyes blazing with angry lights. "I'll make a living with what my father left me. My land is not spent, only unproductive, and there are still plenty of farmers in need of jobs. Starting this spring, every field will be planted."

Stunned silence was the only response she got, until Antoinette Delbert's saccharine tones filled the air. "Would you all come to the dining room, *s'il vous plait?*"

The guests filed through the double wide doorway leading to the dining room, murmuring quietly as they went. Kelsey was certain she knew what they were all whispering. She stood silently to one side, allowing the others to pass her and wishing fervently that she had not come, when a voice behind her ear sent a shiver of warmth through her veins.

"Well done, Miss Tremayne. You've just spoiled half the indigestions in Lewiston."

Without turning, Kelsey nodded. "It serves them right," she declared. "I'm sick of everyone minding my business. Why can't they leave me alone?"

"Because you're young and unattached," Garrett warned, offering her his arm. "And extremely vulnerable to gossip. Shall we go in?"

What none of them knew, she mulled, was that she had no reputation worth protecting.

But as he escorted her to her seat, another thought left her feeling distracted. When it came to Riverview, she and Garrett were unquestionably on the same side. She had begun to sense it during their daily excursions, which she looked forward to far more than she should. And now his unspoken support emboldened her more than words possibly could. Kelsey's spirit soared, making her wish she were home right now, planning her next move for the restoration of Riverview.

With Garrett. The tiny voice inside her was insistent, but she painstakingly ignored it.

". . . don't you agree, Miss Tremayne?"

Her silent musing, thank goodness, was interrupted by her dinner companions, and Kelsey was obliged to take part in the conversation between Justin on her left and Judge Crandall on her right. Something about the river having some scenic value, if she understood them correctly. But any other details she had either missed, or they hadn't mentioned.

At least, she thought, they had all left off talking about her. Until someone mentioned the only other subject she wished to avoid. Her heart sank at the conversation next to her.

"I heard they caught him," Matt Ruther was saying, gesturing with his fork for emphasis. His wife frowned threateningly across the table, but old Matthew had never been known to pay much heed to his wife, or for that matter to anyone, when he had something to say. "They caught him over in Rochester and shipped him back to Kentucky. Heard they cut off his toes to keep him from running away."

"If that's true," Mrs. Gephardt interjected, "then why is that horrible Ogden man still wandering around Lewiston. I don't like him, I tell you, and you men should stand up to him."

"That would be against the law," Justin explained in a deferential voice. "Bart Ogden and his kind are protected by a federal order. Anyone interfering with his business would be in violation of the Fugitive Slave Act."

"Balderdash! The man is scum. Why, he reminds me of that Simon Legree fellow in Mrs. Stowe's book, only worse! He shouldn't be allowed to walk the same streets as the fine people of Lewiston!"

From the murmurs and nods all around the table, Kelsey could tell that on this everyone was in agreement. Several of the other ladies offered their impressions of the popular novel, just recently making the rounds again after having enjoyed limited success when it was first published. Apparently the passage of the Fugitive Slave Act had instigated new interest in the subject of slavery.

Five years ago passions had not run so high, Kelsey recalled. At least not outside her own family. "If it's against the law to stand in Ogden's way, are we then obliged to help him?" Though she addressed her remark to no one in particular, her gaze slid toward Garrett at the far end of the table.

"Of course we don't have to help him!" George Delbert raised his spectacles. "Don't be ridiculous!"

Again all eyes were on Kelsey, but this time she realized it was because they thought she was taking Bart Ogden's side! She opened her mouth to speak, but was interrupted by Antoinette.

"It's not her fault, mon cheri," she said to her husband in a patronizing tone. "She is of good southern blood."

A warning look from Garrett caused Kelsey to drop her gaze to her plate, but inwardly she was fuming. Why were people so quick to assume they knew how she felt! And why did they automatically believe she held the same opinions her mother had?

At Antoinette's prodding, the conversation shifted to the subject of the arrival of a traveling theater group. When Kelsey dared to lift her head, she found that only three people continued to study her. Judge Crandall was looking at her sympathetically. Justin smiled her way, though there was a definite gleam in his eye. She turned her head slightly, knowing by the tingling feeling in her blood that Garrett, too, was watching through hooded eyes. His expression was indiscernable, his blue eyes turning dark and brooding.

The rest of the evening passed in a miserable blur for Kelsey. Instead of finding the support of old friends, she felt more alienated from the townspeople than ever before. And worst of all, the sense of comradery she had experienced earlier when Garrett stood behind her was now gone. She was learning quickly that slavery was a topic rife with controversy.

One other thing she noticed, less unsettling but just as surprising to her, was that Garrett seemed as relaxed and at home in this setting as he was with Stocker Fulton or the men at the dock. He had gained a level of acceptance with people who had shunned him in years past. The men in particular appeared to treat him as an equal, and the women, especially the younger ones, made it clear that they enjoyed his company.

Which made the situation far more embarrassing to her

when the time came to leave and their departure together was met with sly innuendo and knowing glances. The only thing that kept Kelsey from melting with shame was the knowledge that she had withstood far worse, and had survived.

This, she told herself repeatedly, was nothing.

Garrett, however, did not agree. He'd been stewing silently all evening, so when Justin invited himself to follow them out the door, he was more than ready for a confrontation.

"I think it only proper that you let me escort you home, Kelsey. No need to flaunt your unseemly living arrangements. If you were any kind of man, O'Neill, you'd have a care for Kelsey's reputation." Justin did not hide his scorn.

Garrett started toward him, but Kelsey laid a hand on his sleeve, determined not to have the two men adding to the humiliation she had already experienced that night. The muscles beneath her fingers were taut and quivering, evidence of the supreme control it took for Garrett to refrain from thrashing Justin. She could hardly blame him, since she would have loved to take a poke at him herself just about now.

"As all your guests seem to know the details of my situation intimately, I hardly think my reputation could suffer any more. Besides, Justin, it's foolish for you to take me all the way home and ride back in the dark when I can go with Garrett just as well. Please don't make a scene."

Justin's features tightened, his dark eyes narrowing so that he resembled Antoinette when she was about to make a particularly cutting remark. "As you wish, my dear. You've always done exactly what you wanted, and I see you haven't changed in that. But let me warn you, there's something going on out there, and I don't like it."

Kelsey thought she felt Garrett's muscles flinch, or maybe they were the nerves in her own hand. "Are you accusing me of inappropriate behavior?"

"Not accusing, my dear. Warning. Isn't that right, O'Neill?"

Garrett's eyes were cold steel, but his upper lip curled into something between a smile and a smirk. "I've heard you're an expert at discrediting a witness, Delbert, but since no one's on trial, I suggest you leave your tricks in the courtroom. Unless, that is, you're making a formal charge?''

A throbbing ache formed in Kelsey's chest as she waited interminably for Justin to answer, and it wasn't until he shook his head and retreated to the house that she realized she'd been holding her breath. The air escaped her lungs in a sharp hiss.

''Let's get out of here,'' Garrett suggested, his callused hand covering hers as he led her toward the buggy waiting at the end of the short drive. The mingling sounds of high-pitched laughter and a faint rumbling in the distance, which could only be thunder, added to Kelsey's distress as they started for home. She had the vague sense that those guests still inside were finding amusement in her present straits, and that God was somehow murmuring his approval.

''Was it my imagination,'' she asked after several minutes of silence, ''or did we just make our escape from the lion's den?''

''If I had suspected Antoinette intended to serve you up for the main course, I would have warned you. Not that you didn't do a creditable job of defending yourself.''

''And I was worried you might be a target.''

''I learned to shoot back years ago,'' Garrett quipped, unoffended by her admission. ''Besides, nothing breaks down the barriers of class like a hefty sum of cash. Now, having a poor background adds a touch of the romantic to my dashing appeal. At least to most of Lewiston. There are still a few holdouts.''

Was there a measure of bitterness lacing that dripping humor? Kelsey couldn't tell, though she was closer now to understanding his feelings of being an outcast than ever before. It was not a position unfamiliar to her.

''Have you any idea why everyone was so interested in whether or not I sell Riverview? There seemed an inordinate amount of concern, but perhaps I'm just being overly suspicious.''

"You're not," Garrett confirmed. "Actually, I'm surprised you haven't already been approached by the formal committee, though you were, in a sense, since all the members were at the Delbert's tonight."

"What committee?" Kelsey froze, much of the evening's discussions beginning to come together like pieces of a complex puzzle. Only instead of having to guess what the completed picture might be, she knew instinctively.

"The same committee that asked Sheldon for the sale of part of Riverview. The hundred acres to the north and east of the house, to be exact. Prime riverfront property."

"You knew about this?"

Garrett nodded, shifting in his seat so that he could see her face clearly. "I planned to mention it right after you got here, but then when we got off to such a bad start, I was afraid you would sell the land just to spite me. After that, it really did slip my mind. They'd been after Sheldon to sell for years, so the whole thing's been more or less in the background for a long time."

Kelsey couldn't disagree with his logic; there *had* been a short time when she might have done absolutely anything just to spite him, as he put it. But that didn't begin to explain everything. "Why does this committee want Riverview in the first place?"

Coming within view of the row of poplar trees, Garrett urged the horse a little faster. It would be easier to tell over a glass of whiskey, and he could sense by the way she was sitting with her back ramrod straight that Kelsey was as tautly strung as an archer's bow. He would stand less chance of setting her off if she were more relaxed, too. "I can tell you better inside. Why don't you pour us a drink while I stable the horse. I'll meet you in the study in fifteen minutes."

The idea of inviting him in, and its inherent dangers, warred with the myriad questions consuming her thoughts. Curiosity won, but at a price.

As soon as Garrett jumped from the buggy and turned back to her, Kelsey began regretting her decision. At this angle the buggy lantern cast its light full on his upturned face, burnishing his golden hair and turning his eyes into hot blue flames. His arms were outstretched to lift her out of the buggy, but for a moment she saw more there than mere courtesy.

How easy it would be to enter the world offered by those magnificent arms, she mused. How incredibly right it seemed. How wonderfully safe.

How utterly foolish.

The almost magical aura surrounding him dissipated soon enough. With a purely casual motion, Garrett placed his sure hands around her waist and lifted her to the ground, releasing his hold with nary a hint of undue haste or a sign of lingering.

Disappointment lurked beneath her relief, though Kelsey's first thought upon settling her feet on the hard ground was that perhaps she shouldn't have a drink after all. If this were the kind of fanciful mood she was in, then maybe wide-awake and sober was better than relaxed and slightly tipsy.

She was about to suggest that they postpone their discussion until morning, but Bridget chose that moment to set up a welcoming din, which set the horse skittering sideways until Garrett lunged for the bridle, muttering a string of oaths in a deceptively calm voice.

Kelsey raced to the top of the stairs to quiet the dog, turning in time to see Garrett disappear behind the stables. Well, she sighed resignedly. At least she had the satisfaction of knowing she was about to have some of her questions answered.

She only hoped there were not too many new ones raised.

12

Garrett paused at the study door, gripping the frame on either side of his head to prevent himself from swaying, as longing rocked through his body like a surging wave. The tableau that greeted him was exactly like the one of his dreams, from the muted colors fading into darkness around the edges of the small lamp's meager light, to the soft, welcoming expression Kelsey wore. Her dress was the same, and though he couldn't remember for sure if he had always known it was rose, he couldn't be sure, either, that it had not. Even the style of her hair, piled high on her head for the party but now loosened to allow several curls to stray, was as he had imagined it.

"Come in," she welcomed, her voice unaccountably husky. It might have been from the dampness outside, but more likely was caused by the prodigious lump in her throat from the way he was looking at her. Moving slowly, he came to within a few feet of her chair, so close she had to bend her head back to see him.

God, she was beautiful! Garrett ached with every pore in his body to capture her softly parted lips beneath his, to have her tilt her head farther so he could trail his mouth down the slender, graceful column of her neck. He wanted to ease the clinging dress from her shoulders and watch it slip from the tips of her breasts, to cup her fullness tenderly, to explore each velvety inch of her. All evening he'd avoided watching her too closely, afraid someone would see the stark longing in his eyes. Now no one would witness the strength of his desire.

Or the depths of his foolishness.

As if awakening from a trance, Garrett jerked his gaze away from her and took a half step backward, noticing what he had not seen before. This was not the scene of his dream at all. No fire blazed at the hearth, no child rested his head against her knee. Even the expression on Kelsey's face was different, no longer eager and welcoming, but puzzled . . . watchful. He went to the table, hoping to cover his actions by reaching for the bottle of whiskey. He poured himself a generous three fingers.

"Won't . . . won't you sit down," Kelsey said haltingly, disturbed by the strange light in his eyes, and by the way her own body was reacting. For just a moment she had been sure it was desire behind his penetrating stare, and that thought had stolen her breath and made her heart race madly around inside her body. Her breasts throbbed as if he had touched them with his hands instead of his eyes, the nipples growing taut and full, aroused by the feel of his gaze raking across them. The thin wool dress offered little cover against her body's betrayal, and Kelsey fiercely wished she could cross her arms over her chest.

That, however, would be too obvious a gesture, and so she, too, sought to hide her extraordinary response behind the very ordinary act of pouring tea.

"Would you like something to eat?" she asked, offering the plate of tiny cakes she had found in the kitchen. Garrett did not answer, only threw back his head to swallow his drink in one long gulp.

Ignoring the chair opposite Kelsey's, he strode to the divan pushed up under the windows, making a show of stretching his long legs before him as if that were the only reason he had sought the darker end of the room. From here he could watch every nuance of expression on her lovely face, and he told himself it was to better see her reaction to what he said.

"Ever since the Erie Canal was dug," he began without preamble, "the good folks of Lewiston have had their backs up over the trade they lost. Some of the older men remember how it was a long time ago, when much of what was shipped to the upper lakes had to pass through Lewiston by way of the Portage road, because of the falls. Now canal barges bring loads of goods from the east all the way to the town of Buffalo on Lake Erie, leaving Lewiston stopped dead in its tracks. That doesn't sit too well with a lot of people."

"But it's been that way for thirty years. Haven't they got used to the lack of trade by now?" Kelsey wondered what all this was leading up to, and what it had to do with her land.

"More or less," Garrett replied thoughtfully. "There was a shift toward agriculture in the area—your father was one of the first to take advantage of that—and the town has prospered well enough, though it's not growing nearly as fast as Lockport has. That isn't enough to satisfy everyone.

"Now that the suspension bridge is finished, a lot of folks wonder if a new industry can't flourish here, the same kind that's taking hold in the city of Niagara. They have the falls, of course, but there're sights all up and down the river that might appeal to tourists. A committee was formed by the town council to study the suggestion, and the solution they've come up with is to build a passenger railroad along the river from the falls to Lake Ontario."

"Near Riverview?" Kelsey asked.

"Not just near," Garrett said grimly. "*On* Riverview land. If they built this, you'd be able to look out from Sheldon's balcony and see the trains moving along the bank."

She gasped. "Why didn't you tell me about this before?" Garrett's face was hidden in the shadows, but he leaned forward slightly, as if girding himself for battle.

"As I said earlier, I thought if you knew you would sell the land, without thinking it through carefully."

As Kelsey absorbed his words, she remembered the discussion at dinner to which she had paid scant attention. "Obviously, Justin supports this, though I wonder that he didn't mention it before. The way everyone was badgering me tonight, I had the impression there was some great hurry."

"Only in the minds of the men who conceived the idea, and I'm not even sure Justin is one of them. My guess is that George Delbert persuaded his son it would be a breach of ethics to induce you to decide one way or another, since he was Sheldon's attorney and is presumably yours. He probably thought it best that the committee approach you formally."

"Did Papa know about this?"

Garrett paused, gathering his breath. He didn't want to be accused of swaying her thoughts either, though so much hinged on her making the right choice, it was a temptation hard to resist. "Sheldon knew."

Setting her teacup back on the side table, she chewed at her lower lip thoughtfully. The land in question, the strip of riverfront property stretching northward from the house, was too rocky to cultivate. The cliff itself was steep and had always hidden nests of rattlesnakes between the rocks. Clasping her hands in her lap, Kelsey directed her gaze toward Garrett's shadowy form. "How much is the committee offering for the land?"

The figure he named nearly made her gasp again, and she noticed that Garrett's shoulders stiffened and he shifted in his seat. "With money like that," he offered tentatively, "you could refurbish every room in the house and still live comfortably for a year or two."

Though his voice was carefully devoid of emotion, Kelsey sensed there was more underlying his explanation. With a sudden flash of insight, she asked, "Then why didn't my father sell?"

Of course Garrett knew the answer to that, but he couldn't tell her the whole story. Not yet. He could only hope that a sliver of the truth would suffice. "Because it was part of Riverview," he explained, "and Sheldon Tremayne loved Riverview more than almost anything on earth."

His left brow twitched nervously, but he had schooled himself long ago never to show impatience. His gaze flicked over Kelsey's ramrod figure, gauging her mood by the thrust of her chin and the upright angle of her slender back. It was important, not only that she accept what he gave her as Sheldon's reason for not selling that particular stretch of land, but that she adopt it for her own. Unconsciously holding his breath, Garrett waited.

So what if her father hadn't wanted to sell! Kelsey fumed, defiance supplanting her disappointment. He hadn't cared so much for the land that he'd bothered to make proper use of it. He hadn't cared enough for her to see that she'd never wanted any other home but Riverview. Turning that land over to this committee seemed the most appropriate of paybacks!

And yet, reason told her, clamoring for a voice even in the midst of anger, *who would be hurt most for giving in to such spitefulness?*

She would, Kelsey realized with a disconsolate sigh. She didn't want a railroad under her window any more than she wanted strangers gawking and traipsing all over her land. And somehow, trading away part of Riverview, even a relatively small, useless part, seemed too much like selling out. That was not the beast she had set out to conquer.

Garrett saw the tiny shudder that allowed the tension to flow from her, but it seemed that with it came a measure of her spirit, and he was inexplicably saddened. Why was it that any mention of Sheldon caused her face to grow pallid and her energy to wane? Were they merely signs of mourning, or was there more than the normal amount of grief draining her of life?

"If it were up to you," she asked slowly, knowing the answer but wanting to hear it for herself, "what would you do?"

Garrett withheld a relieved sigh that threatened to escape his bursting lungs. Rising, he crossed the room to pour himself another measure of whiskey. "Once I thought having property of my own would be the true mark of success. I dreamed of gazing over miles and miles of planted fields ripe for the harvest, and dozens of ships laden with cargo, knowing they all belonged to me. That's what drew me first to your father. To me, he was the epitome of a successful man.

"By knowing him, I thought I would learn how to make my own way through the world, and that by modeling myself after him I could one day equal his accomplishments." He drained his glass, dropping to the chair across from Kelsey's and hunching forward with his elbows on his knees, his strong fingers laced together and his head raised almost imploringly.

"I'll never be what he was, Kelsey, and it has nothing to do with money or land or even respect. It has to do with honor. And for that reason, I will do anything in my power to keep Riverview intact."

Jumping to her feet, Kelsey clenched her fists at her sides, anger and frustration mounting to uncontrollable heights. "How can you speak of honor?" she said, her attempt at derisive laughter sounding more like weak sobs, even to her own ears. "Was it honor that made him send my mother and me a world away, just so he could carry on his 'business' without interference. Was it honor that prevented him from loving his own daughter? If you knew him so well, Garrett O'Neill, then answer me that!"

Her body quaked with all the pent-up ferocity of a wild animal, cornered and desperate. Garrett was astounded by the depth of her bitterness, but not so much that he forgot the value of his own obligation. "Whether you believe it or not, Sheldon did the best he could under the circumstances," he replied stubbornly.

"Under the circumstances, I should think you'd be a little more hesitant to defend him. Unless, that is," she said sarcastically, "you condoned what he was doing."

Garrett moved closer, resting his hands lightly upon her shoulders. Even through the fabric of her gown he could feel the warmth of her skin seeping through his palms, igniting his blood. The motion seemed to calm her, or at least all signs of her wrath fled, for she raised her gaze to meet his, and her rich brown eyes were more alarmed than angry.

"Whether you think your father's actions were right or wrong isn't really the issue, Kelsey dear. Riverview is. What's in the past is best forgotten, so we should concentrate on the future. Agreed?"

"Agreed." Even while she nodded her head, Kelsey was berating herself for letting him control her so easily. She may as well have been eight years old again! Except that when she was eight, he hadn't looked at her in quite the same way. Had his eyes always been that intense shade of blue, so clear and piercing she felt as if he could read her soul?

"Good." Garrett dropped his hands, thankful that the moment hadn't lasted one second longer, or else he might have given in to the desire that gnawed at him with velvet claws. "Then I'd like you to consider this proposition before you accept any other offers. I'll continue to help you with the farm, provided you take over some of the bookkeeping and office work for the shipping businesses. And since I own half of the house, it's only right that I contribute half the money necessary for upkeep, not just enough to cover the loan. You can wait until after you have a crop to pick up your share. Fair enough?"

It was more than fair, Kelsey realized, certain that Garrett was giving her the better end of the bargain. She was tempted to refuse, unwilling to take advantage of his generosity.

"I . . . I need time to think about it. There's so much to consider. Exactly how much money would I owe you?"

"Not me," Garrett emphasized. "Riverview. We're talking about part of your share of the profits going back into the estate. And the amount can be as great or as little as you wish. How much will it take to get started making this place a little more livable?"

Kelsey quickly did some adding in her head, based on her previous inspection of the house. She would have loved to redecorate completely, but that would mean having that obligation hanging over her head, even if he was willing to foot the initial bill. Instead, she would accept only enough to cover the cost of hiring extra staff for cleaning, and to tackle the most urgent repairs. She named a figure considerably lower than her original total.

The only sign of surprise Garrett allowed was the slight lifting of one brow; he had been prepared to go as high as five times that sum. "I'll supply twice that amount, with two stipulations. That blasted balcony must be the first thing repaired, since you can't seem to stay off it any better than your father. The other is that from now on we take our meals together. It's a burden Hannah doesn't need, ferrying my meals out to the cottage, and I'll be damned if I'll eat another bowl of half-cooked stew. That old stove isn't fit to heat a barn."

Smiling at his exaggerated grimace, Kelsey found she couldn't come up with one good reason not to accept his offer, and several arguments in favor—even a few she didn't like to admit to herself. She was almost tempted to invite him to return to his room in the house after his ill-concealed hint that the cottage was cold, but she decided having him at the table each night would be quite testing the limits of propriety, not to mention her own limits.

"All right then. I can't say that it won't be a relief to know the house won't deteriorate any further. And if you have enough faith in my bookkeeping ability to trust me with the accounts, then who am I to say otherwise? Besides," she added wryly, "I wouldn't want you to starve to death from sampling your own cooking."

"Good. We can start right away. You take care of finding servants and I'll talk to a carpenter when I go into Lockport day after tomorrow."

"It's a deal." Kelsey extended her hand automatically, regretting the impulse the moment his much larger hand surrounded hers. The warmth of his grip vibrated through her palm, and she was seized by the sensation of being hemmed in, or perhaps engulfed would have been a better word. Circumstances were moving more rapidly than she could have expected, and despite her intentions to the contrary, she had just agreed to let Garrett share an even larger portion of her life. It was as if she had no control over events where he was concerned, no curb on her emotions.

It occurred to her that he, too, was conceding a lot for the assurance that she would not sell even a small part of Riverview. She couldn't help wondering what was in it for him.

She would have been surprised to know that at that moment, Garrett was wondering the very same thing.

13

The month of March ended and the capricious skies of April at last gave way to the life-giving sunshine of May, releasing the landscape from winter's clutches with a vengeance as spring blossomed full. Corn and wheat sprouted green shoots toward the yellow brightness above; apple trees laden with pristine flowers looked like mounds of snow. The air was pungent with the rich scent of the earth fulfilling its promise.

Scanning the field with a practiced eye, Garrett calculated the success of Kelsey's newly planted corn crop and mentally measured it against the expenditures yet to be tallied. If all went well, Riverview would make a tidy profit. Not bad, he mused, considering the farm hadn't operated in the black for nearly three years.

Part of their early success, he freely admitted, was due to Kelsey's incessant energy and her willingness—more like a need, actually—to do her share. In the past few weeks he had shaken his head over her zeal on several occasions. She learned fast, worked tirelessly, and most surprisingly of all, proved she had a head for business. He hadn't imagined when he offered her the thankless task of managing his books that she would exceed his skill at juggling figures to make ends meet.

Now Garrett looked up, spotting Kelsey's approach on Ladyfair at the north end of the pasture. He raised in his stirrups to hail her. Though she was still several hundred yards away, he imagined he could see her slow smile, and a familiar ache radiated from his chest as she kicked her horse into a ground-eating canter.

That, he conceded, was his only problem.

If keeping his hands off her had been difficult before, now it was next to impossible. In the past few weeks she had changed before his eyes as surely as the awakening land. She had taken to wearing men's breeches when she was riding, pairing them with the same blouse and short jacket she had worn before. The effect was tantalizing. The incongruous outfit emphasized every womanly aspect of her figure. And unlike the Kelsey of old, she seemed completely unaware of his reaction.

That was the least of it. The haunted expression around her eyes was nearly gone, the sun had turned her skin to the glowing color of honey, and she was quicker to smile at the sight of a bird taking wing or the antics of the children, whom they visited regularly. She had changed, yes. Anyone who saw her now might even believe she was happy.

Garrett, however, knew better.

Hannah apparently felt an obligation to apprise him after she had been awakened twice by Kelsey's nightmare cries, and he himself had seen a light in her room on several occasions, each time long after she should have been sound asleep. He could also tell which nights she dreamed by the way she looked the following mornings.

Some days she was bright-eyed and refreshed, but on some the tension pulled her lips into tight lines, and once he had seen her touch her fingertips to her temples as if her head were wracked with pain. Today her eyes were red-rimmed, evidence of another sleepless night.

"Good morning," he called, lifting one hand in greeting. As Kelsey reached his side, pulling Ladyfair to a halt, Garrett's heart twisted painfully. Her smile—if he had really seen one before—had returned to the carefully prim benediction she reserved for him alone.

"Did you sleep well?" he asked, all too aware of the answer, and knowing full well she would not tell him.

"Where do we go today?" Tugging at the reins to bring Ladyfair around to her customary position at his right, Kelsey ignored his attempt to pry, steering the subject to safer ground. He spurred his horse forward, motioning her to follow. "I was just down at the stables. Lady Luck will foal sometime today and I promised James he could watch. We'll swing by his house to pick him up, then make a stop at the orchard to check with Fulton before coming back. It should prove to be an exciting day. Have you every seen a birth?"

Kelsey felt the blood drain from her cheeks as if the sun's rays had intensified, bleaching her face of all color. Grateful that she was to the side and behind Garrett, she clutched the pommel of her saddle for support, willing herself not to make a sound, other than the one he was expecting. "N-no."

"You don't have to come if you don't want to, but it's a sight everyone should see once. It's quite miraculous!"

The profound awe in his voice only made her misery more acute, and Kelsey was at a complete loss, knowing that if she tried to demur gracefully she would surely reveal the extent of her distress. The alternative, she realized, swallowing the hard knot in her throat, was to bluff her way out of it.

"What happens if Lady Luck doesn't feel like obliging? I mean . . . what if it doesn't happen today?"

"It'll be today. Let's hurry. I don't want her to start before we get there."

At Garrett's urging they broke into a rapid trot, covering the distance to the cottages in far less time than Kelsey would have liked. The fact that they could not speak to one another was the only benefit of riding fast. It gave her a chance to think of a good excuse not to be present in the stables while Lady Luck had her foal. Perhaps, if she was very fortunate herself, one of the children would need her help today. Or maybe she could contrive to make them late.

An hour later Garrett wondered briefly if she was doing just that, but he dismissed the thought immediately. Kelsey may have been secretive about her personal life and her past, but when it came to matters of the farm she was always forthright and open. If she didn't want to watch the foaling, she would have said so.

So why was she acting so strangely? This was more than the result of a restless night, for on those other days she had always made an attempt to pull herself out of a foul mood by concentrating on work. Today she seemed distracted, absorbed in whatever thoughts were dragging at her soul.

"Would you like to bring Esther along? She can ride behind you on the way up." Usually, any mention of the bewitching child brought an instant smile to Kelsey's lips. Garrett twisted in his saddle to see her better, but was disappointed to find her shaking her head vehemently.

"Absolutely not! Esther's far too young for this."

"She's been raised on a farm, Kelsey."

"She was raised on Riverview land. So was I."

"Then you should know that giving birth is a natural part of life. But you may be right. Esther's a sensitive child. The last thing we need is to have her upset Lady Luck." What he was really thinking was that Kelsey seemed more likely to be upset than the little girl. He had almost forgotten how sheltered her childhood had been, and she was apparently nervous about seeing her first live birth. Certain that she would change her mind once she laid eyes on Lady Luck's foal, Garrett rode on, content that he had figured out what was bothering her.

To Kelsey's misfortune, their visit at the cottages was brief, offering her no opportunity for escape. James was ready to go and the rest of the children scampered away as soon as Garrett bestowed on them the requisite sweets. Even Esther, who normally lingered at Kelsey's side until she was forced by her mother to come away, only gave her a quick hug and babbled something about catching tadpoles before she joined the others.

Within minutes she and Garrett were threading their way between high-grown weeds, taking a shortcut to the orchard, where he intended to meet with Fulton.

"Now that the north field is almost cleared, you'll want to decide what to put in it. Since you've already several acres of corn, it might be smart to plant something else, like wheat. On the other hand, there's enough seed to sow another lot. And harvesting will be less costly with only one kind of crop."

"Then why bother to switch?" Kelsey asked, glad for the chance to get her mind off the coming crisis.

"It's as simple as not putting all your eggs in one basket. Corn will bring a larger profit, and faster, but you're less likely to lose both if anything should go wrong."

"Lose the crop?" Now Kelsey's attention was riveted on Garrett's back as he led the way through a patch of overgrown bushes. She'd been so intent on getting the corn in and clearing the orchard, she hadn't given much thought to anything going wrong now.

"It's unlikely," Garrett assured her, "but there's no accounting for the weather. A drought this summer could ruin the corn, or for that matter, too much rain this spring."

Her glance moved automatically to the sky, a crystalline blue that seemed to reach all the way to heaven and beyond. Wisps of white clouds clung to the cerulean backdrop like tufts of cotton, distant and harmless. "The weather's been so mild, it's easy to forget how quickly storms blow in from the lake."

Still, her tone was doubtful, and Garrett smiled to himself at her natural optimism when it came to her land. If only that same attitude extended to other aspects of her life. "Here's Fulton now," he suggested. "Why don't you ask his opinion?

Kelsey did just that, dismounting to inspect his work in the orchard as she posed the same questions to her overseer that she'd just asked Garrett. The man listened intently, offering little but nodding his head at her comments.

"What do you think?" she probed.

He swung a mighty arm around his head, indicating the orchard, looking considerably better than it had just weeks before. All the rotted fruit and dead wood had been removed, leaving nothing but healthy trees frothing with pale pink blossoms. "Corn and apples. Two good crops, sure 'nuff. But it's up to you, miss. I'll do what you want."

Kelsey had to will herself not to turn to Garrett, but she sensed tacit approval in his silence. They were leaving the decision up to her. That knowledge filled her with newfound confidence, even while the responsibility weighed heavily.

"I say we stick with corn, then," she said thoughtfully. "We need every dollar of profit we can manage."

Before long, they were on their way again, though now her thoughts were focused on the possibility of an even larger harvest than she'd first anticipated. It would mean paying off the loan, she realized happily, and returning the money Garrett had advanced for repairs to the house. She would be well on her way to independence.

Glancing over at him, she studied his relaxed frame as he rode easily in the saddle with James perched behind him. He did everything well, she decided, including making himself indispensable to her. Perhaps not purposely, but she didn't like feeling that she couldn't live without him. It was a bit too close to the truth for comfort.

As they approached the stables, a pall seemed to hang over the yard, suffocating Kelsey with a sense of impending doom. She glanced over at Garrett and James, but neither seemed to notice the strange silence or the tension that stretched the air like a sapling pushed to near the breaking point.

"Glad to see ya git here so quick," Benjamin said, startling Kelsey into nearly dropping the reins. The elderly negro limped toward her, so she dismounted quickly to hide the fact that her knees were wobbly and her palms clammy.

"You're in for a real treat, missy. Lady Luck is a fine mare, ain't none finer, and she gonna drop a fine foal, too. We could use another pretty little filly like the one you ridin', ain't that right, Mistah Garrett?"

"That's right." Garrett lifted James from the saddle

and set him down, then swung himself to the ground eagerly. "How's she doing, Benjamin? Any problems?"

"No, suh. Breathin's a might hard, but that's ta be expected. Thing's is lookin' dandy, but we best be gettin' in there, else she'll be done before we know it." A sharp nicker from the stables punctuated this last statement.

Garrett grinned down at James, James was grinning at Benjamin, and Benjamin was beaming at all of them.

Kelsey just wanted to scream.

She wondered how they could stand around as if nothing were happening at all, and then before she could protest, Garrett had clasped her elbow and was guiding her through the stable doorway. Though all the windows were opened except for the one in Lady Luck's stall, Kelsey found breathing difficult in the cloying atmosphere. The combined odors of fresh hay and horse swirled around her, no longer pleasant. Instead, she fought to keep from swaying when Garrett let go of her arm and entered the box in the center of the barn.

Lady Luck was still on her feet, but her sides were lathered with perspiration, rippling like tiny ocean waves as her breath heaved laboriously. "Good girl," Garrett murmured, running his hands expertly over her back and distended belly. "Good girl."

Kelsey felt a movement at her side and looked down to see James tucked beside her at the railing, his feet planted on the second rung from the bottom. "Don't you worry none, Miss Kelsey. Looks to me like she's doing fine."

Now Kelsey's smile was genuine, if a little strained. Garrett had already told her that James had never witnessed a live birth before, yet here he was sounding just as authoritative as . . . as Garrett! Were all men so much alike? she wondered ruefully.

Lady Luck issued another whicker, this one sounding quite a bit more distressed than the last, and Kelsey's attention returned to the stall. "Is she all right?"

Benjamin was just returning from letting Prince and Ladyfair out to pasture, and he poked his graying head around the post Kelsey clung to and nodded. ''Nothin' to worry about,'' he confirmed, echoing James's words.

She swallowed hard, not at all certain she could stay a moment longer. Instead of feeling more at ease, panic was mounting in her stomach like a rising storm, the barn walls closing in around her. Her knuckles were white and aching from clinging so tight to the stable door.

''What's taking so long? Are you sure she's all right? What if something goes wrong?'' She could hear the rising hysteria in her own voice and clamped her jaw shut when Garrett looked up sharply, wariness turning his eyes dark. What Kelsey didn't realize was that his concern was for her, not the laboring horse. She saw only trouble in his expression, and it escalated her own precarious emotions. When Lady Luck chose that moment to drop to her knees, tossing her head wildly as she rolled sideways in the hay, Kelsey felt a silent scream fill her throat.

Garrett was still watching her, and he saw at once her eyes were dilated with terror and something else, something unnamable that caused his own gut to lurch crazily. Quickly, or as quickly as he could without disturbing Lady Luck, he traded places with Benjamin. ''We'll be outside,'' he said tersely, moving behind Kelsey.

She was hardly aware of his hands encircling her shoulders, but when his gentle tugging was not enough to dislodge her fingers from the wooden door and he had to pry her grip loose, she was shaken from her panicked trance.

''Come on,'' Garrett murmured, his voice as soothing as when he had whispered to the horse. ''Let's get you out of here.''

''What's wrong with *her?*'' James asked loudly, clearly impatient with her irrational behavior, yet just as willing to shrug it off as normal for a female. He turned back to watch Benjamin, shaking his blond head.

Kelsey stumbled only once on the cobblestones, but with tiny beads of perspiration dotting a face as white as the apple blossoms on the trees, it was enough for Garrett. He turned her toward him and clasped her hard against his chest, hooking one arm beneath her knees and lifting her from her feet. With long strides, he carried her from the barn, not slowing until he had reached the wide front porch of the house and settled her gently on the top step, cradling her shivering form.

Still trembling violently, Kelsey found it almost as hard to unlock her fingers from behind his neck as it had been to let go of the stall door. Garrett's arms were like a blessed wall around her, holding the horror at bay, keeping her safe within their solid strength, until finally the agonizing waves of pain began to recede.

"My God, Kelsey! What happened in there? I know you were nervous about watching, but I never expected you to faint!"

"I didn't faint," she argued weakly, reluctantly pushing herself away from his broad chest. "I just got a little dizzy."

"That was more than dizziness. You looked as if you were watching someone being murdered!" Garrett held her securely, too intent on finding out thc cause behind her bizarre reaction to admit that he simply didn't want to let her go. Though she was still pale, her eyes had lost that glazed expression, capturing him with their dark luminescence.

It wasn't so much that he had almost hit on the truth that made the trembling begin again as it was the way he was looking at her, his blue eyes full of sincerity, and desire. She wanted to unburden herself, knowing instinctively that he would understand—and care—but it was the unabashed yearning she felt vibrating between them that stopped her, reminding her that the very source of her panic was the same reason she could never give in to her longing.

Now all her earlier fears were replaced by a sorrow so profound her entire body ached with it. And though she knew it wouldn't help matters, the only source of comfort she could draw on was to stay right where she was, if only for a minute more. . . .

Cradling her to him with extraordinary tenderness,

Garrett fought to control the explosive currents pulsing through his body. Some innate sense warned him that if he revealed his passion for her now, he might endanger whatever precarious relationship they had established, and he could admit freely how very much he cherished that bond. He felt his mouth quaver where it was pressed to her temple, but otherwise made no move that could be construed as threatening.

Some time later—minutes, in fact, though Kelsey could have sworn it had been longer—the distant sound of a carriage bouncing toward them along the river road roused her. Glancing dazedly around, she was surprised to see that the midday sun still blazed high above. Swiveling her head toward the road, she watched as the Delbert's carriage came into sight.

Garrett felt her stiffen in his arms and some perverse part of him wanted to hold on, just to see what would happen if she were forced into a confrontation.

"Let me go," she insisted, lowering her head quickly so he couldn't read her eyes. "I'm quite all right now. Go on back to the barn." When he didn't respond immediately, Kelsey lowered her hands to his shoulders, pushing away from him. The thought of someone other than Garrett seeing her in such an emotional state was impossible to bear. She needed time to collect herself before facing an intruder.

His hands dropped from her waist like lead weights. Gratefully, Kelsey scooted herself backwards, putting distance between them. She needn't have bothered, for Garrett rose immediately.

"Call if you need me," he said, his voice graveled and low.

Kelsey opened her mouth to speak, but nothing came out. She wanted to thank him. She wanted to ask him to stay. It even occurred to her to blurt out that she did need him, desperately.

But she said none of those things.

By the time she was able to summon the words, Garrett had turned and was gone.

14

While Kelsey dressed, Justin prowled the study, taking stock of the changes she had already made, calculating his disadvantage by the signs of her contentment. From all appearances she was settling into her old home well, and a surge of impatience shot through him. He had planned to approach her slowly, but perhaps he would need to reconsider his strategy. He paused before the window, one long hand raised to his brow.

That was how Kelsey saw him when she entered the study. She hesitated, not wishing to disturb his deep thoughts. As always, Justin was dressed with offhanded elegance. His clothing was of the finest cut, fitting him superbly, yet she could not help thinking that his dark blue trousers would be torn to shreds after a day of hard riding, and that his coat would fall apart at the seams if subjected to a rigorous day's work. He carried himself with masculine grace, yet his movements lacked the power and command of Garrett's. She couldn't imagine Justin lifting her into his arms so easily.

What was she thinking! Kelsey scolded herself. Thrusting her recalcitrant thoughts away, she stepped into the room.

Justin raised his head and smiled. "My dear, you look lovely, as always." Bowing over her hand, he surreptitiously studied the rose-colored dress. So . . . matters weren't going so well, if she couldn't afford to spend money on her wardrobe, he thought hopefully. "I see you've begun work on the house. Did you take my mother's advice on which servants to hire?"

"Yes, I did," Kelsey replied, then qualified her answer. "Though not all of them. Four were quite enough."

"Were? Don't tell me you've let them go already?"

"It was only temporary, Justin, long enough to complete a thorough cleaning. I explained that to your mother."

And I shouldn't have to explain it to you, she wanted to add, though she controlled her tongue. Just because she was still upset over the events in the barn was no reason to take it out on Justin. After all, he was her friend.

"It's too bad you must stop with a cleaning," he commented, continuing to peruse the book-filled room. The draperies had been washed and were drawn back to allow sunshine to spill inside, and the furniture, polished and fragrant with oil and beeswax, had been arranged more attractively. "This house has a lot of potential, but you deserve so much better."

Kelsey's gaze followed the direction of his, trying to see the room from his eyes. Of course he hadn't meant to be insulting, but she was stung by his remark. She had been quite pleased with the result of her efforts, especially here in the study where she spent a great deal of time.

"I do like the way you've moved the desk to that other wall, and the table closer to the windows. It makes—," he broke his sentence off. "I didn't know you played chess."

"Garrett's teaching me." Lifting her chin defiantly, Kelsey glided over to a chair in front of the hearth and sat down.

Justin made a sound somewhere between a snort and a chuckle. "I didn't know *he* played either."

"Why shouldn't he? Garrett's not the ignorant stable boy you like to pretend he is."

"Of course he's not," Justin responded just a tad too loftily. "Your father saw to that. Unusual, isn't it, for a man of your father's status to undertake the education of a poor boy? But then, generosity was always one of Sheldon Tremayne's hallmarks. Why else would he have sent O'Neill to Europe?''

''Garrett was in Europe?'' Kelsey sat upright in surprise. ''Where . . . when?''

Shrugging, Justin moved to the chair opposite Kelsey's and sat down, crossing his legs comfortably. ''It was about two years after you left, I think. I just assumed he stopped to see you in London. In fact, I'm almost sure Sheldon told my father as much. You didn't know?''

Kelsey shook her head. So Garrett had been in London and had not called on her. Her heart flip-flopped with disappointment. If only he *had* come, so much might have been different.

Though his pose was one of nonchalance, Justin was eminently aware of the effect this information had on Kelsey and it disturbed him to no end. Not only were she and O'Neill working together every day, according to local reports, but they had apparently become quite cozy in the evenings, too, as evidenced by the chess pieces abandoned in mid-game. Leaning forward abruptly, he reached for her hand, gripping it hard when she attempted to pull free.

''My dear, no one knows better than I how close you were to O'Neill at one time. Children who live near one another, even from different families, often seem like brother and sister. But feelings change, usually for the better. I know mine have.''

Kelsey had barely digested the irony of him thinking she and Garrett were like sister and brother when it dawned on her that Justin was gazing avidly into her face and that his expression had grown earnest. ''Your . . . your feelings?''

''Dear, innocent Kelsey. Don't look so shocked. Haven't you always thought about what a good pair we would make?''

''Good pair?''

''Certainly.'' Justin gave her hand another squeeze before dropping it, then leaned back in his chair again. ''The right families, the right upbringing, not to mention the right ages. A marriage between us would be a match even my mother couldn't find fault in!"

It occurred to her to ask him if it was Antoinette who had suggested he propose, but Kelsey was too stunned to do more than smile awkwardly.

"It's a thought, my dear, that you may want to consider." Hiding his discouragement at her less-than-enthusiastic response behind a mask of cordiality, Justin shrugged again. "After all, we have a great deal in common."

And did he think that was all it took? Kelsey wondered if he would still think them such a good match if she told him the truth. Then again, his proposal had seemed rather off-the-cuff. Since he'd hardly professed great feelings of love and passion for her, maybe her past wouldn't matter to him at all.

And neither, she thought sadly, would her refusal.

Keeping her voice purposefully light, she folded her hands in her lap. "You know I'm very fond of you, Justin. But I couldn't possibly marry now. I've simply too much to do and think about right here at Riverview. Thank you very much for asking," she added, almost as an afterthought.

Justin, having no choice at the moment but to swallow defeat, put on his most charming smile. "Perhaps when you are more settled, then. Running the farm must seem very new and exciting to you now, but you were born to be a gentlewoman, Kelsey. Please don't forget what I said."

Relieved that he accepted her answer graciously, she rang the tiny silver bell at her side, summoning Hannah with tea for her guest. By the speed of the woman's response, Kelsey suspected the cook had been standing just outside the door, though Hannah kept her wrinkled brown face expressionless. But there was just a smidgen of a twinkle in her soulful black eyes.

Over refreshments, Kelsey described to Justin some of the progress she had made in the past few weeks, including her success with the bookkeeping. Though she was loath to go into great detail about the bargain between herself and Garrett, it didn't hurt to have Justin know that she was capable of managing her own life.

Could it be that his proposal was only the attempt of a dear friend to help her out of a tight spot? Certainly that was pushing friendship to its bounds, but then, Justin had always been very loyal to her.

Relief seeped over her as she listened to Justin drone on about a case he was trying. She was glad she hadn't hurt him by refusing, though she couldn't deny just a twinge of resentfulness.

She certainly hadn't asked for a proposal, but it would have been nice to think that someone wanted her for herself.

Justin left an hour later and Kelsey was about to spend the rest of the afternoon finishing some of the bookkeeping when footsteps heralded Garrett's arrival in the hall. She looked up to see him in the standing in the doorway, watching her.

"You're feeling better now?" he asked doubtfully. Her expression was still as troubled as before.

Kelsey nodded, struggling to swallow the lump that lodged in her throat at the sight of him. "A little. I'm sorry for the way I behaved."

"No matter. If you're up to it, there's something I want you to see. In the barn," he added as a warning.

Immediately, her heart pounded rapidly. "I really don't—"

"It's okay, Kelsey. Everything's fine." He let a smile creep into his voice, overriding his hesitation to make her come outside. "She's a sturdy filly. James named her Little Lady."

"You mean . . . you mean it didn't die?" Kelsey choked.

Garrett swung his head, stepping forward to take her hand and pull her to her feet. "When I left the barn a few minutes ago, she was already wobbling around, trying to find something to eat. I expect she's found it by now. Come on."

Kelsey followed, her hand held firmly in his, relief and excitement beginning to stir inside her, dispelling her doubts.

This time when they entered the barn she felt none of the pervading sense of doom she had experienced before, and though the memories from the past came swirling back, she was able to thrust them aside in favor of the present.

"Look here," Garrett said, hauling her just inside the box stall. Ladyluck stood drinking peacefully from a half-full pail of water, only lifting her head slightly to see what the commotion was all about before returning to her bucket. Beside her, James knelt in the straw, using a piece of clean sacking to rub the foal's coat under Benjamin's watchful eye.

Kelsey raised herself on tiptoe to get a better look, and the movement drew the foal's attention. All long nose and dewy brown eyes, Little Lady swiveled her head around and bleated a high-pitched whinny aimed straight for Kelsey.

"Oh . . ." Unable to utter more than that single sound, she stood and stared at the tiny, long-legged creature. Tears trembled at the corners of her eyes, and with a quick glance at Benjamin to make sure it was all right, she dropped to her knees beside James. "Oh, my," she murmured, reaching a tentative hand to the foal. "Oh, *my.*"

Little Lady's coat was velvety soft, like touching a perfect night sky. The foal skittered away a bit when Kelsey's hand first made contact, but then she settled down to be petted.

Though he'd brought her out here to see the foal, Garrett's attention was riveted instead on Kelsey. Now the tears flowed freely down her face and a smile hovered on her lips. Only once before had he seen her this way. When she was twelve and he was seventeen, Sheldon had taken them both on a business trip to the city of Niagara Falls.

Kelsey had stared at the magnificent tumble of water with eyes full of wonder and an expression of pure joy on her face that had pierced his soul. There, high above the majesty of the Niagara, he had seen for the first time beyond the pestering child to the woman she would become.

And now, humbled before the miracle of life, he saw within the woman the child that once was.

Overwhelmed with tenderness, Garrett knelt beside her, clearing his throat as he held out his hand for the foal to nuzzle. Carefully, he pointed Little Lady toward her dam. Within seconds the foal was suckling greedily.

The four witnesses watched in silence, until finally James broke the spell with a heartfelt, "Aw, gosh. I ain't never seen *nothin'* like that before."

"Me either," Kelsey answered, laughing with the others. She stood, brushing straw from her dress. Her eyes flickered upward to Garrett's, then leapt away when she saw the intense way he was watching her. "Thank you for showing me this," she said.

I needed to see it, she added in her thoughts.

"She surely is special, isn't she?" Garrett replied. "We forget sometimes, what wonders there are on this earth."

They fell silent again, watching James help Benjamin toss fresh hay into the middle of the stall. But it wasn't like the awkward silences of the past several weeks, when neither of them could think of what to say.

This time, it was because they didn't need to say anything at all.

Hours had passed before Stocker Fulton came by to pick up James, and in an effort to prolong the festive spirit that had so infected her, Kelsey urged everyone to come to the house.

Hannah had already laid out a meal on the large kitchen table. It took no small amount of coaxing to get the overseer seated at the table with his beautiful employer, but James had no such qualms, starting to fill his perpetually empty stomach as soon as Hannah set a heaping plate in front of him. And though the cook refused to sit as long as anyone looked like they might need another bite of her lovingly prepared victuals, even Benjamin finally took a seat at the corner of the oak table.

There was a sense of hesitation present in the room as they all sat down, as if each and every one of the adults was struck by the knowledge that they were breaking a time-honored tradition. Kelsey was determined not to let such feelings destroy the friendly mood, but she wasn't sure how to put the others at ease. Thankfully, James accomplished that for her.

"I ain't *never* ate nothin' this good before," he crowed between mouthfuls, earning one of Hannah's hard-won smiles.

Everyone else laughed, and when Garrett questioned Fulton about the day's work in the field, the dam was finally broken. Amid the clatter of stoneware plates and voices rising and falling, Kelsey was able to question Benjamin further about the science of raising horses, learning for the first time that the man had grown up on a southern plantation known for its fine thoroughbreds.

"When me an' Hannah came north with your mama, ah thought ah'd never lay hands on such a fine piece of horseflesh agin'. This old man'll die happy if one o' these ladies wins a race."

Spurred on by Benjamin's words, the conversation shifted to a discussion of various racetracks. Garrett displayed an amazing knowledge of the horse-racing world, reminding Kelsey that she wanted to question him later about his travels, especially his trip to London. Only James did not join in the talk, for Hannah had decided she had met someone who could wolf down her food faster than she could dish it up, and the two were engaged in a contest that both seemed determined to enjoy.

Kelsey looked around her happily. How was it that she was so entranced by the warm, relaxed atmosphere created by this group of people? She recalled her unease at Antoinette Delbert's soirée, and the false amiability of some of the townspeople as they silently measured her against their expectations, gauging her worth according to what they could gain. There was nothing false here; only joy and friendship.

Garrett looked up at that moment, catching her eye. He was more handsome than ever with his sleeves rolled to his elbows and his shirt unbuttoned at the collar. He had washed up out at the well with the others, flecks of moisture still clinging to the crisp golden hairs peeking through his collar and to the damp curls on his forehead. His eyes looked incredibly blue against his sun-darkened skin and she smiled happily at him.

The look he returned, however, took her completely by surprise. She had expected perplexity, maybe even a little amusement, but not open admiration. It made her heartbeat quicken and stained her cheeks with spreading heat, mostly because she realized for the first time how very much she had wanted him to look at her this way.

And then suddenly there was even more running between them, a pull that was as strong and undeniable as the flowing river. Kelsey swallowed thickly, suddenly conscious of her own appearance. The rose dress, clean when she had donned it for Justin's visit, was now covered with bits of straw, her own sleeves unbuttoned and pushed high up on her arms. So many pins had slipped out of her hair in the barn that she had eventually discarded them all, hastily fastening her unruly locks in a single fat braid, tied with a bit of old cord Garrett had found for her. Mortified, Kelsey felt as if she had never looked worse.

To Garrett, she was never more beautiful.

His gaze was still locked with hers when Hannah plunked a dish in front of him, pronouncing "dessert" in a voice carrying an unmistakable note of glee. Looking up, he caught her perceptive eyes shifting between him and Kelsey.

"If you're gonna sit there gawkin' and ain't gonna eat it, can I have your pie?" James exclaimed, studying the sizable wedge as if he had not had a bite in weeks.

"Aren't," Garrett corrected. He wished the boy hadn't

called attention to his lack of concentration on the meal. "And no, you may not have my pie, since I plan to eat it myself."

James was mollified only after Hannah placed a slice nearly as big on his own plate, but the scrutiny he paid toward inhaling every last crumb gave Kelsey the chance to recover her wits enough to rejoin the conversation between Benjamin and Stocker Fulton. Aside from Hannah, no one else seemed to notice her temporary lapse.

It was with true regret that Kelsey bid good-bye to Fulton when he pleaded the need to return to his own family, taking James with him. The boy's cocky grin remained in her mind long after she watched his skinny figure trudge away into the darkness alongside the overseer.

"After a rather shaky beginning, I'd say James has developed a monumental crush on you."

Garrett's voice caused her knees to lose their starch, but Kelsey did not turn around. "More likely on Hannah's biscuits," she retorted, then rolled her eyes in imitation of the towheaded lad. "I ain't *never* seen anyone eat like that!"

Together, they chuckled over the memory of the enormous amount of food that had disappeared from James's plate, and of the like-sized hug that he had earned from the brusque cook.

It seemed to Kelsey that their laughter rose in the still night air like delicate rose petals of different hues, tossed by the wind until their colors swirl together in an intricate pattern that cannot be separated by the eye, or the heart.

Suddenly, the bond of friendship and trust she had cherished just an hour ago was much more than she had asked for, and not nearly enough. Though he wasn't touching her, the radiant heat from Garrett's body warmed her back, sending tendrils of fire twisting through her veins. She wished she could step away. She wished she could take a step backwards. And she wondered, like a child gazing at the first bright star, what Garrett was wishing for right now.

"I wish—"

Kelsey's heart thudded! Had he been reading her mind?

"—you would tell me why you were so upset this morning. Benjamin was worried, which is one of the reasons why I took you back in." His voice was purposefully low, compelling.

Startled by this change of tack, but relieved that her treacherous thoughts were still secret, she attempted to sound lighthearted. "Haven't either of you seen a case of the vapors before? I guess I'm more squeamish than I thought, that's all."

"Squeamish, hell! A week ago you never so much as flinched when we stopped at Hanson's and he was castrating those bulls."

Kelsey couldn't resist turning to him now, the corners of her mouth twitching irrepressibly. "But I seem to remember quite a bit of flinching on your part," she teased. "And maybe even a groan or two?"

"That's different." Garrett crossed his arms and frowned, but his eyes shone with shamefaced amusement. "I don't know any man who wouldn't react to something like that. It's kind of . . . well . . . personal."

She understood better than he thought. "Just so," she said, nodding smugly.

At first Garrett did not respond to her answer, but then a look of consternation crossed his face, followed by plain surprise, making Kelsey regret her quick tongue.

Oh Lord, what had she done! she wailed silently. She hadn't meant to tell him the *real* reason for her panic. Her mind searched for a way to forestall the questions she could see forming in his eyes, and she lighted on the only subject she could think of that might successfully divert his attention.

"By the way," she said, feigning indifference, "when Justin was here today he made a very interesting proposal."

"Another offer for the land?"

"Uh-unh." She shook her head. "I said a proposal, the real thing. Justin Delbert asked me to marry him."

Kelsey's ruse succeeded, in so far as that every other thought was instantly washed from Garrett's mind. Rocked as if an arctic gale had hit him full in the face, he clenched his teeth together so hard they made a sound like a grindstone in the quiet night. "So what did you tell him?"

"I told him 'thank you very much, but no.' " She watched him run his hand along the rail as if checking to see if it needed a fresh coat of paint, and she was seized by a perverse sense of disappointment that Garrett's reaction had been no stronger than a pained grimace. As if the idea of her marrying someone else was merely an inconvenience, and only a slight one at that.

"So you dismissed him in an instant?" Garrett's tone dripped with sarcasm. "Poor Delbert. I expect he thought he had a reasonable chance. Little did he know you hold exceedingly high standards for the man you will one day marry."

His bitter retort raised Kelsey's ire, and her chin. "As a matter of fact, I don't intend to marry at all—ever! There are only three benefits to marriage for a woman, as I see it. One is security, which I have already, and another is wealth, which I don't want—"

"Where does love come into it?" Garrett drawled. "Or is that merely a pleasant side effect, not to be taken into consideration unless all other criteria are first met?"

"If marriage always means love, and vice versa, then my parents wouldn't have spent the last five years of their lives separated by an ocean." Nor would she be standing here, denying a desire that raged more fiercely in her every day.

"So you *don't* love Delbert." It was a statement of fact, a confirmation that relieved some of the constriction around Garrett's heart, even while it raised another question. "Does he love you?"

"Of course not. He was just looking for a way to help me."

Garrett made a swift movement in the darkness that Kelsey could not see, but it appeared he was angered by the news that she had refused Justin's proposal. Bewildered by his reaction, she reached for him, her fingers coming in contact with his tautly muscled arm. He jerked away as if stung by her touch.

"I . . . I don't think he truly expected to be taken seriously," she stammered.

"And if he had? Would that have changed your mind, or would you have shrugged your pretty little shoulders and sent him on his way with no more than a 'no thank-you' as consolation for a broken heart?"

"I don't understand you at all, Garrett O'Neill! Would you be happier if I had said yes?" If she thought stomping her foot would have helped, Kelsey would have done it then! Never in her life had she felt so helplessly frustrated.

He started to speak, then clamped his mouth shut again with an audible snap and thrust his hand through his hair so roughly, she thought he would tear it out by the roots. After a wordless moment, in which his eyes seemed to burn holes through her with their blue fire, he strode toward the barn, leaving her leaning weakly against the porch rail.

"I don't understand," she repeated into the darkness that had swallowed him. Confusion twisted her mind into baffled pieces, each floating in a different direction like dandelion puffs in the wind. One minute he was kind and solicitous, the next gruff and indomitable. Laughing, then sullen.

But how could she begin to understand him, she realized with a pang, until she understood herself?

Clunking sounds from inside the house intruded into her thoughts, rousing Kelsey. When she returned to the kitchen, Hannah was still there, sawing away at the pump handle, drawing water to clean up the supper dishes.

The table was scattered with dirty dishes and half-full platters, empty mugs and silverware tossed haphazardly down. On the stove, mounds of pots and pans awaited cleaning, and Bridget—always around when you needed her—eyed a pile of table scraps hungrily. "What can I do to help?" Kelsey asked, surveying the room.

Hannah barely looked up from her task even though she'd heard. On other occasions when Kelsey had offered to help she shooed her away fast enough, being a firm believer in keeping a one-woman kitchen. But this time, Hannah thought, the child had a look about her like she was busting to talk and wanting to cry at the same time, so she relented. Besides, there was plenty to do tonight. "You can scrape those plates first, so's that hound of yours don't starve ta death before our eyes."

Kelsey pushed her sleeves higher on her arms and stepped to the table, happy to have something to do. "The meal was delicious, Hannah. You've found a permanent admirer in James Brady. How ever did you know to make extra?"

The cook chortled, her arms elbow deep in a sink full of soapsuds. "Only chile I know that ate more'n James was Mistah Garrett, back when he was 'bout the same size. I sure do like fixin' up a meal fer someone that knows how to 'preciate it. Mistah Garrett, he come an' told me we was havin' comp'ny while you was chattin' with Mistah Justin," she said without pause.

"I'm glad we invited them all in. It was nice to hear the sound of laughter in this house."

"You bin workin' mighty hard lately. No harm in takin' time out to enjoy y'self. 'Sides, you got a lot on yo' mind."

Was Kelsey imagining the subtle query in Hannah's voice? Since the old woman probably heard every word spoken within two miles of her domain it was no use pretending she didn't know what had happened that day, from Kelsey's barnyard hysterics to Justin's surprising proposal, and more than likely even the baffling conversation she and Garrett had just shared.

Kelsey almost asked the trusted servant for her opinion, but stopped short, contenting herself with performing the simple chores. Anyway, if there was something

Hannah wanted to tell her, no doubt she'd hear it soon enough.

As it happened, the old cook was only waiting until the table was clear enough to set a hot cup of tea down before her young mistress. "Sit," she ordered, not unkindly.

Kelsey obeyed, wondering whether Hannah meant to take her to task for refusing Justin, or to interrogate her about her reaction to Lady Luck's foaling. Either way, she was relieved to be able to share her tumultuous feelings with someone.

"Even though your mama said different, ah never did hold with no playin' 'round with men's feelin's. Them belles what gits courted by everythin' in britches and then picks and chooses according to who's got the most land, or the most slaves, or the most kin; why, they generally ends up bein' the saddest bunch a ladies in the world. The ones that end up bein' happy, why they're the ones that marry men who loves 'em, and don't waste no time sittin' 'round waitin' fo' something better."

Kelsey nodded thoughtfully. "I couldn't agree with you more, Hannah. But what has that got to do with me?"

The cook harumphed loudly, banging the teakettle on the stovetop for emphasis. "You sayin' you ain't doin' a little teasin' yourself, maybe just ta get his dander up?"

Was she talking about Justin? Kelsey was truly stumped. "I was not teasing at all. I meant what I said."

"Then why you go tellin' 'im 'bout that other one, an' then say you ain't gonna marry nobody. If that ain't teasin', then ah'm deaf as a one-eared mule!"

As if Hannah had knocked her over the head with her much-used rolling pin, Kelsey finally understood what the woman was getting at. It was Garrett she was referring to, not Justin, though the old dear had her facts confused. "I meant what I said to Garrett, too. I will never get married. You can tease someone only with something he wants, and Garrett isn't the least bit interested in me."

"Hmmmph. Ah may be deaf, but ah ain't blind. You two was made fo' each other like the sun an' da moon."

"The sun and the moon are opposites," Kelsey chided.

"So's men an' women. But the sun an' moon, they both light up in the dark, jes' like you light up when Mistah Garrett in the same room. An' just cuz he ain't speakin' up don't mean he ain't got feelin's too. He just don't know what they is yet."

More disturbed by Hannah's observation than she cared to admit, Kelsey stirred restlessly on her chair, torn between fleeing the now confining atmosphere of the kitchen and pouring out her frustration. She chose a path somewhere in between. "Oh, Hannah," she wailed softly. "Why do men have to be so exasperating?"

To the servant's credit, she did not smile, but only shook her head at the way young folks seemed set on making things harder than they had to be. "Nothin' good ever comes without some bad," she consoled, stifling the urge to snatch the teacup out of Kelsey's grip before it was squeezed into a thousand pieces. "The things what brings the mos' joy, brings the mos' pain, ah 'spects, like love . . ." she narrowed her eyes, watching for her mistress's reaction to her next words, ". . . and babes."

As she expected, Kelsey paled, the only color on her face two pinpoints of flames high on her cheeks. She made a tiny sound, a sigh so gentle, it disappeared in the air as soon as it left her lips. But Hannah wasn't one to miss a clue.

"Then you already know why I'll never marry," Kelsey finally said, her voice sounding resigned, yet valiantly optimistic. She reached down to pat Bridget's head next to her thigh. "But as long as I have Riverview, I can still be happy. The rest I can do without."

Do without *maybe*, Hannah thought, clucking her tongue as she watched Kelsey rise to finish drying the last of the dishes. But happy? Not if she lived to be a hundred.

15

Dacia clamped her strong white teeth down on the spoon handle, her eyes widening to an unfocused stare. Twice she grunted—harsh, tearing sounds that seemed to fill the tiny room—then a whoosh of air followed as she exhaled forcefully.

Patience Goodman longed to blot the beads of perspiration from the straining woman's brow, but she was afraid Dacia would react as she had to her fussing ministrations just moments before: with a low growl of pain that sent shivers of unease rippling through Patience's aged bones.

"There now, dearie," she crooned instead. "Thou must not fight it so."

Through the fog of her pain, Dacia heard the old woman's voice like a distant beacon. But she'd been fighting so much for so long, she could not bring herself to heed the words. She had to fight. Fighting was surviving, she'd learned. Giving up meant death.

Another spasm racked her thin frame, creeping from around her back and building to a huge force centered on the bulge of her belly. Dacia wondered how so fragile a thing as a babe could survive the contractions that must surely be squeezing the life from it, as they seemed to be doing to her.

"Thou will soon be fine," Patience comforted, puttering around the bed like a helpless quail circling her young. She wasn't sure at all if her prediction would prove true, but she did have faith that the Lord had heard her hastily worded prayers and would answer after His own fashion. He always did.

Six hours, Patience thought as she straightened the bedclothes, more out of habit than concern for neatness at this time. It had been six hours since Jonathan Levi had knocked softly upon her door, whispering of the cargo hidden beneath the seat of his wagon. She had been appalled by the condition of the young woman he had carried inside, and even more by the tale of hardship he told before he left to fetch the physician. Dacia—she had managed to say her name before the pain got too bad—had endured much on this journey north. And from the looks of things now, she was about to face a great deal worse.

"More water?" Patience asked, seeing that the last contraction had ended, leaving the young woman on the bed limp, but still lucid.

Dacia shook her head. She had been slipping in and out of consciousness for the past hour or so, and the tiny woman at her side had become her only link to reality. "Don't go away," she croaked. Her throat was as raw as if she had been screaming out loud instead of holding the screams deep inside, but she did not want Patience to move away, even so far as the sideboard.

Patience, having borne six children of her own, recognized Dacia's need and scooted closer. "I shall not leave. Jonathan will return soon with the doctor and thou shall be in good hands then." She did not add that she herself had delivered most of the children in the county, and that Doctor Hampton was only called when circumstances became critical.

As it was, she didn't need to tell Dacia a thing. In the way knowledge often came to her, Dacia knew that death hovered nearby. But she also sensed that it would not find her tonight. In its own way, Dacia's faith was as unshakable as that of the Quaker woman's, even though its focus differed.

While Patience Goodman trusted in the Lord for all things, Dacia looked toward her angel for deliverance.

Another contraction seared through her, causing her vision to grow misted and dark as she tensed against the agonizing pain.

"Do not push," Patience pronounced hurriedly, placing one hand low on Dacia's belly. She could feel the hard, protruding bumps that indicated the child was placed all wrong—feet down and face upward. Not only was such a position dangerous to the baby, for it was likely to strangle to death before the head could be delivered, but the extra strain on the mother would be next to unbearable. Patience had seen such births before, with tragic consequences.

A soft scraping at the door jerked Dacia to greater awareness, and she twisted her head around to see Jonathan enter swiftly, then turn to bolt the door behind him.

An expression of alarm crossed over Patience's wrinkled face, though she quickly assumed the appearance of complete serenity when Dacia looked her way. "Doctor Hampton has been slightly detained?" she asked with false calm.

Jonathan wagged his head. "Thou must care for the girl thyself. The patrollers block the road. To pass them now would be to invite their interference."

Breathing deeply as her contraction receded, Dacia watched the farmer cross toward the hearth, where he kicked the burning logs apart to kill the blaze. Taking his cue, Patience reached for the lamp on the table, turning it so low that only the barest of flames glowed above the shortened wick. The dim light cast eerie shadows across the once cheerful room, and from where he stood, Jonathan's face was bathed in darkness. Dacia shuddered.

"I shall take the wagon to the Lancaster road," he said. "Perhaps I can lead them away from thy house, my friend."

Patience paused but a moment, then nodded quickly. "It is best," she agreed. If the slave catchers burst in upon Dacia now, there was no telling what the result might be. Besides, this was no place for Jonathan, either, though she would have dearly appreciated the presence of someone knowledgeable in the ways of childbirth. "Go, thou, with the Lord."

Dacia opened her mouth to speak, but another fierce contraction gripped her hard, robbing her of the breath it took to voice her fears. Even if she could say aloud what she knew, she realized that the devout Friends would smile upon any warning and attribute her ramblings to superstition and pain.

Perhaps they would be right, she thought distantly, struggling to stay conscious. Perhaps the pain and hunger and weariness was causing her imagination to trick her. With all the strength she could muster, Dacia willed it to be true.

But as Jonathan opened the door and slipped out into the darkness, she could have sworn she saw a shadow follow him—a shadow not thrown by any light of this world. A new set of tremors beset her, not of agony this time, but of horror. Death *would* come tonight—not *to* her, but because of her.

Silent tears of relief and sorrow grew thick in her eyes while the pain receded again, leaving room for anger and shame to take its place. She had learned, over the years, that it was a waste of time to feel sorry for herself. She had not yet learned to stop shedding tears for others.

As Patience settled into her chair for the long vigil to come, Dacia turned her head to the wall and wept.

16

Kelsey rose one morning to the sound of raindrops pelting her window insistently. Her first waking thought was for the corn; the second was one of bemusement that she must truly have the mind of a farmer now.

Leaping out of bed, she reached for her breeches and tugged them over her hips, pausing at the mirror only long enough to determine that her braid was still fastened, then reached for the freshly laundered shirt Hannah had left in her wardrobe. She galloped down the stairs, each step keeping time with the litany pounding in her head. *The corn, the corn, the corn.*

She stopped short when she turned the corner at the landing and saw Garrett at the bottom, one foot perched on the first step. Her heart lurched crazily.

"I was just about to wake you," he said quietly, his pulse beating strange rhythms at the sight of her. "Hannah's rheumatism acts up on days like this; she didn't feel like climbing the stairs so she asked me to come."

"I'm already up," Kelsey said unnecessarily. It would have done no good to tell him that Hannah *never* came upstairs to wake her. This was probably just the old cook's way of trying to ease the tension between her and Garrett. It wasn't working.

For nearly a week they'd circled one another like two cautious animals. Hannah's wise words on the night Little Lady was born rang insistently in Kelsey's head like a warning knell, and Garrett was still seething at the thought of Justin Delbert's proposal.

Whenever they were together, which was far too often

by Kelsey's count, they skirted both subjects, discussing instead anything that came to mind. They talked about what they would do with the extra corn money. They talked about how well James was progressing with his riding lessons. They talked about everything and anything, except what each was really feeling.

Suddenly aware that they'd been staring at one another for too long, Kelsey spoke. "How long has it been—"

"There's no need for you to—"

They both stopped again, until this time Garrett broke the silence. He flipped his hand palm upward. "You start."

"I was going to ask if you knew how long it's been raining." Kelsey descended the stairs, a blush working its way up from the tops of her breasts when Garrett's gaze riveted on a point below her throat. Too late, she remembered she hadn't finished buttoning her shirt all the way, and the collarless garment gaped open in a wide V from the third button, exposing the lacy edge of her camisole and most of her cleavage. "Well? Do you?" she snapped, more perturbed at herself than at Garrett.

He whipped his head up, meeting flashing eyes. "Do I what?"

"Know when it started raining?"

"About dawn," he answered, hiding his own discomfort by turning and pointing toward the west. "But the sky's already looking lighter. It shouldn't last long."

Kelsey didn't know which brought her the most relief; the fact that the rain wouldn't ruin the corn after all, or that Garrett now stood with his back to her, giving her time to fasten her shirt. She had been wearing similar garments for weeks now, but all of a sudden she felt practically naked in them. When had he started looking at her that way, as if he would like to devour her on the spot, or was it just that she had become more aware of him lately?

Garrett held back a wry chuckle as he entered the kitchen, knowing from the sound of her shuffling footsteps that she was fastening the buttons of her shirt as she walked behind him. He was tempted to turn around quickly to catch her in the act, but he was certain she wouldn't appreciate the humor.

Hannah looked up with a knowing smirk when Kelsey slid into her chair before Garrett had a chance to hold it for her. Moving slowly, as if her limbs ached from the effort of walking, the cook laid a plate in front of Kelsey, then placed the other on the same end, forcing Garrett to sit at right angles to her.

He peered at Hannah suspiciously, his mouth quirked in a half-smile. But he did not move. "Until the rain stops," he began after Kelsey had poured tea, "I have work to do at the shipping office in town. You can come along if you'd like, but there won't be much for you to do there."

Did she detect a challenge in his voice? Kelsey's first impulse was to say she would go with him, if only to prove that a little rain wouldn't keep her home, but the thought of the two of them cooped up in that tiny room alone, together . . .

Stop that! she chided herself. Lately it seemed that her imagination had grown vivid with unwanted images, and she was more determined than ever to put a halt to them.

"Don't worry about me," she said blithely, hoping her voice wouldn't betray her treacherous thoughts. "I can keep busy here until the weather clears."

"Then I'll see you later," he said, struggling to keep his gaze from revealing his thoughts.

"Later," she nodded, already looking forward to that moment.

"Fine," he added, pretending to concentrate on his food, when what he really wanted was to have her near him.

"Fine," she agreed, trying not to be fascinated by the way his mouth turned down at the corners when he chewed.

In the corner by the stove, Hannah harummphed, loudly enough to tell them both exactly what she thought.

* * *

Two hours later the rain was still pouring down in torrents, occasionally joined by gusts of wind that rattled the door leading to her father's balcony. Kelsey knelt on the floor, anxiously peeking out the thick-paned window as she sorted through the large crate packed with papers and books.

After the work on the balcony had been completed, she had elected to make her father's old room her own. There was just enough money left from Garrett's loan for new wallpaper and draperies, and though Sheldon's heavy oak furniture was too somber for her tastes, she could "borrow" pieces from the other rooms. The biggest part of the job lay in sorting through the boxes and books and mementos left there. Today would be a good day to start.

She eyed the box before her, then one by one, Kelsey pulled each book from the crate. Some were old and falling apart; those she placed on a pile to discard later. Most of the volumes were in good condition still, and she stacked them neatly to take down to the study.

As she neared the bottom of the box, she pulled out one of the older-looking books. It was some kind of journal, so she placed it carefully aside to study later. She was just about to turn back to the box when she caught sight of a tiny triangle jutting at angles from the book. Hoping that she had not inadvertently torn or bent one of the pages, she opened the book to that place.

A piece of paper, not one of the journal's pages, was tucked into the volume. Removing it cautiously, Kelsey could tell at once that this sheet was not nearly as old. The handwriting, while still scrawling and haphazard, was readable—and heartbreakingly familiar. This, Kelsey realized with a sudden pang, was definitely her father's, though the writing in the book was not.

Instead of reading the single letter, she gingerly flipped through the volume, quickly finding that there were many more like it jammed between the journal's pages. It was not until she had accumulated a stack of some twenty-odd pieces of paper that she stopped, satisfied that she had found them all. Leaving the journal where it was, she gathered the sheaf in one hand and moved closer to the window.

The pages were indeed letters, and to her shock, she saw that they all bore the same salutation. But why hadn't she seen these before? Why hadn't her father sent them?

She began with the page on top. *My dearest Kelsey . . .* Tears choked her, blurring her vision until she had to blink rapidly to clear her eyes in order to continue.

It took only a few moments of reading to draw two conclusions. One was that her father had been as inept at correspondence as he had been at keeping accounts. It would be difficult to understand his ramblings unless the letters were read in the order in which they were written. The other was that somehow her father had believed she had returned his letters unopened. That they had found their way back to his possession was proof of the fact, but Kelsey had never laid eyes on a word from her father for over five years, until after Mabelle's death!

A combination of eagerness and dread engulfed her as she quickly scanned the dates, shuffling the pages in her hand until they were in chronological order, beginning with a date only three weeks following her departure from Riverview. What would her father's words tell her? Kelsey wondered, her hands trembling, making the aged paper rattle ominously.

She was almost afraid to find out.

Rain-soaked and worried, Garrett paced the study floor, torn between going upstairs to confront Kelsey with the troublesome news or waiting for her down here, where the cheerful blaze in the grate could draw the dampness from his clothing and the ice from his blood. Neither prospect was appealing, but because he didn't relish putting off a confrontation, and God knew how long Kelsey would be up there anyway since she probably didn't even know he was here, he gave up stalling and strode to the stairs.

The door to her room hung open, but a quick look inside told him she was not there. Instinctively, he headed for Sheldon's old room. Rain or not, he wouldn't have been surprised to find her out on the balcony, knowing that her concern for the corn had to be at least as great as his.

Pushing the massive door wide, Garrett started in. "Have you looked outside lately—"

The sight that greeting him stopped him short, making his heart tumble curiously. Kelsey was seated on the floor near the window, her legs pulled to her chest and one arm hugging them tight. In the other hand she clutched a sheaf of papers.

But it was the expression she wore when she lifted her tear-streaked face to him that sheared his breath in two. Sorrow, as stark as the poplar trees in winter, turned her eyes into limpid, bottomless pools of darkness. The tears that trembled on her lashes were the only movement he saw as she stared up at him imploringly.

"Kelsey?"

"Oh, Garrett," she choked, her throat thick and fearfully dry. "He . . . he really did love me."

For a split second he thought it was Justin Delbert she was talking about and jealousy slashed through him like a scythe. But then reason returned, and with it the certainty that it was more than a spurned suitor that played such havoc upon Kelsey's emotions. He glanced around the room, seeing for the first time Sheldon's books and papers, his gaze eventually resting on the journal still lying in the middle of the floor.

"These were your father's?"

Kelsey nodded bleakly, tears blurring her vision as she raised the fistful of letters. "I f-found these in a b-book."

Garrett moved to take the papers from her, bending on one knee before her. His arms ached to hold her, to brush the tears from her cheeks with his mouth, but he turned his attention instead to the all-too-familiar missives. "Mabelle always returned your letters with her replies, but I didn't know your father kept them. I suppose seeing them again brought everything back. I'm sorry."

"S-seeing them again?" Kelsey stared up at him,

dumbfounded, and then comprehension washed over her with all its horrifying implications. "Oh, God," she moaned, fresh tears spilling over her cheeks. "It can't be!"

"What can't be?" Now Garrett was thoroughly confused, and completely shaken by her obvious pain. He slid closer, drawing her into his arms tenderly. "What, sweetheart? What is it?"

Kelsey choked back a sob, then took a shuddering breath to answer him. "I never saw one of these letters. Not one!"

"How can that be?"

"I-I don't know. Someone must have . . . someone must have returned them without telling me."

Garrett searched her tear-swollen eyes. She knew the answer as well as he, but he couldn't blame her for not being able to voice it out loud. When a huge tremor rocked her slender form, he cradled her closer, his own eyes burning with pity and anger. "Damn her!" he whispered fiercely. "Damn her!"

"My . . . she must have thrown away the letters I wrote to you and Papa, too. No wonder you were so angry with me."

"I'm sorry I didn't believe you before. I knew that all communication was not broken, because your father sent money regularly. Mabelle's letters implied that you were too busy to be burdened with answering yourself as long as she could assure him that you were well. Shhh. Don't cry, love."

It seemed that she had been weeping forever before Kelsey's sobs finally receded to tiny hiccoughs and the tears ceased to flow. Enveloped in the protective warmth of Garrett's embrace, she allowed the bitter anger to pour from her soul, knowing instinctively that if there was anyone left on earth to understand her pain, it was he. For in a way, he had been as wronged by what had happened as she.

"Oh, Garrett," Kelsey breathed, her hot face pressed against his shirt. "Why would she do such a thing?"

"I don't know, love. I don't know." With his chin propped on the top of her head, her wispy curls tickling his throat, Garrett recalled what he knew of the problems between Sheldon Tremayne and his wife. The foremost had been the cause to which Sheldon devoted so much of his time and money. Mabelle had never tried to understand and accept his beliefs. "She probably thought she was protecting you," he murmured, his desire to comfort Kelsey far stronger than any need for vindictiveness.

"From what?" Kelsey struggled to clear her thoughts enough to make some sense of this. "Surely not from Papa?"

Not from Sheldon, Garrett knew. But perhaps from the consequences of Sheldon's obsession? And his?

Kelsey noticed his hesitation through her tears, and she was dimly aware of his heart's erratic beat as she pressed her cheek against the solid wall of his chest. His shirt was still cool and damp from the rain, but she could feel the heat from his body warming her face through the thin fabric, just as her own shirt provided little protection from his grazing hands. Now the shudders rippling through her had a different source, beginning deep in her abdomen and rippling outward, and she understood suddenly another of her mother's sins.

"Oh, Garrett," she cried softly again, leaning back against his bolstering arm to study his face as she shook her head sadly. "In some of his letters Papa mentions your trip to London. He asks why I sent you away without seeing you."

"You were only following your mother's wishes. When I came to see you at your cousin's estate, the footman told me you were out riding. I came back three more times that week, until Mabelle had no choice but to speak to me herself. She said you didn't wish to see me because you were engaged to be married to someone more suitable than I was." Garrett's voice nearly broke, but he forced himself to go on. "As much as I resented it at the time, I can't fault you for that."

"But I wasn't engaged!" Anguish filled her voice, her

hands clutched at the folds of his shirt. "I wasn't following my mother's wishes because I never knew you were there at all!"

Impotent rage mingled with harsh disappointment, mounting in Garrett's chest with volcanic force. He didn't realize his grip on Kelsey's shoulders had tightened until she gave a small, painful gasp. Her eyes were full of regret, and something he could not name that made him drop his hands from her quickly, before he was completely consumed by it.

Just as fast, Kelsey scooted from his lap, landing back on the heap of dust covers. She averted her gaze, pretending to look once again at the letters, though she knew it was just a ruse to keep him from seeing the blatant longing engulfing her.

"You weren't just calling out of courtesy?" she ventured.

Garrett considered lying, but told himself it was best to clear the air between them once and for all. Deep inside him a distant hope was taking wing, one which he hadn't dared to acknowledge before, and even now would not pursue. He stood, reaching a hand to Kelsey to pull her to her feet. "You'd been gone for nearly three years, and I figured you were old enough to know what you wanted by then. I was pretty damned arrogant, I suppose. I expected resistance from your mother even though I was sure I could support you well enough by then, but I hadn't even considered the possibility you wouldn't want to come back to Riverview with me."

"C-come back with you? Papa wanted me to come home then?"

Garrett smiled ruefully. "We both did. I'd already discussed my plans with Sheldon, and he was in agreement. The only one left to ask was you."

Kelsey didn't need to voice the question, for the answer was written in the glowing intensity of his eyes and the way his jaw was clenched as tight as a vise. "You wanted to marry me," she stated softly, with just a tinge of wonder in her voice. Closing her eyes, she summoned all her strength, willing herself not to shatter into a thousand pieces.

I will not cry for what cannot be changed, she told herself firmly, battling the tears that stung behind her eyelids. *I will not!*

"I said I was arrogant," Garrett said with false lightheartedness. "And also painfully naive. I imagined there would never be another woman for me, nor another man for you."

"And was there? Another woman, I mean?"

Again, he shrugged. "None that mattered. I was pretty well disgusted with the whole female race after that." He waited for her to admit that she'd never loved anyone else either, but she didn't respond.

Kelsey swallowed back a lump the size of an ostrich egg. "I'm so sorry. I can't believe my mother would try to hurt us both like that."

Garrett was inclined to agree with at least half of her statement. Mabelle had never wasted any time showing him false affection, but to keep her daughter from her own father? She had been either completely heartless or seriously disturbed. He wasn't quite sure which. "You don't have to apologize for her, Kelsey. Remember what I said about living your own life, and not having to account for what our parents were?"

She sighed. "I remember, but it's still hard to accept."

Understanding that she needed time to deal with what could only be termed as a betrayal, Garrett tipped Kelsey's chin up with the ends of his fingers. "This doesn't have to affect you for the rest of your life, you know."

"But it will," Kelsey argued gently. "So much has changed now; we can never go back again."

"Then can we not go forward?"

Sorrow spilled from her heart, pouring over until she felt as if inside her burned a cauldron of anguish and bitter regrets. If only he knew how irrevocably her fate was sealed. If only he knew how much at this moment she wished it weren't so. "No, Garrett," she whispered achingly. "It's too late."

His fingertips hovered beneath her chin for just a moment longer, barely brushing her with a touch as gentle and brief as a butterfly's kiss before stepping back, a parody of a smile twisting his lips. "Then tell me this one thing," he demanded, his voice hoarse, yet strangely tender. "If you had known . . . if you had been able, would you have come home with me then?"

Kelsey blinked back scalding tears, knowing that a lie would wound him deeply, that honesty would hurt him more. But when there were so many half-truths and hidden meanings between them, one more lie was too many. Just this once, she told herself, she had to let him see into her heart.

Though they were no longer touching, she felt bound to him, as if he were commanding her answer by force or by seduction. His blue eyes, at once compelling and entreating, mesmerized her so that she could not look away.

"Would you have?" he asked again.

Kelsey nodded weakly. "Yes," she breathed.

Something flickered behind his eyes—elation? triumph?—then was gone in an instant, replaced by the familiar blandness that he wore with such ease. Only his mouth betrayed the depth of his emotion, twitching though he struggled to keep it firm.

"Then it truly *was* my loss."

17

Garrett slogged through the boggy field, thick mud sucking at his boots with each step. All around him, the corn lay in sodden branches on the ground, as if trampled by some heartless beast. He crouched on his haunches, fingering a few broken stalks hopefully.

"What do you think?"

Kelsey's voice was as bleak as the weeping day, making his heart thump lower in his chest. He stood slowly.

"We might be able to salvage part of it . . ."

If it stops raining. He didn't need to say it. It was what they had both been thinking for six days now.

"How much of it?"

"A third . . . maybe less."

Kelsey raised her face to the rain, letting it bathe her wind-chapped face and rinse the sting of tears from her eyes. How could something that felt so wonderful cause so much trouble? she thought distantly. She looked at Garrett again. His rain-soaked mackintosh hung dark and heavy from his shoulders; the hair plastered to his head looked the same, emphasizing his grim expression. How much was he holding back from her?

Aside, that was, from his disdain.

"I shouldn't have told Stocker Fulton to plant more corn," Kelsey said dejectedly, the wind whipping her words away so that Garrett had to turn in order to hear her. "You were right. I *don't* know enough about farming to save Riverview."

Garrett started to reach for her, then dropped his hand abruptly, feeling wretched enough without having to see her pull away from him again. ''You took a gamble and it didn't pay,'' he conceded, ''but that doesn't make it wrong.''

''How can you say that?'' Kelsey flung her arm wide, her forlorn gaze scanning the dismal lands. ''I've lost everything!''

Garrett looked again. Two weeks ago the field had been blanketed with bright green shoots so thick and healthy, Stocker Fulton had hinted at a record crop. Now the corn lay flat to the ground, an endless, hopeless wasteland that pulled his gaze all the way to the line of poplars guarding the house, green spires blurred by a drizzle that showed no signs of letting up.

What bothered him more than the lost crop, however, was the defeated slump in Kelsey's shoulders. He knew this crop was important to her, but it surprised him how easily she blamed herself. This was not the self-assured young girl who had left five years ago, nor was it the independent woman he thought had returned. Her complete lack of confidence disturbed him, more because he sensed that its source lay deep within her, that losing the corn had only brought it to the surface.

''Shall we go in?'' he suggested, seeing her shudder from the cold. Her trousers were mud-splattered and wet above her new riding boots, which she had probably ruined stomping through the field. She had stuffed her hair up under a floppy hat she found in the stables, but now damp tendrils clung to her neck and cheeks, having worked their way down from beneath the wide brim, making her look bedraggled and somehow more vulnerable than ever. It made Garrett's heart ache with every beat.

Wordlessly, Kelsey turned and began trudging toward the house, cutting a muddy swath through the fallen corn. She couldn't stand to see the pity in Garrett's eyes; it was hardly better than the smugness she had half expected. Not that she wouldn't see *that* soon enough, she thought ruefully. Justin had sent a message saying he would call that afternoon, no doubt to remind her that he was still willing to save her from herself.

If only it weren't too late for that.

In all of Riverview there was only one room that was always warm and snug, and though Kelsey hadn't remembered the house being so miserably damp when she was a child, now she couldn't wait to make her way to the kitchen.

She knew Hannah would have the fire stoked high to combat her rheumatism, and a cup of something hot and soothing just half a minute from readiness. The idea was comforting.

" 'Bout time yo' come in outta the cold," she clucked as soon as Kelsey rounded the half-open door. "You'll catch your death, if y'ain't careful."

"I've been hearing that all my life," Kelsey retorted gently, helping herself to a cup of tea from the sideboard. "I've never yet met anyone who died from a little rain. Besides, I wasn't the only one getting wet."

"Well, if Mistah Garrett was here, ah'd be givin' him a piece o' mah mind, too. Traipsin' around those fields like a hired hand. As if that'll make the rain stop fallin'."

"I'm afraid even that wouldn't make much difference now. The corn is just about ruined."

"Hmmph. Wouldn't be the first time, wouldn't be the last."

Kelsey watched as Hannah lowered her creaking body to the rocker in front of the fire. She wished she could explain how she felt without inviting a lecture, but she'd heard just about enough logic for one day. Justin Delbert had already come and gone, and as she had expected, he had argued dispassionately for her to listen to reason.

"Be practical, Kelsey," he had said in that smooth, controlled tone that always made her feel like sticking out her tongue at him. "I could settle enough on you, even without selling, for you to hire an estate manager to straighten out the mess your father and O'Neill made.

You would be free to concentrate on the things a lady should.''

''And what, may I ask, would that be?'' she had asked pointedly.

''Now, Kelsey. There's no need to take that tone with me. You forget, I've known you all your life. Why, no woman in Lewiston could hold a candle to you, if you would only spend some money on yourself. The fact that you're in such dire straits that you can't even buy a decent wardrobe, simply breaks my heart!''

No doubt it did, Kelsey thought with a heavy sigh. At least as much as Justin's heart was capable of being broken. When she had politely refused him, again, he had given her a smile that as good as said to her, *No matter . . . I can wait.*

Perhaps his wait would be shorter than he expected, she thought despondently, seating herself at the table. She sipped slowly at the steaming brew, then lowered the cup to the table, curling her fingers around it to capture its reassuring warmth. Without the money from this crop, she couldn't pay her share of the bank loan.

It seemed there was nothing left for her but to sell the river property. Or accept Justin's other offer.

But when she said as much to Hannah, the cook let out an angry snort. ''Don't you go doin' that now! An' don't you go marryin' that Justin Delbert jest ta satisfy a bunch o' pryin' folks. He won't make you happy, no way.''

''Justin is a dear friend, and he's been very sweet to me, but I won't marry him.''

''Then you gonna marry Mistah Garrett, like he wants?''

Kelsey shook her head sadly.

''Don't see why not!'' Hannah exclaimed. She grabbed an iron poker from the hearth and gave the dying fire a vicious jab.

''Oh, Hannah, please try to understand. Even if he really wanted me—not just because of some sense of duty, or out of loyalty to my father—but because of me . . .

even if he wanted me, we just wouldn't be suited to one another.''

To Kelsey's surprise, the woman leaped from her rocking chair, facing her with hands on her hips and skinny arms cocked high. ''Yo' thinkin' yo' too good fo' him now, missy? But he ain't too good ta ask for help when no one else'll give it, an' he ain't too good ta ask ta worry hisself sick over yer crop!''

Stunned, not only by the vehemence of Hannah's attack, but also because she never realized her meaning would be so misconstrued, Kelsey shook her head helplessly. ''Oh, *no,* Hannah! I don't think that at all!''

''Well, it shore 'pears like it, the way you take Mistah Garrett for granted.''

Was that what she'd been doing? Kelsey swallowed thickly, and she had the terrible urge to cry. ''I never meant to,'' she said softly. ''I . . . I do appreciate everything he's done.''

''D'ye love him?''

Words sprang quickly to her lips, the same words of denial she'd been spouting all along. But somehow, this time she couldn't speak them, and whether it was the way Hannah's lips pursed at her, firmly but gently, or because she was too tired and weary to fight it anymore, she didn't now. Tears sprang to her eyes and she hunched her shoulders forward. ''Y-yes.''

''Then marry 'im.''

''It's not that simple. I'm not . . . I'm not good enough for him. I'm not good enough for any man.''

Hannah remained motionless, but her wrinkled face lost some of its starch. ''Where'd you git that fool notion, chile?''

''Because I'm like . . . because I'm like my mother. Some women just aren't capable of . . . of loving a man,'' she finished in a hushed voice.

''Pshaw! Nothin' wrong with yer mother, an' ain't nothin' wrong with you. She had no business tellin' you otherwise!''

''But why would she say that?''

"Why would who say what?"

Kelsey nearly jumped from her chair at the sound of Garrett's voice, and her heart beat erratically against the walls of her chest. Had he heard?

"Where you been?" Hannah demanded gruffly, whisking another cup from the sideboard and slamming it onto the table. She seemed determined to keep Garrett from repeating his question, and for that Kelsey would be eternally grateful.

"Ah cain't be expected ta keep this tea hot forever. A body's got 'nough ta do 'round here without havin' folks bustin' into the kitchen at all times!"

Her ploy worked, at least so far as steering his thoughts away from whatever he might have overheard, but Garrett was not so easily fooled that he didn't see there was something wrong with Kelsey. Her chin trembled the way it always did when she was trying too hard to keep it upright.

"I talked to Fulton," he said, pulling up another chair across from her. From the corner of his eye he saw Hannah lace his tea liberally with whiskey before she placed it in front of him. "It might not be as bad as it looks. He said it rained like this in '47 when he was working for Thompson, and they salvaged half the crop by digging extra drainage ditches."

Kelsey could barely lift her eyes to meet his, and even then it was hard to see through the tears. "Are you just trying to make me feel better?"

"Yes . . . no . . . dammit, Kelsey! This isn't your fault!"

She watched as he took a long swallow of his drink, then sucked in a mouthful of air to counteract the burning liquor. "That doesn't change the fact that I could lose everything I've worked for," she said.

"Everything *we've* worked for! Don't forget I'm in this with you too. And I'm just as much to blame."

"It was my decision. It was my mistake."

"It's the same one I would have made." His voice softened, compelling her to listen. "I wanted you to have a say in how the farm is run, but I never would have let you do the wrong thing. In your place, I would have opted for planting corn and so would Stocker Fulton. It was a calculated risk and we lost, but it's not the end of the world."

He had leaned forward, gathering both her hands in his, and the effect was like a jolt of electricity to Kelsey. her fingers tingled against the callused flesh of his palms, but she could no more draw her hands away than she could tear her eyes from his entreating gaze.

Her brown eyes widened and Garret felt himself swirling in their depths. Something passed between them, more powerful than desire, more intimate than any kiss, and he felt as bound to her as he had on that day more than five years ago when he had let her go, believing in his heart that she would come back to him.

"There're still the apples, you know. The orchard is looking better than ever and this rain won't hurt it a bit. If we can save enough of the corn to hold us over until the apples can be picked, we'll be all right."

"I-I don't know. Do you really think so?"

His throat tightened as her shoulders lifted hopefully. He prayed to God he was right. "Don't you trust me?"

Kelsey dipped her head without breaking the threat of contact between their eyes. "Y-yes. I don't have any other choice, do I?"

Garrett squeezed her hands harder, wishing she hadn't put it quite that way, as if trusting him were merely the better part of a bad bargain. "We always have a choice," he answered roughly.

But deep in their hearts, they both knew it wasn't true.

Nestled in a corner between two great lakes, the Niagara frontier was protected from the arctic freezes that paralyzed the rest of the state for most of the winter. The lake temperatures usually remained stable from first frost to last, resulting in the kind of wet, moderate weather so precious to farmers everywhere.

Usually, but not always.

After three weeks of unending downpours, Kelsey thought she had seen the worst. What she didn't know was how much worse it could be.

On a night similar to many others when she'd had trouble falling asleep, Kelsey bundled herself into a blanket and found a book to lull herself. Bridget, too, had been unusually restless, padding back and forth to the window several times before settling down in front of the grate.

She hardly noticed the cold or rain, in the way one grows immune to the sights and sounds that are in indelible part of existence. She did notice, however, when the wind began its keening wail, pounding the drops against her windowpane with vicious force. The flame in the fireplace danced higher as a breath of cold air pushed through the crack beneath her door, and Kelsey debated whether to add more wood to the blaze. But she was still snug in her bed when the cadence of the rain changed altogether, bringing her to her feet like lightning.

Starting first for the door to the balcony, Kelsey stopped when she realized that to open it would be to become immediately soaked. The pounding at the windows was unlike anything she'd ever heard before, and for a second she wondered if someone were outside throwing gravel at the house.

Then understanding came in one sickening instant. It wasn't gravel she heard, it wasn't even rain anymore. It was sleet.

"Oh, my God!" she exclaimed out loud. "It's May! This can't be happening." Bridget looked up from her rug at the hearth but did not move, wisely deciding to enjoy the fire's heat while she could.

Hurrying to the window, Kelsey held her hand in front of her as if to ward off the icy scourge. Her fingertips touched the cold pane, causing four small circles of mist to form on the glass. To her dismay, the mist crystallized as soon as she removed her hand, proof of how terribly cold the wind must be. For a long moment she stood motionless, watching the sleet accumulate on the ledge outside. Before too many minutes passed, she could no longer see out the window anyway—it was one solid sheet of ice!

As frigid as the temperature was outside, Kelsey felt as if her heart were ten degrees colder. Her stunned senses could barely fathom the cause of such a freakish turn of events, but the consequences loomed in her thoughts like a death knell.

She knew that beneath the arctic winds swooping across the lake, her apple blossoms would freeze and wither away.

And with them, her last shred of hope.

Stocker Fulton shook his shaggy head, fingering the thin branch with surprising gentleness. "That's it. If there'd been more wind, the ice never woulda stuck. Less, and the blossoms woulda thawed out right here on the branch." He shrugged with the age-old acceptance of a true farmer. "There's next year."

Stomping his feet to keep the circulation flowing through his toes, Garrett cast a bleak gaze upward into the rime-covered trees above him. Many of the branches had cracked beneath the weight of their unwelcome burden, and the ground below was littered with broken limbs.

"Always did think it was odd that somethin' so bad could be so purty," Fulton said. "D'ye think she'll want ta see it?"

"No, she doesn't want to see it!" Garrett's response was harsher than he intended, and he turned so the other man could see his regret. "She doesn't need to see it. She was up all last night during the storm."

"All night?"

Nodding, Garrett started the long walk back to the barn. Having deemed it too slippery to ride Prince, he'd trudged out this morning just as soon as it was light enough to see, knowing that the conscientious overseer would beat him anyway. After hours of inspecting nearly every tree in the hope of finding some undamaged, the two men were ready to concede that nature had won this round.

But the worry uppermost in Garrett's mind was Kelsey. He'd spent the better part of the night in the kitchen at Riverview because the stove in the cottage had finally begun to spew black smoke. Dozing fitfully, he'd tried to snatch some sleep for himself in Hannah's old rocking chair, knowing that the day ahead would be a difficult one.

That's where Kelsey had found him. He was jolted awake by the sound of slippered feet whispering across the floor, though what had truly startled him was the blank expression on her face as she moved the kettle to the front of the stove.

"Hannah's still sleeping," she had mumbled when he started to speak. With movements as mechanical and stiff as a machine's, she reached for the tea implements stored on a shelf near the door.

Overwhelmed by the need to offer comfort, he had risen to stand behind her. "I'll go out soon. It may not be as bad—"

"Don't! Don't say anything!"

Her voice was raw, and so was the pain that had tremored through it, making Garrett want to still her shaking with his arms and drown her words with his lips.

Now, homeward bound, he fought the lethargy brought on by the cold with his concern for Kelsey. She had not been willing to face him. Such a reaction was natural, he supposed. He had asked her to trust him, and her trust had been for naught.

That wasn't your fault, he told himself.

She may not see it that way, his mind argued.

Then that's her problem, not yours.

"She'll sell the land now."

"I don't think so. She's a game one, I'll wager. And likely to give it a go again next year."

Garrett looked up with a start. He hadn't realized he'd spoken that last sentence out loud until Stocker Fulton answered him. Now the man was waiting for a response.

"She *can't* wait another year. Even if I pay the bank loan, which I'm quite sure she'll refuse, there are other expenses to be considered." But the only consideration that truly mattered was Kelsey's state of mind. If she decided she was finished, then nothing he could say would convince her otherwise.

Except, he admitted silently, for the one thing he had vowed never to allow.

And even then, he couldn't be sure it would work.

18

On any given Saturday afternoon, a body passing through the village could look across to the Frontier House and spot the heart and soul of Lewiston. Businessmen congregated on its wide gallery to enjoy a cigar after their noon meal, tradespeople stopped to put the final touches on deals negotiated during the week, and ladies on their way home from market paused to pass the time, nodding their greetings as they secretly wished that they, too, could recline in one of the many rockers lining the porch, or hitch one leg over the spindled railing.

After last week's ice storm, the weather had grown remarkably mild again, seeming to draw the citizens of Lewiston to this familiar spot. At least the male citizens. Such impromptu meetings were one of the traditions reserved for men only, and today was no exception.

It was just as well, Garrett thought as he surreptitiously studied his companions lazing in various positions around the verandah. For all their appearance of relaxed conviviality, there was little pleasure in the subject they discussed.

"Damned if I don't wish there was something more I could do. But my hands are tied!"

Murmurs of agreement rose in support of Judge Crandall's statement, and Garrett joined with the rest, glad that, at least in this, there was almost universal agreement among the town's leading citizens. "He held up one of my deliveries yesterday with a long and unnecessary search. I'd have gladly had him tossed off the property if it wouldn't have given him so much satisfaction to see me fined for impeding a so-called lawman in his investigation.''

''Best to ignore him,'' George Delbert concurred, never opening his eyes. His chin bobbed on his chest so that it appeared he was dozing, but his occasional and very pointed comments were proof that he was as alert as ever.

''How can we ignore someone like Bart Ogden?'' Matt Ruther protested. ''You can smell him from fifty paces, and he looks like the worst kind of river scum.''

Justin stirred from his chair. ''Our only recourse is to petition Congress to revise the Fugitive Slave Act.''

''Too slow,'' someone cut in. ''That could take years.''

''Not if all the free states band together.''

''And have the South do the same? That would mean war!''

Silenced by the grim thought, the men on the porch peered at one another speculatively, each wondering exactly how strong his peers would stand on such an issue. A few, Garrett knew, would back it with their lives—in fact, some of them already were doing so. By prearranged agreement, he carefully avoided meeting the eyes of any of those men. Even though the others seemed to oppose the law that made Bart Ogden's nefarious business legitimate, he couldn't be too careful.

''War can be avoided,'' Judge Crandall said solemnly, ''if all men act with reason. It's up to us to set a good example for everyone else. Prudence,'' he said, looking up to meet Garrett's gaze, ''and caution are the keys.''

Justin watched the exchange through narrowed eyes, automatically suspicious of anything O'Neill did which could be considered out of the ordinary. Why did Judge Crandall's words suddenly sound like a warning? And for what?

''Lookee there.''

All heads swiveled in the direction Ruther pointed. Sauntering toward them was Bart Ogden, one hand cradling a shiny new shotgun, the other dangling at his waist, the thumb hooked in his beltless trousers. A tattered hat was pushed up high on his forehead, so that all could see the derisive grin twisting his beefy, unshaved face. The planked walkway groaned beneath his weight as he idled forward, stopping just in front of the inn. Ruther had been right, Justin Delbert thought, sniffing distatefully. Fifty paces gave the man more than his due.

"Waalll, what've we got here? Town meetin'?" Ogden settled the stock of his rifle on the ground beside his huge, slime-encrusted boot and leaned on the barrel. "Jest the passel o' folks ah been lookin' fer. Caught me another darkie the other day 'n ah thought a bunch o' nigger-lovers like y'all'd wanna know. A real purty one, too," he added lecherously, spitting a huge wad of tobacco on the ground. He swiped a dirty shirtsleeve across his yellow-stained mouth, smearing tobacco juice across his cheek. "Cain't say as ah was sorry ta send her back with one o' mah men; she were a right mean gal . . . ," his grin widened, ". . . but ah knocked it outta her."

Garrett stood from his seat on the railing, his hands balled into fists at his side. He was vaguely aware of movement behind him, but his fury was aimed at the gaping excuse for a man standing before him. He was about to launch himself from the porch when a firm hand settled on his shoulder, and Judge Crandall's low voice registered in his brain.

"Easy, son. Think of what's at stake."

Slowly, Garrett's Irish temper cooled, though he remained standing, staring openly into Ogden's pig-eyes as if daring him to continue. The men around him were mumbling, disgruntled by the slave-catcher's bold challenge, but none did more than cast disparaging glances at the man from the Mississippi swamps.

"Whatsa matter, O'Neill? Was she one o' yours?" When Garrett refused to be baited, Ogden continued with an exaggerated shake of his head. "That's right! I fergot you don't have many darkies around yer place anymore."

Garrett felt the muscles in his chest constrict, forcing the air out of his lungs. He prayed to God no one would say anything that might send Bart Ogden snooping around

Riverview again. He'd had enough trouble from the man already.

"Why don't you and your friends just clear out of this town? You're wasting your time here." Justin Delbert eased smoothly from his chair, taking a place just behind Garrett's other shoulder. One by one, the other men stood also, forming a solid wall of strength against Ogden.

Unperturbed, the man spat again. "Ah don't think so," he said, raising one shaggy brow. "Ah think ah'll jest bide mah time. That's right, ah'll just bide mah time."

Bart Ogden hefted the rifle to his shoulder and hitched his trousers up a mite in preparation to leave. Before he did, however, he eyed Garrett for a long moment. "That Miz Tremayne is one fine-lookin' woman. You tell 'er ah said howdy, hear?"

With that he turned and ambled away, but an evil chuckle drifted back to the men on the porch, causing a great deal of indignant muttering.

"Despicable!" Matt Ruther pronounced, though his eyes slid to Garrett suggestively. "No sense of decency whatsoever."

After a few more minutes of discussion, in which Garrett did not take part, the others began to leave in twos and threes until the only men left on the verandah were Garrett, Judge Crandall, and Justin Delbert.

The judge had dropped his restraining hand from Garrett's shoulder, but still stood at his side. "Hits close to home, doesn't he? But he's only trying to rile you."

"The fact that the man is breathing riles me! Thanks, though, for stopping me from making a mistake."

"It's never pleasant to be the target of viciousness."

Garrett nodded as the judge picked up a panama hat from his rocking chair and stepped down into the street. He knew well enough that his friend referred to more than the question of antislavery, and that bothered him as much as if Ogden had out-and-out accused him of harboring fugitives. That, at least, he could deny. But Bart Ogden wasn't the only person in town looking askance at his and Kelsey's living arrangements, and for that he could only blame himself.

"He's right, you know. You've made Kelsey vulnerable to a lot of rumors."

He'd almost forgotten Justin was still there, but now Garrett swung around to face him. "It's none of your business!

"It's my business when your ungentlemanly conduct threatens to ruin her life."

"And how is that?" Garrett's tone was acerbic.

Justin grew flustered, but managed to stand his ground when he thought about the evidence he was accumulating against his rival. "Look, O'Neill," he said placatingly. "I don't want to stir up any more gossip than already exists. *I* know your relationship with Kelsey is purely for financial reasons, but others may not see it that way. Can't you think of her best interests?"

"Is that what you were thinking of when you asked her to marry you?" Garrett asked. "Or have you stopped eyeing that piece of land as if it were hiding a gold mine? Don't talk to me about best interests."

Justin was furious, and somehow ashamed that Garrett O'Neill not only knew that he'd asked Kelsey to marry him, but had cast aspersions on his proposal by implying that it was less than sincere. It never occurred to him, however, that Garrett could have gotten such information only from Kelsey. "And what else do you want from her? You already took more than you were entitled to when Sheldon was alive. Do you want it all?"

Yes, Garrett wanted to shout, but he held the impulse to voice his desire out loud, especially to one who would purposely choose to misunderstand. The land, the money, the prestige . . . they all meant little to him in the face of what was more important. "Don't we all?" he said cryptically, looking past Delbert toward the row of shops just up the street.

Justin pivoted, following Garrett's attentive gaze. Kelsey was just coming out of the apothecary. A basket swung on one arm as she gathered her skirt with the other hand and crossed Center Street. She didn't seem to notice the two men watching her while she strolled the planked walkway, pausing occasionally to peer into store windows.

Garrett's heart thumped mightily at the sight of her, and he couldn't stop his mouth from curving upward ever so slightly. She was wearing a navy skirt and a white blouse that made her look as young as a schoolgirl, and for once she had left her hair billow about her shoulders, with only the top pulled back from her crown in a puff that framed her face like a halo.

"Excuse me, Delbert," he said, leaving the other man on the steps of the Frontier House as he strode toward Kelsey. Today was the first time in a week she had left the protection of Riverview. The loss of both crops had left her depressed, as he'd expected, but she seemed to be getting over that gradually. He only hoped the reason wasn't because she'd been talking to Justin Delbert about selling the river property after all. Maybe the time for patience was over.

As he neared Kelsey, he summoned a smile. She was facing the other direction, and so didn't see him until his reflection shimmered behind hers in the plate glass window.

"Hmmm, beautiful," he murmured in her ear, inhaling the fresh scent of the rose perfume she wore.

Kelsey spun around. "Garrett! You startled me." His chest was scarce inches from her flushed face, forcing her to look up into his crinkled eyes and lay her hand on his arm to keep from losing her balance.

"Sorry," he chuckled. "Couldn't help it. Are you ready to go?" He watched as she fought a losing battle with the blush that rose from her prim collar, flooding her cheeks a becoming shade of pink.

"Yes." Kelsey looked down at her fingers dancing fitfully across the top of the basket handle. Nibbling on her lower lip, she tried to hide her agitation. "Yes, let's go."

Garrett's eyes were drawn to her restless hands, and to the basket that swung on her arm as lightly as before.

"Did you get everything you need?" he asked, one brow slightly raised.

She did not answer, only started across the street to where the buggy was hitched behind the Frontier House. In two strides he caught up with her, clasping her arm gently.

"Is something wrong?"

"No, it's nothing," she said, shaking his hand from her as she turned to smile a little too brightly. "I'm not going to shatter like a piece of glass, you know. You've been watching me all week as if you expect me to fall into pieces at the slightest sound. Really, Garrett, I'm fine."

He wished he could believe her, but something in the pitch of her voice told him she wasn't all that sure herself. It made him wonder if it was unchivalrous of him to take advantage of her uncertainty, but after Justin's comments and Ogden's sly innuendo, he had made up his mind that there was only one course of action left to take.

Together, they reached the buggy, Garrett lifting her onto the high leather seat before pulling himself up beside her. Kelsey did not mind that he was pensive on the way home. With each turn of the wheels her wrath lessened, so that by the time they were halfway to Riverview there was little left of her anger but a lingering aftertaste like sour wine.

And so she was startled when he raised the very subject she'd been trying to forget.

"The gossip has been getting worse, Kelsey. I'm not saying so to hurt you, but it's time we did something about it."

"So *that's* what the big discussion was about up on that porch. I wondered." She sighed, uncertain how to explain that it didn't matter to her anymore. That she couldn't *let* it matter.

Garrett turned the horse north on Second Street with a savage slap of the reins. "We were discussing business, not you. Your name did come up afterward, however.

Delbert is still concerned about your reputation, and with good cause."

"Justin's only concern is for himself," Kelsey retorted.

"That's not how it looked to me."

She paused. That's what she had thought, at least until today. It had been easy to pretend to herself that Justin's dire warnings were created to further his own aims, but that very morning she had been snubbed by three different women, and had been refused service in one of the shops she had entered.

But since it was just something she would have to live with, she decided to make light of the situation. "I'm surprised at you, Garrett. I would have thought you'd be the last person on earth to worry about what others think."

"I'm not worried for myself."

"Well, don't worry for me either! I've lived without the good opinion of those around me before, and if there's one thing I learned, it's that people will find something to hold against you sooner or later unless you spend most of your time bending over backwards to keep that from happening. I don't intend to waste my time trying."

They had cleared town and were headed away from Riverview on a road that was little more than a rutted path, trees closing in around them as the buggy bounced along determinedly. Garrett had allowed the horse to slow to a walk in order to negotiate the uneven ground. Now he hauled back hard on the reins.

"If you think being the only American among a group of foreigners is the worst that can happen to you, try going hungry for a while."

"I hardly think I'll starve because Mrs. Porter won't extend me credit."

Garrett's jaw clamped hard, his blue eyes flaming. "So that's—" He stopped, his voice turning to a feral growl. "I ought to go back there and strangle the old biddy!"

"It's not your fault, Garrett. And it's not so bad as all that, really."

"No? What happens when she refuses your money at all? Or when she asks her husband to stop buying your corn? Or Mrs. McGiver gets old man McGiver to boycott the shipping company, all because you're sharing a house with a shanty Irishman."

Kelsey sucked in her breath. She hadn't thought of it that way, but surely he was wrong. She hoped. "Background doesn't have anything to do with it," she protested.

"Perhaps not." He turned to her, noticing at once that, though her words were staunchly resolute, her eyes flickered with uncertainty before she shifted her gaze away. "And perhaps there's nothing to this at all. But are you willing to risk everything you've worked for?"

Kelsey settled her gaze on his hands, resting motionless on his muscular thighs. They were clean, though rough and callused, the nails trimmed square. Not the hands of a dandified aristocrat, but the hands of a laborer. They reminded her that for every minute she had worked, he had worked twice as hard. She lifted her eyes to his.

"What else can we do?" As soon as she asked it, she knew what he would say, and she was swamped with dread laced with anticipation. In a way, she'd almost been expecting this.

As if his heart weren't slamming against his rib cage or his throat swelling up like he'd been struck with some rare disease, Garrett shrugged and said, "You could marry me."

There, it was out. It surprised him how easily the words had come, when for a week they'd been locked up in his throat, refusing to budge. This was the solution he had wanted to give her, if only she would listen.

Four little words, Kelsey thought. Four *important* little words. And yet they rolled from his mouth as easily as if he'd said, "Fine weather we're having" or "How do you do."

You could marry me.

She didn't know whether to laugh or cry. Once upon a

time she would have died to hear those words, as indifferent as they sounded, but now she couldn't help thinking that even Justin had put more emotion into asking for her hand.

Summoning her most annoyed tone, because she knew it was her best defense against tears, she drew her shoulders straighter and pinned him with an indignant glare. "Why do men think marriage automatically solves any problem a woman could possibly have?"

"It would solve this one."

"Only to create more. Besides, I told you before that I would never marry."

"But you never told me why."

That much was true, and she had sworn to herself that she never would. But he was waiting for an answer now, and she owed it to him to offer some kind of explanation. "I can't marry you," she whispered hoarsely, then cleared her throat and repeated louder. "I can't."

It wasn't much of an answer, but the way her lower lip trembled despite the unyielding set of her chin told him more than he wanted to know. It was not just stubbornness, and he was certain that she felt no more of a class barrier than he did anymore. Whatever her reasons, they were very real and very painful. That could mean only one thing.

"There *was* someone in England, then."

"Y-yes." Her voice nearly faltered. But this was not a lie, merely a truth that would be easy for him to accept. "Yes, there was."

"Did you love him?"

"I . . . yes."

"And are you still hoping to marry him?"

"No."

"But you'll stay true to him anyway."

Kelsey wished she could see past the stony set of his face to what Garrett was really thinking. This last statement had been as dispassionate as the rest, and some perverse part of her wanted more of a reaction. Instead, he merely reached for the reins tied around the buggy's brake and chucked them over the horse's back.

So she *had* met someone else in Europe, Garrett fumed. No doubt that was the reason she had not hurried home, even after her mother's death. Then what had gone wrong? His mind churned with unasked questions, but his heart seized up like a rusted gear, bringing the truth crashing home to him. All these weeks he'd been pretending that he'd stopped loving her.

The truth was, he never would.

19

From the kitchen door, Garrett watched Kelsey flee from the yard atop Ladyfair. Aside from a slight clenching of his right first there was no indication that anything untoward had occurred, but Hannah didn't need a map to see which way the road lay. She thumped her rolling pin down on the table vigorously. "Best let her go. She's needin' time to think things out."

Since he had just arrived himself, and the decision to follow Kelsey was only a half-formed thought, Garrett's response was to raise one brow in surprise. He then shook his head wretchedly. "I'm afraid she's already made up her mind about this. She'll sell that land in order to keep this house, not even realizing what's at stake. Why does she persist in the belief that she must do this alone?"

"Seems to me when a body's been alone for long, he tends to forgit what it's like to need folks. Ah reckon ah remember hearin' you sayin' you never needed no one."

"How old was I then?" Garrett smiled grimly, swiping at his hair in a telltale gesture. "Twelve? Thirteen?"

"Thereabouts. Point was, you growed outta it. Kelsey ain't had time to yet. She's been through a lot more'n you or me knows. Ah 'spect 'bout the worse thing Mistah Sheldon ever done was leavin' that chile to stand up to her mama all by herself. Problem was, as good as Mabelle was at passin' out blame, Mistah Sheldon was at takin' it. Kelsey's too much like him that way. Her head's sayin' her mama was wrong, but her heart ain't listenin' yet."

"Wrong about what?" Garrett straddled a chair and

rested his elbows on the table, his fingers locked tightly before him.

" 'Bout everythin'. Mostly bein' happy. She's got it in her head she don't deserve happiness. Ah ain't figgered out why, yet, but ah reckon you kin find out as well as me."

"You're wrong there." He laughed harshly. "She won't tell me what happened while she was in Europe any more than she'll take another dime. I'd gladly pay off that loan tomorrow if I thought she wouldn't march down to the bank immediately afterward and demand that Mr. Snowden give the money back."

Hannah had been measuring out flour for a piecrust, but she stopped suddenly, frozen in midair. Ever so slowly, she tilted her head to one side. "Maybe she won't take no help, but as far as ah kin tell, she don't hold no objections to givin' it."

Garrett instantly thought of Micah. He also remembered that Kelsey had adamantly refused to have anything to do with continuing to help other fugitive slaves. "If you're suggesting we ask her to assist with the station, I've already done some probing. She knows she could lose Riverview if we were caught."

"Ah ain't talkin' about that," Hannah insisted, turning with her hands on her hips. She shook her head at Garrett as if he were a recalcitrant schoolboy. " 'Ah'm talkin' about you." When he only stared at her with a perplexed expression, the cook waved her arm irritably, sending up a cloud of white flour. "You gotta make her think she's doin' *you* the favor. Kelsey's near as stubborn as this ole woman, but she ain't gonna tell you no for nothin'."

"She already has," he grunted. And yet, Hannah's idea did make sense. If he could only persuade Kelsey. Coerce was probably a better word. "Don't you think your suggestion is slightly dishonest?"

"You sayin' she wouldn't be helpin' you, if you was to talk her outta sellin' that land? That ain't no lie, way ah'm thinkin'. It'd be best for everyone." Hannah harrumphed loudly as Garrett's face relaxed into a smile. She could only guess at *how* he would talk Kelsey around, but there were some things she would have to leave to chance.

"Hannah, I don't know whether you're a she-devil or a genius. How'd you get so smart?"

Waving her arm again, she shooed him out of her way, embarrassment bringing the gruff tones back to her voice. "Ah ain't so smart. You git on outta here now. Ah got work to do."

Now it was Hannah's turn to watch from the door, as this time Garrett strode toward the stable so fast it came to her mind that he hardly needed a horse. "No, sir," she muttered, turning back to her kitchen. "Ah ain't so smart."

But as her hands worked the dough into a perfect circle, a smile creased her careworn face.

Kelsey rode Ladyfair south along the river, taking care to avoid the paths that were likely to carry other people. The only time she moved onto a main road was for the ride up to the top of the escarpment. The trail she followed was a difficult one, but the last thing she wanted right now was company. Too many battles raged in her mind; too many emotions wrangled for her heart.

Ladyfair was content to let her mistress hold her to a comfortable walk, leaving Kelsey free to sort through the muddle of thoughts in her head.

Why? Why had Garrett suggested marriage? He said her reputation was at stake, but surely he was as immune to the gossip of others as she. He'd lived with it most of his life; she had only had to learn to deal with such spitefulness more recently.

And he certainly didn't love her. Though he had admitted to wanting to marry her once before, even then he hadn't mentioned love. In fact, he had made a point of telling her that both Sheldon and he had wanted her to come home. Almost as if it had been a joint decision, she mulled. He'd been fond of her, of course, but hadn't that been the extent of it?

The memory of their farewell kiss on the river's edge spun through her mind like a gossamer web. Softly clinging, yet easily whisked away. Affection, youthful desire . . . love. They were too distant, too fleeting to give credit to them now.

Now there were too many complexities to consider.

Kelsey was nearing the spot where the river made a sharp bend toward the southeast, creating an elbowlike bulge on the Canadian side. From her vantage point high above, she could see the rushing water struggle unsuccessfully to make the turn, instead swirling into a vortex formed within the circular canyon. Even at this distance, the roar sent up by the captive stream was monumental, made more imposing by its relentlessness.

Dismounting, Kelsey tied Ladyfair to one of the evergreen trees that topped the gorge and edged her way closer to the precipice. Between the rim and the trees was a grassy space of about ten feet.

It was here that she decided to stop.

When Garrett found her, she was gazing over the eddying water with such a rapt expression on her face that he hesitated to interrupt. Apparently she had not heard him ride up, but with the river overpowering even the sounds of the birds, he wasn't surprised. Carefully, he made his way toward her.

"Amazing, isn't it?"

Kelsey snapped her head around, astonishment clearly written in her wide eyes. "What are you doing here?"

"It should be pretty obvious. I followed you." Dropping to the ground beside her with contrived casualness, he followed her example by gazing out over the water. "This has always been one of my favorite spots."

"Then I'll leave you to it," she said, rising abruptly. Before she could take a step, Garrett snatched her hand with the speed of an adder.

"Don't go."

Kelsey turned to argue, but her eyes locked with his, and for a moment she was as paralyzed as if he *had* stung her with some mind-numbing drug. Though his grip on her hand was gentle, it was just as unbreakable as the spell of the whirlpool. ''I . . . I should get back. I told Hannah I'd help her make pies to take to Mrs. Fulton today, and then—''

''She's not expecting you for a while,'' Garrett interrupted, drawing her toward him. At Kelsey's puzzled look, he chuckled. ''Hannah told me to find you.''

''She did? Why?'' Suspicious, yet unable to resist his tugging hand or his persuasive smile, she knelt as far away from him as his outstretched arm would allow.

''Because we need to talk.''

In the time she had had alone to think, Kelsey had arrived at several conclusions. One was that nothing, or no one, would deter her from her decision to stay at Riverview.

The other was that she owed Garrett an explanation, one that would not only satisfy him as to why she felt so strongly about her home, but would eliminate all possibility of his wanting to marry her, no matter what his reasons. Though it shamed her to be forced to confess, Kelsey knew she had no choice.

She just hadn't thought the time would come so quickly.

''I've wanted to ask you—''

''There's something I need to—''

They both stopped, the awkward silence that followed broken only by the constant pounding of the river below.

''Go ahead,'' Garrett finally said. Confident that she no longer intended to bolt, he released her hand and leaned back against the thick trunk of an elm tree.

She glanced at him with trepidation. He looked so relaxed, one leg stretched before him, the other knee bent, his fingers laced together behind his head. If only he wouldn't look at her so intently, as if he could divine her thoughts merely by peering into her eyes!

''Hannah said I've been taking you for granted,'' she said in a rush. ''Maybe she's right, a little, but I didn't want you to think I don't appreciate everything you've done for me.''

Garrett remained still, but his heart surged with renewed hope. ''I had something to gain, too. Remember, I consider Riverview my home. But you're welcome,'' he added gently.

She parted her lips as if to speak again, but then lowered her eyes to her lap, giving him the opportunity to study her openly. In the past few weeks he had watched her regain her confidence and it filled him with mixed emotions. Sheldon's letters had revealed the full extent of Mabelle's vindictive hold on her. Garrett wanted more than anything to see Kelsey put that behind her. On the other hand, he didn't want her to stop needing him, either. Not when he was only beginning to realize how much he needed her.

''Is that all?'' he prodded.

''No-no.'' Kelsey puckered her brow, struggling to choose the right words. ''You're entitled to more of an explanation than I gave you before. I couldn't tell you when I first got home because . . .''

''Because you weren't sure you could trust me?''

She looked up gratefully. ''That's right. I was too—''

''And now you can.''

''Wh-what?''

''Trust me.''

Now I have no choice, Kelsey wanted to say, but she merely nodded her head. ''This isn't very easy for me.''

''Take your time. I'm not going anywhere.''

Somehow, that very thought *did* make her feel better, though she would have preferred him to stop staring at her as if she was going to disappear into thin air at any moment. She plucked a broad leaf from the ground next to her, appearing to study it closely, when in fact she was remembering another time when she had sat in a grassy glade with a handsome man.

''I suppose you've figured out by now that I wasn't very happy in England.''

''I gathered as much.'' Holding back the impulse to

smile, Garrett watched her tear the leaf she held to tiny shreds, then brush them from her lap emphatically. Her voice vibrated like notes from a violin, but she held her chin as firmly as ever.

"My cousins were not exactly the most gracious of hosts. I think the only reason they allowed us to stay with them so long was that Mother paid them a portion of the money Papa sent to her. Even so, Lady Margaret never let me forget that in her eyes, we were the 'poor relations.' Her attitude may have been part of the reason my mother was insistent that I make a good marriage. She said that was the only worthwhile accomplishment to which a 'lady' could aspire. You can imagine her reaction the time I told her I wanted to study to become a teacher."

For the first time since she began, Kelsey smiled, but Garrett saw that it was a smile tinged with sadness and regret. His chest grew tight with anger toward the woman who had dared to steal away a young girl's dreams.

"Lord and Lady Kelsey sponsored me at any number of balls, but after three seasons I believe they had quite given up on me. There I was, nearly nineteen years old and not an eligible suitor in sight."

"Were the men all blind?" Garrett asked abruptly. It occurred to him that it was during that time that he had approached Mabelle himself.

"Only human," Kelsey shrugged. "I had made up my mind not to have anyone if I couldn't—" She broke off, realizing her near slip.

"If you couldn't . . . ?"

"If I couldn't choose my own husband," she finished quickly. "Mother and Lady Margaret rarely asked my opinion of any of the gentlemen they introduced to me." Her lips curved playfully. "But they never could figure out why none payed a second call."

Garrett was almost afraid to ask, but curiosity outweighed caution. "What did you do to the poor sots, pray tell?"

"Not much," Kelsey said, waving her hand dismissively. "A little pepper here, a misplaced pin cushion there . . . it's not difficult to dissuade a person who isn't all that keen on pursuing you in the first place. I saved the most convincing act for the few gentlemen who proved to be extraordinarily persistent."

"Which was . . . ?" Too intrigued to remember that at least one of the gentlemen in question had eventually won her over, Garrett grinned encouragement.

"Keeping in mind that many Europeans still consider the United States to be an uncivilized wilderness, it was only natural to regale my suitors with tales of life in the wilds, including the time I was bitten by a rabid squirrel while out picking corn with my Indian friends."

"Bitten by a squirrel?" His astonishment gave way to sheer amusement when she rolled her eyes and chattered her teeth in an adept imitation of the furry creatures. Garrett laughed out loud at her antics.

"Of course I assured them each that my fits passed quickly, and were never more frequent than twice a day. It almost always worked." This last statement hung in the air between them like a cloud, gloomy and near bursting.

Finally, Garrett managed to gird himself enough to bring up the subject they'd both avoided. "I already know that you fell in love, despite your attempts to avoid it. Won't you tell me about this paragon?"

Kelsey winced inwardly at his disparaging tone, but she managed a weak smile. "In many ways he reminded me of you," she chided gently. "He was charming, irreverent, and not the least bit fazed by my acute case of rabies. In fact, Robert swore to me that he'd almost caught it himself during a hunt, but had managed to defend himself by biting the fox first." She paused, reluctant to add to his unease, but determined to continue what she'd started. "That's when I knew we would get on together."

"He sounds . . . he sounds rather unconventional." That was the most charitable comment Garrett could offer.

"That's what I liked best about him," Kelsey confirmed. "Robert had a way of laughing in the face of convention that drove people to distraction. And yet, he was considered a most eligible bachelor. Fortunately for him, maintaining the considerable wealth he was born with was one of the conventions he did believe in." She paused, then added quietly. "Marriage, however, was one he did not."

Garrett fumed silently. It was clear now that this cad had stolen her heart and then broken it. It was no wonder she had sworn off men altogether. "I think I understand now," he whispered in a hoarse voice, "why you don't want to marry anyone." *Why you don't want to marry me,* his thoughts echoed.

"No! No, you don't!"

Kelsey's vehement denial took him by surprise, and he looked up sharply to see tears pooling in her dark eyes.

"Don't you see? I *can't* marry now!" Her voice shook with self-reproach. "Not after the way I disgraced myself."

And now Garrett did understand, though he almost wished he didn't. Every muscle in his body knotted up like ropes, seeming to pull him in all directions. He didn't know whether he was angry at her, or angry *for* her. But before he could bring himself to respond, Kelsey drew in a shaking breath to speak.

"You warned me once about . . . about men. You told me some men wouldn't stop with a kiss, but I didn't pay any attention until it was too late."

"You were young, Kelsey," he ground out. "Young and naive. But you aren't the first young girl to make such a mistake, and I daresay you won't be the last."

Against his derision, she might have held out. His gentleness, however, breeched every defense she had. The tears she had blinked away now spilled freely, scalding her cheeks with their bitterness.

"H-how can you . . . how c-can you bear to look at me," she whispered guiltily, "when I can't even s-stand m-myself?"

"Because when I look at you," he began, "I see a

great deal of strength and character. The shame you feel is only in your heart, Kelsey. It's not written on our forehead or sewn onto your dress."

"But it did kill my mother!"

"Only if she allowed it to, or wanted it to, which I daresay she did. To regret your foolishness is one thing. But you can't let guilt cripple you for the rest of your life."

Kelsey raised her head defiantly. "Then tell me it doesn't make any difference to you!

"It doesn't make any difference to me."

Not until after he said the words did Garrett realize that he meant them. It was obvious, however, that Kelsey didn't believe him. With the back of her hand she scrubbed the last of her tears from her eyes, then peered at him doubtfully.

"Why not?"

The truth nearly sprang from his tightly pressed lips, but he held it back, knowing instinctively that she wouldn't believe that either. Instead, he remembered the wisdom of Hannah's advice, and his original purpose in seeking Kelsey out. "Because I still need to ask for your help," he replied evenly, "and the past has nothing to do with it."

She regarded him suspiciously. "With what?"

"With the present. Or the future. It's the future I'm thinking of, Kelsey, yours and mine . . . and Riverview's."

When he saw that at least she seemed to be listening, Garrett sat up straighter, resting his elbows on his knees. "I want you to reconsider what I said before. You were too surprised to think your answer through. That was my fault, I suppose; please hear me out now."

His compelling tone drew her baffled gaze, but it was pure impulse that made her jerk farther away from him and scoot backwards on her bottom. "I haven't changed my mind."

Before she could get too far away, he reached for her

hand. "Please listen to me, Kelsey. It's the least you can do."

That much was true, she told herself, not wanting to admit how good his warm hand felt around her ice-cold fingers. She nodded warily. "I'm listening."

"Good. Because we haven't much time to reach an agreement on this. What I said earlier about the businessmen boycotting us is a real concern, but it isn't the only one. I'm more worried about Bart Ogden closing in on the men who are operating this last station of the Underground Railroad."

Kelsey wrinkled her brow. "Are you talking about the committee's railroad? The one planned for the tourists?"

"Hardly." Garrett smiled. "It's a sort of code name for the people who work together to help fugitive slaves reach freedom. The underground part is because it's secret. Safe houses are often called stations, and the men who run them are conductors. Thus, Underground Railroad."

"I see. But what does that have to do with Riverview? I don't want you to put it in danger."

"I won't, and I haven't." *Not yet, anyway,* Garrett thought to himself. "But Ogden remains suspicious, and the only way I can fight him is to throw him off track. Our getting married—and soon—would accomplish that, since you've already stated once in public that you don't condone antislavery activities."

"I never said that!" Kelsey spouted, before realizing she'd played right into his hands. Garrett's half-smile was proof.

"What you said at the Delbert's party and what you meant can be construed differently. The point is, that's how other people, Ogden in particular, perceive you. It should be easy enough to nurture the seeds you've already planted in their minds." He picked a stone from the ground beside him and weighed it in one hand, hefting it twice before tossing it over the cliff's edge a few yards away.

Kelsey found the action disturbing, but not as disturbing as the distant clattering the rock made as it bounced down the side of the gorge. Holding her breath, she waited for the final splash that would signal the end of its descent, but she could hear nothing except the continuous rumble of the current. It drowned out the sound of Garrett's stone, if it had made it to the bottom at all.

She drew air into her aching lungs. "If I do this—allow people to make this assumption, I mean—then Bart Ogden will leave us alone?"

Garrett wished it were so simple. "I hope so. Will you help me?"

Risking a glance in his direction, Kelsey found him watching her pensively. She didn't believe for a moment that he couldn't somehow manage to thwart Ogden without her playing a part in it, but what he said did make sense. On the other hand, she still hadn't changed her mind about endangering her hold on Riverview. "I just don't think this would work," she sighed, shaking her head. "We're too different. If we married, it would be for all the wrong reasons."

"Wrong? According to what standard?"

There was a touch of bitter irony in his voice, just enough to cause Kelsey's throat to thicken. Certainly he didn't think she was refusing him on the grounds of his background. And yet, he had said almost the same thing to her when he thought she had turned down his proposal before.

She laid her hand on his sleeve, touching him voluntarily for the first time since the day Little Lady was born. "It's just that . . . well, the whole thing sounds so mercenary!"

One lip twisting upward, Garrett covered her hand with his. "Many great unions were begun with less. You'll keep your home, and I'll avoid possible arrest."

"But all my possessions would revert to you. What good would that do me?"

"I'll sign the house over to you, if that's what you want. On one condition. The property, *especially* the strip alongside the river, must not be sold." When she appeared to question this unusual request, Garrett explained, ''Right now, that stretch of the river is isolated. If the town council gets their hands on it, there'll be a constant stream of tourists clambering up and down that riverbank. It'll be crowded, spoiled . . .''

''And difficult for runaway slaves to hide.'' It was clear enough to Kelsey what he was getting at. She wouldn't, however, let him force her into a promise that was at cross-purposes to her own goal. ''I didn't want to sell the land anyway,'' she warned, ''but that doesn't mean I condone the use of Riverview as one of your 'stations.' What's the use of going through with this if you're arrested anyway?''

Garrett's hand tightened briefly. ''*If* I'm arrested for aiding and abetting the escape of 'human property,' the usual sentence is six months in jail and a fine of one thousand dollars. Not a small punishment, but one I'm willing to face. You, however, could not be held responsible or liable.''

''Six months!'' Kelsey's heartbeat quickened. ''I had no idea!''

He couldn't resist a grin. ''You'd miss me, then?''

His blue eyes glittered irresistibly, and Kelsey realized suddenly that it sounded as if she'd agreed to his peculiar proposal. She tried to pull her hand away, but his grip on it was unbreakable. ''You're purposely confusing the issue!'' she accused. ''I won't be hoodwinked into anything, least of all a marriage I don't even want!''

''Don't want?'' The smile slipped away from Garrett's face, replaced by a look of such intensity that Kelsey's insides coiled as tightly as a serpent preparing to strike. Though only their hands touched, it was as if a current of electricity raced from his palm to hers, bonding them inexorably together.

''Don't want, love? Or *can't* want?''

''What's the difference!'' Snatching her hand away, Kelsey started to rise.

''There's a great deal of difference, if you'll only look beyond your stubbornness to see. We were meant to be together. Perhaps not in quite the way we once wished, but at least in a way that can still mean something to both of us. We have much to build on, Kelsey. We can give one another a good life, happiness, children. . . .

"Look at me!" He had followed her to her feet, and now grasped her elbow, spinning her around to face him. But instead of mutiny, her expression was filled with such abject misery that he was momentarily stunned. Her dark eyes shimmered with a sadness so profound that he dropped his hands to his sides in surrender.

She could barely raise her eyes to meet his. "I can never have children, Garrett. I . . . I'm sorry. But now you can understand why I have to say no."

It was as if the blast of a shotgun had caught him full force in the chest. Shock left him speechless, even while his mind was already pulling together the threads of clues that had led to this all along.

The blank look on his face was just the reaction she'd expected, and so was the way he roughly swept his hand through his hair. What she didn't anticipate was his next statement.

"All right, then, no children. That doesn't alter anything else."

"Doesn't alter—?" Now it was her turn to grope for words. "But that means . . . you can't want . . ."

"I want you. And despite your many objections, I know what you want, too. Why do you deny how we feel about one another?"

"How *you* feel!" she whispered weakly. "Not me!"

"They why did you tell Hannah that you love me?"

Her face grew heated. "You heard that?"

At least Garrett had the grace to look sheepish, though it passed quickly. Kelsey shook her head with disbelief, stunned at having been caught. "That means nothing," she insisted lamely. "I meant that I loved you . . . like a brother."

Garrett wasn't sure whether to laugh out loud or shake her until her teeth rattled. Instead he clasped her shoulders tightly, drawing her against him with gentle force.

"Is this how a brother would hold you?" he murmured, wrapping his arms around her when she tried to wriggle free. He clamped one hand on the nape of her neck, holding her head still while the other pressed into the small of her back, propelling her closer. "Is this brotherly affection?" he taunted.

Kelsey struggled to keep herself rigid, but his strength was nearly as overwhelming as her own traitorous body. Every inch of her burned from the heat of his hard-muscled length pressed against her. "Oh, Garrett," she pleaded weakly. "P-please don't do this. It . . . it won't prove a thing."

"Then indulge me." His voice was a taunting growl.

She had expected his kiss to be hard and demanding, but instead it was gently emphatic, more irresistible than all the brute force in the world. She tried not to kiss him back, but her own lips betrayed her, opening wantonly to allow him access. She told her hands to push him away, but instead they circled his broad shoulders and twined through the thick curls brushing his collar. Her mind screamed that this could not be happening, but the rising torment in her blood warned her that it was, and that it was happening with a speed and ferocity she could not have imagined.

And then, quite suddenly, it was over. She couldn't hold back the gasp of disappointment that escaped her when he broke off with a strangled groan. Still holding her tight to him, he brushed her temple lightly with his lips, moving his mouth over her eyelids and cheeks as lightly as a spring mist. His ragged breathing gradually steadied, and his embrace gentled.

"Can you deny, now, that you want me, too?" he murmured.

With no more resistance than a newborn kitten, Kelsey leaned against him, tears gathering in the corners of her eyes. "Oh, Garrett, I do want you. But . . ."

"But nothing." He cupped her chin, raising her head until her gaze met his. "Consider this one of the pleasant bonuses to our bargain."

"But kissing is only part . . . there's more . . ." Her hands grew clammy just remembering, and she closed her eyes helplessly.

"Yes, there is more." Tenderness spiraled through him at her shyness, even while he silently cursed the man or woman who had instilled this kind of fear in Kelsey. "There's so much more than you've ever dreamed of, my love. Pleasures beyond your wildest imagination. Do you trust me?"

There. He was asking her again. Deep inside, Kelsey was at war with herself. Garrett had never let her down before, but then, he didn't know as much about her as he thought.

"But you agreed not to . . . that we wouldn't have children?"

His rich chuckle sent shivers of anticipation down Kelsey's spine and sent a blush rushing to her cheeks. "There are ways, my love. There are ways."

He was tearing down the wall between them, brick by brick, and she was beginning to run out of arguments. Beginning to wonder why she had even begun to think she could win.

"Any more reasons?" he teased.

Chewing on her lower lip, Kelsey frowned. "We don't always agree on everything."

"What two people do?"

She sighed helplessly, making one last feeble attempt. "You think I'm too stubborn and prideful."

"I can live with that."

"You're an early riser and I like to sleep late."

At that moment, Garrett knew he had won. Seized by a profound sense of triumph, yet loath to startle her further with his exuberance, he instead turned her toward the edge of the precipice, where far below the river pounded against its banks. With his hands wrapped around her middle and his jaw nestled against the side of her head, he held her close, enfolding her in his arms the way he wanted to encompass her into his life.

"Look down, Kelsey," he whispered, directing her

hesitant gaze to the whirlpool swirling beneath them. "There's something between us—there has been since the beginning, more powerful than that current. I've been fighting it for so long I can't even remember why I was trying. All I know is that I feel like we've been swept up by something beyond the control of us both. I don't want to fight anymore, love. I don't want to fight it."

His voice mesmerized her, drawing her into its warm haven as surely as the vortex below captured and held whatever chanced into its relentless stream. Though they stood less than three feet from the edge of the world, Kelsey felt safer than ever before. The hardness of his chest was like a fortress behind her; the gentle clasp of his hands at her waist burned with the promise of what lay ahead. She was filled with the dawning knowledge that she had no choice but to trust Garrett this last time, because one thing was gloriously, excruciatingly clear.

If she did not, she would regret it for the rest of her life.

20

There were not many places on earth where the gods still roamed, and many men, calling themselves enlightened, refused to acknowledge that they ever had. But at the place named Niagara—*thunder of waters*—by the ancient Iroquois, it was easy to believe there were forces at work beyond the realm of nature.

For thosands of years the Iroquois had worshiped at her brink, sending sacrifical maidens, and less valued goods as well, into her awesome and demanding clutches. When white men first viewed the falls on the river Niagara, they fell reverently to their knees, dumbstruck by its majesty. Now thousands upon thousands of touring visitors lined her banks every year, struggling to grasp the enormity of countless tons of water pouring two hundred feet into the churning mist below.

The tiny city of Niagara Falls, perched on the edge of the river's high banks, was just realizing the potential value of catering to these astounded guests, and thus had recently taken its first steps toward competing with Saratoga Springs for the crowds of wealthy sightseers.

Kelsey was amazed by the changes to the city since her last visit when she was thirteen, but more so by what had not changed. She had expected age and experience to have temepered her excitement, but when she and Garrett approached the river, she was again overwhelmed by the tremendous power passing just beyond their reach. "So much water!" she exclaimed breathlessly, transfixed by the rushing flow.

They stood on an embankment that jutted out over the

river at the top of the falls, from which they could look across the Niagara to the Canadian side or gaze down into the churning waters that plunged beneath their feet to the river basin far below. Several other sightseers stopped near them, but Kelsey had glanced only briefly at the tophatted men and elegantly dressed ladies. The myriad rainbows created by the sunshine and mist were far more fascinating.

Garrett leaned closer to her ear so she could hear him over the cascade's incessant roar. "Whenever I come on business I stop here first and last. I keep wondering if it'll run out."

"Me too! When I was small I thought all the water in the world ended up here."

"And not in your cornfield?" he asked, grinning slyly.

It amazed Kelsey that she could laugh in return, when just a few weeks ago she would have sworn she would never laugh again. But Garrett had asked her to trust him, and so far he hadn't let her down.

Only three days had passed since they had returned to Riverview after reaching their agreement. Immediately upon arriving at the house, Garrett had filled out a bank draft for the remaining balance on the loan. Then, first thing Monday morning they had taken the buggy into Lewiston together, where they stopped to have George Delbert act as notary in the signing over of Riverview into Kelsey's name. She had breathed a sigh of relief when the plump attorney informed her that Justin had taken his mother to Lockport for a two-day shopping excursion. She was not yet ready to face his certain disappointment.

Though George carefully perused each and every document involved, it was clear he was satisfied that Garrett was at last returning Riverview to its rightful owner.

By silent consent, neither made mention of their plans to marry: Kelsey because she wanted to cherish the secret knowledge to herself for as long as possible, Garrett because he wasn't sure whether George Delbert's reaction would be a favorable one, and he didn't want anything to throw doubts into Kelsey's head.

For the same reason, he had urged her to agree to a private ceremony the next day, performed in Judge Crandall's chambers.

She had not anticipated having second thoughts, but now that the deed was done, Kelsey was tormented by doubt. In a sense, she had not saved Riverview at all, but had merely allowed Garrett to do so, she derided herself. Perhaps her mother had been right to tell her that marriage was the only worthy accomplishment a woman could achieve. Her futuile attempt to manage the farm certainly hadn't proved Mabelle wrong.

The problem was that, even though Garrett had offered her a chance she had long since given up as hopeless, Kelsey wasn't sure she could succeed at marriage any more than she had at farming. She had let him convince her it was the only reasonable choice for them both, but now she wished she had listened to her head instead of her heart.

"Seen enough?" Garrett inquired, breaking into her thoughts.

Kelsey laughed nervously. "We just got here. Can't we enjoy the view a little longer?"

"For a few more minutes then," he conceded. "I want to check into the Cascade House before dark. We can come back later, if you wish. The waterfall isn't going anywhere."

"Neither is the hotel." Uncertain why she was suddenly so reluctant, Kelsey closed her eyes, letting the sound and scent of the water surround her. The constant rumble reminded her of approaching thunder, only no storm was ever so violent and enduring. The mist created by the pounding stream rose to envelop her senses, and she breathed deeply of the pure, moist air. It had not the tanginess of the ocean, but was filled with a rich, cleansing scent all its own.

"The river is life itself," Garrett said behind her, his voice low and melodic. "Deep and endless, in some places turbulent, in others calm, but always moving and changing. Love is that way, too."

Kelsey forced herself not to lean back against him. It was too easy to lose herself in his hypnotic spell. She had already fallen victim to his charm by agreeing to this, but she couldn't forget that it was a marriage of convenience for them both. "I always thought of love as a flame," she contradicted. "A flame burns hot for a short while, but eventually it dies out. And the river *did* stop once. Remember when it froze up one year?"

Garrett remembered, but just now he was more intent on finding out why she had turned skittish at the last minute than on recalling the spring several years before, when an ice floe had dammed up the river. That was how she was acting, he thought uncomfortably. Like she was holding her emotions behind a frozen wall. That wall, he knew, was part fear. It was a wall he was determined to breach.

"Fire can be rekindled, Kelsey. And the ice in the river," he added in a slow drawl, "eventually melted. It's time to go."

They were no longer talking in generalities and they both knew it. Kelsey felt a wave of helplessness wash through her as she succumbed once more to the seductive command of Garrett's voice. Maybe he was right about love being like the river, she thought as he led her away from the water's edge. Her fingers automatically tightened on his arm when she turned her back on the powerful stream.

She certainly felt as if she had jumped into a dangerous current that was only sweeping her faster and faster into unknown waters. It somehow helped, though, to have Garrett's strength to cling to.

But the questions still raged through her mind, blending with the cacophony of the river and the damp, cloying air. Was he there to rescue her? Or would she learn that he was the one who had pushed her in?

* * *

Kelsey paced the floor of her hotel room from the bed to the window and back again, all the while plucking nervously at the lace trim above her breasts. Oh, Lord! she implored silently. Why doesn't he just hurry and get this over with?

She looked askance at the huge tester bed in the center of the room, which somehow managed to appear both comfortable and forbidding at the same time. Furtively, she glanced in the direction of the window again, almost hoping to find it wide open and offering her easy escape. She sighed. There was no use delaying the inevitable. If she were going to change her mind, she should have done it before now.

Self-consciously, her fingertips flew to one of the thin lace straps that skimmed her shoulder. A rush of indecision raced through her. Made of silk so finely woven it was almost transparent, the sheer gown clung to her in the most indecent places, the lacy bodice revealing far more of her cleavage than it hid. And the color, instead of providing protection, was a pale rose that actually enhanced every shadow and curve of the flesh beneath it. She'd never in her life seen anything like it. There was no doubt in Kelsey's mind, however, that Garrett had realized the gown's capabilities completely when he had chosen it for her that day, along with several other outfits.

"This is insane," she whispered disparagingly, flinging herself toward the bureau with every intention of finding something more comfortable—an old blanket would do nicely—to wear. But before she had taken three steps, a firm rap on the connecting door to Garrett's room sent her whirling around.

"Come in," she yelled automatically, forgetting in her nervousness that she was standing square in front of the lamp. She remembered, though, the instant the door swung open and Garrett entered.

He paused in the doorway, and for a fleeting second Kelsey wondered if he had forgotten something. But then she saw his eyes flicker with an intense light that sent a shiver of apprehension skipping down her spine. She raised her arms to cross them in front of her, but before she could cover herself, Garrett had shoved the door shut behind him and was moving toward her, clasping her wrists gently.

"Don't," he whispered, his voice more compelling than even his burning gaze, which wandered appreciatively down the entire length of her body. He may as well have been touching her, the way her skin tingled and puckered beneath his perusal. His eyes continued their loving caress, even after he released her hands, allowing her to turn away.

"You're not afraid, are you?"

"No," she lied. If he'd asked her if she was nervous, she might have admitted as much, but he had already seen too much of her fear. Besides, the sooner this was started, the sooner it would be over with.

She had stopped near the foot of the bed. Now she faced him again, raising her chin slowly as she let her hands fall back to her sides. Unconsciously she squared her shoulders, unaware until it was too late that the motion only emphasized the high thrust of her breasts, now threatening to burst from the lacy bodice. It took all her willpower not to wrap her arms around herself again, but instead she managed to meet his blatant stare, even though the blood rushed through her veins so fast it was making her dizzy.

"What t-took you so long?" she stammered hoarsely, not sure whether her tone was seductive or not, but quite certain from the expression of barely suppressed desire on Garrett's face that it didn't matter one whit.

"I would have changed faster if I'd known you waited so eagerly," he said, his smile tight, as if he were having trouble controlling his own voice. For the first time, Kelsey noticed that he had traded his frock coat and cravat for a shirt of fine ivory lawn. The thin fabric draped his shoulders in a manner that was graceful, yet supremely masculine. A row of small buttons remained unfastened to a point halfway down to his belt buckle, offering her a glimpse of the hard, flat plane of his chest. With his tight-fitting trousers and highly polished boots, he could have passed for a buccaneer—all he needed was a sword in his belt and a patch over one eye, she thought. Few women would have complained about being taken hostage by the likes of Garrett O'Neill!

"Why are you looking at me that way?" His tone had gentled again, but a trace of amusement laced his words.

"What way?"

"As if I were a wild beast about to devour my dinner."

Kelsey laughed nervously, perching on the edge of the bed. "Is that how it looked? I was thinking of you as a ravishing pirate, but come to think of it, you do look more like a lion with that mane of gold hair."

"And do you feel as if you're about to be ravished?"

Kelsey shrugged. "I suppose so, but the word ravishing sounds far too romantic for what's going to happen."

Garrett suppressed a surge of exasperation at her pragmatic tone. She acted as if this meant less than a childish kiss.

But something in the way her gaze fluttered from here to there, not lighting anywhere for long—especially anywhere near him—showed him the true extent of her distress.

"I told you before, I won't do anything you don't want me to. But I thought—" He hesitated. "I thought since you knew what to expect . . ."

"That was different." Kelsey turned her head so he couldn't see her shamefaced grimace. How could she tell him she'd been too intoxicated to remember much of that single incident with Robert, other than the horrendous stab of pain and the incredible sense of guilt that had followed? It was bad enough that she had been used in that way, but to admit that she had been unable to resist somehow added to her dishonor.

Garrett felt as if his heart had stopped, then resumed its beat at a pace much slower than before. His arms were leaden weights at his side, and though he took several steps toward Kelsey, it seemed as though her trembling form still hovered in the distance.

He lashed himself inwardly for reminding her of the other man she had loved. All his attempts to woo her would be for naught if he kept dredging up her past like the heavy silt from the bottom of the river, allowing it to muddy what lay between them. "Yes, it is different," he said thickly, sitting beside her. "But that doesn't mean it can't be sweet and good."

His long fingers encircled her wrist gently, raising it. He turned her hand over, pressing a kiss into the palm of her hand that made tremors cascade through her with the pounding fury of the waterfall. Her own fingertips curled inward, tracing his jaw tentatively.

"I-I hope so," she breathed, unable to say more as he lifted his azure eyes to hers. His ardent gaze spoke of a need so profound that she blinked back tears. Perhaps she had lost her chance to experience that once-in-a-lifetime kind of love, she thought achingly, but maybe having someone need her, for whatever reason, was almost as good. God knew she needed him.

Garrett drank in the sight of her as if she were a healing draught, his hands absorbing the petal-softness of her skin as he caressed the length of her arm. The flesh of his palms tingled as they skimmed her lightly, cupping her smoth shoulders protectively and spreading to encompass the narrow breadth of her bare back. Slowly, he pulled her closer, until her gasping breaths played against his chin and her silk-covered breasts brushed his shirt. Impatience burned at him like a fiery whip but he quelled it, his desire to bring pleasure to her greater at this moment than his own yearning.

"Kelsey, love. Open your eyes and look at me."

His words were tender probes, compelling her to respond. When she lifted her eyelids cautiously, it was to find him watching her with that familiar little half-smile he always wore when he was uncertain what to say next. This glimpse of his vulnerability bolstered her courage.

He cleared the thickness from his throat. "You must . . . *should* tell me what pleases you, darling. Show me what you want."

What she wanted? Kelsey might have laughed out loud, except that a wave of longing pounded through her, pushing away everything in its wake except the feel of his hands scorching her flesh through the thin fabric of her gown. She couldn't tell him what she wanted because she didn't know, but what he was doing to her now felt so impossibly wonderful that she didn't want him to stop, either. "Oh, Garrett," she moaned when he swept one hand around her midriff to cradle her breast. With the pad of his thumb, he brushed the point of silk until her nipple turned pebble-hard against the cloth.

She twisted toward him, unknowingly pressing for more of the same, and somehow she was on his lap, with her own hands beginning a faltering exploration of the flesh beneath his open shirt. Her lips parted as she exhaled a pent-up breath.

"Like this, my love? Like this?"

As if through a distant fog, she heard Garrett's insistent plea, but she could only answer him with another stifled moan as his mouth took over where his hands had stopped.

Now her parted lips found his brow, and she inhaled his scent and tasted his skin as if it were sweet nectar. Her fingers were nestled in the soft waves of his hair as she held him dearly, her fear for what would follow overcome by her fear that he would stop.

And Garrett did stop, but only long enough to ease her onto the bed so that he could dim the lamp and remove his boots. Kelsey's eyes reflected the light like twin moons, no longer filled with trepidation, but radiating her trust and newfound desire. With as much patience as he could muster, he lowered himself to the bed beside her.

"God, you are beautiful," he murmured, his gaze sweeping her from her tousled hair to her dainty feet, then up over the length of her calf. The hem of her nightgown was twisted around her thighs, and he slipped his hand beneath the lacy trim, beginning a smooth ascent toward heaven.

"Garrett, I—" Her words were cut off when his mouth claimed hers, his gentle kiss driving all thought of protest from her mind. With the tip of his tongue he traced her lips until she shivered with delight and want, finally opening to him wholeheartedly.

She heard the unsteady rasp of his breath and her own short gasps, punctuated by tiny moans that forced their way through her constricted lungs. When his hand slipped upward along her thighs her muscles tightened instinctively, but his gentleness urged them to part.

"Don't be afraid, my love," he breathed. "I won't . . ."

His words were muffled as he ran his mouth along the side of her neck, fanning the hot fire inside of her. The tremors that shook her had nothing to do with fear any longer, and though her mind dimly imagined that Garrett was about to say he wouldn't hurt her, another part of her welcomed it, welcomed anything that would assuage the fiery need that was rising toward a blazing crescendo.

And then, it seemed his hands were everywhere. Stroking, cupping, probing. She felt herself melt into liquid fire, ignited in the pit of her stomach and burning ever outward, until the flames licked at her groin and turned her blood into molten lava. And through it all she clung to Garrett—his broad shoulders were her anchor in a sea of flame; his voice, inciting her with whispers like sparks, was her beacon.

The heat inside her fanned yet higher, surrounding, engulfing his sweet intrusion until she arched her back convulsively, greedily, grasping for each wave of exquisite pleasure before it slipped beyond her reach. And he continued to bring them to her, until at last she cried out in surrender, her body growing still and the raging inferno giving way to warmth and wetness.

She trembled within his embrace, but Garrett felt her gradually relax. Slowly, tenderly, he moved his hand upward, his fingers splayed across the satiny skin of her stomach.

He willed his hands to remain steady, though his jaw

was clenched so tightly he could hear his teeth grind together like the planks in a ship's hold. Kelsey's erratic breaths stirred upon his chin. It was a potent lure that he forced himself to ignore. To kiss her now would be to lose himself completely, and the echo of his promise was all that kept him from giving in to the consuming need that throbbed through his aching loins.

Nestled against his side, Kelsey listened to the staggering beats of his heart as it thrashed around inside his chest. Her hand curled limply within the folds of his shirt, and one leg was thrown over his thigh, her nightgown pushed high on her hips, no longer a hindrance.

"How do you feel?"

Garrett's drawl rolled through her head like a sunshiny day. "Wonderful," she whispered, a lazy smile stretching her kiss-swollen lips. She yawned contentedly.

"We've had a busy day. You should get some sleep."

Utterly replete, Kelsey did not notice at once that his gentle tone hid a sharp-edged discontent. It was not until she shifted in his hold and brushed her arm against his belt buckle that she realized that he was as fully clothed as when he'd come in.

He saw the direction of her startled glance and reached to brush a stray wisp of hair from her cheek. "I made a promise, love, and I intend to keep it. Had you forgotten?"

"N-no. It's just that . . . what about you?" Her face was already flushed from passion; now it grew red with shame. She'd been so consumed by what had happened to her, she hadn't given a thought to Garrett's pleasure. Just as she hadn't given a thought to the possibility of becoming pregnant tonight. She had trusted him implicitly and he had not abused her trust.

His heart flipped over at the confused look on her face. Tipping her chin up with his knuckle, he smiled ruefully. "Consider this my wedding gift to you. I wanted to bring you pleasure. Was I right in guessing that your experience before was somewhat . . . lacking?"

Kelsey frowned pensively. "Yesss, but—"

"Then this truly was special?"

Special didn't come close to describing the way she felt. "Oh, Garrett. Nothing like this has ever happened to me before. But I feel so . . . so selfish." His chuckle warmed her, but not as much as the look of tender possessiveness in his sapphire eyes. How could she ever have doubted that he cared for her?

"Enjoy it. Tomorrow may be a different story altogether. But for tonight you deserve some rest. I know you haven't been sleeping well."

That much was true, but Kelsey doubted she would rest easy tonight either, knowing that she hadn't come close to holding up her end of their bargain. The problem was, her knowledge of the love act was rudimentary, at best. She didn't have the vaguest idea what he had in mind for tomorrow night. Her "experience"—as he had put it—with Robert had been severely diminished by her semiconscious state at the time.

Sensing her bewilderment, Garrett carefully disentangled himself and eased off the bed, drawing the wrinkled coverlet over her.

"Where are you going?" Even in her groggy state Kelsey was surprised.

"Just into the other room." He traced a light caress across her lips, but it nearly cost him his restraint. He didn't know what he would do if she asked him to stay; he only knew that if he didn't leave now, he couldn't be held accountable for his own actions. Bending to retrieve his boots, he cast one last, lingering gaze at the figure on the bed. Kelsey's languorous stretch only increased his aching desire, but her fluttering eyelids and weary sigh brought a smile to his mouth, held rigid against his own needs.

"Sleep well, love," he murmured softly, glad that at least one of them would.

21

Justin huddled back into the comfort of his leather chair as he studied Kelsey with bleak eyes. Though he gave no outward sign of distress, his gut cramped painfully at the sight of her sitting across from him. *Good God!* he swore silently. *What had she gotten herself into?*

She wore a stylish gown of sprigged muslin and matching gauze shawl that was more decorative than functional, as befitted the warm day. A wide-brimmed straw hat lay on the cushion next to her, its yellow streamers dangling to the floor. The picture of fashion, he thought miserably. But beneath his silent perusal she fretted nervously, patting at the chignon pinned at the nape of her neck.

"I wish you'd say *something,*" she complained softly. "Justin . . . ?"

"What would you like me to say? That I'm happy you turned me down in favor of a lowbred Irishman? That I don't think you're making the biggest mistake of your life?"

Kelsey bit her lower lip and sighed. "I hoped you would wish me well. We've been friends for a long time, and I never . . . I never lied about my feelings for you."

"That much is true," Justin conceded, "which is why I do you the same courtesy now by telling you exactly how *I* feel. What, pray tell, were you thinking?"

She wished he wouldn't use that courtroom tone with her, as if she were a criminal and he the judge. She had stopped to call on him out of a sense of fairness, but she was of no mind to submit herself to an interrogation.

Besides, she couldn't possibly tell him that Garrett had aroused her passion to the point where she couldn't have refused if she wanted to!

"I was thinking," she retorted saucily, "of the very things you've been pointing out to me these past few weeks. It's not as if I haven't been chaperoned—"

"A negro slave hardly qualifies!"

"Ex-slave! And Hannah is certainly as qualified as anyone. But since others persist in holding the same opinion as you, it's far more proper that Garrett and I are married than to have continued our living arrangements as they were.

"And then there's the simple matter of the businesses. I can't manage the farm without him, he and I share the others, so marriage was the more expedient method of handling our affairs."

"You wouldn't lower yourself to marry me for financial reasons, but you've done so with O'Neill. My God, Kelsey! Aside from the fact that he hasn't a social connection worth two bits, there's every chance in the world that he's up to his neck in the same idiotic crusade your father was involved in."

"That's not true!" She wasn't sure which disturbed her most, his slur against Garrett or the implied one against Sheldon. But now Kelsey's irritation was truly becoming a force to contend with. "I won't listen to this, Justin. I didn't come here to be insulted, but to ask for a favor because I thought you were my friend!"

"Here, wait! Don't leave!" Jumping to his feet as she furiously gathered her things, Justin reached her side before she could rise from her chair. "I didn't mean to hurt your feelings, darling. Believe me, I *am* your friend. Please let's not let this come between us."

Lowering his chin a notch, Justin peered at her through puppy-dog eyes. Kelsey struggled to quell the anger quivering through her like a taut bowstring. Anger not so much at him as at herself for hoping this would not happen. Releasing her pent-up breath in a rush, she frowned. "Friend or not, if you persist in this kind of behavior I shall not call on you again. I won't listen to slander against my husband, Justin. I can't."

"I see," Justin replied slowly, hunkering down on a chair.

She wasn't at all sure that he did see, but how could she make him understand something she wasn't sure she understood herself? "I know this came as a great surprise to you," she consoled gently. "I didn't come here to hurt your feelings either, or to make you think that our friendship is threatened."

"Then why did you come?"

His tone was so desolate and hopeful all at once that Kelsey's heart went out to him. Truly he had reacted so badly *because* he felt protective toward her.

Which only made the small deceit she was about to commit seem larger by the moment. But she had promised Garrett, and she was bound to see it through. She drew a bolstering breath.

"Actually, it's the very thing you just brought up," she said in a rush. "I know very well that my father ruined his health and his fortune by committing himself to this cause, as you put it. All the more reason why I want nothing to do with it. And Garrett has also promised to stay clear of these people and their activities."

Justin snapped his head up, obviously startled by her statement. The Adam's apple in his throat jumped like an acrobat and he swallowed thickly. From disbelief, she surmised.

"As well he should."

"The trouble is, many of the people who knew my father—that horrible Ogden man, too—assume that Garrett is somehow involved. You have so much influence in this town, Justin. If you were to accept our marriage, then perhaps others would as well and the speculation might die down. It would be a tremendous help to m—to us," she amended hastily.

He was tempted to bellow out his repugnance there and then, but Justin forced himself to study her face calmly, letting his own turbulent feelings settle while he tried to discern hers. At first glance her expression was as composed and tranquil as a summer sky, but beneath it he could see the roiling clouds that heralded a storm of violence and power. They told him—as if he hadn't already guessed—that Kelsey was suffering from some great disturbance of her own.

Relief welled up in him, for it could only be one thing. Some way or another, O'Neill had coerced her into marrying him against her will. "Was that part of your deal?" he asked angrily. "That you would provide him with instant acceptance?"

Kelsey recoiled at his bitterness, but she had a hard time faulting him since his accusation wasn't so far from the truth. It was no use trying to convince him that Garrett had married her for love; Justin wouldn't believe it any more than she did. "Is it so wrong to enter into a partnership that is mutually beneficial?" she asked defensively. "You don't seem at all impressed by the fact that he's provided me with the money necessary to keep Riverview forever, not just a temporary solution. I had far more to gain from this than Garrett."

"I doubt that. It's only been two days, my dear. Perhaps an annulment isn't out of the question?"

Kelsey's eyes flew to her lap. "No," she whispered achingly. "That won't be necessary." Though Justin was too well-mannered to come right out with it, she could guess what he was thinking by the way his high cheekbones flushed a shade darker. If he only knew the truth, she thought woefully, he would probably launch himself to Garrett's defense so fast it would make her head spin. She rose hastily, suddenly uncomfortable in the face of all this emotion from the person she had counted on to remain steadfast. "I had hoped you'd be happy for me—"

"I would be," Justin said, grabbing her arm, "if I was certain that you are happy. Are you, Kelsey? Are you sure you've done the best thing for yourself?"

The false smile she flashed him made her cheeks ache. "Of course I'm sure."

"Then it seems I have no choice but to bow to your decision." Slowly, he released his hold on her elbow. "All I ever wanted was what's best for you, my dear. I give you my word I'll help in any way I can—"

"I'm so glad! Thank you, Justin. And do tell your mother I'll call on her soon. I'm sorry she wasn't home to hear my news firsthand."

Justin could only stand agape, not realizing until she was already out the door in a swirl of lace and ribbon that he had just agreed to endorse her marriage to a man he was growing to despise more with each passing minute. How had things gotten so out of his control?

Like an automaton, he turned toward the window, catching sight of her just as she drove away in the buggy. It certainly looked to him like she was hiding something, he rationalized. But surely that was only her pride.

Pride! Of course that was it! With a surge of exaltation, Justin felt the blood returning to his limbs. Kelsey was a proud woman—he had *known* as much, hadn't he? She would never admit that giving in to O'Neill wasn't her idea, just like she wouldn't own up to knowing about his secret occupation.

But just because she wouldn't admit that she needed his help didn't mean Justin couldn't give it to her anyway, albeit indirectly.

Feeling more pleased with himself by the second, he strode toward the glass case that held his law books and selected a volume from the shelf. In this he was confident. Every guilty man carried within him a shred of innocence—just as in every innocent man there was a measure of guilt. The trick, as he had learned over the years, was to know how to use each to one's best advantage—in this case, to help Kelsey. With a smug chuckle, Justin carried the book back to his desk and settled down to read.

After all, he had just given her his word.

Her visit to Justin's office upset Kelsey more than she expected, and she spent the entire trip home mulling over everything he had said. His angry words fueled her own doubts about what she'd done, but not because she questioned Garrett's motives; rather, they pointed to *her* shortcomings.

Flicking the reins across the horse's back testily, she examined her own conscience. Justin was absolutely right. When he had offered her financial protection in return for marriage she had been appalled, and yet look how easily Garrett had convinced her to do the very same thing.

But was that so very different from what many young women did, she wondered. According to her mother, her primary aim all along should have been wealth and security. Love needn't have been a factor.

But it was, Kelsey admitted. She loved Garrett. She had loved him all her life. That was the reason she had accepted his offer. Not for money or prestige. Mabelle had lied and schemed to keep them apart, but it hadn't worked.

Kelsey's mood lightened at the thought, and she briefly considered turning the buggy around and surprising Garrett at the shipping office. She was suddenly overwhelmed with the need to see him. Their honeymoon in Niagara Falls had been cut short when Garrett had awakened her that first morning with news of a telegram calling him home. She recalled that her shyness had quickly dissipated in the rush to pack her newly purchased belongings. On the long ride home, however, Garrett had seemed distant, as if his mind were far, far away. She hadn't been able to help wondering if his reserve was due to disappointment.

Then when they had reached Riverview late last night, Garrett had insisted that she get some sleep and not wait up for him, claiming that he wanted to check the situation at the loading dock immediately.

Kelsey had no idea what time he'd returned. She remembered that she had still been awake when the clock struck two and that he hadn't been home yet. But he'd been there that morning, she knew. Hannah had told her as soon as she came downstairs that Garrett had breakfast early and left before daybreak.

The cook had also informed her that Justin had stopped by three times during the two and a half days she was gone. There'd been no mistaking Hannah's wrinkled frown or agitated sniffs. Kelsey wasn't sure whether the servant was miffed at Justin for pestering, or at her for encouraging his friendship. Either way, a talk with Justin had been warranted, and despite the upsetting nature of their discussion, she was glad now that she had taken care of the matter.

It gave her time to concentrate on more important things.

A warm breeze stirred past her, gently lifting the brim of her bonnet and whispering through the trees lining the path. Kelsey looked up, surprised to see that she was almost home. The row of poplar trees swayed gracefully in the distance, their tiny spring leaves winking back and forth, waving to her as the buggy made its final approach to the house.

Just as the buggy rounded the corner to enter the drive, voices rose to interrupt her thoughts. The wall of trees still blocked her view of the house but she could hear low-pitched grumblings mixed with Hannah's lashing commands.

"Git that no 'count horse off o' that grass!" she ordered. When Kelsey came within view, she saw the old cook shaking a frail-looking arm at the offending animal. Surrounding her were three men she did not recognize, but their scraggly appearances and ill-kempt clothing reminded her of someone. Anxiously, Kelsey hurried the buggy forward and reined in just before the kitchen door.

"What is the meaning of this!" she demanded, glaring at the sneering men. Hannah looked up quickly, an expression of fear passing over her wizened face as she spotted her young mistress. But Kelsey was more concerned with the swaggering man who appeared around the corner of the house, his blackened grin sending a shudder of apprehension down her spine.

"Well, well. The purty little gal ah was hopin' ta see."

Angling his head slightly without ever taking his eyes from her, Bart Ogden spat a stream of brown juice from the corner of his mouth. The filthy mess landed on the kitchen porch, bringing a fresh spate of muttering from Hannah. But the woman did not flinch from her post in front of the door.

"What do you want with me?" Kelsey asked frostily, stepping from the buggy with as much dignity as she could. She would have liked to knock the leer from his face with her buggy whip, but she realized that to incur his anger would only endanger Garrett. It was her job to appease the man without turning his suspicions toward her husband.

"It ain't exactly you ah was lookin' fer," Ogden amended. "But ah 'spect ye'll do fer now. Where's that nigger-lovin' Irishman o' yers?"

Her fingers tightened around the hilt of the whip and her chin jerked up a notch. "I'll thank you to refrain from using such foul language in my presence."

"Foul language?" Ogden's jeering grin widened. "Which is that offends ya, niggers or Irishmen? Personally, ah can't abide neither 'less they knows their place. Ah reckon this one appears to be a mite uppity," he taunted, shrugging toward Hannah. "Lucky fer her she's too old ta bring much on the auction block. Only thing ah hate more'n a uppity nigger is a uppity Irishman. Where is he?"

"If you're referring to my husband, Mr. Ogden, then I'm afraid you'll have to speak to him at his office." Kelsey's teeth were clenched so tight the words barely squeaked out, but she was afraid to say more for fear of saying the wrong thing.

"Husband, is it?" Ogden hooted. "Ah thought things was cozy up here! Ah already been to the dock an' yer *husband* weren't there, so ah hurried on over here ta have a look 'round. Ya don't mind, do ya?"

Garrett wasn't at the dock? Kelsey's mind sought frantically for the correct response. If she allowed Ogden his search, it might help put his mind at rest about Garrett's involvement. On the other hand, she wasn't 100 percent certain he wouldn't find something incriminating. She threw a helpless glance to Hannah, who gave her a slight nod.

Taking a deep breath, Kelsey peered at Ogden coldly. "I don't know what it is you expect to find, but since it appears the only way to be rid of your obnoxious presence is to allow you to look for yourself, then I suppose I must. But let me warn you now," she said imperiously, "if I find one dirty footprint, one speck of filth on any of my belongings, I'll have you arrested for wrongful destruction of private property. Do I make myself clear?"

His only response was a slight narrowing of his beady eyes. Then he flicked his hand, signalling his men to begin their search. "Folks that break the law oughtn't ta be so snooty," he finally chortled.

She and Hannah remained out in the yard while he and his foul-smelling cohorts combed the house. When Kelsey tried to question the cook, Hannah hushed her sharply.

"Don't say nothin' yet," she whispered.

Kelsey wasn't sure whether she was just being cautious or if she actually knew something she wanted to keep Ogden from hearing. It was all she could do to stand silently by while her home was being invaded and her privacy destroyed, but she kept reminding herself that this was a part of what Garrett had asked her to do for him.

When Ogden and his men finished inside the house, their search took them to the stables. The two women followed as closely as they dared, and Benjamin joined them as the foul man slammed from one stall to another, kicking over troughs and knocking against the walls as if they were lunatics trying to find a way out. Kelsey wasn't even certain what they were looking for, until a shout from within the new tack room made her blood drain to her toes.

"In here, boss!" one of the men called. Ogden paused

long enough to sneer gleefully at Kelsey, then he strode into the small room.

The ruckus they'd caused before was nothing compared to the din of breaking wood and curses that flew through the door. Kelsey took a step forward, but Hannah's firm grip around her waist held her back. "Ain't nothin' you can do now, chile," the woman whispered fiercely. "Ain't nothin' nobody can do."

It seemed she was right. Within moments the loud cracks and smashing reports ceased, followed by an ominous silence that was almost worse than the previous cacophony had been. Ogden returned to the main room of the stable, followed by the man with him. Both wore wide grins as they marched into the yard.

"Thought ya was too damn smart fer Bart Ogden, heh?" With a swaggering lurch, he hoisted his pants up higher over his protruding gut. "But ah'm better 'n a coon dog when it comes ta sniffin' out a hidey hole."

Sniffing disdainfully, Kelsey took a step away from Hannah's protection. "I have no idea what you're talking about, nor do I care. But I warned you I'd send for the law—"

"Go 'head, Miz *O'Neill.*" His emphasis on Garrett's name caused her heart to leap. "An' while yer explainin' ta the sheriff all the trouble ah caused, don' ferget ta show 'im what's under the floor in there. At least what's left of it."

Under the floor? Kelsey fought to conceal her own surprise. So she had not imagined that whispered conversation. Apparently there was some kind of crawl space where the man who spoke with Garrett had hidden until she was gone. But that still didn't mean fugitive slaves had ever been concealed there!

"What you found proves nothing you didn't already know," Kelsey bluffed, drawing on her memory of that first confrontation with Ogden. "Everyone is aware of what my father stood for, but he's been gone for months. *I'm* responsible for Riverview now!"

Ogden was momentarily nonplussed, but the leer returned to his face before Kelsey even noticed it was gone. ''Mighty brave words.'' With that, he turned to leave, his band of bedraggled men sauntering behind him.

It seemed there was only the one horse between them, and the other three began arguing over whose turn it was to ride until Bart Ogden swatted them away and mounted himself. The poor nag staggered beneath his weight, then set off at an uneven trot with the rest of the men following as best they could.

''No 'counts!' was Hannah's pronouncement as they watched them disappear behind the line of poplars.

''He said there's a room under the floor . . . ,'' Kelsey wondered out loud, recalling his words, ''. . . at least what's left of it?'' The rending noises would account for that last statement; the men had probably ripped up the floorboards in their search. But something in the way Ogden's words had slid by like oil made her turn back toward the stable questioningly. Could it be . . . ?

At that moment, a wisp of smoke curled through the open door, and Benjamin's shout punctuated her thoughts.

''Get some water, quick!'' he called, limping from the back of the building. ''Them bastards set the tack room on fire!''

22

Without a thought for anything beyond the next few moments, Kelsey dashed into the stables, snatching up a blanket from near the door as she passed through. Smoke billowed into the main part of the building from the tack room in the rear, but she ignored the source and turned instead for the center stall where Lady Luck stomped around fretfully, her foal at her side.

Bejamin's shouts had summoned the two stable boys, who had been sent off to guard the other horses in the paddock when Ogden's men first arrived. By great good fortune, Stocker Fulton had been close by as well, and he led the youngsters in passing buckets of water to Benjamin, while Kelsey worked at calming the mare.

Using the blanket as a blindfold, she was able to lead the frightened animal from the stall with no trouble, though she paused uncertainly when the foal remained huddled inside instead of following her mother. "Come on, baby. Come on," Kelsey urged gently, though her voice was nearly drowned out by the shouts of the others. "Follow me. It's all right."

"What in hell—?" She straightened at the sound of Garrett's voice, relief pouring through her like life-giving water through a parched desert. "Thank God you're back," she breathed. "I wasn't sure—"

"Get out of here. Now!"

In three long strides he was at her side, tugging at Lady Luck's halter to get her moving once more, and Kelsey had to scamper to keep up once the mare was headed for the open door. She threw a glance over her shoulder to make sure he was following with the foal, then turned her attention back to guiding the blindfolded horse out into the fresh air.

She had just removed the blanket from the mare's head when Garrett's hand closed around her upper arm, jerking her abruptly around. Her surprise turned to something more riveting when she saw the ill-concealed anger flashing in his eyes.

"What in God's name do you think you're doing?"

His voice was no more than a raw whisper, but it had all the effect of a roar on Kelsey's nerves. The trembling that she'd kept well under control in Ogden's presence and had ignored during those few minutes of frantic activity after the fire was discovered now seized her entirely. Her lower lip quivered from the effort of opening her mouth to respond, but she never had the chance before Benjamin hobbled up to them.

"Fire's out," he pronounced, automatically running a protective hand over the mare's back. He shook his wizened head dolefully, then turned to them. "Not much damage, Lord b' praised. Someun' shoved a torch under the floor in the new room. Wood was too green ta catch. More smoke 'n anythin'." His eyes flitted anxiously to Garrett's as if he wanted to say more.

"I'll take a look later."

"Don't you think we should check now?" Kelsey managed. "There might be evidence of—"

"I said I'll look into it later." With no more than a curt nod to the gathered men, Garrett clasped her elbow tightly and spun her toward the house, cutting off her startled protest.

Clamping her lips together, she silently hurried to keep up with his long, angry strides. Ignoring Hannah's questioning call, he sped them through the kitchen door and into the house. When he seemed about to drag her bodily up the stairs, Kelsey dug her heels into the carpet and pulled back resentfully.

"I'm not moving one more inch," she claimed, "until

you stop pulling at my arm like I'm some kind of criminal."

"Whatever possessed you to go inside that building?" he ground angrily, turning on her with blazing eyes.

Kelsey's spine stiffened automatically. "For the same reason you did. To save the horses."

"Don't ever do anything like that again, do you hear me? Never!"

Anguish was etched across his soot-streaked face, anguish so deep and fierce, it pierced Kelsey's indignation and lanced straight at her heart. Tears sprang to her eyes, not from his harsh grip on her arms, but from the raw fear that contorted his features, turning his mouth into a tight slash.

Then her irritation melted away completely, dissolved by the knowledge that his anger toward her was fueled by his concern. Earlier today she had wondered how much he truly cared for her; now she knew.

"I wasn't in any danger, Garrett. Not really." Sensing that his fury was ebbing, she laid her hand on his bare chest. "But I couldn't stand by and watch everything that's important to me disappear. Please don't be angry."

Nibbling on her lower lip, Kelsey watched as he clenched his eyelids shut. Beneath her hand his chest hardened to steel, making her wonder if he was even more furious than she first thought. Then he opened his eyes to narrow slits, peering down at her. "I'm sorry I lost my temper. You're right, of course. I'd forgotten how much Riverview means to you."

Somehow, his bland apology was more disheartening than the ferocious glare she'd seen just moments before. Not to mention that he'd taken her meaning all wrong. It was as if a mask of indifference had fallen over his features, cool reserve. At least when he was furious she knew he was feeling something for her besides brotherly concern. With a dispirited sigh, she dropped her hand from him. "Now I know just what you meant about steering Ogden away from here. But perhaps now that he's found the crawl space empty, he'll leave us alone.

"He won't come near you again, I promise you that," Garrett said menacingly.

Kelsey's expression grew thoughtful as she met his gaze in the mirror. "What do suppose he hoped to accomplish by setting that fire? Surely he realized that the hiding place was no longer being used."

"Why do his kind do anything?" Garrett's hands rested on her shoulders with a light grip, though they still flexed tensely. "He's like a creature completely without reason; a man obsessed with a mission, undaunted and unstoppable."

His words hung in the air between them, suspended by the unspoken recollection that leapt through both their minds as if they were joined by a common thread. *A man obsessed with a mission.* That was how he had once described Sheldon, and though he now regretted such a harsh accusation, Garrett knew that Kelsey had neither forgotten, nor amended it. Her face was locked in a frozen smile, but beneath his fingers her shoulders shuddered gently.

"Go on up," he said abruptly. "I'll send someone with hot water for a bath."

Without another word, she obeyed.

The sky had turned to indigo by the time Kelsey stepped from the brass tub, wrapping a huge sheet around her as she moved closer to the hearth. She couldn't deny that taking a bath had been a good idea, but the emptiness in Garrett's voice when he prompted her to come upstairs still left her feeling hollow inside. She could understand his anxiety after the fire, she could even understand his anger at her rash behavior.

What she could not comprehend was his dismissing her like a recalcitrant servant the moment she mentioned Bart Ogden's name. A more natural reaction would have been pure wrath at the man's obvious insolence, not the icy wall that surrounded Garrett's emotions.

Kelsey edged closer to the fire, bending so that her hair fell in a cascade over her shoulder. With strokes more vigorous than was necessary, she brushed the auburn waves until they crackled. And what about now? Where was her husband now?

In the doorway of her room, Garrett stood transfixed by the graceful arching of her neck as she bent forward. Her hair shimmered with molten fire as it captured the dancing lights and sent them radiating outward, as if her auburn locks were the source and not the reflection. His fingertips ached to touch those silken flames, to bury themselves in the luxuriant fall that had entranced him for more years than he cared to remember.

He remained silent while she forced the brush through the thick mass of hair with undue vigor, knowing that her frustration was justified, but unable to put it to rest. His only consolation, meager though it might be, was that the angry helplessness he felt now was undoubtedly greater than any she might be feeling. Greater, he admitted to himself, because it was fueled by guilt.

"Kelsey?" His voice passed roughly through his scorched throat, the tone low and gentle, but it brought her head snapping upward like a spring trap. Her dark eyes sought his. Ruefully, he knew he had no answers for the questions lurking there.

"If you brush any harder," he said evenly, "you'll tear your scalp off. Let me do it."

"Y-you?" Surprise warred with far greater emotions as he approached her slowly, holding out his hand for the hairbrush she clutched in her frozen hand. He stood behind her in the mirror, and his image drove her breath away. His expression was rigidly controlled, his movements deliberate as he took the brush from her hand. But his eyes, though carefully hooded, spoke to her of unaccountable wretchedness.

"Did you know I've always wanted to try this?" Garrett asked. With long, sensuous motions, he stroked her hair from the crown of her head to the middle of her back where the soft waves ended.

Kelsey held herself immobile, paralyzed by the bewitching sensations that crept over her limbs. She knew if she gave into it, she would melt away completely beneath his tender ministrations, and a part of her still fought the waves of delight that coursed through her each time his hands smoothed over her thick hair.

"G-Garrett, that's enough," she choked, pressing her palms against the top of her dressing table.

Silently, he laid the brush down beside her, but instead of backing away, he placed his hands on either side of her head, sliding his fingers beneath the heavy fall of her hair.

"Don't you like when I do this?" he murmured, tugging gently until she sighed with pleasure.

"It feels wonderful, but . . ."

"But what? You don't want to feel good?" His voice was hoarse and teasing. "I thought we'd settled that issue?"

When his hands dropped to her shoulders and began gently massaging the knotted muscles, Kelsey nearly moaned out loud. Little by little, the tension was streaming out of her like melting snow until she could barely summon the power of speech. "But I . . . I wanted to make *you* feel good."

Garrett sucked in a quick breath, his hands freezing at the back of her neck. Then his low chuckle broke the silence. "I'm not sure what makes me want you more, your sweet innocence or bold candor." With one finger, he traced the curve of her shoulder in a feather-light caress. "You are making me feel good, just by letting me please you. The pleasure is *supposed* to be mutual."

Of course she had known that, Kelsey thought dazedly as he drew her up from the dressing table, wrapping his arms around her waist as he trailed a string of kisses along the path his touch had just marked. But she also knew just *how* men found their pleasure, and since he'd already promised not to risk getting her pregnant, she didn't know exactly what else he planned to do. The only thing she did know was that she had no choice but to trust him.

Turning within his embrace, she met his ardent gaze shyly, but with growing confidence. The high emotions of the day had drained her of all but the need to feel his strong arms around her. Her glance flickered downward from the thrust of his obstinate jaw to the flat plane of his chest, and without thinking she traced her fingertips along the same path, sensing the need in him by the way his muscles jumped and quivered beneath her hand.

"I want . . . will you show me what to do?"

Intense longing surged through him, warning him that it had never been more than a heartbeat away. The sight of her chin, lifted high yet still trembling with uncertainty, filled him with a tenderness beyond any he had ever known. He wanted nothing but to enfold her into his arms and protect her from the world, even knowing that she would fight such a suffocating hold—and that the threat she feared most came from him.

With gentle restraint, Garrett kissed her upturned lips, his tongue skimming lightly over her sweet mouth until she opened to his skillful foray. The dressing gown she wore provided little protection in the face of his rising desire as he cupped one breast, teasing the burgeoning peak with his thumb until it pressed insistently against his palm.

Kelsey shuddered involuntarily, reveling in the play of his muscles beneath her seeking hands and the expertise with which he aroused her flesh to a relentless, exquisite fervor. Nearly mindless with need, she strove to get closer to him, blindly fitting her hips intimately against his growing hardness.

His response was forceful and instantaneous. Garrett crushed her to him fiercely, lifting her from her feet as he gathered her into his enveloping embrace. Kelsey's lips parted in a wordless expression of surprise, then softened as they met his eagerly.

There was no way she could stop the torrent of sensations that ripped through her veins like a shearing wind, driving away all thoughts, all feelings except the one indelible presence that was the essence of her existence. *Garrett.* She wanted to shout it with exultation and hope, but his mouth was moving over hers insistently, eliciting more from her soul than mere words could express. And she was answering him with more than words. Within his unyielding clasp she was trembling like a weak-kneed schoolgirl, except that it was no longer fear of the unknown that shook her, but rather anticipation of the joy she knew was yet to come. Her hands crept behind his neck, her fingers dove into the rich thickness of his hair, all to show him that her desire matched his.

All the restraint, all the care he'd taken with her in the past was gone now, replaced by a raging passion that flooded through him. The dam that had been years in the making took only moments to crumble in the face of his desire, his need—his love.

For an instant Garrett wavered on the brink of an abyss that was nearly as compelling as it was frightening. The bonds of the past conspired with the reality trembling in his arms to draw him closer to that soul-shattering plunge, but his mind scrambled and clawed for a hold, finally clinging to the only thought that could save him: he had already broken one promise to her; he would not disregard the other.

No matter how difficult it might prove to be.

With one powerful motion, Garrett lifted her high and carried her to the bed, laying her gently upon the smooth coverlet. He expected to see timidity, even embarrassment in her eyes when he backed away enough to remove his clothing, but instead they shone with love and assurance.

Slowly, with only the briefest hesitation, Kelsey tugged at the ribbon that held her gown in place over her breasts and shrugged the sheer fabric away.

"Oh lord, you are beautiful," Garrett whispered as he gazed down at her. As quickly as he could, he shed his shirt and trousers, kicking off his boots haphazardly. When he was completely undressed, he turned to her almost languidly.

She could only stare with utter fascination at the sheer splendor of his maleness. His calves and thighs were as muscular as his chest, though not massively so. Lean hips, tapering torso, all molded to sinewy perfection beneath flesh that rippled with a thin sheen of perspiration. Inevitably, her gaze drifted to the proud evidence of his virility, and though she struggled not to make a sound, she knew her eyes had grown wide with astonishment.

With total lack of self-consciousness, Garrett returned to the bed, kneeling above her. Kelsey tried not to flinch, but when he reached for her hand such a jolt of electricity shot through her that she couldn't help but draw a sharp breath.

"I won't . . . hurt you," he whispered throatily, lacing his fingers between hers and raising them to his mouth. Carefully, reverently, he turned her palm over and placed a kiss on the soft, padded flesh there. Then he watched her as he drew the tips of her fingers into his mouth one at a time, sucking gently on each until she shivered like a fawn ready to spring away into the dusk.

Kelsey had thought she knew what to expect, but nothing had prepared her for the onslaught of erotic sensations and images speeding through her veins and tripping into her thoughts. Their wedding night had taught her much, but she was just beginning to realize there was an entire world opening up before her, inside of her, and Garrett held the key to the door.

With his hand he brought her closer, with his mouth and tongue he drove her beyond the entrance, but when he nudged her knees apart and raised her hips slightly, Kelsey stiffened automatically, fearful of taking the next irrevocable step.

"Shh," he murmured against her ear in a strained voice. "Don't worry . . . don't worry."

His words, heavy with both reassurance and need, broke through the last barrier of opposition as if it were no more than transparent tissue wrapped around her heart. All the tension fled from her body, except for the winding coil that tightened within the core of her being. This time, when Garrett probed at the intimate softness, she allowed him entrance.

He penetrated her slowly, with one long, bold stoke

that seemed to touch the very center of her. Now she felt herself grow taut again, not with resistance, but with the need to hold him fast to her. Nevertheless, his gentle rocking motion caused him to slide easily within her womanly passage, deftly, surely . . . agonizingly.

Myriad sensations swelled together inside her—fire running hot through her veins and ice dancing across her flesh—while her hips matched and held the rhythm of his in a timeless counterpoint of love.

Garrett responded to her increasing frenzy with bare restraint, his teeth gritted forcefully in order to maintain the tenuous reign on his own passion. For his own sake as well as hers he drove her toward the peak of ecstasy, hoping beyond hope that it would not come crashing down upon both of them. And then, when he could trust his control no longer, he pulled away from her warmth, spilling himself instead into the cold void that was not Kelsey.

Arching spasmodically, she emitted a soft whimper at his sudden absence, unable to bear in silence the vast emptiness she felt when he rolled away from her. No longer was she filled with his satin heat, no longer did his comforting weight envelop her. Fighting for her breath, she quelled the feeling of abandonment that left her frustrated and oddly bereft, though he had not moved more than a few inches away.

Garrett saw the flash of turmoil that tore away the fog of rapture from her eyes. Tenderly, he gathered her close to murmur words of sweet nonsense into her hair, sensing that she was too confused for conversation and too embarrassed for silence. He wished there was something more he could do or say, but the brutal reality was that he had done as much as was allowed him. That Kelsey realized this herself was evident by the sigh that whispered past his chin.

Gradually, her limbs began to relax against his, and with aching slowness he caressed the silky skin of her hip before backing away enough to look at her flushed face.

His blue eyes, full of soothing concern, only made Kelsey more uneasy. She squeezed her eyelids shut miserably.

"It's okay, you know," he comforted, clearing the gravel from his voice. "Marriage, like anything else, takes patience and practice. A great deal of practice. You won't be disappointed next time."

Glancing up, she saw the grim amusement forming a smile on his lips. Searching for a smile of her own, she shrugged resignedly. "I'm not disappointed, but I'm afraid you are."

He shook his head, placing a light kiss on her brow. Disappointment hardly covered it, but Garrett wasn't about to let her see that it had taken every ounce of willpower in him not to betray her trust. He wouldn't be able to hold his resolve if she tried any harder to please him. There was precious little satisfaction either way.

Easing over to the side of the bed, he bent to retrieve his pants and shirt from the floor.

"You're leaving?" When she realized what he was doing, Kelsey's heart thumped painfully against her ribs and a huge lump of tears lodged in her throat.

"I have to, love, if you want me to keep my promise. I'm far too human to stay. Besides," he said, averting his gaze, "there are certain things I have to take care of."

Though it hurt her desperately that he had to leave, it did make a certain amount of sense. And of course, he knew best. Eyes brimming with unshed tears, Kelsey managed a thin smile.

Garrett hid his expression as he fought inwardly with his own conscience. The trust she had placed in his keeping was ill-deserved, but there was no way he could change that without hurting her more. Dropping to the side of the bed so that he could yank on his boots, he pondered his choices.

To tell her now would be too great a risk, both for the fragile ties of their relationship, just now ripening with bright promise, and for the other people whose lives depended on his discretion.

To keep the truth to himself for a while longer was the only alternative. If she learned of his deceit later, at least by then the safety of his charges would be assured. And he could always hope that the bond between Kelsey and him would have strengthened enough that she would accept his decision.

It was a meager hope, Garrett thought bleakly.

But for now, it was the only one he had.

The acrid stench of smoke mixed with soaked canvas still permeated the air of the tack room as Garrett poked his way through the debris. Glass from the shattered window glistened in the lantern light, deadly, pointed shards that looked like the icicles that had hung from their apple trees a scant three weeks earlier. Blackened wood that was once the blanket box where he had found Kelsey's boots lay in a heap at his feet, a grim reminder of how near disaster could strike. And how quickly.

A hasty inspection showed him that Benjamin's earlier assessment had been correct. The damage from the fire was limited mainly to the outside wall and the contents of the box. The smoldering saddle blankets and old leather had generated a great deal of smoke, but had never really roared out of control.

"It ain't a pretty sight, is it?"

Startled, he spun toward the fire-gutted wall, holding the lantern high. Light and shadow danced over the soot-streaked planks. Garrett froze, then consciously forced his muscles to relax as a dark figure slipped into the lantern's glow.

"Micah," he muttered relievedly.

The large man gazed around slowly, taking in the condition of the room as well as the tormented expression on his friend's face. "Warning?" he asked bluntly, grunting when his question elicited a curt nod.

"What else? In broad daylight . . . in front of witnesses."

Micah grunted once more. It was hard to tell if Garrett's mood stemmed from anger or disgust. Or both.

"It's by the sheerest luck that no one was hurt," he continued, viciously kicking at a piece of fallen wood. "If more of the horses had been inside, or if the fire had gone undetected a little longer. And just two days ago—"

He stopped, catching himself before voicing the phrase out loud. Two days ago there had been more in this tack room than blankets and harnesses. Wordlessly, he set the lantern on the scorched windowsill, then pulled at the boards that had once concealed the shallow space beneath the floor. Now they were splintered and broken, hacked apart with an axe by men who were more malicious than they were smart.

When he raised what was left of the spring door, smoke that had been trapped beneath the floor billowed upward, driving them back a few steps. Micah covered his nose and mouth with one hand, coughing, though he quickly returned to the opening and peered inside cautiously, shaking his head. "We were lucky this time."

The odor burned at Garrett's eyes and throat, bringing back with potent impact the terror that had crashed through his chest when he saw Kelsey dash inside the stable just as he galloped into the yard. With a silent groan, he turned away from the gaping hole in the floor and marched savagely into the undamaged part of the stables. One by one, he slammed open each shuttered window until fresh air streamed through the building.

Still it couldn't erase the desperation from his heart.

"My friend . . . Garrett!"

When Micah's urgent whisper finally penetrated his anger, Garrett stopped suddenly, his head bowed as he leaned against one of the thick posts in the center of the stable. "It would have been my fault," he ground out. "It would have been my fault if she'd been killed . . ." His mind settled on an image of Bart Ogden's leering face. ". . . or worse."

Behind him, Micah dared not move from the relative

safety of the tack room. Instead he waited until the distraught man shook his head dazedly, straightening as he turned.

"It has to end. Soon," Garrett said in clipped tones. "Ogden knows, and it's only a matter of time until he catches us unaware. I won't risk . . . I won't have lives at stake because he's watching me."

Eyeing him questioningly, Micah answered softly, "They know the risks. Most of them've been living with danger of one kind or another since they were born. None of them expects this part of the journey to be easy just 'cause it's the last."

"Nor should they be subjected to more danger than necessary," Garrett offered in dry rebuke. "I'll see Levi tonight. Other arrangements will have to be made."

He turned to go, but Micah's large hand caught his shoulder, urging him back. "Ogden or no Ogden, Riverview is still the safest place. I doubt Levi'll see it any other way. You know there's three more waitin' for me in Batavia. Where else they gonna go?"

Garrett met the other man's penetrating stare, reading the unspoken question that was there, compelling him to examine his own motives. As much as he wished events had not brought them to this, they'd shared too much for him to ignore it. "Whatever Levi decides," he relented gruffly, "I'll abide by it."

For a long moment Micah remained silent, as if waiting for something more. Then, with a smile of sadness in his dark eyes, he dropped his hand and nodded a brief farewell.

The expression on his friend's gentle face was the same one Garrett had seen on Kelsey's when she watched him leave her room just an hour before, and he felt a piercing sense of guilt that circumstances would force him to betray one of them.

He started to speak, but no words came easily, no explanation would suffice.

And before he could utter his usual phrase of friendly caution, Micah was gone.

23

Dacia woke from a restless sleep, her heavy eyes lifting, her hand reaching swiftly for the small bundle nestled within the curve of her body. Once certain that all was well, she withdrew her hand so as not to wake her sleeping child, though she curled around him just a bit closer, wishing to share her own meager warmth. The fast, steady rhythm of his tiny pulse reassured her, filled her with hope.

It also allowed her to spend a few moments taking stock of her own situation.

Though Dacia knew little enough about the vagaries of childbirth, instinct told her that after so many weeks, she should have been feeling well by now. But her limbs still shook like saplings, unable to bear her weight, and the fire in her blood raged and waned by turns, leaving her weak and ill.

Of course she *did* understand that the circumstances of her son's birth had led to her condition, just as she understood that there was no use bemoaning those facts now, when it was too late to change them.

Still, she couldn't keep her thoughts from skimming back and forth over those two days the way a hand keeps reaching for an itch—fretfully, like it's got a mind of its own. The fever had so ravaged her memory, she could hardly recall the face of the kind woman who had eased the babe from her womb, nor could she picture the earnest-sounding man who had crept back to the little house just hours after the birth, whispering that it was time to go.

The only thing she did remember, clear as a starless night and just as black, was the feeling that had clutched her heart at the sound of gunshots behind them on the wagon journey afterward.

Dacia had not seen what happened—at least not with her eyes—for she and her baby had been hidden beneath the wagon's rickety seat. But two men had helped her into her hiding place, and after a bumpy, bone-jarring ride, only one lifted her out. His youthful, clean-shaven face had been wet with tears as he carried her into an abandoned barn, and it was with a choked voice that he handed her over to the others who waited there too. She remembered wanting to thank him, to offer some words of comfort in return for his care. But the illness had already claimed her tongue, and she'd done no more than watch him as he drove away to search for his father's body, lying somewhere along the road.

That had been days—no! *weeks* past, Dacia thought. It had been weeks that she'd lain in this empty barn, tended by a woman who crept furtively in by night with food and water. Dacia could tell by the woman's nervousness that it was dangerous for her to stay in one place for long, but there was no helping that. She could not walk more than a few yards at a time, and even then at great cost.

Outside, a nightbird hooted softly. The tiny body at her side stirred. Cautiously, Dacia raised her hand over her child's head, a protective gleam entering her eyes. The woman had come and gone already, so whoever was creeping toward them—and she was certain there was someone!—was a threat.

When the barn door cracked open she tensed, knowing not how she would fight for her child, only that she would. Her wobbly limbs grew rigid, her ragged breaths shallow.

"I come from Gabriel."

The words whispered through the darkness, falling on her ears like a psalm. For a moment Dacia refused to believe them, but then they came again, deeper, more slowly.

"I come from Gabriel."

And then the speaker stepped before her, crouching to get a look at her face in the darkness. She met his gaze bravely, knowing now that the time for fear was past.

"I am a daughter of Gabriel," she said, responding in the way the woman had taught her.

"Then come."

The man was large, and he lifted her effortlessly, hardly waiting until she had gathered her babe to her breast. She would have preferred to make her own way with assistance, but he gave her no chance to try, merely lifted her high in his glistening black arms.

"Let me walk," she demanded, her voice thin and weak.

"Faster this way. There's two others waitin' outside, and we got miles ta go tonight."

Despite the truth of his reply, Dacia wriggled uncomfortably. She even tried pinning him with the regal stare that worked so well with other men, but he only glanced down at her tolerantly.

"The last person who helped me ended up dead," she warned as he carried her through the barn doors into the night.

"There's worse things."

"For who?" she argued. But she knew now that this man understood as few others had. The knowledge brought her peace, and with it a sense of unity she had never known before, even while it frightened her with its strangeness. "Who are you?"

He paused then, letting a shaft of moonlight fall over them both, so that they could take measure of one another before the journey began. Then gradually, gently, a smile pulled at his face. "I'm Micah," he whispered hoarsely, "and you'll be just fine now. Just fine."

24

"Where are we going now?" Garrett asked.

"It's a surprise." Standing in her stirrups, Kelsey scanned the horizon with an imaginary spyglass, throwing her arm forward as she pretended to spot something in the distance. Laughing, Garrett followed.

Days like this had been rare in the past few weeks; not because of the sunshine and fine weather, for the early part of June always boasted fair skies and warm temperatures, but because lately Garrett had been spending an inordinate amount of time at the shipping office. Only on three occasions since their wedding had he remained at Riverview past breakfast. One was on the day after the fire. The second was shortly after when they traveled together to Lockport for a day of shopping. Today was the third.

With an effort, Kelsey forced herself to forget the tension that had grown between them like one of the taut wires on the suspension bridge across the river. Too many nights she had lain awake long after he returned to his own room. She could no longer blame insomnia on demons from the past. Her thoughts and feelings were firmly entrenched in the present, with Garrett.

"Come on," she shouted, looking over her shoulder. Breathlessly, she urged Ladyfair up the last rise. "This is what I wanted to show you."

Coming alongside her, Prince tossed his head against the reins, obviously impatient to race across the open field below them. So she wasn't the only one chafing over

Garrett's unusual devotion to his desk, Kelsey thought wryly.

Not that she blamed him. It was almost as if they were both trying too hard to ignore the restrictions she had placed on their relationship, at least until it was impossible to ignore them any longer. Unwillingly her thoughts drifted to the late spring nights. If they avoided one another by day, once the sun set they seemed to be drawn together by a force so inpenetrable that neither could deny it.

As if they would want to. Kelsey felt a familiar tightening in her abdomen that never seemed to go away completely. It wasn't that she was unsatisfied. Physically. Garrett was a skilled and considerate lover, and she herself had done her best to learn how to please him in ways both imaginative and tender.

And yet, she could not deny the aching emptiness that throbbed deep within her each time he left her side. Though he denied it, she knew he felt the same lack of fulfillment. It was in the way he looked at her when he thought she wasn't paying attention, with eyes as burning and intense as a caged beast's. And it was in the way he didn't look at her, too, using any excuse he could grasp to spend time away.

It was time they both needed, Kelsey understood, but that didn't ease the gnawing hunger that seemed to grow more insistent every day. So she had thrown herself into her work in the same manner as he, spending long hours on Ladyfair overseeing the progress of Riverview's bounteous acres. With Stocker Fulton's expertise and the added labor that Garrett's financial assistance had provided, they had managed to save more of the corn crop than any of them had anticipated. In the meantime, work was begun on clearing the vineyards, which were expected to produce as early as next season.

Kelsey was proud of her accomplishments, though she was quick to remember that she had not done it alone. That was one of the reasons she wanted Garrett to share in the excitement and triumph she felt today, gazing over the latest proof of Riverview's success. Sloping downward for several hundred yards lay several acres of freshly turned land. The pungent aroma of damp earth was like perfume to her, and she drew in a deep and satisfied breath.

For today, at least, they could both pretend that nothing was wrong.

Reining in beside her, Garrett glanced over in time to see her breasts heave beneath the open V of her blouse. The movement evoked an immediate and undeniable reaction that sent the blood boiling through his veins.

One would have thought, he pondered ruefully, that an adult man, a married man at that, could exercise more control over his own impulses. But where Kelsey was concerned, he was finding that control was the last thing he wanted to exercise. In the past few weeks he had questioned her carefully about her reasons for believing she could not bear a child. More and more he was convinced that her fears were a by-product of Mabelle's and hopefully groundless. But until she came to this realization herself, patience was in order.

If he concentrated only on what she was trying to show him instead of letting his mind wander over the luscious curve of her backside in those damnable trousers, or his thoughts drift to the wisps of curls that caressed the nape of her neck, then he would have no troubles. Directing his gaze toward the stretch of land she indicated with her hand, he kept his tone purposefully light and free of the tightness that had seized the rest of him. "This" he asked playfully, amusement pulling at the corners of his mouth, "is . . . it?"

She pouted at him with mock exasperation. "I suppose you don't know what this means," she challenged. When he shook his head laughingly, she heaved a dramatic sigh. "And I thought the Irish were natural-born farmers! It's barley. We planted last week, and look! It's already starting to sprout."

Garret peered intently at the ground, then swung from the saddle to get a better look. Leading Prince by the reins, he strode to the edge of the cultivated field, crouching on one knee to examine the tiny green shoots that were, indeed, sprouting from the earth.

"Barley," he repeated thoughtfully, fingering one of the slender plants. "You sowed barley?"

Kelsey dismounted also, jamming her fists against her hips. "Of course I did. I told you weeks ago that Stocker had the field cleared. It was just a matter of deciding what to put in it, and I chose barley."

She pursed her lips when she saw his indulgent smile, misunderstanding its meaning. After the debacle with the corn it hadn't been easy for her to commit herself again, but it was important that she maintain control of the farm. Turning failure into fortune was only possible if she overcame her hesitation and went back to making decisions. Now, it seemed, Garrett was questioning her judgment.

"For your information, barley is an extremely hardy grain. Its growing season is shorter than most other crops, so the late start won't affect the yield. You've been cooped up indoors for too long, Garrett O'Neill, when you can't even tell a cash crop when you see one."

Her sharp tone wiped the smile from his face as he stood slowly, finally turning to meet her indignant glare. "I wasn't distrusting your decision, Kelsey. Only wondering why you didn't mention it to me before."

"I would have," she retorted, though some of the wind had been knocked from her sails by his gentle tone. "But you're usually gone all day, and at night it just never seemed the right time to bring it up—"

She stopped short, warmth creeping over her face. Biting the inside of her cheek, Kelsey lowered her head, pretending to tighten the girth on Ladyfair's saddle.

Garrett frowned with exasperation but it was aimed only at himself. She had no way of knowing that his enforced distance had less to do with her than with his own ragged emotions. He took a step closer, grimacing as she flinched when he touched her squared shoulder. "I'm sorry I've been neglecting you lately. What you've done with the farm is nothing short of remarkable. I hope you know how proud I am of you."

"You . . . you are?" Disbelief warred with exultation, but she'd lived so long with the former that it was hard to let go. She chopped at the air with one hand dismissively. "I'd reserve judgement if I were you. Look what happened to the la—"

"Stop it, Kelsey! Just stop it!" Catching her wrist in midair, he pulled her around gently. She did not resist, but neither did she give in completely. Her back remained as straight as a rake handle, her shoulder blades as sharp as prongs. It was the expression in her eyes, however, defiant and puzzled at the same time, that softened his voice to velvet. "Stop undermining your accomplishment here. There's nothing wrong with a little well-deserved pride. Enjoy it—"

"—while it lasts?" Kelsey finished. She could appreciate what he was saying, though his strange behavior the past few weeks was hardly confidence-inspiring. But she would never, *ever* let him know how much she depended on his approval. "I'm just trying to be realistic, Garrett. Seed does not come with a written guaranty. Nor does anything else, for that matter."

"No, it doesn't, " he replied thoughtfully. It was easy to understand her implication. "But hard work increases the odds, as you're proving here, whether you'll admit it or not. So does having faith in yourself."

Faith in herself. Kelsey drew an unsteady breath, ducking her head sideways. How could she have faith in herself when she couldn't even manage to succeed at the one thing every woman ought to be able to do? When Garrett suggested she see a doctor she had refused, afraid of revealing the deepest, darkest part of her secret. Did he know how much his incredible patience wounded her? That every time he gazed at her with tenderness and understanding, she felt the full weight of her own shortcomings pressing down upon her?

Because it was easier to pretend they were still talking about the barley than to face the truth, she slipped from beneath his hands, looping Ladyfair's reins around one wrist as she moved away from him. "I suppose you're right." She shrugged, careful not to let him see the tears that threatened to spill from her eyes. "One of the reasons we chose to sow barley is because Justin told me that Guenther Schultz has finally signed a contract for that new brewery he's been talking about. We'll have a ready market for the grain and our own source of hay for the horses as well. What *could* go wrong now?"

"Nothing!" Garrett insisted, coming up behind her. Prince nuzzled Ladyfair, forcing him to keep a tight grip on the reins, but he wrapped his free arm around Kelsey's waist, drawing her back against his chest. The slight tremor in her voice had not escaped him, nor did the delicate scent of rosewater as he lowered his head to her hair.

He ached profoundly, and it was with more than just wanting her. He longed for the secrets and the silence to be over, to be rid forever of the chains that bound them—and kept them apart. Beneath his hand he felt the frantic rhythm of her heart keeping time with his own erratic pulse, and though he knew it was a fool's wish, he whispered another promise he could only hope would prove true.

"Nothing will go wrong now, sweetheart. Nothing will go wrong now."

The frigid river water slapped at his thighs stubbornly, defying Garrett's efforts to complete this mission with the minimum of discomfort to himself and to his passengers. Even in June the current was swift and bitterly cold, and he knew that one wrong move could result in an icy plunge into the river, and almost certain death.

But despite the cold spray bathing his head and shoulders and the slippery footing that constantly challenged his sense of balance, he couldn't squelch the feeling of immense satisfaction that surged through him. In a matter of seconds they would be free of danger, another journey successfully completed.

A dull grating noise signaled the hull touching rock, and Garrett leant a shoulder to edging the craft toward a firmer mooring. On the other side of the small boat Micah did the same. Soon the sound of splashing oars was replaced by the hushed preparations of those on board as they stood ready to wade the rest of the way to shore. Black as pitch, the moonless night covered the movements of the others, but Garrett followed their actions with his ears.

And with his soul.

Once on solid ground the three men and two women would huddle together in disbelief. Then one by one, they would drop to their knees in reverent prayer. Only after Micah urged them to hurry would they follow the footpath up the embankment—not as steep as the one they'd come down, but treacherous nevertheless—until they reached the top and the welcoming friends who would start them on their way to new lives.

The scenario rarely differed, Garrett thought. Only the faces and the names changed. The relief, the joy, the gratitude: Those things endured, those things made it all worth while.

Until now.

Until now, the danger had only added to the heightened awareness, the sense of vitality that always left him invigorated and utterly pleased with what he had done. Normally he had to check himself against feeling too much pleasure, counting on the very real peril and a kind of forced humbleness to bring him back to earth.

Tonight he needed no reminders. Guilt kept his emotions shackled to the ground.

"Ready" came Micah's strident whisper as he sidestepped down the bank in the darkness. In truth, such caution was not necessary on this side of the river, but both men had formed habits that were difficult to break.

Soundlessly, Garrett eased the boat backwards until it floated clear of the shore, then held it steady while Micah climbed in. Once he had boarded, he picked up one of the two oars, matching strokes with his friend as they made their way back across the river. Automatically he listened for any telltale sounds that might mean their mission that night had been detected, but only the river raised her voice.

The black water continued its endless journey toward the lake, oblivious to the affairs of the men who rode her. It was only fitting, he told himself. It was by man's design that a configuration of nature should become a boundary between two worlds, a symbol intended to divide instead of to join. It seemed somehow right that the Niagara would resist such human pettiness by challenging them every inch of the way.

Letting exertion clear his troubled mind, Garrett rowed.

Her dream returned that night.

Though she should have known it was inevitable, Kelsey was amazed by how vividly the pain and frustration seemed to her when she woke with a silent scream ready to burst from her lips.

Knowing that any chance for sleep was gone, she scrambled out of bed and into a robe, splashing cold water on her face from the bowl on her dresser. "Oh, God," she moaned in a broken whisper, leaning against the bureau with both hands clutching the polished edge for support. "What's wrong with me?"

Other people had dreams, she knew. Even nightmares. But why, when she was happier than she had been for years, was she continually haunted by events that should have been put behind her long ago?

A steady clicking outside her door broke into Kelsey's thoughts, and she immediately recognized the sound of Bridget pacing the hallway. That was strange. She distinctly remembered Garrett putting the dog outside before they had come up to her room. Since Hannah had long since gone to her bed, it was unlikely that the cook had let Bridget back inside, and so Kelsey was puzzled by the dog's presence now, though not ungrateful.

"What are you doing up at this hour?" she whispered as Bridget slipped into her room. "Did I wake you?"

Something had. As if sensing her mistress's restless mood, Bridget continued to pace in circles, stopping occasionally to stare at the door that led to the balcony. Once she even whined softly, and Kelsey took the hint.

"Good idea. I can use some fresh air, too."

The sky was black and starless, the scent of the river permeating the air. She could tell it was very late by the way even the night creatures had fallen hushed and still, leaving only the sound of the water far below to fill her ears.

It brought Garrett's words of several weeks ago back to her, and she hugged her arms tight around her middle to ward off the aching desire that sped through her at the thought of him.

There are some thing you can't stop, he had said. Some things that were as unchangeable as the river.

Had he meant love? The question hovered in her mind, pricking at her with nagging fingers. No, he hadn't said anything about love, though she recalled with a blush that she had admitted to it. *His* feelings were still painfully unclear.

Except, of course, for his desire. Each night he came to her, masking desperation with gentleness, passion with patience. And each night he left her again after an achingly sweet kiss that somehow left her yearning for more. Her mother had once told her that the marriage act was a thing to be endured, despised. She had been wrong about that. Maybe she had been wrong about everything. History did not always repeat itself.

Bridget had joined her on the balcony, and while Kelsey peered into the blackness, the dog shuffled around her legs uneasily, occasionally lifting her head to scan the dark horizon. When the chill air began to turn her skin to gooseflesh Kelsey started back inside, but Bridget suddenly froze, a low growl rising from her throat like a waking beast.

The hair on the back of Kelsey's neck bristled as she

stared out into the night. Something or someone that shouldn't be out there was nevertheless present. And since Bridget rarely raised her hackles, even for strangers, Kelsey was alarmed.

"Shhhh." More to calm her own fluttering stomach than to quiet the dog, she stretched her hand over Bridget's neck. She cocked her head, trying to discern any unusual sounds, but could hear only the steady shushing of water against the rocks along the riverbank. Kelsey edged closer to the balcony railing.

Now she heard what Bridget, with her far superior senses, had detected first. A faint rhythmic splashing, growing louder with every second, followed by a dull scrape. No voices yet, but Kelsey was positive that the distinctive sounds were oars dipping in and out of the water, and then the hull of a small boat bumping across the flat rocks that lined the river bank just below the house.

Who would be out on the river at this time of night? Not fishermen, she was sure. But why else? Straining to hear, Kelsey listened for telltale voices, or even the sounds of the boat casting off again, for there was no way up the steep cliffs at that spot. The mysterious boater would have no choice but to move on, assuming his landing here was accidental.

After a few minutes passed, however, and not another sound had floated up to the house, Kelsey released her pent-up breath. "Where did he go, Bridget? Can you still hear him?"

But Bridget had already disappeared, and when Kelsey went back into the room, she found the dog curled up on the foot of her bed as if nothing unusual had happened. Kelsey stood on the threshold, her eyes moving from the dog out into the blackness and back again. "Don't tell me I was imagining things!"

Bridget only gazed at her beseechingly.

Puzzled, Kelsey returned to the balcony, leaning far over the repaired railing. Even in full daylight she couldn't have seen all the way down to the river from this angle, and on a moonless night like this it was difficult to make out the edge of the precipice. She was half tempted to go outside and look for herself, but since Bridget seemed undisturbed, she decided there must not be anything down there at all.

Perhaps she hadn't heard the boat leave, or maybe the whole incident had been the product of too many sleepless nights. If stress could trigger nightmares, certainly it could also cause her to hear things that weren't there.

She came inside and closed the door to the balcony softly, leaning her forehead against the wood panel for a moment. But she hadn't imagined Bridget's initial reaction, or the fact that Bridget was here at all when she should have been outside. She looked over at the dog, now snoring peacefully with her snout resting on her paws.

Kelsey gave her head a doleful shake. Chances were she would never know for sure what had caused the sounds, or whether or not she had really heard them at all.

Perhaps she should wake Garrett to see if he had seen anything. Halfway to the bed, Kelsey stopped short, realizing how illogical she was beginning to sound. If he *had* heard the same disturbance, he would already be investigating. To wake him now would be pointless, since whatever had caused the noise was probably gone.

Still, the very idea of entering Garrett's room held a certain delicious appeal. How did he look when he slept? Would he wear the same angry frown that appeared so often when he was deep in thought? Or would his mouth be relaxed, gentle?

Would he awaken quickly, or would his eyes drift open with languid slowness, absorbing her presence with the same equanimity with which he handled his business every day?

The very thought of waking him made her heart stop for a moment, then start again with a beat that was much too fast. A shiver ran through her body, but with it came a measure of the same caution that sent him to another room in the first place.

What would he think when he found her near his bed? Would he believe her if she said she heard a noise, or would he assume she had come to him for some other reason?

Kelsey considered the consequences. Perhaps, she wondered, that wouldn't be so bad. She was as tired of resisting as he probably was. It might simply be easier to give in.

But that thought startled her so much that she suddenly became aware of her hand on the latch, her bedroom door hanging open by inches. Jerking her hand away as if the brass knob were red-hot, she pressed her palms to her cheeks.

"What a coward you are," she scolded herself miserably, turning back to her cold bed. "What a bloody coward."

By the time the two men had landed on shore again and dragged the small craft beneath a clump of bushes, they were both breathless from exertion. It was not until they reached the place where safety allowed them to relax that Micah finally spoke. Leaning his broad back against a wall, he wiped his brow with a meaty forearm and heaved a deep breath.

"Message from Levi says two more tomorrow. No moon again, so what time you want me ready?"

"Tomorrow?" Garrett's eyebrow shot up doubtfully. But meeting the other man's steady, patient gaze forced the protest from his lips. Levi Hoffman was the unofficial stationmaster of this final leg of the Underground Railroad. His dedication was unshakable, his judgment beyond question. Besides, Garrett had already tried to convince the older man that Riverview was no longer a safe depot. Tried, and had failed.

"Two hours after midnight, then," he responded gruffly.

Now it was Micah's turn to lift a puzzled brow. "So

late? We'll be pushin' close to dawn by the time we're done.''

''I said two and I meant it!''

His sharp reply sliced through the air like a knife, leaving behind only a weighted silence. Sighing, Garrett shoved a shaking hand through his hair. ''I'm sorry. These past few weeks've been rough, but I've no right to take it out on you.''

Micah laid a dark hand on his shoulder. ''No need to explain, my friend. I think I know what you're feelin'. Two in the morning it is.''

Darkness swallowed Micah as he moved beyond sight, leaving Garrett to ponder his actions alone. His capable accomplice probably did have an idea how he was feeling, but it was a safe bet that he didn't know the true extent of it, since Garrett had only given the briefest account of his conversation with Levi.

Within days after the fire he had concocted a reason to go to Lockport, and while Kelsey was busy exploring the many shops there, he had arranged to meet with the busy man in an empty room above one of the taverns.

The smile that had softened Levi's gaunt features receded swiftly when Garrett gave an account of the damages, as well as relating his suspicion that the blaze was a warning from Ogden.

''It's a certainty that he knows I'm part of the system,'' Garrett had acknowledged grimly. ''With the room beneath the stables made useless and the slave catchers watching so closely, I think we'd be wise to direct our efforts away from Riverview for a while.''

''I disagree.'' Always blunt, Levi had lifted one crooked finger to the curtain covering the window, edging the tattered lace aside to catch a glimpse of the street below. Satisfied that he had not been followed, he let the lace drop and turned back to Garrett. ''*Every* depot is being watched, which is reason to steer even more travelers your way. Despite your concerns, Riverview is still the safest and fastest route to freedom.''

''But Ogden—''

"Ogden, and those like him, are just a few of the many roadblocks we have always had to contend with. Rest assured, if he had any evidence at all, he would have acted by now."

Levi's conviction did little to ease Garrett's troubled mind. The man was leaving him no choice but to admit that Ogden was just a small part of his problem. "Setting the stable on fire is action enough. If it were only me . . ."

"Yes, I know," the Quaker said gently. "If it were only your life to consider you would not be hesitating. But remember this. They are the lives of many you hold in trust. Personal concerns must not stand in the way."

Lifting his eyes to the older man's, Garrett realized that Levi Hoffman had known his reasons for coming here from the moment he'd walked in the door. He tightened his lips, emitting a harsh stream of air. "Then I have to tell her. It's not fair to let her go on believing I've stopped, when in truth the station is now more active than ever."

"You cannot do that," Levi said thickly, even a little sadly. "You may be sure of her loyalty, though I sense you're not as certain as you'd like to be, but it's more than a matter of discretion. An unintentional slip of the tongue can be just as tragic as a deliberate betrayal."

And so he had not attempted to argue further, Garrett recalled. But with every day that passed in which Kelsey gazed at him unsuspectingly, with every night that found her entrusting herself to his arms, he wished he had persisted until Levi changed his mind.

Wrenching his thoughts back to the present, he searched in the darkness until he found a rag to wipe the perspiration from his brow and the mud from his boots. Tonight's crossing had been uneventful, by the grace of God, but each day increased the risk of discovery. Sooner or later his luck would run out.

Self-doubt was an emotion largely unfamiliar to him, but lately Garrett had found himself wavering over every decision like a woman trying to pick between two hats.

Starting with the one decision that was irrevocable.

He'd convinced himself that marrying Kelsey would put an end to the wariness between them, or at least ease it somewhat, but instead they'd been circling one another like two leery wildcats, not knowing whether to pounce or to retreat. He had been confident that Kelsey's fears would magically disappear once she realized the depth of his love, yet she remained as perplexed as ever. Slinging the soiled cloth to the ground, Garrett sighed with utter disgust.

Worst of all, he had counted on someone else to make the road easy for him. He was learning the hard way that sometimes there were no easy roads to take.

And he was already too far down this one to turn back.

25

"Kelsey, my dear. I never expected to find you here!"

Guiltily, her head shot up, then Kelsey forced the sheepish expression from her face as she smiled at Justin, who was approaching her from across the street. With a quick glance back toward the shop window to make certain Mrs. Porter was not watching still, she greeted him.

"Where else do you suppose I would be on market day," she quipped. In truth, it had taken her days just to get up the nerve to return to the place, and she was still angry with herself for letting the woman's previous snub bother her so. Fortunately, news of her marriage had preceded her, and while the shopkeeper was not particularly jovial, she at least let Kelsey make her purchases and leave the store relatively unscathed.

Only Justin's unexpected appearance made her feel as if she'd been caught filching gumdrops from the candy jar; but perhaps that was because she was still a bit ashamed of having practically eloped in the wake of *his* proposal.

"I heard you were still working in the fields like a hired hand," Justin said as he fell into step beside her. His tone made it clear how he felt about such behavior.

Kelsey ignored it. "There's not much to do now that the planting's done. Stocker Fulton assured me there's no way I can make the barley grow faster, but you can be sure at harvest time I'll be back out there."

Justin's eyes grew shuttered. "It's a shame you have to work so hard, my dear. I missed seeing you at the

Schultz's party last week. You were invited, weren't you?"

Thrusting her chin forward, Kelsey turned on him. "You know I wasn't, but what you don't seem to realize is that I don't care. One silly invitation doesn't mean the entire town has turned against me. Things are not as bad as you seem to think."

"Aren't they? Then why was your stable burned down?"

Kelsey had trouble keeping her voice from rising irritably. "It wasn't burned down, Justin. And you know as well as I that the reason had nothing to do with my relationship with Garrett."

"Aside from the fact that he is your husband," Justin said dryly, "and that his actions are the cause of Ogden's ignoble attentions."

"You don't know that! Why—"

At that moment a young couple with two young children walked past them, nodding a friendly greeting. Kelsey walked along on silence, until they were out of earshot.

"I didn't mean to—"

"You must know that—" Pressing her lips together tightly, Kelsey waited while Justin went on.

"I didn't mean to argue with you, my dear. It's just that I can't help but be concerned."

"Your concern is unwarranted. Everything is fine at Riverview. The fire was put out before it really got started, the horses were not harmed, and the crops are doing well."

"So I've heard." As he walked her to where the buggy was tied, Justin gazed at the clear blue sky thoughtfully, as if rehearsing what he was about to say. "If everything is going so well, Kelsey, then why are you not happy?"

She pursed her lips in a frown. "What makes you think I'm unhappy?" she asked after a few tense moments had passed.

"I know you too well. It's in the way you talk about everything but what is truly important. Do you know that you never mention your husband by name? And that when you do your eyes get this kind of agonized light in them, as if it's too painful for you to think of him?''

Kelsey was so stunned by his assessment that she could not respond. What he said was probably true, she admitted miserably. Though not for the same reason he seemed to think.

Embarrassment swept over her, laced with no small amount of vexation toward herself for not hiding her emotions better. It had never occurred to her that others would see that she was still plagued by doubt. That Justin had automatically assumed the fault lay with Garrett did not surprise her, but it filled her with shame nevertheless. And hardened her resolve.

She could not summon the power of speech until he had helped her into the buggy and placed the reins in her unsteady hands. ''You are mistaken, Justin. Garrett . . .'' She nearly choked, her throat was so tight. ''Garrett and I are very happy together. You do us both a great disservice by suggesting otherwise.''

He did not answer at first, but after a long moment he peered inquisitively at her flushed face. ''I apologize, then, for speaking out of turn. It won't happen again.''

After a strained good-bye, Kelsey steered the buggy into the center of the street, leaving Justin standing on the boarded walkway in front of the store. She did not wave to him, even though he lifted a hand in farewell, nor did she look back.

If she had, she might have seen the glimmer of satisfaction in his eyes.

Garrett leaned on the paddock rail, arms crossed before him as he watched one of the horses graze peacefully on the far side of the field. Too peacefully, he decided, examining the animal with a practiced eye. In fact, the mare had barely moved in the quarter hour he'd been standing here, not even to lower her head for another mouthful of grass. Unless he was mistaken, another foal would be born within the next twenty-four hours.

When he saw Benjamin cross from the kitchen to the stable he signaled for the man to join him. In less time than it took to ease his weight from his stiff leg, Benjamin's sharp gaze had seized on the mare, a wide grin splitting his wrinkled face.

"Six hours," he predicted quietly.

Garrett peered again at the horse. "Eight," he replied, holding out his hand.

Benjamin took it, sealing their wager with a firm shake. "Six, and ah'll add an extra case if'n she throws a filly."

"Done. We're due for a colt, old man. Double or nothing."

Benjamin accepted the increased stake with supreme composure. "Ain't lost a bet in forty years," he warned cheerfully, " 'cept but one. An' that didn't have nothin' ta do with a horse. Miz Kelsey done took longer ta make her 'ppearance than what anyone 'spected." He grinned again. "Jest lak a woman."

Garrett's laughter drifted through the field like a welcome breeze, the sound causing the mare to lift her head. Her roan coat glistened in the sun, clearly highlighting the rippling movement that shimmered across her side and around her swollen belly. Then, as if nothing had happened at all, the mare lowered her head again.

"Six," Benjamin pronounced once more before turning to limp back to the stable.

Garrett was still chuckling when Kelsey came out of the house. He glanced in her direction once, then looked again, his laughter dying, replaced by a stronger, more potent emotion.

She was wearing a white dress of the sheerest muslin with an underskirt the color of apricots. Puffed sleeves gave the gown a look of youth and innocence, but the scooped neckline and tightly sashed waist hinted seductively at greater charms. He had not seen this dress before, except in its box, but it swayed around her as if it were made for Kelsey alone, and only she could fill it to perfection. The effect on his system was like a splash of cold water.

Hot water, he amended hastily as blood steamed through his veins. His hands, now clenched around the top rail in a white-knuckled grip, ached to span her slender waist and test the smooth ascent of her breasts as she sauntered closer.

Kelsey was breathlessly aware of his lingering gaze, and it was all she could do to keep from retreating back to the house. Her fingers wound tighter around the wicker handle of the basket she held, but she raised her chin resolutely.

"I brought us some lunch. I thought perhaps we could picnic in the clearing by the river." As if a bribe were necessary, she added, "Hannah fried chicken."

Only the nervous tremor in her voice kept Garrett from pulling her hard against him. He studied her eyes for some sign of what this meant, but could find nothing except the same staunch determination with which she faced any task she found unpleasant, from mucking out the stables to having tea with Antoinette Delbert. Strangely disappointed, he returned his attention to the mare.

Kelsey released her breath with a measure of chagrin. It was going to take more than a pretty dress and fried chicken to breach the walls she had erected between them. The problem was, she didn't quite know where to begin. Mabelle's lectures on womanhood had never included the art of seducing one's husband.

From the stable behind them came the sound of Benjamin's tuneless whistle, and somewhere in the distance Bridget barked, yet still she felt certain Garrett could hear her pounding heart above the rest. He made no move, however, except to place one foot on the bottom rail as he leaned against the fence.

A whispering breeze ruffled his sun-streaked hair, making her yearn to do the same with her fingers. From his side she gazed longingly at his harsh profile. His tanned features were hard as granite, looking to be carved by the sun and wind, and yet Kelsey knew that a smile could turn his face into one of boyish playfulness, an appeal even more potent than the compelling magnetism she felt emanating from him now.

She wavered between moving closer and stepping away, knowing that either could be a mistake. Instead she followed his gaze into the paddock. "Is she all right?"

The mare had taken a few steps closer to them, still grazing occasionally but mostly staring straight ahead with a look of intense concentration. Garrett wondered if Kelsey were feeling the same sense of panic that had beset her when Lady Luck dropped her foal, but when he glanced over he saw only concern, with just a touch of curiosity.

"She's fine now. Benjamin was a bit worried when we first got her. She'd been sadly neglected by her previous owner, who didn't even realize she was carrying a foal until a few months ago. He was willing enough to sell her when she first started to show signs of illness."

"What kind of illness?" If her question sounded earnest, Kelsey didn't care. All her attention was focused on the mare.

"Nothing serious, thank God," Garrett explained. "She was overworked and malnourished. Rest and a healthy diet were all she needed"

"And the foal? Will it be all right, too?"

"As best as we can tell. We've done everything possible. Nature will take care of the rest." When several minutes passed and she didn't say anything, he risked another glance in her direction. Her gaze was fixed on the horse, but she chewed her lower lip thoughtfully, as if her mind were miles away. He was about to ask if something was wrong when she spoke suddenly.

"Are you saying that sometimes . . . that circumstances can play a part in whether or not a foal is born healthy and whole?"

Garrett peered at her questioningly. "Circumstances? If you mean proper care, then yes."

"And might it be the same way for . . ." she paused, her voice dropping low, "for people?"

"I'm no physician, but yes. I believe it is somewhat the same."

Kelsey sensed that he was waiting for her to explain, but when she met his gaze, she saw only the tenderness and friendship she had hoped to find before. Faltering, she dropped her eyes to the basket, where her fingers danced nervously along the handle. "I suppose . . . I suppose you'll want to stay here, to make sure everything's all right."

"We have a few hours. Six or eight, at least."

The note of amusement in his voice caused her to look up again. But before she could say anything, he took the basket in one hand and clasped hers tightly in the other. "The clearing did you say? Shall we ride or walk?"

"Umm, walk, please. I . . . I'm not wearing my habit."

Garrett looked at her out of the corner of his eye. "Yes, I've noticed."

Kelsey felt a blush rise all the way from the top of her breasts to the roots of her hair. She had wanted him to notice, hadn't she? Then why was she suddenly feeling like a rabbit cornered by a hungry wolf?

With her hand still engulfed in his, she had no choice but to follow as he led the way to a thicket of brambles, holding the prickly bushes aside until she was through. He hadn't asked which clearing, she recalled with a happy glow in the pit of her stomach. Though there were several along the river, only one was bound to her heart by memories. Garrett's too, she thought with a small measure of triumph.

It had been years since the path had been trimmed back or the grass clipped, but that mattered little to Kelsey when they reached the secluded spot. Aside from a bit more privacy, nothing had changed since the day more than five years ago when he had kissed her good-bye.

Briefly, she recalled, too, that this was the spot where she had encountered Micah, but all that seemed so far behind her now, while what had happened years ago was like yesterday.

Garrett helped her spread the blanket Hannah had packed atop a delicious-looking assortment of food, and they lost no time in unpacking their feast. It was, Kelsey thought ruefully, a good excuse to keep from talking. By now most of her resolve and all of her courage had fled, and though he continued to chat amiably, it was all she could do to respond in a voice she only hoped sounded normal.

She was making a valiant effort, Garrett decided less than halfway through their meal. Valiant, but not quite convincing. The awkwardness that had become a familiar part of their relationship in the past few weeks now escalated to forbidding heights, and he wondered what it was she had brought him here to tell him. He reached for her hand. "You're as skittery as a fawn today. What is it you're so nervous about?"

"I'm not nervous." Kelsey tried to pull her hand away, but his grip was firm. She could tell by the insistent look in his eyes that it was too late for her to change her mind now. She twisted her head and to the side. "Well, maybe I am, a little. There's something I wanted to talk to you about, and I'm not sure where to begin."

A sickening jolt shot through Garrett, the muscles in his chest contracting instantly. It couldn't be that she had changed her mind . . . could it?

"Why don't you say it?" he urged, choking back the bitter anxiety that rose in his throat. "That's usually the best way."

Kelsey fiddled with the plate on her lap, then thrust it from her abruptly. He was right, she told herself. She should quit stalling and simply tell him what was on her mind. "Do you remember when I was asking you about the mare?" she began.

"Is that what this concerns? Horses?"

"No—not exactly," she stammered. "It concerns me . . . us. Oh, Garrett, it's so hard to explain."

She had kept her face averted, but he didn't need to see it to know the anguish there. It was in her voice, in the way her hand trembled in his like a frantic bird. Moving closer, he eased her back against his chest so that she was sitting within his protective embrace. He rested his chin on the top of her silky hair. "I think I know what you're trying to say," he crooned gently. "Are you still worried about having a child?"

"Y-yes . . . no!"

A bright, shimmering hope lit inside him, radiating outward like a beacon of light. He could barely speak. "You're not?"

"I-I don't think so. At least, not as much. Before, I kept remembering—"

She stopped. There was no way she could explain without telling him everything. It was a risk she knew she could no longer avoid, and yet it seemed as if her entire life balanced upon this single moment. She was willing to trust him with everything she had in her power to give, but if he rejected that trust how could she bear to live?

"Remember what, darling? The things your mother told you?" He felt her heart beat against her ribs, and he wished he could ease her panic. He would dispute whatever tripe Mabelle had passed off as advice and reassure her if necessary.

But when she spoke again, it was *his* heart that slammed against the wall of his chest, knocking his breath away.

"I had a baby," she whispered agonizingly. When he did not respond she kept talking, rather than bear the silence that stretched around them like a deadly weight. "I had a baby. That's why I couldn't come home to you and Papa. Mother was so upset and humiliated that her heart failed, but before she died she made me swear I would never tell Papa, or come home with my bastard child and bring shame to the family."

"Oh, God," Garrett groaned, squeezing his eyes closed against the wrenching pain. His arms tightened around her, pulling her closer, and he felt a shudder wrack her slim form. "Why didn't you tell me before."

"I-I couldn't." Tears flowed down her cheeks, but they were tears of relief as well as sadness. He had not pushed her away with anger or disgust, as she had half expected. "I was so ashamed. And it . . . it hurt so to think about it."

A thousand questions clamored in his head, all demanding explanation, but only one was important enough to voice out loud. "What happened?"

Her body stiffened, resisting the answer with every ounce of her strength. Then Kelsey grew limp in his arms, unable, *unwilling* to fight it any longer. "I told you about Robert, but what I didn't say was that he tricked me into going to his room. I was so nervous, I drank too much champagne. The next thing I knew, it was morning and a maid was peering at me as if I were some kind of leper. Robert left a note of apology and then promptly discovered he had business in France. While I . . . I had to face the disgrace. Mother was furious, of course, but she kept it all a secret until we learned I was pregnant."

Kelsey paused for a breath, surprised that once she started, it was all so easy to say. It helped that Garrett's expression was concerned, but encouraging. "Lord and Lady Kelsey were appalled, of course. I was hidden in an upstairs room, with only my mother to wait on me. Then, after several months, she had a stroke."

Garrett knew she was leaving out a great deal. Mabelle would not have nursed her daughter with sympathy and care; rather, the woman probably spent most of her time railing against Kelsey.

"I wrote to Papa that she had died, but that I wished to stay in Europe. Mother convinced me that Papa would be ashamed, and since I already thought he didn't want me home . . . well, you can see why I couldn't tell him the truth. When he sent me money for expenses, Lord Kelsey demanded that I pay him for room and board. Except that once Mother was gone, I was lucky to get one meal a day."

Garrett stroked her back lovingly, nuzzling her hair. "And the baby?"

"She . . . she was born too soon. She was born too s-soon and she d-died."

The tears came hard and fast now, but to Kelsey's surprise, the incredible grief she had kept deep inside seemed more bearable now that it was allowed to surface. Or maybe it was because Garrett was holding her tenderly, absorbing some of he pain. As soon as her initial spate of crying eased, she found herself wanting to tell him the rest. The loneliness when Lord Kelsey cast her out shortly after the birth, the hardships she endured while earning money for passage home, and most of all the guilt, knowing a single mistake had brought nothing but death.

He listened in silence as she poured out all the sorrow and horror that had poisoned her for so long. And when she ran out of words, he held her quietly, possessively, willing her to take whatever strength she could from his warm embrace.

"My love," he whispered hoarsely, an overwhelming sense of protectiveness filling his heart and his voice, "tell me what I can do to help you. I want to help."

Kelsey nuzzled closer to him, wiping her damp cheeks against his shirt. "You already have," she breathed. "I was afraid you would be angry because I kept the truth from you for so long." She felt a muscle jump beneath her hand, but she decided that it was merely a reaction to her movement.

"You had reason to keep your silence," he replied evenly. "I can understand."

"But I should have trusted you. What kind of marriage do we have if we can't trust one another?"

What kind, indeed, Garrett thought grimly. Her innocent plea only served to make his sin of omission seem more dastardly. But not for long, he pledged to himself. Not for long.

After several minutes of gathering her composure within the circle of his arms, Kelsey shifted around so that she could see his face. Lines of care creased his brow, disappearing beneath the golden hair that fell over his forehead. His blue eyes were penetrating, yet gentle, with just a telltale hint of redness around the rims that made her heart swell with love. Very gently, she pressed her hand to his cheek, as if it were cut of the smoothest marble. "I-I'm sorry that I've let all this stand between us. I don't want it to—"

"It hasn't, darling. I'm glad this is out in the open now, but I won't have you blaming yourself for not wanting to have children. After what you've been through, it's only natural."

"But it's not true anymore!" Kelsey gazed at him with a mixture of shyness and hope. "That's what I've been trying to tell you. I was afraid that my baby died because something was wrong with me, but mostly I thought I couldn't bear to risk that kind of heartache again. I don't want to be afraid, Garrett. I want to be free of the past. Everything's different now and . . . well, I just want us to be happy together."

Her dark eyes shone with an inner light he had never seen there before, far more compelling than seductive words or bold kisses. Cupping her face in both hands as if it were the most fragile thing in the world, he bent his head over hers, his mouth poised just a hairsbreadth from her trembling lips. "I will make you happy, sweet Kelsey."

Her heart throbbed surely, gloriously, infusing her with a heat that spread through her limbs and ignited her soul. He kissed her slowly, deeply, drawing a response that rose from so far within her that she felt nothing but the growing web of need that clung to them. Her skin tingled as every pore opened to absorb the feel of him holding her.

Garrett moved his hands to her head, driving his fingers through her tangled curls, loosing the shiny ribbon that was a poor rival to the satin darkness of her hair. He tilted her head back farther to lengthen their kiss, and her lips parted willingly, invitingly. Welcomingly.

She shifted slightly so that she could span his shoulders with her hands. Beneath the soft fabric of his shirt, his muscles were like iron encased in velvet, and she could not get enough of touching him. Her fingers searched for and found the softness at the back of his neck, twining through the golden locks like tiny creatures burrowing for shelter, for comfort.

His hands framed her face, his eyes questioning, his voice unsteady. "Kelsey, if we don't stop now . . ."

The shattering need in his eyes made her limbs weak and her pulse bold. Drained of despair, her heart ached to be filled with what was new and wondrous. Excitement and desire had replaced the nagging doubts, telling her she would be his for the rest of their lives. She breathed against his burning lips, "I don't want to stop . . . please, don't stop."

26

With infinite care, Garrett eased her onto the blanket, elbowing the wicker basket aside. The overgrown bushes provided a screen of privacy, enclosing them in a room with walls of spring greenery and a ceiling made of the cloudless sky. He seemed hesitant still, so Kelsey reached for him, drawing him down until his weight pressed full upon her.

Her eyes sparkled with tears of joy, turning so dark and rich that he felt as if he could journey into their depths and never return. Tracing the line of a single tear that had slipped down the side of her face, he let his finger capture its moisture, changing it from a trail of sorrow into a path of wondrousness. And then his mouth followed where his hand had touched . . . tasting, soothing, healing.

Kelsey arched higher, her lips seeking his, her arms pulling him closer. His weight was like a comforting blanket upon her, a heated contrast to the cool ground beneath them and the air swirling over her sensitive flesh. An urgency filled her, borne of desperate need and delirious hope, and she pushed at his shirt eagerly, trembling with anticipation.

He was surprised by her fervor. Surprised, and incredibly aroused. Her hands enflamed his skin with a burning desire for more; her supple body was provocative and impatient. Slowly, with painstaking restraint, he slipped the muslin dress from one shoulder, smoothing her alabaster skin with aching fingertips. She shuddered at his touch, lightly, delicately, escalating his passion to greater heights.

It was the first time he had seen her in the full light of day, but Kelsey's initial shyness soon melted as he removed each layer of her clothing. His eyes had darkened to a deeper shade of blue, flecked with colored lights that shifted and moved like a kaleidoscope with the stream of emotions flowing between them. His own clothing was quickly dispatched and he stretched his length next to hers, thigh to thigh, lips to seeking lips.

"My God, you are beautiful," he murmured thickly, hardly tearing his mouth from hers long enough to speak. Without the barrier of clothing she was like a blaze of heat next to his skin, and he felt his blood begin to churn and boil.

No hell could flame as hot as this, Kelsey thought distantly, nor heaven be as filled with such ecstasy. Everywhere his hands touched left her shivering with delight, and he *was* touching her everywhere. The emptiness she had felt before was fast becoming sated with sensations she had never known existed, let alone wished for. Yet now she wished for them all, craved them all, knowing she would not be complete until he gave them to her.

He kissed her slender throat and collarbone, easing his weight lower until his mouth caught and held the rosy tip of her breast. Laving the budding peak with his tongue, he gently massaged the other until it, too, pebbled beneath his thumb and forefinger.

It seemed to Kelsey that there was a taut wire stretched between her breasts and her womb, tightening with exquisite pain and pleasure at the same time. Her hands clenched in the thickness of his hair, feeling his pulse throb at a tempo matching her own. Then slowly, reluctantly, he raised his head enough to meet her heavy-lidded gaze.

"Sweet Kelsey, are you sure?" In the final instant of control, before it escaped him completely, he wanted to be certain. Perhaps it was in the back of his mind that, if she drew away from him now, he could withhold his trust for just a few more days. But her instant response left no room for doubt.

"Love me," she murmured, her lips brushing against his forehead. "Love me, Garrett."

His touch became more intimate, exploring the curve of her hip and the flat plane of her belly. She gasped when his fingers became entangled in the damp curls at the juncture of her thighs, seeking entrance.

He was not surprised to find that she was as ready for him as he was for her, though he had reckoned on her having misgivings at the final moment. But with a small cry of triumph and elation she lifted her hips, making his way clear, inevitable.

She was hot and tight, giving and taking, and the sensations that spilled through his body tore restraint from him like a hurricane wind. Gentleness was no longer in him as passion drove him closer to the mindless release to be found only in her arms. His mouth sought hers again, stifling a moan that tumbled from her lips, not of pain or fear, but of exultation.

The small amount of discomfort she felt at his sliding intrusion slipped away in the face of a much more compelling need, and Kelsey opened herself to him with total abandonment, letting his love fill her heart and her body and her mind, until there was no room for anything but him.

He started to slip away and she clutched her hands tighter in protest, but he entered her again, faster, deeper than before, and a whole new range of pleasure flashed through her. Time ceased to exist, the world fell away, life began and ended with this.

And then his movements grew stronger, building the fire inside her to raging inferno. She rose instinctively to meet his powerful thrusts, searching for release from the desperate ache that consumed her entire being.

Nothing that had come before prepared her for this, nothing that happened after would ever be as exquisitely beautiful. The rippling waves began deep inside her and unfurled quickly, suddenly, and she heard the sob that was her own as if from a distance. Every nerve in her body screamed for fulfillment at the same moment that his final, magnificent thrust sent the flames shooting through her limbs, quenching them at the same time.

Garrett's own mouth formed around a wordless shout as release shuddered through him, joining them with invisible chains that would never again set them free from one another. Their hearts were irrevocably fused, their souls forged into one by love.

Lifting himself slowly, he searched her eyes, finding in them the answers to all the questions he had ever asked, all the trust he had ever wished for. "I love you, Kelsey," he whispered brokenly.

Her heart responded to his claim with a gentle swell, tears blurring her vision. Now, however, she did not need to see to know the truth of what he said. She could feel it still within her, around her; the very air seemed to quiver with the brilliant purity of their love.

"And I love you," she replied, aware that she was crying, yet unable to keep her emotions from flowing freely. "I have loved you all my life."

Tenderly, reverently, Garrett kissed the tears from her face, rolling to his side without breaking the bond between them. One hand still clutched her hair, not wanting to let go, while the other smoothed a path over her trembling flesh from hip to shoulder. "Somehow," he murmured, "I always knew it would be like this. I once told you we were meant for one another, my love, but it goes far beyond that. You are so much a part of who I am and what I long to be that I can't begin to separate myself from you. I don't want to."

Words seemed inadequate, so Kelsey merely clung to him with all the fervency that was left in her, enjoying the safety and comfort of lying in his arms. It was quite some time before she found the strength to move farther, and even then it was only to lift her head to meet his gaze. "Do you think . . . ," she began hesitantly, "do you think we started a baby?"

Garrett shifted slightly, turning her in his arms so he

could look full upon her face. "Perhaps. There's no way to tell, yet. Would it bother you if we had?"

Kelsey chewed at her lower lip. A part of her still wanted to cringe in terror at the idea of becoming pregnant, but she recognized that attitudes so ingrained would take time to dissipate completely. Just now, however, she was too full of trust and hope to let those old fears bother her. She was determined not to let them. "No, I meant it when I said I wanted to have a child. I just think it would be nice to know, so we could look back on this day and remember how very special it is."

"This day will *always* be special to me, baby or no baby. It's you I love, Kelsey. If we have children, they'll be the fulfillment of our love. If not we'll still have each other. That's what's important."

If she could have captured this moment in glass to preserve for all time, Kelsey would have done so. "Oh, Garrett," she sighed happily, resting her cheek on his broad shoulder. "You were right. I always knew we could be this way together, too, only I didn't dare hope for it. Did you know I dreamed of us?" Stifling a giggle, she recalled some of her more imaginative fantasies. "Sometimes," she admitted sheepishly, "I quite embarrassed myself."

His throaty chuckle lifted wisps of hair from her brow, caressing her skin like a satin breeze. "Those kinds of dreams, sweetheart, are meant to come true. So long as they are about you and me, of course."

He felt, rather than heard her silence, though in no more than a dozen heartbeats she sighed and spoke. "I've had other dreams, too. Nightmares, really, about the time when I was desperate and ill, before . . . before my Amanda was born. Some nights—I suppose when I'm not sleeping very soundly anyway—I wake up before they get too horrible. But once in a while the dream goes on and I feel myself losing her again. I try so hard to hold her close but there are always people tearing her away. And that's when I hear the crying."

All through her soft recital Garrett had remained still,

but now his eyes narrowed quickly. ''Crying? Do you mean *you* cry out?''

''No, it's always a baby's cry. It seems so real. Last night—''

''You heard it last night?''

''I *dreamed* it last night, and the night before. But I have a feeling I won't be dreaming it again.'' Kelsey nuzzled closer, incredible satisfaction and peace of mind combining to make her drowsy. Now she was certain she could rest without interruption for days. ''Perhaps,'' she whispered lazily, ''we've hit upon a cure for insomnia. I feel terribly relaxed, you know.''

He did not answer, only continued to stroke her hair gently. Gradually, her limbs grew heavy entwined in his, and her lips fell open slightly, her feather-soft breath fanning his chest.

When next Garrett looked down at her with a troubled frown, she was fast asleep.

27

The first day of summer burst forth in a morning as glorious as any Kelsey had ever seen. Flinging open the balcony door, she tiptoed to the railing, hugging her cotton wrapper around her. Like old friends, the line of poplars tipped and waved in the gentle breeze, each small green leaf winking at her conspiratorially as the wind flipped through the treetops. She lifted her arms high and stretched, inhaling deeply of the morning air, which was fresh and exhilarating, hinting at roses and the moist scent of the river.

It would be a wonderful morning, she decided happily, to treat herself to a luxurious bath before she went to check on the brand new colt born last evening.

The kitchen was sparkling clean and completely empty, so she peeked through the window to see if Hannah had stepped out to the yard. No one was in sight, but the market basket usually balanced on a nail next to the back door was missing, meaning the cook had gone to town. Since the sun was already arching over a thin line of clouds in the distance, Kelsey knew it was much later than her usual rising time.

A slow smile curved her lips. Somehow she wasn't surprised.

As if last night hadn't been enough to make her pleasantly tired, Garrett had awakened her before the sun was more than a hint of pink light slipping through the curtains in her room. His tender kisses had teased her out of a deep slumber, only to have him whisper that he was off to Lockport to arrange for a load of spring wheat to be shipped to Montreal. His departure, however, had been slightly delayed.

A heated blush suffused her cheeks at the memory and she was glad Hannah was not there to witness it. The old woman would have been, in her own words, plum tickled to see that the two of them had come to their senses. But to Kelsey it was all too new, too wonderful to share. She wanted to hold each moment like a thousand precious gems, to be taken out and examined privately, then tucked away in a secret corner of her heart.

Rousing herself from such fanciful thoughts, she filled two kettles with water from the pump and stoked the fire until it roared. Once the water was set to boil, she pulled her cotton wrapper tight around her, sitting down in Hannah's rocker.

Immediately, she noticed that the chair was not in its usual position in front of the stove. That was odd. Hannah was extremely particular about keeping her chair centered exactly over the braided rug that covered the floor between the stove and the table. Time and again, Kelsey had seen her fuss about, looking for the perfect spot where the curved rockers swayed smoothly without the slightest creak or groan coming from the floorboards. Kelsey gave the chair a tentative push.

A piercing squeak made her smile. Sure enough, Hannah would shift the rocking chair to its rightful place just as soon as she came back. Kelsey lifted her feet, leaning back and forth gleefully as the wooden planks beneath played their grating tune. Now she remembered doing the same as a child, purposely rocking faster and faster until a tormented Hannah would shoo her from the kitchen with some treat or another. Likely that was why the old woman fretted over the chair now; she probably recalled those days as a peculiar form of torture.

Kelsey's expression softened. Silently, she thanked God for Hannah's loving nature. The cook had always treated her childish pranks with amused tolerance, intuitively understanding her need for freedom from Mabelle's suffocating hold. And when that hold had continued to threaten her happiness, Hannah had urged her to confront her doubts and see them for the silly fears they were. Kelsey would be eternally grateful. Thanks to the old woman's loving concern, she was far happier than she ever dreamed she could be.

Of course, Garrett had had a hand in that, too.

Of its own volition, a smile emerged from her lips and she ducked her head to hide it, though no one else was in the room. She slowed the rocking chair to a soothing, rhythmic pace, trying to lull her suddenly pounding heart into a like beat.

Why was it, she wondered, that two people could be so very different in some ways, and yet their joining be as miraculous as a perfect rosebud, fragile and light, yet promising to blossom into a thing of such beauty and radiance that one could barely comprehend its reality?

Closing her eyes tightly, Kelsey continued to rock back and forth. And how could it be real, she mused, when ordinary emotions ceased to exist, supplanted by feelings more vibrant, more utterly resplendent than anything she had known before?

For several minutes she basked in the knowledge that, even if these wonderful feelings did not last forever, at least she had experienced more in the past twenty-four hours than many people did in a lifetime. Surely her own parents had not, she thought sadly. If they had, then perhaps events might have taken an altogether different turn.

The sound of steam venting through the top of the kettle interrupted her thoughts. Rising quickly, Kelsey put aside her dreamy notions and hurried to attend to her bathwater.

It was when the chair rocked to a halt, bringing an end to the incessant creaking, that she heard the faint echo of a new sound. Her limbs locked, Kelsey froze with one hand outstretched toward the stove, the other clutching her wrapper with a white-knuckled grip.

All her senses were riveted on the oval rug beneath her feet. It was from that direction that the noise had come.

For a long moment she could hear nothing but the bubbling water, demanding her attention with tiny, insistent pops, but soon the terrifying sound came again. A tremor worked its way from her feet clear to the top of her head, where she was certain her hair was standing on end.

It was the sound of her nightmares, as distant and unreal as in the blackest of nights, and Kelsey couldn't help wondering if she was going mad. Until yesterday she had considered the possibility, but passion had overruled all other emotions, causing her to forget the spectres that haunted her. Now they had come back. She nearly moaned.

From outside, Bridget's strident bark as she warned away a flock of sparrows plunged through the air, chasing away the cobwebs of dreams and bringing Kelsey full awake. This wasn't another nightmare, she thought, snapping her head up, her expression narrowing to a concentrated frown. Nor was she imagining things. From somewhere nearby, below her, came a constant, high-pitched wailing that could have only one source.

A baby.

But where? Kelsey hurried to the stove, snatching a potholder to shove the boiling kettles from the heat. For a brief moment she debated calling out, but Benjamin would have driven Hannah to the market. Aside from the stable lads, whom she'd not seen or heard yet this morning, there was no one else to help her search. She would have to find out for herself.

Swiftly, Kelsey grabbed the arms of the rocking chair and propelled it against the wall, then reached low for the edge of the braided rug, flinging it aside with a strength that might have surprised her had she stopped to take note.

At first she could see nothing but the smooth boards that made up the kitchen floor. Dropping to her hands and knees, she inspected each plank carefully, running the tips of her fingers along the cracks between them. Without the thick wool of the rug to muffle it, or perhaps because her ears were now tuned to the distant sounds, the baby's cries seemed louder now, more persuasive than ever.

"Oh, God," Kelsey groaned. How could the sounds be coming from the ground? There must be somewhere else! She lifted her head, peering around for some clue. The fruit cellar!

On the opposite wall was a door that led to the small, underground room where Hannah stored perishable food. Kelsey had often played there as a child, and in fact had stepped inside just yesterday to fetch a bowl of chilled butter for the cook. Though the crying did not seem to be coming from that direction, she scrambled to her feet, rushing over to yank the half-sized door.

Ignoring the candle placed on a shelf, Kelsey hurried down into the stone-lined room. A multitude of scents rose to greet her, from the ripe odor of last year's apples and the spicy fragrance of Hannah's dried herbs, to the peculiar tang of dank, mouldy earth. Kelsey had to stoop low, for the ceiling was a mere five feet from the floor. By stretching her arms out, she could almost touch the shelves on either side. Crouching down, she swept her hands in wide circles across the floor, remembering only after the cool earth met her palms that it was made of hard-packed dirt. Frustrated, and straining to hear if the crying was louder, she stood again. Either the wails had stopped or she had moved farther away from them, not closer.

One thing was patently clear. There was no baby in here, and never had been.

Retreating up the steps, Kelsey closed the door behind her, turning to face the disorder she had created in the kitchen. "Maybe the entrance is somewhere else," she whispered to herself, struggling to recall if she had ever seen anything odd, which might have been a doorway. Certainly Mabelle had never mentioned an underground level below the house, but her papa had designed Riverview, so surely he had known.

And what Sheldon once knew, so, likely as not, would Garrett.

A sudden hissing from the stove jerked her attention back to the present, and Kelsey hurried over, using a potholder to lift one kettle of water farther away from the heat. She scurried back to her room to throw on some clothes, her bath long forgotten. If only Garrett were here. He would help her find—

Kelsey stopped short. Find what? A baby? In a cellar she wasn't even certain existed?

Until now she had been so intent on finding the source of the crying, she hadn't paused to consider the meaning of such a thing. But now the wails had faded to silence and her heart had ceased its excited patter, allowing her to contemplate what she was about to do, and why.

You're searching for a dream, a voice inside scolded.

Not a dream. Not in the middle of the morning!

What difference does that make? It can't possibly be real.

But it is! I know it is!

How can you be so sure?

It was this last thought that leant a sense of urgency to her purpose, giving wings to her feet as she sped up the last few stairs. She wasn't sure at all, but there was only one way to find out, and waiting for Garrett to come home wasn't going to do that poor baby, wherever it was, any good. Not to mention her own state of mind!

By the time she had thrown on the first dress that came to hand and donned a pair of sturdy shoes, Kelsey was beginning to doubt her sanity again. Even if Riverview had a cellar—and just because she didn't know about it was no proof that one did not exist—how on earth would a baby have gotten inside?

What she had probably heard, she rationalized, was some kind of animal, perhaps a cat or a bird, and for some reason the sound had carried up through the floor instead of the windows.

Or maybe the crying *had* come from within her own mind. She had heard of people who claimed they were bothered by strange sounds, ringing and clanging and such, just before going deaf. Could that be what was happening to her?

At this point, she thought ruefully, tying her hair back with a ribbon as she bounded down the stairs, even the thought of portending deafness was preferable to the alternative.

Kelsey returned to the kitchen for one more look.

One more look turned into several, each as hopeless as the last. But when she bent down to replace the braided rug so she could push the table away from the wall, she caught sight of a small knothole in one of the planks. Now that the sun was streaming brightly through the kitchen window, it was clear that what had appeared to be a dark circle earlier was really a hole in the floor. Kneeling, she peered into the tiny opening.

Only blackness met her eye, so with a resolute frown on her face, Kelsey stuck a finger into the hole and tugged lightly.

To her utter astonishment, that slight movement was enough to cause a section of the floor to rise soundlessly, and with more ease than she could have imagined she swung the trapdoor all the way up, then back down again, marveling at the smooth workings of a pair of well-oiled hinges. The door was so expertly fitted into the surrounding planks that she might never have found it, and certainly would not have looked twice had the sounds of crying not compelled her to search.

Relief welled within her, along with a sense of determination that wiped away her earlier thoughts of deafness and insanity. No dream had created this hiding place, and no nightmare would keep her from learning its secret.

She propped the door open again, then scurried to the cupboard for the lantern Hannah always kept there. After a quick check to make sure there was plenty of oil, Kelsey lit the wick and approached the opening.

The hole itself was about two feet square, and she could see the first rung of what appeared to be a wooden ladder reaching into the darkness. Holding the lantern down into the entrance, she tried to ascertain the size and depth of the space below, though she knew it would be difficult to tell until she lowered herself into the gaping hole.

Kelsey set the lantern down long enough to knot the hem of her skirt up around her knees, then started down, reaching for the light when her head was level with the floor.

She didn't realize she had been holding her breath until her foot touched solid ground at the bottom of the ladder and she was able to turn around to see what was behind her. Expelling a lungful of air in a rush of disappointment, Kelsey held the lantern high, viewing the tiny enclosure with a rueful frown.

It was a cellar, all right. As bare as the poplar trees in winter. Even the rows of shelves lining one wall were empty, as if they had been built and then forgotten. For whatever reason Sheldon had designed this room, it appeared he had never used it. There was nothing to be found here, especially not a baby.

Loath to give up too quickly, yet afraid she would find nothing, Kelsey hung the lantern from the ladder and began a cursory search of the empty chamber. Unlike the fruit cellar, these walls were constructed of wood panels, with the floor laid from planks similar to those in the kitchen. The room had obviously been planned with care, which alluded to some purpose or intent beyond the more usual storage cellar. But now its only wares were dust and cobwebs.

"Good Lord!" she exclaimed with a shiver of revulsion as she walked into one of the clinging gossamer threads. With a swipe of her arm she cleared the air around her face. Her voice echoed through the tiny chamber, sounding at once louder and more distant. Like the cries she had heard just minutes ago.

More convinced than ever that this room held the answer to the puzzle, she circled toward the wall of shelves, continuing her search. With both hands Kelsey reached over her head to feel along the highest of the flat boards. It was just beyond her reach so she raised up on her toes, inadvertently pressing her body against the lower shelves. As she did the wood gave in to her weight, and though the movement could have been only a scant quarter of an inch, it was enough to make her jump back with a startled cry.

A moving wall! Kelsey stood squarely in front of the mysterious partition. Tentatively, then with growing firmness she pushed, uttering a satisfied cry when the wood panel gave way to pressure with a creaking groan. Just like a door, the wall swung inward, revealing another small enclosure behind it.

Snatching up the lantern, Kelsey slipped into the narrow fissure, first making sure that the panel would not close behind her. Fear and anticipation shimmied up her spine. She had no intention of stopping her exploration now, but she didn't want to be trapped inside either!

The next room was no larger than a closet, yet she had no need to search further. She knew as soon as her foot caught on one raised floorboard that there was another trapdoor here.

This one was not as well hidden as the hatchway in the kitchen, but there was no need, she realized, because the closet itself was so thoroughly concealed. Again she lifted the planked aperture slowly.

The scent of damp earth rose to fill her nostrils, and a puff of air rising through the opening caused the lantern to flicker, casting eerie shadows on the closed in walls.

Raising one hand to her breast to calm her pounding heart, Kelsey lowered the lantern into the blackness below.

28

Kelsey lifted the lantern above her shoulder, surveying the stone-walled cavern as she reached to bottom step of yet another ladder. How many had she come down now—four?

With each descending level, the rooms had grown smaller and more primitive. This one was as cold and damp as a cave, though the chisel marks on the straight walls were proof that it had been constructed by man, not nature. Still, the rock-hewn sides were beaded with moisture, the dankness filling her nostrils with an earthy scent; not unpleasant, but hardly comforting.

"Is anybody down here?" She didn't really expect an answer, but the sound of her own voice lessened the solitude. Her words faded to nothing in the blackness beyond the lantern's circle of light. Edging closer to one wall, Kelsey peered into the dark, making out an odd shape cast into shadow against the carved rock. With one hand she reached hesitantly, prodding the chest-high mound with a shaking finger.

It was made of cloth, or at least was covered by one, and Kelsey quickly looked around for a place to set the lantern down. Seeing none, she held it higher, tugging at the dark fabric until it gave way.

The canvas sheet dropped heavily to the floor, revealing a stack of assorted crates and a pile of burlap sacks. Shifting the lantern to her other hand, she lifted one of the wooden tops. To her surprise, the lid lifted cleanly from the box. She raised herself on tiptoes to peer inside, thrusting the lantern high so that the light fell into the opened crate.

"Apples?" Reaching inside, she picked up one of the round fruits. Though it was wrinkled and small, the conditions down here had preserved the apple well. But surely not for more than a few months? she questioned silently. Replacing the apple, she pulled the cover back onto the crate, using it as a resting place for the lantern as she moved to another box. This one was smaller but just as easily opened.

"Cheese!" The round wheels were quickly identified by their pungent odor. The next crate revealed ropes of dried beef wrapped in newspaper, the headline of the *Lewiston Register* appearing boldly on the first piece she unfolded. The date beneath the banner was less than two months old. *After* she had come to Riverview.

How did this stuff get down here? And more important, who had been using her home without her knowledge? Kelsey was more than puzzled; fear niggled at her, refusing to go away. How many nights had she laid upstairs while a stranger invaded her privacy?

At least she wasn't insane, she thought wryly, refusing to examine the potential danger involved. Certainly there was no baby, but there *had* been someone. And maybe that person had inadvertently caused noises that *might*, from a very great distance, sound like a baby. She knew she was stretching for possibilities, but what else could she think?

Carefully, Kelsey returned everything to its original place, conscientiously adjusting the canvas cover. Sooner or later the owner of this contraband would have to return, but in the meantime she didn't want him to know he'd been discovered. It would be far more satisfying to catch him in the act of trespassing. Preferably with Garrett and the sheriff to back her up.

She moved to the ladder and was about to climb up when a noise scraped through the room, making her turn so fast the lantern swayed wildly, throwing bizarre shadows on the stone walls. Panic clutched at her throat, but she managed to hold the lantern still and croak, "Who's there?"

When silence was her only answer, Kelsey breathed a ragged sigh. Perhaps she had disturbed the contents of one of the boxes, causing them to shift. Or maybe there were mice down here. Laughing uneasily at her cowardice, she turned toward the ladder. But for some reason, a cold chill raced up her spine like an icy wind shifting the air.

And then she heard it again. At first it was the same as before—a scraping sound not unlike the one Bridget usually made when nudging against a door—but it was followed by a faint mewling, muffled, though still quite distinct. It was coming from the direction of the crates!

"Is someone there?" Kelsey wished her voice wouldn't quiver so, but she could no more control it than the trembling in her knees. Now she was certain that she was not alone, and for a moment she was torn between investigating further and fleeing up the ladder. She didn't want to run into whoever was down here.

And if she did? Drawing herself up straighter, Kelsey raised her chin bravely. This was *her* home.

As soon as she sped back to the pile of crates she saw what she had missed before. Part of the wall behind the stash of food was made of wood, not stone, and in that wall was a tiny door. There was no knob or latch, but she could tell by the positions of the hinges that the door swung toward her, with just enough gap for the tips of her fingers. With an abrupt nod to giver herself courage, Kelsey pulled on the wooden portal.

Though the darkness beyond the doorway was as thick and unbroken as black velvet, she sensed right away that she would not be met by an empty room. Faint whispers, rhythmic and hushed, filled the air with expectancy. And then a piercing wail jolted through the quiet like the scream of a wounded beast.

Several things happened at once then. Kelsey dropped her lantern with a startled gasp, spinning back toward the opening at the same instant that someone rammed into her from the side, shoving her to the hard rock floor. Before she could call out, a sweaty palm clapped tightly over her mouth, hauling her to her feet. She heard the door behind her click shut, and dread swept through her with sickening speed.

"Who is she?" a frightened voice asked. The man's soft accent reminded her of her mother's on the rare occasions when it had not been sharpened with bitterness, but Kelsey could see nothing since the lantern's flame had been snuffed out.

"Light a candle," someone growled behind her ear. Kelsey squirmed, but his iron-hard arms gave no mercy. He seemed to be gigantic, taller and stronger than anything human, and more frightening. A helpless wave rolled through the pit of her stomach.

Within moments the quick flash of fire and odor of sulphur told her a match had been lit, and soon a small flame illuminated the face of the man who held a crude candle so high it nearly touched the low ceiling of the cave. Her widened eyes met his as recognition jolted through her.

"You can let her go," he said quietly, motioning to her captor to loosen his hold.

A third man stepped forward into the light, peering at her warily. His dark face was blank with fear, the only white showing when he rolled his eyes at the one who had held her in his unyielding grip. Kelsey shivered as the hulking black man stepped from behind her, and she stared up at his towering physique. She was lucky he hadn't snapped her neck!

"How did you find us?"

Kelsey whipped her gaze back to the man with the candle. There was none of the kindly shoemaker in his demanding tone; only the same determination and fear she had witnessed in him that night on the riverbank. "Micah!"

"How did you find us?" he repeated relentlessly.

"There was crying . . ." She cast around for the baby she knew must be here with them, her eyes finally coming to rest on a shadowed figure huddled in one corner. "I thought I imagined it. But I didn't, did I?"

"I tol' ya we should'n' a brought 'er," the large man rumbled at the smallest man.

Standing between them, Micah raised a hand to order silence. His gaze still probed Kelsey. "Does anyone know where you are?"

"N-no. Garrett . . . had to go to Lockport today. I thought you made it to Canada," she said abruptly. "At least when I didn't hear anything I hoped you had. Have you been down here all this time?"

Curiosity had displaced her fear once she remembered that Micah had not harmed her that first time and was unlikely to do so now. She glanced around the room, noticing for the first time that it appeared to be a natural cave.

Motioning to the other men to step away, Micah beckoned for her to follow him. She hesitated only an instant, then moved closer to the opposite wall where he waited.

"I did make it to Canada," Micah explained softly. "But some of these other folks needed help findin' their freedom."

"Is she a friend of Gabriel's?" the large man spoke up insistently.

"Who is Gabriel?" Kelsey did not miss the sharp glance Micah threw her way, nor did she miss the hiss of air as the person propped against the wall inhaled deeply.

Micah's hand sliced the air in a dismissive gesture. "There is no Gabriel. It's only a code name we use for anyone who helps us on our way."

"Well, someone must be helping you now. How did you get into my house?"

His full mouth curved, though the smile did not reach his eyes. "How do I know we can trust you?"

Kelsey paused, returning his stare. "You don't, except that I helped you once before. Even though you wouldn't take much."

A sudden moan from the person bundled against the wall drew her attention. She crouched low. "Are you hurt?" she asked gently. From behind the folds of the blanket a pair of clouded eyes peeked out at her. Then the blankets parted and the figure lifted a squirming object toward Kelsey.

"Dacia!" Micah's deep voice reverberated through the cavern, but the frail woman appeared not to have heard. She let the blanket fall away from her head, revealing a face too thin and drawn, and hair lank and matted.

Kelsey was shocked by the woman's condition, but not as shocked as when she brushed the woman's hands and found them dry and so hot she felt as if she'd been branded. But the object wrapped in an old linen sheet soon occupied her every thought, for as quickly as she clasped it to her chest it wiggled and emitted another lusty cry.

"Oh dear God!" Kelsey whispered as a thousand emotions rocked through her at once. She uncovered the baby's head quickly, realizing that it might have suffered from lack of air while its mother was trying to keep it from crying out. But just as compelling was the deep sense of longing that poured from her soul when the tiny warm body snuggled closer to her, searching hungrily for something to eat. Her hands trembled so much she was afraid she might drop the babe, and so she reluctantly held it back to its mother.

The woman named Dacia shook her head adamantly, though it was obvious the movement cost her considerable effort. A racking cough prevented her from speaking right away.

"She's sick," Kelsey cried softly, turning to Micah. "She's too sick to be down here."

Micah shook his head. "There isn't any place else. She knew the risk before she came this far."

Anger at his apparent callousness filled Kelsey, and she touched the woman's feverish brow with her fingertips. "Don't worry. I'll get a doctor and—"

"No doctor!" For the first time Micah's voice frightened Kelsey. He took a step closer to her, standing over her with one large fist clenched around the candle, the other balled into a dangerous weapon. She glanced back at the woman, whose glazed eyes were beseeching.

"We have to do something to help her! It's too cold and damp down here. And this baby will soon be sick, too, unless it's properly cared for."

At her mention of the baby, Dacia stirred restlessly, struggling to speak again. She lifted one burning hand, clutching Kelsey's wrist weakly. "Take . . . my baby," she pleaded, her voice rasping. "You . . . take him."

Kelsey's chest constricted into a hard knot, but she nodded her head. "I'll help you," she promised. "I'll take care of your baby until you're well."

Again Dacia shook her head, but her ravaged face relaxed into some semblance of a smile. "I know . . . you," she wheezed. Her features grew pained as she was shaken by another fit of coughing, though her grip on Kelsey's arm never loosened until after she slipped into unconsciousness.

Before she did, however, the woman moved her lips to whisper, forcing Kelsey to bend close enough to hear.

"My . . . angel," Dacia breathed. Then her hand fell away limply and her head rolled back. She said no more.

Garrett unsaddled Prince hurriedly, rushing through the grooming with quick, precise motions. Usually he enjoyed lingering over the task, using the time to mull over the day's events while giving the horse his due. Today, however, he had far more important work waiting for him, not the least of which was supplying Kelsey with a belated explanation.

His journey today had been successful on two counts. Initially, he had wanted only to put Bart Ogden to the test by pretending to try to slip through town unnoticed. Sure enough, the man had followed on his broken-down nag. The pair had been easy enough to lose, however, once Garrett reached Lockport and the second part of his mission. The most important part.

Before he had a chance to ponder further, Prince tossed his head, signaling Benjamin's approach in the stables.

"Back early," the older man observed, automatically lending a hand with the tack Garrett had tossed to the floor to be cleaned later. "Any troubles?"

"None I couldn't handle. Ogden tried to follow me, but I lost him on the Lower Mountain Road. Got to Levi with the message and then ran into our friend Bart on the way back." Garret stopped currying and turned to Benjamin's gleeful chortle. "He was mad, all right. For a minute I thought he was going to ram me on that poor beast he calls a horse. I almost wish he had, too. A charge of assault against an unarmed citizen is about all Judge Crandall needs to have that scum banned from the town limits."

" 'Cept that'd be takin' too big a chance," Benjamin replied. "Cain't have you gettin' hurt now. Not with folks dependin' on ya, not ta mention the missy."

At this reference to Kelsey, Garrett's lips curved generously. "Levi Hoffman finally agreed—after quite a bit of persuading—that I should tell her when the time is right. I say the sooner the better. Has it been quiet today?"

Benjamin followed his employer as he led Prince to a box stall, latching the door firmly after making sure the feed bucket and water trough were full. "Ain't heard a peep outa nobody since Hannah an' me come back from town. Thought the missy'd be out by now ta see the colt. But she ain't showed her face yet."

At this news, Garrett paused. It was unlike Kelsey to stay abed this late, or even to confine herself to the house unless the weather made it necessary. On the other hand, he grinned inwardly, their lovemaking last night and this morning had been passionate and fulfilling, like a stage play finally brought to a satisfying conclusion. Who could blame her for spending a lazy day recalling it?

Hastily, he went over the plan for that night with Benjamin, checked in on the mare and her new foal, then strode toward the house, wondering how responsive Kelsey might be to a reprise of last night's performance—or better yet, to rehearsing a brand new scene.

But when he stepped into the kitchen, the scene he found was not the one he had in mind.

Hannah bustled past him, mumbling under her breath and casting him a warning that he dared not try to interpret. Stacked high on the oak table was a pile of blankets and linens, and next to it a tray loaded down with all manner of eating utensils. Several loaves of freshly baked bread lined the cooling rack next to the oven and the pleasant aroma of steaming soup—chicken, he guessed, filled the kitchen with fragrance.

"Smells good," he said cautiously, glancing around for a clue as to what in God's name Hannah was up to. A sound from the doorway drew his gaze. He looked to see Kelsey enter, one hand balancing an armful of even more blankets, the other dragging a mattress. It gave a soft whuumph when she let it drop to her side, a single feather flying from a hole in the ticking. When it floated up past her face, she snatched at it impatiently.

"Good morning, love." His attempt to move toward her was blocked by Hannah, who pushed past him again with another tray of food. "What are you two doing?" he laughed apprehensively. "Preparing for an invasion?"

Kelsey tossed the blankets onto the table with an angry thump, spinning toward him. "We're preparing for guests," she spat. "As if you didn't know!"

Garrett stared at her incredulously, then his eyes narrowed as he scanned the floor, finding immediately the clues he had missed. The rocking chair, always carefully in place, had been shoved against one wall and the braided rug was skewed toward the center of the room. One look at Hannah confirmed his suspicion. She nodded her grizzled head brusquely, then muttered something about seeing to the bedrooms and sped from the kitchen.

He braced himself as he raised his gaze to Kelsey. She was visibly shaking, though not with the passion he had hoped to find, but with unmitigated rage. The flashes of light he'd always admired in her dark eyes before now danced irately, pinning him with their fierceness.

''How could you? How could you have lied to me like that?''

Her voice quaked, though he sensed it was not anger that made it so. ''Kelsey, I—''

''Don't touch me! Don't you dare come near me!'' Turning on her heel, she flung herself toward the stove, making a show of stirring the soup that was bubbling loudly. For a long moment it was the only sound in the room besides her ragged breathing. Clenching her teeth, she willed herself to stay calm when she heard Garrett approach with heavy steps.

''I was going to tell you myself,'' he said evenly.

''When?''

''Today . . . now. Just as soon as I got the chance.''

''What kind of chance were you waiting for?'' she taunted, keeping her back to him. ''A chance like the one you had yesterday when I told you I'd heard the baby crying? Or last week when we talked about my father? Or this morning?''

Her bitter laughter did more to deflate his hopes than all the anger in the world. It was too much like the way she'd sounded when she first came back to Riverview, demoralized and spiritless.

''I couldn't tell you,'' he explained levelly, ''because it wasn't my secret to share. Many people are involved in this network, and each one depends on the absolute discretion of the others. With no exceptions. It took weeks of arguing, but this morning I gave them an ultimatum. Believe me, Kelsey—''

''Believe you!'' She slammed the stirring spoon to the stovetop with a loud clatter and hunched her shoulders forward. ''That's been my trouble all along! I believed everything you said, including your promise not to do anything to risk Riverview. But you lied!''

Now Garrett felt his own ire rise, not so much at her as at himself. Striding across the room, he snatched her shoulders and turned her to face him.

''Let me go!'' she hissed, her eyes brandishing fire and her cheeks aflame. ''Let me go!''

"Not until you listen to me." Maintaining his grasp even though she fought to be free, he pulled her toward him. It was easier to keep her still with both arms wrapped around her like barrel hoops, his chin clamped down on the top of her head. He could not see her face, but her breath raged hot and erratic against his collarbone. "Listen to me, Kelsey. Listen to me."

His crooning voice was like a balm, cooling her anger and making her limbs grow lethargic. She *wanted* to listen to him. Wanted to hear his words of defense.

But she couldn't let herself! "I know exactly what you're going to say, Garrett O'Neill, and it won't change a thing. Micah admitted to me that you and he have been transporting runaway slaves all along. Using my land and my stables and *my* house!"

"Our house," he reminded her harshly. Though her resistance had eased somewhat, he didn't make the mistake of letting her go. Her soft, pliant body felt ripe and desirable pressed against his. Her full breasts teased at his chest and his hands itched to do more than clutch her upper arms. Lowering his mouth to her hair, he inhaled the hypnotic fragrance that was a mingling of rose-scented soap and her own sweetness.

She stiffened her back, unwilling to show any sign of the way his nearness affected her. If he had stayed on the other side of the room she could have easily shot daggers at him all day, but in his arms, she was afraid of giving in to him—of giving in to herself.

And the worst of it was, as anger slipped farther and faster out of her grasp, it left room for other, more anguished emotions. A sense of defeat gouged at her already sore heart, leaving it raw and bleeding. "It's no wonder you were so hostile when I came home," she blurted, disillusionment weighing her words. "I could have ruined everything for you. And when I wouldn't sell you the house outright, you bought your way in."

"Kelsey, don't!" He could feel her pain through every pore in his body, but short of shaking her until her teeth rattled, he couldn't think of any way to stop her from tearing herself apart. "Don't turn this into more than it really is. I know you're disappointed because I couldn't tell you before now, but that doesn't have anything to do with us."

"Doesn't it?" Her voice rose to an hysterical pitch, and though she knew she was probably being irrational, she pushed away from him with herculean strength. Once clear of his arms, she quickly put the table between them. "Then I have only one question, Garrett, and please do me the favor of telling the truth this time. Before we were married, when you were living in the cottage, how did you get people in and out of the house?"

Now her tone was like acid, and though he knew he deserved part of her anger, he couldn't help rebelling. "Not under your stubborn little nose, that's for damned certain! The runaways stayed in the room under the stables. I was the only one who went in and out of the cellars for food and supplies."

"And then? After we were married?"

"Once Ogden started bearing down on us, we had no choice but to use the cellar. It's the safest hiding place in the county."

"Of course," she responded tartly. "Papa would have seen to that. You must have gone to great lengths to hide your panic when you found out I could lose it all to the bank. And here I thought you were so noble to help me out of a spot. It was really yourself you were helping, wasn't it?"

"Kelsey, I won't deny that I was concerned about how your presence would affect Micah's and my network. But I wanted you to succeed with Riverview for your own sake, too."

"You deliberately led me to believe you were *not* involved in helping slaves escape, but that was never true, was it?"

Garrett shook his head slowly. "No, it wasn't."

"And when you asked me to marry you, because you claimed we would both benefit, was this . . . ," she swept her arm toward the floor, underneath which was the hidden room, ". . . was this one of the reasons?"

Garrett paused before answering, squaring his shoulders, though his eyes reflected a bleakness she'd not seen in them before. She had allowed her heart to fasten on to a glimmer of hope, but Garrett shattered it with his next words.

"I won't lie to you anymore. At the time, yes, having access to the house was a consideration. But only one, Kelsey."

"I see." She ducked her head so he could not spy the tears forming in her eyes or the way her chin was quivering. Her limbs felt wooden and lifeless, her stomach like lead. Mechanically, she began to count the number of loaves on the bread rack. Only the thought of that sick woman and her poor baby kept Kelsey from racing out of the house to find solace somewhere far from Garrett and the anguish he'd brought to her.

Miserably, he tried to think how to explain so she would understand. He tried to summon the words, though the set of her shoulders and the determination in her stance warned him he would fail. This was the scene he had been dreading for weeks; the reaction he had feared would come to be. Except that the devastation tearing through him now was far, far worse than he ever could have imagined. "No, I don't think you do see," he said without emotion. "But I hope you will when you have time to think about everything that's gone on between us. In the meantime, what do you plan to do?"

"You've given me no choice," she retorted angrily, stacking the loaves into a basket, "I'll do what I have to."

"Which is?"

The question was spoken softly, impassively, but the doubt was there in his voice. The slight inflection in his words, the way his brow flicked upward just a fraction of an inch. After all this, he still didn't trust her.

A new kind of pain spiraled up through the numbness in her body, this one less unexpected than the rest, but no less potent. She could barely lift her eyes to meet his, and when she did, she found his gaze watchful and guarded. "I won't betray you," she said, her tone mocking him. "But neither will I make it any easier for you to manipulate me than I already have. There's nothing between us anymore. Starting now."

He moved as if to take a step forward, but she raised her hands palm outward to ward him off, stopping him short. They both froze, an instant turning into several as their gazes locked. Her eyes were shards of ice, staring at him venomously, but within the space of a heartbeat they began to melt, until one small tear hovered at the corner of her eye, then spilled onto her cheek.

Despair ricocheted through his chest, but before Garret could summon words of reassurance, of comfort, Kelsey had turned and fled.

29

There are times when the line between dreams and reality becomes blurred and indistinct, difficult to perceive and impossible to control; dreams of such incredible purity and impact they convey a truth undeniably real, and reality obscured by pain and anguish so excruciating that even a nightmare seems preferable. As Dacia's fever rose and fell, she experienced the agony of reality and the blessedness of dreams, flitting back and forth between two shadowy worlds, belonging to neither, existing in both.

The land that she went to in her rare moments of sleep was one of beauty and peace, sloping green hills and clear blue skies stretching to infinity. She found herself longing to traverse those gentle knolls and valleys, knowing that the journey itself would be as wondrous as the unnameable joy she would find at journey's end.

But most of the time she hovered in a state of semiconsciousness, beset by racking pain and horrifying fear. With each breath she felt as though knives were slashing through her insides, tearing her lungs to ribbons and leaving her drained of strength. With each heartbeat she knew the terror that followed her still, threatening to rip away what was more precious to her than her own soul.

Yet she found herself denying the tranquility of that netherworld, clinging to the pain and the fear as if they were her only link to salvation. Somewhere in her ravaged mind was the knowledge that without them, she would die. Now, as always, fear meant hope; pain meant life.

Only two things kept Dacia from letting go of the imaginary rope that hung suspended over certain death. She was not certain when it had begun or whether it was from the dream or from reality, but if it was a vision she saw, it was the most beautiful, miraculous vision a soul could ever want. As long as her freedom angel continued to bring her comfort, she knew she could face her fear.

And as long as her baby's cry still pierced the fog surrounding her, Dacia wanted to live.

Kelsey bent over the frail form lying so dreadfully still on the bed and reached a hesitant hand to Dacia's brow. The woman's gray-tinged skin and sunken cheeks bore the look of death, and for a moment she was certain the flesh would be cold and lifeless. But when her fingers grazed her brow, Dacia stirred uncomfortably, startling Kelsey. The skin beneath her hand was warm; not the frightful chill she had expected, nor the scorching fever that had raged through Dacia's thin body for the past four days.

"Micah! Micah, come here!" Her rasping whisper woke the man dozing in a nearby chair, and in an instant he was on his feet and bending over the bed. Though he masked it well, alarm turned his black eyes to hot coals, vibrating through the length of him as he reached awkwardly for Dacia's hand.

"Is she . . . ?" The question never quite reached his lips.

"Her fever broke. It's a good sign."

Micah did not move or speak, except for a humble lowering of his head. Kelsey could almost see him will the strength from his body to Dacia's, a transfer of spirit that brought her both profound faith and acute, poignant grief.

Fighting tears, she straightened and backed away from the bed. It only hurt, she rationalized, because with nursing the sick woman and child, she had not had time to heal herself. The throbbing pangs that had become an indelible mark upon her heart would soon fade, she prayed, once she could get on with her *own* life, putting this ordeal behind her. She would learn to live without Garrett because there was no alternative.

Yet she knew, deep in the farthest reaches of her soul, that her lies were worse than any Garrett had ever spoken, because they were not lies of necessity or obligation.

They were lies of the heart.

When Micah stood up after placing Dacia's hand gently upon her breast, Kelsey swallowed back the burning lump in her throat, smiling tremulously. "She's better, don't you think?"

Unwilling or unable to let his optimism show, Micah shrugged his huge shoulders. "Better let Hannah take a look. Ah'll get 'er."

"No, you stay here with Dacia. I have to get another bottle anyway." On her way out the door, she stopped for a quick check on the baby, who slept peacefully in a makeshift crib fashioned out of a bureau drawer straddling two chairs. They still did not know if the child had a name, but Kelsey had taken to calling the little boy Gabriel because Dacia had often muttered in her sleep something about angels. Reaching a hand to straighten the thin blanket around his shoulders, she whispered softly . . . hopefully. "Your mama's going to be fine now, darling. She's going to be fine."

The infant stirred his tiny head covered with fine black curls, then quieted again, his mouth making small sucking movements even in his sleep. She smiled tenderly. "I'll be right back with your dinner, Gabriel."

A sound from Micah made Kelsey look up. He was studying her quizzically, a frown pulling down the corners of his mouth.

"Why you callin' him that?"

"We . . . we don't know if he has a name and I have to call him something," Kelsey explained sheepishly. "You said Gabriel was some kind of code, and Dacia keeps talking about an angel. Calling the baby Gabriel just made sense."

Micah's frown deepened. "Don't let no one outside this house hear you sayin' it," he warned. "Garrett's in enough trouble as it is."

"G-Garrett?"

"It's him we call Gabriel, and word's been spreadin'. If that bastard Ogden ever heard he was so close, he'd be on 'im like a hound on a fox."

Kelsey felt a shudder work up from the base of her spine, as much from the sound of Garrett's name as from the potential danger. "I wouldn't tell anyone," she said quietly. "You should know that by now."

Micah's expression softened. "I 'spose I do. If it hadn't been for you insistin' on givin' her your room, Dacia might've died. That babe, too," he gestured toward the sleeping infant. "You ain't so dead set against helpin' as I thought."

Kelsey shook her head sadly. "It wasn't that I didn't want to help, Micah. I just can't lose everything I love in the process. Can you understand that?"

Pausing thoughtfully, the man lifted one shoulder in silent acknowledgment. His gaze drifted back to Dacia, whose breathing was now effortless and calm. "Time was I woulda said no," he admitted. "But now I think I know what it feels like to want something so bad for myself that nothin' else matters."

Kelsey realized this had not been an easy admission for the proud man. He had reluctantly allowed her to move Dacia and Gabriel to the upper part of the house before he and Garrett ferried the other two slaves to Canada that very night. From the moment of their return, Micah had not stepped from Dacia's side for more than a few minutes. Three days they stood vigil, and in that time Kelsey had come to respect his dignity and courage as he described to her some of the dangers and ideals he and Garrett shared.

Long before his own capture, Micah had been a link in the chain of dedicated men and women who helped runaway slaves find freedom in Canada. Though there had been other routes, Riverview had always been one of the safest hiding places in the county, since the cellars beneath the house were nearly impossible to find and the caves leading between them and the riverbank unknown to all but a few.

Kelsey recalled her astonishment when she first heard this, and the deep frustration she felt at having failed to see what was happening, though she'd been given many clues: the voice in the stable, which she knew now had been Micah's; the mysterious sounds she had heard late at night, but had brushed off as her own fitful imaginings.

Remembering these instances, however, only increased her sense of betrayal. Garrett could have taken any of those opportunities to tell her the truth, yet he had not.

As if reading her mind, Micah rumbled gently, "He wanted to tell you, you know. But he couldn't."

Now it was Kelsey's turn to shrug, though the tears sprang back to her eyes as quickly as summer rain. "He lied to save himself the trouble of finding a new way to help your people. I don't begrudge you shelter . . . especially now," she said, gazing fondly at Gabriel, "but I do resent being used that way."

Micah said nothing, yet his thoughts churned, sorting through what he wished he could say and what was better left unspoken. She didn't know much about bein' used, that was for sure. But he could see how it would appear like that from her way of thinkin'. He could even understand why she figured her world began and ended with a piece of land and a drafty old house. Hadn't he felt a keen sense of loss at knowin' he would never return to the little shop he had built with his own hands?

But to blame it all on a fine man like Garrett? Now *that* Micah could not comprehend if he pondered on it for a lifetime.

"You ought not to judge him so hard," he said hesitantly. "You ought not—well, you just ought not to judge him so hard."

He turned back to Dacia before he could see the indecision that flashed through Kelsey's eyes. He could only hear the steel in her voice as she enunciated her reply.

"Your loyalty is commendable, but I'll never forgive him for what he did to me. I'll go get that bottle now."

The gentle closing of the door marked her exit. Micah lowered himself carefully to sit beside Dacia, lifting her dainty hand into his own large, callused palm. Though he knew she could not hear him, he spoke to her of both the sorrow and the hope in his heart.

"I don't know if when you wake up outta this sickness, you're gonna feel for me the way I been feelin' for you, but at least ain't no one gonna stop us from tryin'. Soon we're gonna be free, girl. No more chains."

He raised his head to peer sadly after Kelsey, adding with a meaningful whisper, "Especially the chains you can't see."

In the following week Dacia improved steadily, nursed in turns by Hannah and Kelsey and guarded over by a steadfast Micah. Fortunately for them all, baby Gabriel seemed to have suffered no ill effects from having been born in darkness and transported through the cold and rain less than twelve hours after his birth. Aside from hunger, which Hannah quickly dispatched with a formula of cow's milk and corn syrup, he was as healthy as a weeks-old infant ought to be.

For Kelsey, who watched both her charges with a mixture of fretful concern and pride, time was moving forward far too slowly. She yearned for something, anything, to keep her mind from straying to thoughts of Garrett, but since most of her day was spent simply sitting and watching Dacia, it was impossible to keep from mulling over every second they had spent together up until now.

Up until a week ago, she amended inwardly, frowning as she carried a sleepy Gabriel to his bed and tucked him in for his morning nap. It had been a full week since she'd seen her husband, though if she were completely honest, she was as relieved as she was disappointed.

Their last conversation had turned into a quarrel every

bit as virulent as the first, ending with Garrett storming silently from the bedroom, leaving Kelsey clutching Gabriel tight in her arms to hide the trembling frustration mounting within. Now she wished she could relive that afternoon, not so that she could put an end to the discord, but because she had thought of several more arguments she would like to throw at him!

Hannah stepped into the bedroom just in time to see Kelsey pacing furiously from one end of the oblong rug to the other. In the bed Dacia slept peacefully, oblivious to the dire mutterings jabbing the air above her head. Gabriel slumbered also, innocently unaware that he was in danger of having his crib knocked from its precarious perch each time Kelsey whipped past, her flounced skirt flaring angrily behind her.

"Why don't you give that mare o' yours some exercise," Hannah suggested with a tactful whisper, positioning herself in front of the temporary crib before damage could be done. "Benjamin been complain' 'bout how them horses is gettin' worrisome. Ah'll sit a spell 'fore time to fix dinner."

"Are you sure?" Kelsey stopped in mid-stride, suddenly pleased by the prospect of getting out for an hour or so. A good ride might help her burn some of the restless energy pent up inside her, and perhaps fresh air would provide her with a fresh perspective.

Hannah nodded perfunctorily, moving to the rocking chair near the bed which, while not as comfortable as her own in the kitchen, had been an adequate substitute in recent days. "Don' you come back without an appetite, hear?" she called softly. "Ah, don' want ta see you 'til time ta sit down at the table."

Kelsey did not answer, having already sped from the room, but Hannah peered after her with a satisfied grin on her face nevertheless. If things went the way she planned, it'd be long after dinner before her young mistress returned, hopefully with a much improved attitude. It hadn't been Benjamin who had mentioned the horses to her. But Garrett had, just before galloping out of the yard on Prince. Hannah considered it fate that Kelsey had not looked out the window and seen her husband for herself, just like she was certain that fate would not allow the two estranged lovers to ride in separate directions.

Fate would not be that unkind. But if fate wasn't up to the task, Hannah declared to herself confidently, she was more than prepared to lend a hand.

Garrett had just decided to find a place to stop and rest Prince when his eye caught a flash of vermillion behind one of the apple trees in the distance. In a split second his thoughts raced back in time to the day when Kelsey had hidden from him playfully, taunting him with a dress of the same color. As if the vision were painted on a canvas in his mind, he could see her now as she was then, eyes dancing and lips pouting sensuously, soft pink and oh, so ripe to be kissed.

Though he knew, with bitter realization, that her purpose today was more likely to escape than to beckon, he could no more ignore this unintentional lure than he could still the sudden hammering in his heart. Tugging on the reins until Prince obeyed with a tight turn, Garrett headed for the orchard.

The previous week had been a difficult one, fraught with danger and the added tensions of having a sick woman poorly hidden in the house. His one attempt to reason with Kelsey had gone poorly, and though he would have liked to try again, more pressing concerns had kept him away.

As he approached the place where he'd last spotted her, he could see that Ladyfair was hobbled to one of the apple trees. The mare raised her head and whinnied at Prince, who snorted in return. But Kelsey was nowhere in sight.

Garrett dismounted at a short distance, tying his horse safely away from the mare and scanning the cool avenues created by the many rows of trees. On foot she could not have gone far in the time it took him to arrive, yet he could see no sign of her red dress amidst the brown and green of the orchard.

No sign, that is, until the telltale whisper of rustling leaves drew his gaze upward. Three trees away, he spied a dainty slippered foot braced atop one of the lower limbs, and a spill of scarlet where her skirt draped between the leaves.

"I did not know," he drawled sardonically, "that this was a native habitat for redbirds. Particularly the wingless variety." Moving swiftly to just beneath her so she could not escape, Garrett peered up among the branches.

"No doubt you were not aware because you are insensitive to anything or anyone who does not fall along with your schemes," Kelsey replied acidly. The moment she heard Prince's pounding hoofbeats coming in her direction, she had scrambled up a tree in the hope that Garrett would not find her. It seemed, however, that luck was not with her today. "Generally speaking, birds do not like to be disturbed. Nor do I."

"Whether you wish it or not, Kelsey, I think it's time we talked. We can't go on like this forever."

"If you've been so anxious to talk," she retorted, "then why haven't you come anywhere near me for days?" As soon as the words passed her lips, she wished she could bite them back. They sounded far too much like a complaint. Fortunately, Garrett either didn't notice or chose to ignore her slip.

"Someone has to keep an eye on Bart Ogden. He's been drinking his way through Lewiston, boasting on how he once trapped a free negro on a false charge of theft, then shipped the man to Kentucky where he was sold at auction. He claims he pocketed a hefty fee for that one, but not as much as he'll get for three that are supposedly headed this way. No one has the guts to remind him that he tried to do the same with Micah Ramsey but failed. And I don't dare provoke him now."

"Has he mentioned Dacia?" Kelsey couldn't help herself, but she had to know if the woman was in immediate danger.

''Not that I can tell,'' Garrett answered. ''Not every missing slave is posted for reward. On the other hand, Ogden obviously has no qualms about capturing the wrong person. We have to keep as close a watch now as ever.''

His tone was slightly reproving, making Kelsey clamp her mouth into a firm line. She wouldn't let him trick her into admitting she cared about what happened to the fugitives.

''Why don't you come down where we can discuss this without my getting a permanent crick in my neck? Besides, I don't want you to fall.''

''Don't bother to pretend concern for me. I'm quite through with talking to you, since I can never be certain whether you're telling the truth or not.'' The leaves blocked her view of his face, but she could sense his anger in the way his voice hardened ruthlessly.

''Come down here, Kelsey.''

''I will when I'm ready.''

He paused for a moment, then said evenly, ''All right then, have it your way.''

As swiftly as a striking serpent, he reached high and clasped the branch just inches away from her foot, hanging all his weight on the limb until it creaked ominously. Kelsey struggled to climb higher, but there was nowhere else for her to go and she felt her balance slipping rapidly.

''Garrett, don't! You're going to make me fall!''

''I'll catch you.''

Considering that prospect and all it implied, Kelsey quickly lowered herself to the next branch, viciously yanking at her skirt when it caught on a twig. As gracefully as she could manage, she swung from the limb, dropping to the ground at Garrett's feet. ''Are you satisfied,'' she spat angrily. ''Now I've torn my dress.''

''That's too bad. It's one of my favorites, you know.''

There was no sympathy, only an odd intensity in his voice that made Kelsey look up curiously. His eyes seared through her, their consuming blaze tempered by the smile that fought to stay on his lips.

"I-I'd better go back," she faltered, uncertain whether he intended to lash out at her or sweep her into his arms. One, she decided, would be as undesirable as the other.

"Not yet." With one hand he caught her arm, the other reaching behind her to twine in her unbound hair. Before she could do more than open her mouth to protest, he lowered his head, locking her in a kiss that sheared her breath in two.

An unbearable longing shuddered through her, and with it the knowledge that even while she resisted him, she could not deny herself. Her body seemed to press against him of its own accord, her arms seeking the angular strength of his shoulders, her hips drawn to the hardness of his, warning her that what he had once given to her with tenderness, he might now force upon her with cruel harshness.

And she would be powerless to stop him, because her hands and lips and heart had long ago ceased to obey her mind. Even her thoughts were straying beneath his compelling onslaught.

"Stop it . . . oh, Garrett, stop!" She wasn't sure if he'd heard her, or even if her appeal had been spoken out loud against his mouth. But when he drew back, holding her away from him at arms length, Kelsey felt a rush of indescribable loss.

With barely suppressed passion still raging in his hooded eyes, he turned away from her, leaning against the apple tree with deceptive casualness. She could see the tension ripple beneath the back of his linen shirt. It reminded her that for all the sins she could lay at his door, lack of restraint had never been one of them. She wasn't certain what might have happened had he ignored her plea; she only knew that he was the one who had stopped, not she.

Kelsey took a stumbling step backwards. "Y-you shouldn't have done that."

"Yes, you're right," he said thickly, "this is not getting us any closer to solving our problem. I had hoped that with time . . ." His shoulders lifted imperceptibly.

"Time doesn't change what happened. You lied to me about everything."

"I withheld the truth," Garrett corrected, turning slowly. "Out of necessity. Out of caution."

"Caution! Neither you nor my father exercised caution. He gave up everything he owned, including his wife and daughter, and you sacrificed our marriage. Do you call that caution?"

Desire had made way for agitation in his cerulean eyes, and he chopped at the air with one hand. "Sheldon loved you, and the letters proved that. I don't know why he did what he did. I suspect he chose to bury himself in this cause partly to redeem himself for letting his marriage fail. But that has nothing to do with me. I love you. Why else would I have married you?"

"B-Because you wanted Riverview," Kelsey stammered, so shaken by his admission that she could hardly think. She'd never heard Garrett speak such a harsh truth about her father.

"It's true I needed Riverview to continue this work," he insisted gently, "but I could have had it by other means. I could have bought your mortgage from the bank, or offered you enough money to sell that you might have given in. Instead I tried to find the solution that would give me what I really wanted. You, Kelsey. Only you. I thought that was what you wanted, too."

A lump formed in her throat, but she quickly forced it back, swallowing the answer that nearly sprang from her lips. "What I wanted," she said emotionlessly, "was to keep my home. That's the only thing that matters to me."

Garrett began to stride away angrily, but before he had taken more than a few steps he spun back, raking his hand through his hair. "You accuse me of committing the same sin as your father, but you're the one who's most like him. You've become blinded, Kelsey. Blinded by a single goal that doesn't allow for compassion or compromise."

Pretending to examine the hole in her skirt, she bent her head to hide her quivering chin. "At least I never lied to you about that."

A long moment passed in which Garrett said nothing at all, then his words came slowly, mournfully. "It seems there's nothing I can do to make you understand."

Because the tears hovered too close, because she was afraid of what her answer might be, Kelsey only shook her head.

When she finally looked up, Garrett was gone.

30

Kelsey stared at her bewildered reflection, wondering how the person in the mirror could be the same one who came here just a few short months ago. The features remained the same, but fear and uncertainty had been replaced in her dark brown eyes by stubbornness and delusion. Was that a shadow of herself she saw, or an incomplete outline of the woman she might one day be? Neither one, she thought forlornly, was very comforting.

With a mournful sigh she leaned forward over her dressing table, cupping her chin in her hands as she continued to search her image for answers to the questions that had been plaguing her for days now. Ever since their encounter in the orchard, Garrett's voice continued to haunt her thoughts.

I love you, he had said. He had lied to her before, but he had never uttered those words in quite the same way. This time, could she believe him?

Just as troubling, though far less pleasant, were the echoing claims he had spoken just before he left her. He had said she was like her father, and that obsession was as much a part of her desire to save Riverview as it had been her father's to destroy it. If that was true, Kelsey mulled, then was there nothing left for her to cling to?

Another comment Garrett had made puzzled her as well; that he did not know why Sheldon had acted as he had. Before now Garrett had always defended her father unquestionably, but his statement reminded her of something George Delbert had revealed in her first interview with him—that it was Garrett who had been the tempering influence on Sheldon. She had not believed it then, because she hadn't wanted to admit that her father had lost control of his own life to such an extent. Now, however, it seemed it was true.

A rustling sound from the bed gained her attention, and she turned to see Dacia easing herself up onto a stack of pillows. Her dark curls fell in a sleepy tangle to her shoulders and her heavy-lidded eyes looked up slowly.

"Good morning," Kelsey said, rising to carry a breakfast tray from the dresser to the bed. "Gabriel was up early. Hannah took him downstairs so he wouldn't wake you."

Momentary panic flashed in Dacia's eyes, then she nodded calmly. "You take such good care of him. I shouldn't worry."

Kelsey hated to tell the woman that in this case, they all had good cause for concern. Ogden had come to the house twice since their clandestine houseguests had arrived. Each time he'd been rebuffed, but it couldn't go on forever.

"He's a wonderful baby," Kelsey replied instead, adjusting the pillows behind Dacia's back. "So happy and content. I just love to hold him." There must have been a wistful note in her voice, for Dacia looked up sympathetically.

"You'll have one of your own soon, I expect."

It was left unspoken in the ensuing silence, but both women were aware of the unlikelihood of that sentiment, given the strained relationship between Kelsey and Garrett. From the instant she had become completely conscious, Dacia knew of the sadness her benefactress wore like a chain around her heart.

On the few occasions when Garrett had entered the room to have a word with Micah, Kelsey's every movement became mechanical and strained. When he looked at his wife, Garrett's eyes were desolate and anguished.

It didn't take much insight for a person to see that something was terribly wrong.

Kelsey stood back as Dacia began to eat her breakfast methodically. She was glad to see her patient acquiring an appetite, though she realized that the sooner she regained her strength, the sooner her new friend would be ready to leave.

"I'm glad you didn't mind that I named Gabriel," Kelsey said, sitting in the rocking chair next to the bed.

"Gabriel's a fine name," Dacia nodded, laying down her spoon. "When he was born I hardly knew my own name, much less what to call him. I don't understand, though. Why Gabriel?"

Briefly, Kelsey explained about the code name Micah had used, but when she mentioned Dacia's own muttered references to angels, the woman lowered her eyes shyly.

"It wasn't your man I was talking about," she murmured in a low voice. "It was my very own freedom angel. My mama always told me to watch out for her to set me free, but I knew I had to find you all by myself.

It took a moment for Kelsey to understand what the other woman was saying, but then a rush of emotion filled her chest. "You mean, you thought *I* was the angel?"

"You *are* my angel. You keep me safe, you're helping me get well again . . . and soon you'll make me free."

Dacia resumed eating as calmly as if they'd been discussing the weather, but Kelsey was stunned. Never had anyone trusted her so unequivocally. It left her both euphoric and strangely sobered.

Very gently, for she knew that Dacia was resistent to the idea, she made a suggestion. "I'm not really going with you to Canada. Micah will be the one. And the way he watched over you while you were unconscious, you should consider him your guardian angel, not me."

"Hmmph." This time the spoon clattered to the tray. "No man carried me this far, no man's going to carry me home. I'll swim across 'fore I let him tell me how to do for myself."

"But Dacia," Kelsey protested softly. "I think Micah cares for you a great deal. He was terribly worried when he first brought you here. Why won't you give him a chance?"

The woman's stubborn silence was all the answer she would give, and with a resigned look Kelsey gathered the breakfast tray and returned it to the bureau. It was too bad Dacia could not return Micah's feelings. It would be a lot easier to see her and Gabriel leave if she knew they would be well cared for on the other side of the river.

Glancing over at the bed, Kelsey saw that Dacia had scrunched down into the pillows as if to sleep again. She would have thought nothing of it, except for the troubled frown that told her the issue was not so easily passed off after all. Why was she being so obstinate? Kelsey pondered as she carried the tray down to the kitchen. Didn't Dacia want to be loved?

She would have been surprised to know that at that moment Dacia was wondering the very same thing about her.

The water was black. Black as midnight and as deep and mysterious as the heavens, which had long since given up its hold on her. Though she choked and screamed, Kelsey could not stop the inky, swirling waters from covering her, clutching at her clothing and twisting around her legs, weighing them down so that she could barely move. Her arms flailed, seeking something to keep her from the water's deathly grip, but her fingertips only brushed the stars, unable to cling to those elusive points.

And then she heard the voice calling to her; not the same vicious tones that had haunted her dreams before, but another . . . more familiar. More beloved. Garrett reached out to her, his strong fingers embracing her arms, his warm hands pulling her out of the icy depths, and in the moments between sleep and wakefulness, her heart rejoiced that he was here.

Her eyelids fluttering, she strained to see him in the darkness.

"Wake up, Kelsey! Darling, wake up!" Garrett gave her shoulders another gentle shake while peering worriedly as she mumbled and tossed her head. He'd always thought insomniacs were light sleepers, but she resisted waking like a tired child who fights to keep his eyes open.

Groggily, she forced herself to absorb her surroundings as she came awake. She was in her room, but lying on the trundle bed she had used ever since Dacia's arrival. From behind the dividing screen she could hear the steady rhythm of Gabriel's breathing, and the stirring noise that told her his mother was no longer asleep.

"Wh-what is it?" Kelsey whispered. "Did I wake you?" Struggling to sit, she glanced at the window. "What time is it?"

"Nearly dawn," Garrett answered tersely. "Get dressed."

He left the room as silently as he had entered, leaving her to puzzle out his odd request while she obeyed. Why would he wake her up so early? And why the urgency in his voice?

Though Kelsey tried to hurry, her limbs were strangely lethargic, her head spinning. When she craned her neck to button the back of her dress, she found herself growing dizzy and was forced to sit down for a moment to calm her racing heart and gather her wits. What was wrong with her? She'd never had so much trouble waking up before, even when her nightmares had been at their worst.

"Are you all right?" Dacia peeked her head around the screen, shuffling to Kelsey's side.

"I'm fine, but you shouldn't be out of bed. You'll have a relapse."

"I've been walking around for a week now," Dacia said dismissively. "What's going on?"

"I don't know yet. Garrett just told me to get dressed. Do you think—?" She stopped suddenly, not wanting to frighten the other woman unnecessarily. Dacia, however, was wagging her head slowly.

"No danger now," she murmured in a low voice. "Not now."

Relief flooded through Kelsey's veins, boosting her spirits a little. "Then I'd best hurry down to see what

Garrett wants. I'll tell you what happens later. In the meantime, you get some more sleep."

Dacia lent Kelsey a hand with the buttons, then watched silently as she finished dressing, ending by pulling a pair of sturdy slippers onto her feet. Even in the darkness she could see the effort it cost, for Kelsey hesitated again before rising, as if she needed to rest between every movement.

"You're the one that should take care of yourself," Dacia admonished easily. "You've been awful peaked lately."

"Only because I haven't spent much time outdoors." That was partly true, but Kelsey wondered if her state of mind hadn't more to do with the weariness she felt. Regret was an exhausting load to bear.

Wishing Dacia good night, she tiptoed down to the kitchen, certain that was where she would find Garrett. Instead, Hannah lifted her turbaned head in greeting as Kelsey entered the room, and Micah waited for her beside the open trap door. Garrett was nowhere in sight.

"What's going on?" she asked, still whispering. A single taper burned in a candlestick on the table, and next to the opening in the floor sat an unlit lantern. Hannah was bending to light the stove, though it was far too early to begin breakfast preparations.

"Come with me," Micah said without explanation. Wordlessly, he climbed down the ladder into the cellar.

After a quick glance at Hannah, who nodded grimly, Kelsey followed. She had a suspicion she knew why Garrett had summoned her now. There must be another traveler in the furthermost hidden cellar, and he wanted her to see for herself, realizing that once she had taken a personal interest in anyone it would be difficult to refuse her help.

In a way, it angered Kelsey that he knew her so well when she wasn't even certain she knew herself any longer. More and more it was becoming clear to them both that she was as determined to protect Dacia and Gabriel as anyone. Since the day in the orchard, she'd been giving a lot of thought to what Garrett said, and she now realized she'd judged him too harshly. She had assumed that he shared the fanaticism of her father, when in truth, she was beginning to admire his sense of honorable commitment.

The problem was, it was difficult to tell him how she felt.

Difficult, she admitted ruefully, but not impossible. Not if she swallowed her pride and asked for his understanding.

Micah helped her down the last rung and continued to lead the way through the labyrinth of rooms, until at last they reached the final one where the fugitives usually remained hidden until they could be taken across the Niagara. When she stepped inside, Kelsey raised her hand to block the strong light that shone from three lanterns positioned around a pallet.

"Micah, I can use your help here." From a spot next to the pallet, Garrett signaled to his friend to put his lantern down and to lend a hand with the writhing form lying at his knees. Kelsey's gasp echoed through the cave.

"Bring me one of those blankets," Garrett ordered her. "Then find me a straight needle and some thread in that box over there. We've got some stitching to do."

Though his shoulders twitched and trembled, the young man on the floor did not say a word as his fate was decided by those who knelt over him. Kelsey could not see his face clearly, but the man appeared to be not more than twenty, his flesh—at least that which had not been laid open with a whip—was smooth and firm, the color of dark honey.

"How did this happen?" she asked as soon as she'd returned to Garrett's side with the implements he requested.

"Ogden had him. Tried to get him to say where the others in his party had hidden. Micah went in to cut this man loose while I distracted the bastards with a show of fireworks from the woods surrounding the shack they've holed up in."

"Wasn't that dangerous?" The inane question was out of her mouth before she could recall it, causing Garrett to glance at her sharply.

"Dangerous, but necessary. Much longer and this boy would be dead . . . along with the man we had to leave behind. *His* skull was broken."

"Kicked 'im they did," the young man on the floor rasped, grunting when Garrett touched a clean cloth to his bleeding back. " 'Til 'e didn't scream no more. They was gonna do me next."

"Someone nearby heard the noise and got word to me. We already picked up three of the others who knew about these two getting caught." At a jerk of Garrett's head, Kelsey peered into the darkened corners of the cave, spotting those fugitive slaves who had been spared Ogden's brutality by a mere stroke of good fortune. Before she could remark, Garrett continued, his words flowing erratically as he pulled the torn edges of the young man's flesh together with needle and thread.

"They would have all been safe," he insisted, pausing to swipe at his brow with his sleeve, "if Ogden hadn't walked into the general store in Lockport this morning and seen Levi Hoffman's daughter buying three pairs of cotton trousers. He knew the Quakers make their own clothing, so he watched and waited until Levi tried to sneak these men out of town in a hay wagon. That's when all hell broke loose."

The unpleasant chore completed, Garrett sat back on his heels, wrists on his knees as he let his blood-covered hands hang over the floor. His voice was weary and resigned. "Levi's the most cautious man I know, and still this happened. One man dead, another only half alive."

Kelsey's heart pounded in her throat as his implication became clear. No matter how careful, the more people who knew about the secret route through Riverview, the greater the chance that Ogden would find out, even inadvertently. He had not kept the information from her out of lack of trust, but for the increased security of the people who relied on him for safe passage.

''Oh, Garrett,'' she whispered brokenly. ''I had no idea . . . no idea at all. It's . . . Ogden committed murder!''

''Unfortunately,'' he spat the bitterness from his mouth, ''the law in this country doesn't quite agree. That's why we'll have to get these men out of here tonight.''

From the other side of the pallet, Micah made a questioning sound. ''Full moon,'' he mumbled.

''I know, but I'm pretty sure Ogden got a look at me after I set fire to that barrel of shot. It won't take the mind of a scholar to figure out that the fire and the escape were not coincidental. By tomorrow morning he'll come down on this place with a swarm of men.''

After dousing all but one of the lanterns, Kelsey helped make the injured man as comfortable as possible while Garrett went up to fetch the meal Hannah had prepared. In a few minutes she followed him.

''Garrett?'' she called softly as she poked her head up through the floorboards in the kitchen. He paused before hefting a large basket in one hand, then moved over to where she was climbing up through the trapdoor.

''One of us should stay with him all day in case he runs a fever. Micah can stand the first watch.''

''I'll take a turn,'' Kelsey volunteered quickly. His sideways glance made her blood tingle. In the pale gray dawn she could see how very tired he was. His clothing was rumpled and soiled, his boots caked with mud, his trousers ripped open in two places. Weary lines etched his brow and creased his cheeks, drawing her gaze to his thinly compressed lips.

''You have enough to do already,'' he said gruffly.

''Dacia's well enough to take care of Gabriel with Hannah's assistance. I *want* to help, Garrett.''

He was almost unwilling to meet her eyes, afraid of the disappointment he would feel when she turned from him again. But her expression was full of mute appeal, softly beseeching him to stop. Though her hands were still, pressed against her skirt, he could see the tension quiver through her like a taut bowstring. She was waiting for his answer, but she was offering him something more—a chance for reconciliation.

The next moments hung suspended in time as he fought a battle within himself, one of pride versus love. He wanted nothing more than to haul her into his arms, to press her close to his heart and murmur the words of reassurance he so desperately wanted to give her. His hand tightened on the basket handle, the wood slat digging into his palm, waking him to the likelihood that she was not asking for love at all, but only comfort from the ugliness she had just witnessed.

If that were so, he thought, then he had nothing to share, for the horror was still fresh in his own mind, too. And until he was certain she would accept more, he could not risk exposing his heart. Not now. Not today.

"You can help by staying close to the house," he ground out roughly, unable to keep the emotion from his voice, disguising it as brusqueness, "From that balcony of yours you should be able to see anyone approaching from a long way off. Keep an eye out for Ogden."

There was so much she wanted to say, yet Kelsey could only nod. Her eyes burned dry and hot, but she refused to let him see how much more wounding was his disdain than all the anger in the world. In learning to believe in him she had lost his respect; weeping would not make it otherwise.

Drawing herself straighter, she watched as he swung his agile body down into the gaping hole, managing the heavy basket with ease. When he was through and had lighted a lantern within, she saw him look up at her.

"Close the door behind me, Kelsey."

His whisper rose to her ears like a harbinger of doom. She nearly scrambled down after him, crying out her sorrow and forgiveness at once, but before she could move, he had turned away from the opening and disappeared into the darkness below.

31

The day passed slowly for all the residents of Riverview, but none suffered from the tedium as much as Kelsey, relegated to the high balcony far away from the rest. Her only respite had come when Hannah called up from the yard, urging her down for a bite of lunch. She had obeyed eagerly, hoping that she might share the meal with Garrett, but only the cook occupied her kitchen, too busy preparing huge amounts of food for the travelers to take with them to pay much attention to Kelsey's low spirits.

As expected, Dacia was more than ready to take over the care of her child. Though she remained short-winded and easily tired, her health had certainly improved enough to spend brief periods of time sitting up. Little Gabriel still slept a great deal of the day, so her task was not too difficult. Once during the afternoon, while Garrett was presumably guarding the visitors in the cellar, Micah came up to see Dacia. Though Kelsey was beset with curiosity, she could hear little more than murmurs through the open door to the parapet. When Micah left Dacia remained silent, not even offering an explanation when Kelsey stepped inside, purportedly for a glass of water. She couldn't help noticing, however, the new light that shone in her friend's eyes.

Now dusk streaked the sky, coral ribbons lacing overhead like the streamers on a young girl's bonnet. A breeze rippled through the poplar trees, making them sway in a graceful dance, reminding Kelsey of the first time her papa had ever brought her to his hideaway in the sky. She supposed she had been only four or five, for it was one of her earliest memories. Sheldon had lifted her to the railing, holding her securely around the waist as she wriggled forward for a better look at the ground below.

"What do you see, Kitten?" he had asked.

She remembered giggling when he pulled tighter, tickling her as his fingers clutched her thin side. "Trees and clouds. Lots of them."

"And land," he added. "Land as far as the eye can see; riches beyond any I could have imagined. Do you know what that means?"

"Mama says it means I can have a pony. Can I, Papa? Can I?" Sheldon had hugged her and laughed, but now she recalled with a poignant ache the answer he had given.

"Land is only as valuable as the crop we sow, and richness is measured not by what we keep, but by what we give away. Remember that, my kitten, and you'll always bear wealth in your heart." Then he brushed a kiss on the top of her head. "And yes . . . you may have a pony."

Now her eyes stung with unshed tears at the memory. Why hadn't she remembered this before? It wasn't excuse enough that her young life had been filled with disappointment and heartache. Had she but heeded her father's advice, so much might have been different. Now she could only pray that she had not remembered too late.

Crossing her arms and rubbing her shoulders briskly, Kelsey paced the balcony from end to end. Garrett had left already, wanting to gain Odgen's attention while it was still light enough to see. Besides, it was a five-hour ride to Lockport and back, which would give Micah plenty of time to make the crossing as soon as the sun set.

"Please, God," Kelsey begged out loud, "keep him safe."

It never occurred to her that before the night was over, she would be the one in need of prayers.

Justin Delbert slapped the reins hard on the rump of his carriage horse, impatience wearing at him like an ill-fitted shoe. Fortunately, the river road was dry and free of ruts after such a long spell of fair weather. Pushing the animal harder, he increased their speed to a reckless pace.

Try as he might, it was hard to replace his smug grin with a proper expression of concern, but he knew if he didn't master his features soon Kelsey would be sure to notice. He struggled to keep his mind on the more sober aspects of his mission.

She was sure to be upset, he told himself. Perhaps she would even cry, though that prospect wasn't at all displeasing. He had visions of himself consoling her, patting her gently on her slender back as she clung to him uncontrollably. With a shiver of anticipation, Justin snapped the reins again.

The carriage wheels clattered noisily as he made the turn into the lane of poplars, yet he was still surprised by the reception waiting for him when he drew up to the drive in front of the verandah. Kelsey stood on the top step, hands propped on her hips and head held high, and Hannah glared at him fiercely from behind her mistress, attempting to hide an ancient shotgun behind her skirt. He thought he saw something flash at an upstairs window, but decided it must have been the last of the sunlight reflecting on the glass pane.

''Hello, Justin,'' Kelsey said cautiously, not budging from her stance as he climbed down from the two-seater. Hannah continued to frown at him as if he were a wolf out to snatch her little lamb. The analogy made him smile to himself; in a sense, it wasn't so far from the mark.

''I need to speak to you. Alone,'' he added meaningfully. With an agitated ''hmmmph,'' Hannah marched from the porch, her skinny frame rigid with indignation.

''We can talk out here,'' Kelsey suggested.

After glancing around, he nodded, stifling his irritation at not being asked into the parlor, at least. But they would have privacy on the porch, and the evening was still warm and pleasant . . . almost dreamy. Enough of that! he warned himself firmly. He was here for a reason.

"I have some rather disquieting news, my dear. Perhaps you should sit down." Even in the dusky light he could see her expression of surprise, though she declined his suggestion quickly.

"Please, just tell me what it is, Justin. I'm quite busy."

"At this hour . . . ? No, never mind that. I don't doubt that O'Neill keeps you waiting on him hand and foot. He is here, isn't he?"

Her nervousness was obvious, and now that he looked closer, her complexion was positively waxen, dark half-moons shadowing her lower eyelids. She appeared to have lost weight in the past few weeks, or perhaps it was the dowdy dress she was wearing—he couldn't tell.

"Did you want to speak with Garrett, or with me?" she challenged, meeting his gaze with a frankness that startled him.

"You, of course. But it's about your husband that I've come. Rumors abound that he is up to his neck with these runaway slaves. I know you didn't believe it before, Kelsey, but I'm afraid the proof is a matter of public knowledge now."

This time he was certain that she turned a shade paler. Her cheeks were a ghastly white, her eyes burned anxiously. "What do you mean, public knowledge?"

"I mean that Judge Crandall issued a warrant to search the premises of Riverview less than an hour ago. Bart Ogden swears O'Neill set fire to his place last night and made off with one of the slaves he was preparing to transport back to his owner. The man says he'd going to hunt him down tonight to lay claim to the missing "property."

"And what if Garrett doesn't have anything to do with it?" Kelsey demanded. "What if Ogden finds him alone?"

"At the very least, he'll probably have your husband arrested for arson, which will be difficult to prove in a trial. It's Ogden's word against O'Neill's, and all rumors notwithstanding, no one in this town will want to see one of their own go to jail on the testimony of that scum."

"I'm relieved that you think so."

Her reply was sarcastic, but Justin sensed the concern lurking just beneath the surface. His own anger swelled unaccountably, and he took a step toward her, his hands quaking as he clenched his fists. "I must say you're taking this well. Seeing as how Ogden could descend on you at any moment, I don't think I would be as calm. But rest assured, I don't intend to leave you to face him alone, any more than I'll let that Irishman you married be the ruin of you! I'll get you out of this now, Kelsey. I swear I will!"

For the first time, her shoulders slumped defeatedly as she reached for one of the verandah posts, leaning into it for support. "There's no need for you to stay, Justin. It'll all be over soon. Hannah's here with us. It'll all be over soon."

He interpreted the conviction in her voice as wishful thinking and was reluctant to leave her in such a distraught state. Taking her cold hand between his own clammy palms, he chafed it gently.

"Perhaps," he suggested quietly, "this will be over sooner than you think."

Garrett sauntered along the planked walkway which skirted the edge of the canal, occasionally glancing back, but always moving slowly enough so that anyone following would have no trouble keeping up.

As he had expected, several men had followed him along the Lower Mountain Road, and he was certain he recognized Ogden's nag in the lead. Not wanting to make it too easy for his trackers, he had urged Prince to a gallop at a point where the road curved out of sight. Now in Lockport, he was waiting for the flustered men to catch a glimpse of him again before he led them on another merry chase among the denizens of Canal Street.

He was not particularly worried about whether the men would find him. Knowing the ilk of Ogden's cronies, it was a safe bet they would gravitate to this district sooner or later. Still, impatience gnawed at him. He almost wished they would spot him, just to keep the night progressing as planned.

For the next quarter of an hour Garrett continued to meander along the sidewalk, allowing his thoughts to wander as he stopped occasionally to peer into one or another of the waterfront saloons frequented by barge men and drunkards alike. In some cases, he recalled with a frown, the two were one and the same.

He briefly wondered if any of the bartenders would recognize him now. There'd been a day when his face poking through an open doorway brought instant recognition, and was more often than not met by friendly cajoling, if not always success.

"Yer pa's not here, laddie. Try O'Shaughnessy's."

For a split second Garrett thought he'd been transported to another time, but then a spindly legged boy of about twelve darted past him, heading for the next establishment down the canal road.

"Hold on there, son." He watched as the boy skidded to a stop, looking over his shoulder suspiciously.

"Who, me?"

"Are you looking for your father?"

The lad shrugged noncommittally. "Ya seen 'im?"

Garrett hesitated, wondering whether delving too much into his own past was a mistake. "Not exactly," he replied. "Do you live nearby? Are there more of you at home?"

Now the youth's cautious gaze narrowed suspiciously. "Close enough to holler. And yeah . . . there's eight of us, countin' Ma and Pa. Who wants ta know?"

Garrett let a rueful smile pull one corner of his mouth upward. "I used to live a few blocks from here when I was a boy. You reminded me of myself."

The lad's gaze scanned him from head to toe, then he shook his head doubtfully. "You don't live on the canal anymore, that's fer damn sure." He shuffled his feet impatiently. "Gotta hurry. Ma said if'n I don't find 'im by ten o'clock I should come home anyway . . ."

"Then you'd best get along." Garrett's chest ached at the mixed expression of shame and concern on the lad's thin face. Fifteen years suddenly seemed a very short time ago. "Here, son. Take this." He flipped a gold coin into the night, watching it arch like a shooting star, winking with reflected lantern light until the youth snatched it deftly from midair.

"What's this fer? I don't have time to run no errands—"

"No errands. It's yours to keep. Or to spend. There must be something you've been wanting to buy."

Now the boy's eyes widened to silver orbs, making him look younger than before. "I seen this book in Larson's about trains. Think this is enough to get it?"

Garrett's smile broadened. "I expect it is. You buy that book tomorrow. But in the meantime, don't tell your . . . don't tell anyone about our little conversation."

"I won't, sir."

With a knowing wink, the boy turned and sped into the darkness as if he was afraid to stand around long enough to let his benefactor change his mind.

More slowly, but with a lighter step than before, Garrett followed.

Kelsey's head was bent low as she tugged the loose-fitting breeches over her hips. Her dark hair swung loose around her face, hiding the odd-colored tinge of her pale cheeks. She *had* been losing weight, she thought irritably. It'd been a few weeks since she'd worn them, yet she remembered that before she'd always had to struggle to get them on.

"You'll need a belt," Dacia advised. "Are you sure you're up to this?"

"I am if you are. Besides, we haven't much choice. You and the baby *must* get out of here tonight with the others."

"But that doesn't mean you have to go along."

Kelsey straightened with a sigh. ''Someone has to hold Gabriel in the boat. You'll need to save all your strength for yourself. Are you ready?''

Dacia nodded from the bed, having donned the warm clothing Hannah laid out for her and wrapping the baby in several blankets. Her hands trembled nervously as she lifted her infant son close. Kelsey hoped that her own fear was not so apparent.

After quickly convincing Justin that he could be of more use in Lewiston stalling Bart Ogden if he was able, Kelsey had smothered the sense of unrest she felt about the ease with which he had departed. It was almost as if Justin had thought of something else he had to do, so eager was he to be off.

Still, she'd had more imperative things to worry about, and so had hurried into the cellar to caution Micah of a possible search. Together they made the decision to let Dacia cross with the party tonight, but Kelsey's sudden insistence upon going along had not been well met by the apprehensive negro.

''Garrett ain't gonna like this,'' Micah had warned just a few minutes before, for perhaps the tenth time.

Surprisingly, Dacia was just as reluctant. ''What if something happens to you?'' she continued to press. ''You have to think about—''

Kelsey jerked her head up from tucking a shirt into her waistband. ''Think about Garrett? I *am* thinking of him, and I know he'd want me to help. Nothing's more important than seeing you and Gabriel to safety.''

The woman shook her head slowly. ''I was talking about *your* baby.''

Silence strained through the room like a guy wire, threatening to snap at the slightest sound. Kelsey felt her whole body tremble, though whether it was from shock or relief, she could not be sure.

''How . . . what makes you say that?'' she faltered, staring at Dacia with wide, questioning eyes.

''All the signs are there. Changes in your appetite, tired all the time. Is your cycle past due?''

"O-Only a few weeks." Kelsey was stunned. She had attributed her ill health to stress and unhappiness. It never occurred to her that she might already be carrying Garrett's child. The thought left her both frightened and elated.

"A few weeks is enough," Dacia confirmed. "That's why you've got to take care of yourself. Your man's not going to like knowing you took this kind of risk with his own flesh and blood."

"I suppose you're right," Kelsey sighed, dropping to the edge of Dacia's bed in numb disbelief. "But he can't possibly know. Not when I didn't even realize . . . I'll just have to go anyway."

With renewed determination, she leaned just close enough to Gabriel to get a glimpse of dark curls and one tiny, perfectly shaped ear. "I'll tell him when we get back. He'll understand why I had to take the chance."

A short rap on the door signaled that Micah was waiting, so Kelsey hurried to finish donning the masculine garb before tying her hair back into a hasty braid. "Are you ready?" she asked Dacia again, her glance taking in the other woman's ashen features and thin, frail body.

"I've been ready for a long time," she replied confidently, hugging her baby closer. "You hear that, Gabriel? Tonight's the night we'll be free."

"We'd best go then," Kelsey murmured, turning her head toward the shuttered window to hide the sudden rush of tears that filled her eyes. The moon had yet to appear from behind a wall of thick clouds; not a thin ray of light would guide them to freedom. Only a beacon of hardship and hope.

For tonight, she prayed silently, it would have to be enough.

When he finally spotted Ogden's man, the scrawny bastard was already well into his cups. That was odd, Garrett thought, troubled by a niggling sense of unease. If this one had been sent to follow him, then why was the sad excuse for a scarecrow propped up at a corner table, looking for all the world like he planned to stay the night?

Swaggering purposely, he found himself a seat at the nearest available table, which by luck was occupied by two barge men from Albany, one of whom was snoring peacefully with his head in a puddle of ale. ''D' ye mind?'' Garrett asked, swinging a chair around to straddle it between his legs. The surly-looking man grunted his consent, barely glancing up.

''Time fer a brew,'' Garrett announced loudly, dredging up a good-natured grin. ''Got a lot of riding ahead of me tonight, that I do. I'll be needin' plenty of fortification.''

Again the man grunted, but since Garrett wasn't really playing to this audience, it hardly mattered. It was the slave catcher whose attention he sought, and a quick glance over his shoulder assured him he had it.

''Name's O'Neill,'' he said, leaning toward his unwilling listener. ''Not many familiar faces to be seen this fine night. But that's just as well.''

From the corner of his eye he saw the scrawny man bend closer, with a gloating expression in his eye that made Garrett's heart thump erratically. What in hell was going on? Deciding he'd had enough equivocating, he rose to turn his chair around in the opposite direction.

''Your face, now, is a familiar one,'' Garrett crooned menacingly. ''I've seen you with Bart Ogden on many occasions, not the last of which was earlier this evening. Where is the son of a bitch now?''

The scarecrow chortled into his ale, spewing foam and amber liquid across the filthy table. ''Don' know . . . don' care. Ah earned my wage already.''

''Doing what?''

Garrett didn't really expect an answer, so when the man merely wiggled his eyebrows deceptively, he grabbed his skinny forearm so hard the pewter mug of ale went flying through the air.

''Were you following me? I saw you long before I left

Lewiston. Did you see where I went? How much do you know?"

Despite the intimation of fear that appeared in the man's rheumy eyes, he raised his stubbled chin until it pointed at Garrett defiantly. "You got no call ta blame me," he hissed. "Ah ain't the fool what tried ta trick Ogden."

"Tried to—" His gut clenched with terror, and Garrett struggled to keep from strangling his prey on the spot. "What are you talking about?"

"You figger it out. Ya think ah'd be sittin' here jabberin' if'n you was really up ta sometin' here in Lockport? Ah ain't that stupid! No, siree!"

"Then tell me," Garrett growled, "how stupid are you?" He still retained a manacle hold around the man's wrist, and it took only a slight twist to bring an expression of startled pain to his face. "Are you stupid enough to think I would lead you anywhere but to Hell? Or stupid enough to believe I wouldn't cover my back?"

The slave catcher emitted a grunting whine, but with his senses dulled from alcohol, he was unable to break the iron grip that threatened to snap his arm in two like a dry twig. "Ah don' know," he wailed. "Ah don' know!"

"Tell me," Garrett murmured dangerously, "where your boss is, and just maybe I'll let you crawl back to Mississippi in one piece."

"Ya cain't threaten me!" His shrill voice piped up with genuine alarm. The tavern's constant din had already waned; now it fell to dead silence as Garrett stared hard into his face. Those patrons who were still sober enough to understand chuckled at the slave catcher's obvious discomfort as he squirmed and twisted, but dared not move.

"Where is Ogden?" he repeated softly, threateningly.

"I don'— Ow! Ya cain't do that, ah say! Ya cain't— He's headin' fer yer place! I don' know when . . . sometime tonight!"

Kelsey! Fear clutched at Garrett's gut, multiplied when he remembered the not-so-subtle hints about trying to trick Ogden. How could he have been so careless?

Under different circumstances Garrett might have enjoyed seeing this fellow lick spilled ale from the floor, but just now the clamoring alarm ringing in his head had him sailing through the door with all the speed of one of his blooded stallions.

His boots pounded a relentless rhythm on the planked sidewalk as he sprinted for his horse. He paid scant attention to the passersby who stepped quickly out of his way, not to the young voice that hailed him as he vaulted onto Prince's saddle.

Garrett had no time left to confront his past; not when his entire future was at stake.

32

He drove Prince harder than ever, yet the magnificant stallion gave him everything he asked for and more, as if somehow sensing the urgency of their mission. The wind beat at Garrett's face, stinging his eyes and burning his cheeks raw, while night creatures scurried from their path, frightened by thundering hoofbeats and the dark swirl of his cape as they flew past. Hurry! Garrett persuaded silently. Hurry!

Perversely, he cursed the clouds that hid the moon though he knew they provided necessary protection to the others. Darkness forced him to stay on the main roads when he otherwise would have whipped through forest trails to save even a few precious minutes. Everything hinged on his getting back to Riverview in time to prevent a catastrophe.

Half expecting to find Ogden holding Kelsey and Micah at gunpoint, he pounded into the yard, sawing so hard on the reins that Prince reared high into the air. But the grounds were strangely silent. Leaping from his horse, he cast his gaze over the hushed terrain.

Had he arrived in time? He prayed it was so even while his heart rose in his throat with fear as the kitchen door swung open, framing Hannah's stooped posture with lantern light. She took a faltering step out onto the small rear porch, clutching the railing with a frail hand as she squinted into the darkness.

"Mistah Garrett? That you?"

The sound of her voice told him she'd been weeping—

was still—and a wave of terror rippled through his limbs as surely as if his own life were hanging by a thread.

In a way, it was.

"Where are they?" He hurried toward her, stopping suddenly to suck in a sharp breath when he was close enough to see the extent of her injuries. One eye was nearly swollen shut, a trickle of blood traced a spidery line from the corner of her mouth to her trembling chin. The hand holding the railing shook violently, but in the other Hannah gripped an ancient horse pistol that hung nearly to her knees.

She gestured weakly. "They come 'bout ten minutes ago. Kelsey 'n Micah had left by then, but they's after 'em.

Garrett relieved her of the heavy gun, then eased her back into the kitchen with one arm around her thin shoulders. "Are you hurt badly?"

"Ah'll live. Dug this old thing outta the cupboard while those sons o' bitches was tearin' up the house. Thought they'd knocked the gumption outta me, but ah got 'em. Not a one cared to test me when ah showed 'em the bizness end o' this here gun."

His concern for Hannah was soon eclipsed by a greater worry. "Did they find the tunnel?"

"Nope. Chased 'em out before they could. They headed for the riverbank, but ah couldn't keep up with 'em enough to tell exactly where. Woulda shot at 'em, too, 'cept ah didn't have time to load this thing 'fore ah showed it. Good thing them good-fer-nothins didn't figger it out . . ."

Her voice trailed off when she realized Garrett was no longer present. By the time she moved back to the door, he was already across the yard and vaulting into the saddle.

"Bring her back safe now," Hannah called into the darkness. There was more she wished she'd had time to say, but the relentless hammering of the horse's hoofbeats as they faded into the night told her it was too late. Too late for words, too late for cautions.

She lifted her face to the dark sky. Garrett could no longer hear her, but maybe someone would. "Bring her back safe," she prayed. "Bring 'em all back safe."

Bart Ogden trampled through the rose garden Sheldon Tremayne had planted as if it was no more than a bed of weeds, not even noticing as thorns caught and snagged his ragged coat and patched trousers. All his attention was focused on finding a way down from the cliff to the riverbank below.

There had to be a path somewhere, he thought stubbornly. If that damned old woman hadn't pointed a gun at his gut he might have found something inside the house to steer him in the right direction. But even when he'd raised his hand to her, threatening to blacken her other eye, the scrawny bitch held the pistol level.

"I don't much care if your men kill me," she had declared. "But you'll be the first one to die."

Something in her tone had warned Ogden she meant what she said, so he had reluctantly obeyed her command to leave the house. But there wasn't nothin' to stop him from catchin' the rest o' them runaways now. Besides, he could always go back and arrest the old lady later, after he took care of O'Neill.

Ogden couldn't hold back a brief chortle even though he was still angry about not knowing the way down. Tricking O'Neill just felt too damned good! About now he figured Harvey was gettin' ready to hit the Irish bastard over the head, as instructed. An' now *he* was gonna catch his wife!

"Here's somethin'!" Wade called.

Rushing to his cohort's side, Ogden peered through the space in the prickly hedge. The hedge itself was nearly as high as a man's head, but on the other side he could see a shelf several feet wide with an unblocked view of the river. Without hesitating, he shouldered through the gap held open by Wade.

Fifty feet below, the Niagara hissed softly, a tumbling black ribbon that reminded Ogden of a huge, deadly viper. The startling thought reminded him of the warnings he'd heard about rattlesnakes on these rocky cliffs, and his glance darted from his feet to the shadowy piles of stones and loose brush all around. ''Watch out fer rattlers,'' he warned Wade, then realized his mistake when the man immediately jumped backwards into a thorny rosebush.

''Ain't goin' down if there's snakes! Ah'm skeared of 'em.''

''You'll come down if ah tell ya,'' Ogden sneered. He had no love for the slithering creatures either, but he wasn't about to lose sight of several thousand dollars' worth of prime flesh on account of a mere rattlesnake. He thought of his heavy clothing, donned even though the June night was warm and humid. ''Ain't nothin' gonna bite ya. Ya smell too bad. 'Sides, y' kin hear the rattle 'fore it strikes.''

It occurred to Wade to ask how long, but he was too used to following Ogden's orders without question to change now. He edged out onto the cliff.

''Quiet now. See if'n ya kin make anythin' out.''

The two men stood side by side, staring into the inky night as if they could conjure up their quarry by will alone. When no sounds could be heard except the constant rushing water, Ogden took a step closer to the edge.

''If'n we go down,'' he reckoned, peering at the barely discernible path, ''we might miss 'em if they's gone to another spot. We got the best chance o' spyin' 'em from up here.''

Wade wouldn't argue with that. Despite his deplorable lack of education, Bart Ogden hadn't become one of the most sought-after slave catchers for nothing. His uncanny instincts were well known among others of his ilk; he claimed he could smell a darkie a mile away, and it often seemed to be so. Wade glanced sideways at his boss. ''Think ye'll find 'em?''

Ogden continued to stare down at the undulating stream of black water. One hand twitched impatiently and his nostrils flared wide, but otherwise he made no movement.

"We'll get 'em, by Christ." His whisper could barely be heard above the Niagara's steady rumble. "We'll get 'em."

With Gabriel bundled snugly in his blankets and pressed against her chest, Kelsey made her way through the dank passageway, focusing on the thin bead of light cast by Benjamin's lantern several yards ahead. Behind her, Dacia, too, was bound in several wool blankets and Kelsey's riding cape, secure in Micah's arms as he strode purposefully toward the mouth of the cavern.

The rest of their party followed silently, the four young men willingly casting their lots with those who promised them a chance at freedom. Kelsey glanced back once to make sure they were still behind Micah, but the lantern's glow had reached its limit. She heard the scuffling sounds of their feet as they crept haltingly along, but she could see nothing beyond Micah's shadowed form.

At the cave's entrance Benjamin halted, turning to wait for each of the travelers to gather around. When all had reached the narrow fissure in the wall that marked the opening, he turned the lantern down until it flickered out completely. The cavern was thrown into total darkness, and to her left Kelsey heard the hissing sound of an indrawn breath. Then Benjamin's reassuring voice.

"This be it, now," he warned. "No talkin', no dawdlin'. Git straight in the boat. Micah will take the starboard oar. One of you boys take the other. Miss Kelsey'll sit in the stern with Dacia and her babe, and you other three sit aft. Ready?"

Not waiting for a response, Benjamin placed the lantern on the cave floor and slipped his skinny frame through the crack, pushing at the protective covering of bushes on the outside with both arms. When he'd stepped through, he held the branches for the others.

Kelsey came first. Despite the heavy clouds covering the moon, she could see better outside than within the confines of the cave. She turned to watch as one by one the men moved through the brush toward her, and she couldn't help wincing at the whisper of the leaves and the crackling of the branches as they strained within Benjamin's hold. When Micah pushed through with Dacia held high against his chest, a corner of her cloak snagged a twig, causing it to bend and finally snap. The sound echoed like a gunshot across the gorge, threatening to reveal their whereabouts.

Kelsey's gaze whipped upward to the precipice now high above them. She hoped Garrett's plan was working and that Bart Ogden and his crew were miles away. If so, then they were safe; it was Garrett who might be in more danger. Breathing a prayer for his safety, Kelsey lowered her face to the tiny bundle in her arms, pressing her lips against Gabriel's black curls. *Please, God,* she entreated silently, *guide each of us home tonight.*

Micah led the way to the spot where the boat was hidden against the riverbank, gesturing wordlessly to the younger men to drag it from its hiding place. Two of the slaves waded into the water, heading toward the clump of bushes he indicated. Waist high in the rapid current, they moved to bring the boat closer to the rest of the group.

Kelsey could see that one of the men—a boy actually, appearing no older than sixteen—stumbled often. His eyes were widened to bright rings of terror and he repeatedly swiveled his head from one side to the other as if expecting danger. In his nervousness he nearly lost his grip on the small rowboat just as they were pushing it toward the bank, but the other men clung to the weathered sides, guiding it back to where it belonged.

While the men labored to hold the craft steady, Micah stepped up to the boat, lowering Dacia gently into the stern. Turning, he took Gabriel from Kelsey long enough for her to settle next to the baby's mother, then handed the child into her arms. After the men were situated, Benjamin bent to give the craft a weak shove. With the current as strong as it was, that was all it took to see them moving inexorably toward the center of the river.

"Take the oar," Micah whispered to the young man seated beside him. He wished one of the others had taken the spot, one not so jumpy, but at his command the boy clutched the wooden hilt with both hands. The oarlock rattled ominously, causing them all to glance around with apprehension.

Despite the time of year, the air over the river was chill, and Kelsey raised a fold of the blanket over Gabriel's head. The baby was sleeping peacefully, oblivious to the tension and danger surrounding him. Kelsey noticed Dacia watching her, and she smiled in the dim light.

"When he's bigger, I'll tell him how he was carried across the river by a freedom angel," Dacia whispered fervently.

A warning shush from Micah prevented her from answering, but tears filled Kelsey's eyes and she reached for the other woman's hand, hoping that her comforting squeeze conveyed the depth of the emotions she was feeling. She would miss Dacia and little Gabriel, but more important was the knowledge that now they would begin a new life, a better one.

As the boat edged out into the center of the river, Micah rowed with strong, sure strokes, guiding the craft into the fastest part of the current. Kelsey watched the shore grow indistinct, the water seeming to grow darker and the roaring sound to intensify as they drew farther away from the land. She glanced quickly at Dacia to see if her friend was distressed, but the young woman had shifted her body to look the other way, her face was wreathed in a smile so utterly serene, Kelsey wondered if she had fallen into a peaceful sleep.

But Dacia was fully awake. All her senses were tuned to the air surrounding her, as if she could divine the actions of those she could not see. And then, with no warning, the smile fell from her lips and her eyes grew wide and stark. "No," she whispered, so faintly that only Kelsey could hear. "Not now!"

In that instant the clouds shifted, revealing a moon as brilliant and large as the midday sun. Moonbeams danced upon the water, reflecting the light like river stars, millions of them, twinkling brightly.

"Keep rowing," Micah growled, but the boy beside him was already frozen with fear. A strangled phrase escaped from his throat as he pointed up toward the high bank.

As Kelsey watched in horror, the boy's body heaved suddenly, and then a split second later the sound of a gunshot cleaved the night air.

Oh God, no! she screamed silently, clutching Gabriel tighter. Helplessly, she watched the oar slip from the dead boy's fingers before Micah could lunge for it, the sudden movement rocking the tiny vessel precariously. Another shot echoed from the riverbank.

This one thunked into the side of the boat, splintering the aged wood near the water line. The frightened slaves cried out despite Micah's calming words.

Twisting her head, Kelsey looked back to where Riverview was but a shadow on the high cliff. She could barely make out the two figures outlined on the edge of the rock but she knew that in the water they were a clear target. She threw a panicked glance at Micah.

The strong man was struggling valiantly with one oar to keep the boat afloat and in line with the shore, but he was rapidly losing ground. They had begun to spin into the current and already icy water covered her feet.

"Listen to me," Micah demanded as a third shot slapped the water less than a foot away. "If this boat sinks, we're not gonna have a chance. There's only one way for us to go now."

"B-But ah cain't swim," one of the men whispered in a terrified voice.

Eyeing him sympathetically, Micah heaved a reluctant sigh. "Then you'd best start learnin'. Fast."

Bart Ogden raised the rifle to his shoulder once more, sighting on the largest of the darkies in the boat. Though he couldn't tell for sure, it looked a lot like the Ramsey fella what got away, which was enough to raise the bile of vengeance in his gut.

"Get 'im, boss," Wade encouraged him in a strident voice.

Ogden took careful aim, slowly squeezing the trigger. The rifle slammed back into his shoulder painfully, but he shouted with glee. "Whooeee. Lookee there."

Before the echo had finished reverberating across the gorge, the tiny craft upended, spilling her passengers into the water. Ogden squinted to see if he could make out the one that was O'Neill's pretty wife, but from this distance they all looked the same. "We got 'em now, by gawd! We got—"

The words were knocked out of him, along with his breath, as a heavy weight hurled him into the air and over the cliff. Landing on his back upon a ledge several feet below with a soundless *whuush*, he clawed at his attacker ruthlessly.

"Goddamn!" Ogden muttered when he could finally draw a lungful of air. His filthy hands were embedded in a furry coat, and when he opened his eyes, it was to face a gaping, slavering set of teeth. "Help!" he squeeked. "Wade, help me!"

"Cain't," his companion called weakly.

Expecting to have his throat torn out at any moment, Ogden continued to beg for help. It took several moments for him to realize that the massive beast atop his chest had no intention of doing more than holding him in place.

"Up, Bridget, up."

In an instant, the huge dog retreated, but not before she coated Ogden's face with a slurping tongue. Repulsed, he used his dirty sleeve to swipe at his cheeks. "Get this damn hound away from me," he complained, so intent on keeping his distance from the dog that he forgot it was not Wade who called the animal off.

He remembered, however, when the click of a pistol cocking drew his attention upward.

"On your feet," Garrett O'Neill ordered in a strangely choked voice. Standing tall, his feet braced for battle, he looked like some Teutonic god with the moonlight turning his hair to silver and gold and the wolfhound at his side. Ogden nearly shivered at the thought, then chuckled evilly, half at himself; there wasn't nothing to be afraid of.

"You ain't got a chance now," he boasted. "You can take me in if'n you want, but ah got proof o' what you been doin'. With me an' Wade both testifyin' that we saw yer wife helpin' them niggers across, you ain't got a chance."

A feral light blazed in Garrett's eyes for a moment, but then they turned as hard and cold as the steel-barreled gun he aimed at Ogden's chest. "Who says I'm going to take you in?" he asked without emotion.

And now Bart Ogden felt fear. In all the years of his experience, he'd relied on the basic goodness of other men to give him an edge. A good man hesitated to harm another person, even one who was despised. A good man was trusting when trust was unwarranted.

Up until now he had prided himself on judging the weakness of another man by the depth of his compassion, and he'd had Garrett O'Neill pegged as a prime milksop. But that was before the Irishman's tolerance turned to malice. Now his gaze was filled with a violent light and utter lack of remorse, which Ogden found strangely familiar.

"What ya gonna do?" he asked anxiously, sliding to his feet. Standing, he felt a sight less impotent against such unbridled hatred, though he remained at the disadvantage.

Garrett stared down into Ogden's beady eyes. His mind thought instantly of a serpent, coiling to strike even in the last moment before death. When the man grinned nervously, his glistening lips stretching to expose black gums and pointed, broken-off teeth, he even looked like a poisonous viper.

But he was a man. The pistol in Garrett's hand was

steady, though inside he quaked with indecision. Could he kill a man in cold blood? Even one as scurrilous as Bart Ogden?

He very nearly lowered the gun, but in that instant his captive lifted his greasy head triumphantly, as if sensing victory. The grin on his face turned into a sneer, compounded by the taunting words that fell from his twisted mouth.

"So honorable, eh O'Neill? But where'd all yer high-minded holiness git ya? Ah don' see any o' them darkies helpin' ya now. An' ah wonder what yer wife was thinkin' when she drowned in the same water with 'em? Ah bet it weren't honor, no siree! Ah bet—"

Ogden stopped short. Even in the darkness he could see and feel the blast of heat emanating from the eyes staring down at him; pure, unadulterated fury, unhampered by conscience.

With no more compunction than if he'd been shooting a snake, Garrett willed his finger to squeeze the trigger.

"Look out!"

The shout came from his left at the same moment the pistol kicked back. He knew immediately that he had misfired, for Ogden launched himself toward the embankment, scrambling among the rocks for a hold. A hard body slammed into Garrett's side, knocking the gun from his hand. He felt himself pitch forward, realizing with sickening clarity that he had underestimated both the number and effectiveness of Ogden's men.

The handful of brush he grabbed on his way down the side of the cliff ripped free from the ground, scattering pebbles and dirt all around him. Landing on the same ledge where Ogden stood waiting, Garrett clenched his jaw against crying out when his left arm was pinned beneath his weight. It seemed he lay still for a long time, summoning his breath and listening to the tumbling rocks continue their descent to the river far below, but in fact it was only a few seconds before Ogden stepped near, his ragged boots just inches from Garrett's face.

The same boots, he recalled distantly, that had bludgeoned a man to death less than twenty-four hours ago.

"Thought ya was so smart, huh? Ah reckon if'n ah jest toss ya into the river, no one'll know ya weren't drowned with the rest o' them no 'counts."

Deep inside, a part of Garrett almost welcomed death. To live now without Kelsey would be worse than any hell he could imagine, and yet the need to see Ogden there first outweighed even the anguish in his empty heart.

"You won't get away with it," he said menacingly, with far more bravado than he ought, considering his position. Bridget whined softly but he knew she would not attack without his gesturing command. The other two slave catchers watched from several feet above as if viewing a drama, and from the way they were elbowing one another and guffawing, seemed to be enjoying themselves thoroughly. Ogden, too, wore a satisfied smirk, though he hadn't moved. It was clear from the way he stroked his bearded chin that he wasn't quite sure how to proceed.

"Ah 'spect ah oughtta shoot ya first," he mulled out loud. "Jest in case yer a better swimmer than ya are a shot." Cackling at his own humor, he peered up at his cronies. "Throw down mah rifle, ya worthless bastards."

"Cain't," Wade answered in his usual manner. "It went over the side when ya fell. So'd his."

Cursing, Ogden scanned the ground around his feet.

Garrett, too, had begun to search the hard rock beneath him for the pistol he had dropped. It was possible that the slave catcher was right, that the gun had sailed over the precipice into the gorge below. But there was also a chance that it had been stopped by the same ledge that broke his fall. As unobtrusively as possible, he turned his head toward the pile of rubble nearest the bank.

Ogden saw the glint of metal and dove for it at the same moment that Garrett rolled for the gun. The pain from his sprained arm lanced through his whole body like a shearing sword, but he managed to reach out with his right hand and clasp the barrel of the pistol in a frantic grip. Ogden's hand, clawing and hard, came down on top of his.

"Give it up," the man croaked. "Give it up!"

Garrett lurched to his knees, shouldering Ogden away, but neither man eased his grip on the firearm. The back of his hand ached from the pressure of Ogden's sinewy fingers and Garrett knew it was only a matter of time before the other man realized the extent of his injury and took full advantage. With another shove, he tried to offset the burly man and break his grip.

Tried, and failed.

Ogden saw that his own grasp made it impossible for Garrett to let go of the gun, yet he was loath to release his hold for even a minute. Blindly, he reached his other hand behind him to fumble for a rock, egged on by the shouts of his cohorts and the ragged, straining rasp of Garrett's labored breath. His own breathing rang heavy in his ears, nearly drowning out everything else. But in the split second that his hand closed around a large rock, Bart Ogden heard a sound that would haunt him for the rest of his life.

Disturbed by the vibrations of falling rock and drawn by the warmth of human flesh, one of the many rattlesnakes that holed up in these cliffs had emerged from its shelter. Poised less than two feet from them, it sensed both the heat and movement of the hands that held the gun.

Ogden froze with fear, seemingly mesmerized by the ominous whirr of the rattler's tail.

Garrett reacted with lightning speed as he tried to snatch his fingers away from the barrel of the pistol.

The serpent, however, was faster. With its mouth wide in what looked to be a shout of exultation, the snake struck hard, writhing in ecstasy as its quarry twitched and flailed beneath deadly fangs.

With an angry cry, Bart Ogden repeatedly smashed the

rock he held against the triangular head, but he was too late.

Even in the throes of death, the snake expelled its lethal venom.

33

It was nearly two days before Kelsey gathered enough courage to face the Niagara again, even though this time it was to cross in the relative comfort of a farm wagon over the suspension bridge, with the added luxury of dry clothing and a soft blanket thrown over her shoulders against the morning dew. She had dared to look down from the bridge at the swirling water only once, but it was enough to turn her hands to ice and her limbs to jelly. After that, she'd kept her eyes closed until they reached solid ground, determined to put that horrible night behind her and to concentrate on better things.

And there *were* better things. For one, she was alive when by all rights her grave should lie in the treacherous river, along with the two young men who died there. She might have died too, she shuddered, but for the grace of God.

That's not much better than looking at the water, she chastised herself. *Keep thinking.*

All right then, there were her friends. Micah's quick actions had saved most of their lives. Before the boat could sink into the murky depths, he had urged them all into the water, then used his massive strength to heave the craft over. Enough air was trapped beneath the hull and waterline to keep the boat floating. They had clung to the tiny vessel desperately, letting the current take them out of harm's way. Aside from the boy who was shot, only one other man did not survive the ordeal. At some point—Kelsey had never been sure when—he must have lost his grip and slipped beneath the dark waters to his death.

Think about Dacia, she told herself. *Dacia's alive, too.*

With Micah's aid and more strength than anyone suspected she had, the other woman made it to the opposite shore. Her hands had trembled when she took her baby from Kelsey's protective arms, weeping silently, joy and relief shivering through her frail form. Little Gabriel was the only one of the lot still dry when they stumbled onto land, for Kelsey had done her best to hold him up out of the water, placing him high on the bottom of the overturned boat while they pushed it to safety.

Think about your own child, her heart whispered secretively.

Now her face softened into a private smile. Throughout that harrowing night her thoughts had constantly returned to the life she carried within, giving her the stamina to continue whenever her weary body cried out in protest. Then, in the day and a half that followed while they recuperated in the home of a farmer named Witcop and his boisterous family, she had hugged the knowledge to herself, letting her newfound joy surmount her constant concern for Garrett.

And what about Garrett? she fretted worriedly. *What had happened to Garrett?*

Micah had discussed with her the possibility of Garrett's having been arrested earlier that evening, which might explain Ogden's inopportune arrival on the riverbank. But Kelsey was more concerned that he'd been involved in a scuffle with the odious man and was hurt and wondering why she hadn't come to him. She had wanted to send a wire assuring him they were safe, but both Micah and Mr. Witcop suggested that such a message might provide Ogden with proof of her part in the scheme to help the slaves escape. As soon as it was feasible, they claimed, the farmer would transport her home.

Home.

And Garrett. She smiled to herself. Her mind was never far from her husband, just as her whole body knew the constant ache of longing to feel his arms around her. These past two days had stretched to years in her heart, but they would soon be behind her. Then she would have nothing to think about but the future.

Now azure bands streaked across the sky, dawn pressing in, driving the night away as the farm wagon lumbered onward. The new lightness gave her hope, the rising birdsong filled her heart. And as always, the deep color of the northern sky reminded her of Garrett's eyes.

Shifting restlessly, Kelsey refrained from asking the placid man beside her to speed up. From his worn felt hat to his scuffed boots, he seemed the sort who forever traveled through life at the same pace. Contentment circled his grizzled head like a halo, peace was in the myriad lines radiating from his smiling eyes.

"Won't be long now," he assured her with an easy grin.

Kelsey returned his infectious smile, wishing some of his serenity would rub off on her as well. Living with his happy family, even for a short time, had made her impatient to start a new life with Garrett. There was so much she wanted to tell him, so much she needed to say.

"I'm just anxious to see my husband," she explained unnecessarily.

"I guess you do have a might to tell him, don't you," Mr. Witcop teased lightly. He was no learned man, but it didn't take one to see the yearning in her bright eyes or the love that shined from her face like a beacon. He suspected that when she did get to her man, there wouldn't be much talk at all. "He'll be glad to see you."

Beneath the blanket, Kelsey pressed her hand to her belly. "Yes," she replied softly, "Yes, he will."

It was almost time to start breakfast, but Hannah could not summon the energy to rise from her rocking chair to cook. Never in all her days had her bones felt so dead-weary at this time of the morning. Never had grief stretched her heart so thin she thought it would tear into pieces.

"Oh, Lordy," she wept, swaying back and forth feebly. Even the creaking floorboards, which in earlier days would have had her bustling to rearrange the chair, could not penetrate her sorrow. No use fixing breakfast anyway, she mourned. No one would eat it.

From outside she heard the uneasy whinnying of Garrett's horse, fretting because he hadn't been ridden lately. Benjamin clattered a bucket noisily inside the stable, solitary in his chores, having sent the boys away for a few days because he didn't believe young ones ought to be around a house of gloom.

And gloomy it was, Hannah thought sadly. Even the bright sun, bursting with lightness and warmth, could not pierce the darkness surrounding Riverview. She sniffled loudly, wiping her cheeks with the dishtowel clutched in her gnarled hand.

The rattling sound of wheels on the distant lane made her scowl irritably. More visitors, she sighed inwardly. Hannah dragged herself to her feet. The stove needed to be lit and there was water to boil. She might not have the heart to cook breakfast, but a soul could always use plenty of coffee.

Last night had been proof of that.

Her thoughts drifting to the previous evening, Hannah frowned. Justin Delbert had appeared at the front door, stone drunk and raving. Luckily, no one else except her had been up to a visit, but that didn't seem to matter much to young Justin. He'd wept in her arms like a baby, pouring out his grief and guilt and regret until finally, nearly an hour later, he'd slipped into an alcoholic stupor. It took two pots of coffee to coax him into Benjamin's buggy after that, but at least she could be thankful no one else had heard his unlikely confession.

Justin Delbert had told her, though she hadn't really wanted to hear it, all about his jealousy toward Garrett and his misguided love for Kelsey. He said he had only wanted to free her from a marriage he believed she had not wished. He had thought that if Garrett were arrested,

Kelsey would have grounds for an annulment without risking her own reputation.

And worst of all, he cried helplessly, he had revealed to Bart Ogden that something was planned for that terrible night. If he'd known Kelsey were going along or that her life was at risk, he wouldn't have done it, he swore. Now it was too late.

Hannah choked back a sob of her own. Regrets were no more than wasted breath, but she couldn't help feeling sorry for the young fool. Sometime when he was sober she would tell him that what he had done probably hadn't made all that much difference. Bart Ogden was still boasting, though from a jail cell, that he'd figured the whole plan out for himself.

Still, Hannah had a hunch Justin Delbert would pay for his arrogance for a long while. Maybe even the rest of his life.

The sounds outside had grown much louder, stopping only when a vehicle halted outside the kitchen door. She was puzzled. Why hadn't they come to the front? Who could it be?

Carefully, her joints aching, she made her way to the door, opening it slowly. From the high seat of a sturdy farm wagon, a kindly looking man nodded to her, tipping his hat. On his far side a woman was climbing down, her head covered with a paisley shawl, her features bent low as she tended to her footing.

"I got all the eggs I can use," Hannah called gruffly, her voice hoarse with unshed tears. "Milk, too."

Despite her refusal to sample their wares, the woman continued to dismount from the wagon. The cook had turned to go back inside and was preparing to close the door firmly when a familiar voice called to her.

"Hannah?"

Closing her bleary eyes tight, Hannah mumbled to herself. "It cain't be," she muttered superstitiously. "It cain't be."

"Hannah?"

The voice was louder now, more distinct as the young

woman moved closer to the porch. Daring to look over her shoulder, Hannah felt tears scald her cheeks, her wizened face growing puckered and tight.

"Oh, Lord," she cried, turning to stumble forward, hands outstretched. "Oh, Lord! My baby!"

Kelsey rushed toward the weeping woman, flinging her arms around her quaking shoulders. Tears tumbled from her own heart as well, but they were tears of gladness, of homecoming.

"Don't cry, Hannah," she soothed, laughing at her own sentimental reaction. "I'm home now. Dacia and the baby are fine, too. They're with Micah now, and they're all—"

The words died on her lips, silenced by the stark recognition that Hannah's weeping was deep and profound, not tears of rejoicing but of something more bitter. Pulling away slowly, Kelsey ran her uneasy gaze over her friend, noticing for the first time the black bombazine dress that Hannah always saved for special occasions. Her glance shifted to the house, unusually silent, and then to the stable, where Benjamin stared at her from the wide entrance as if he were seeing a ghost.

"What's . . . what's wrong?" she faltered, her eyes telling her what her heart refused to understand.

And then her gaze turned to the kitchen door and the fluttering wreath of black silk ribbon that hung there. It had been fashioned with loving care, each bow crisp and precise, each tassel uniform in length. She had seen hundreds of them hanging from doorways in London and marking the entrances to shops, but never had their impact jolted her with such overwhelming anguish.

Pain seared through her, dulled only by shock and disbelief. She felt her knees buckle and her weight shift forward, Hannah's arms supporting her where just a moment ago she had been the one offering comfort.

A scream bubbled from deep within her chest, threatening to tear her throat apart. She opened her mouth to let it out, but did not know if she had the strength, or if the cry would remain locked inside her for all eternity;

pulsing, growing, and eventually smothering the life from her.

Instead, Kelsey closed her eyes tight, fighting the dizziness that offered blessed release. "Oh, God," she whispered, her lips barely forming around the words. "Oh, please God, no!"

Why was it, Garrett wondered achingly as he stared down at the river below, *that everything good hid within it the promise of pain?* Love was elusive, life unreliable, and beauty deceiving.

Like the river.

Woodenly, he hefted a flat rock in his hand and flung it from the cliff, watching its quick descent until it hit the water with a distant splash. The circle of ripples it made was quickly broken up and dispersed by the river's current. Within moments no sign of the stone's presence remained.

Only the river.

For a long time, he wasn't sure just low long—hours? days?—he'd been standing on this spot, drawn by the mesmerizing flow of endless amounts of water. To keep his mind occupied, he'd attempted to estimate in gallons and barrels the exact numbers, but the figures evaded him, much like all the answers he'd been trying so hard to find.

Only one image held clear in his muddled head, only one name rang true when he tried to remember something, anything, else.

Kelsey.

He remembered what she looked like on the last morning he'd seen her, her eyes begging for his love. He could see her trembling lips in the moment just before a kiss, her hair fanned out on a blanket of grass at this very same place. He heard her voice in the breeze that whispered around him, taunting and melancholy, soft and sweet.

"Garrett?"

He lifted his head unsteadily.

"Garrett . . ."

A part of him didn't want to turn, fearing the spectre of madness almost as much as the pain of living without her. But some rational part of his mind forced him to look, and when he saw her hesitate at the edge of the clearing, his heart surged with rampaging emotions, not the least of which was utter disbelief. And yet, her tremulous smile looked real. So did the tears that spilled freely down her pale cheeks.

He swallowed, trying to force his voice past his constricted throat. "Kelsey? Love?"

Launching herself at him, Kelsey flung her arms around his broad shoulders, not even minding when it took several moments before he raised his own arms to encircle her waist with a forcefulness that drove the breath from her body.

"Kelsey, my God! How did you . . . ?" His voice trailed as he lowered his mouth to hers in a kiss that was both crushing and tender. She arched against him as if she wanted to be even closer, and he obliged by pressing her hips tightly to his.

She was nearly delirious with joy, still weak and trembling from the thought of losing him, finding herself even more weakened by the knowledge that he was here. "I thought you were dead," she sobbed against his lips. "And then Hannah told me that you thought it was *me*. But I'm alive, Garrett! And so are you!" She stopped talking then to return his soulful kiss.

Her lips bore the salty tang of both their tears, mingling with the essence that was hers alone. Garrett drank of it like a man tortured by unquenchable thirst, and still it was not enough. Longing raged through him like the water below, unceasing and eternal, filling him and emptying him at the same time. He wanted to never let her go. He wanted her inside of him, to be inside of her.

But most of all he wanted to know.

With more difficulty than he could have imagined, he turned his face into the shimmering fall of her hair, breathing deeply. "Tell me," he whispered hoarsely, "what happened."

Haltingly, achingly, Kelsey explained everything, from the moment she learned of Ogden's search warrant, to that very morning when she'd nearly lost her mind with grief, assuming that Garrett must have been the one who was dead simply because *she* was still very much alive.

Then he took a turn relating to her the events of that tragic evening; just two nights ago, now aeons behind them. "Ogden was arrested, charged with causing a fatal accident. I suppose now the sheriff will let him go. If he survives."

"Survives?" For a brief instant Kelsey wondered if Garrett *had* clashed with the slave catcher and come out the victor, and was shocked by the secret thrill of pride and elation that rippled through her.

"Snakebite," Garrett pronounced tersely. "He might die yet, but the doc says he's probably too ornery. Regardless, there'll be a restraining order forbidding him to step foot in this county again. He'll have to ply his business elsewhere, minus one arm. The other men have already scattered."

Relief that the worst was truly behind them now engulfed Kelsey, and she laid her head on Garrett's shoulder, her hands still splayed across the solid warmth of his back. She wasn't certain whether it was her heartbeat or his pounding through her, or if they had finally become one. "I'm so sorry, my love, for all the trouble I caused. I let my own selfish beliefs stand in the way of what was right. And not right just for everyone else, but right for *me.* Nothing matters now except being with you."

Very carefully, he tipped her chin up to gaze into her eyes, shining brightly with more love than he'd ever thought possible. "And I was wrong, too. Love should be a sharing, marriage a union. There should be nothing between us, ever again."

As if to demonstrate his meaning, Garrett eased the wool shawl from her shoulders, slipping his hands behind her head to run through the rich, dark curls. "It's warm enough now, don't you think, to dispense with some of this excess clothing."

His rough voice vibrated through her, making her tremble to the very core. She reached up on tiptoe to answer him with a kiss, and when his mouth slanted over hers she opened to him completely, without hesitation or doubt. They had ceased to exist in her heart.

Together, they dropped to the soft ground that would be their bed once more. Kelsey felt as if his hands were everywhere at once, softly seeking, exploring, inciting her to wilder heights. Her borrowed clothing fell away easily, and with fingers both shy and frantic, she helped Garrett to undress, too.

He touched her with feather-light caresses as if she were as fragile and precious as rare china, and with every stroke to her smooth skin, he felt her response growing, meeting his. When he would have delayed their joining to give her more time, she arched eagerly, welcoming him, enticing him, until he could no more hold himself back than he could let her go.

Kelsey had never felt this before, the untamed abandon that swept her senses and scourged her mind of thought. It consumed her, it filled her. His movements became more demanding, but not more so than hers as she lifted herself to him, clung to him, giving and taking until the two became a single entity, joined together. Forever.

His exultant shout was muffled against her hair, but she felt it as though it had come from her own lips, her own throat. It was not until later that she realized it nearly had, for her own splendorous moan had been mingled with his in a cry of fulfillment that rent the air, flying straight up to the heavens.

It was a long while before their breathing became steady once more and their hearts resumed a pace that was only twice as fast as normal. Kelsey reveled in the feeling of satisfaction and safety she felt lying in his arms, and in the knowledge that it would last forever. Even the things that had once frightened her most had lost their grip on her heart.

And that thought reminded her that their happiness would soon be complete. ''There's one more thing I have to tell you,'' she murmured haltingly, taking a deep breath. She wasn't certain why this had suddenly become so difficult, but the knowledge that his joy would only increase hers bolstered her courage.

''What is it, love?'' Sensing her indecision, Garrett gathered her closer, gently massaging her spine, draining the tension from her body.

''I'm . . . We're—'' She lifted her head so that she could see his expression, and Kelsey felt her doubts melting beneath the intensity of his loving gaze. ''I'm going to have a baby.''

A thousand emotions pulsed through him, none of them eclipsing the sheer happiness he felt. Pulling her closer, he buried his face in her hair and said thickly, ''Are you sure?''

His words echoed the moments many weeks before, when they had conceived the life inside of her. It seemed only fitting to Kelsey. ''I'm very sure,'' she nodded, her voice husky. ''And what I didn't know, Dacia confirmed.''

''I meant, are you sure you want this?''

His eyes were so full of tenderness and concern that she felt as if her heart would overflow. ''I think I've wanted this all my life. I'm not afraid now, Garrett. Not as long as you're with me. Loving you has freed me of all that.''

''And I love you, Kelsey. I've loved you ever since that day when you were six. No one has every stayed inside my heart the way you have, or meant more to me than my own life.''

This time his kiss was gently compelling, an end and a new beginning. She felt her spirit drawn from deep within her soul, lifted higher and faster and farther than it had gone before.

Within their hearing, the river continued its unflagging journey to the sea. Around them, the land that was theirs lay fertile and rich with promise for the future. And high above, deep and blue and endless, was the sky.

ABOUT THE AUTHOR

Robin LeAnne Wiete was born and raised in New York State. After marrying her college sweetheart in 1976, she lived in Cincinnati, Ohio, for several years, where she worked for a national investment firm. It was largely through the enthusiasm of a co-worker there that she discovered a deep and abiding passion for historical romances, and decided to write one of her own. FREEDOM ANGEL is her third historical romance.

Ms. Wiete has recently returned to Cincinnati with her husband and two children. She spends her nonwriting time enjoying her family, reading, and working with other writers.

She welcomes comments from readers at the following address:

P.O. Box 58608
Cincinnati, Ohio 45258